DARK WITCH

Iona has always felt a powerful connection to the home of her ancestors. So when her beloved grandmother confesses an extraordinary family secret, she can't resist visiting County Mayo to discover the truth for herself. Arriving at the beautiful and atmospheric Castle Ashford, Iona is excited to meet her cousins, Connor and Branna O'Dwyer. And when she lands a job at the local riding school she finds herself drawn against her will to its owner – the hot-tempered but charismatic Boyle McGrath. Perhaps in County Mayo she has found her true home at last. Iona soon discovers that some old legends can return to haunt the present...

DARK WITCH

DARK WITCH

by

Nora Roberts

Magna Large Print Books
Long Preston, North Yorkshire,
BD23 4ND, England.

British Library Cataloguing in Publication Data.

Roberts, Nora
    Dark witch.

    A catalogue record of this book is
    available from the British Library

    ISBN   978-0-7505-3972-2

First published in Great Britain in 2013 by Piatkus

Copyright © 2013 by Nora Roberts

Cover illustration © Mark Fearon by arrangement with
Arcangel Images

The moral right of the author has been asserted

Published in Large Print 2014 by arrangement with
Piatkus Books, an imprint of Little, Brown Book Group

Magna Large Print is an imprint of Library Magna Books Ltd.

Printed and bound in Great Britain by
T.J. (International) Ltd., Cornwall, PL28 8RW

To the power of family,
those born, those made

When shall we three meet again?
In thunder, lightning, or in rain?
When the hurlyburly's done,
When the battle's lost and won.

– WILLIAM SHAKESPEARE, *Macbeth*

1

Winter 1263

Near the shadow of the castle, deep in the green woods, Sorcha led her children through the gloom toward home. The two youngest rode the sturdy pony, with Teagan, barely three, nodding with every plod. Weary, Sorcha thought, after the excitement of Imbolg, the bonfires, and the feasting.

'Mind your sister, Eamon.'

At five, Eamon's minding was a quick poke to wake up his baby sister before he went back to nibbling on the bannocks his mother had baked that morning.

'Home in your bed soon,' Sorcha crooned when Teagan whined. 'Home soon.'

She'd tarried too long in the clearing, she thought now. And though Imbolg celebrated the first stirrings in the womb of the Earth Mother, night fell too fast and hard in winter.

A bitter one it had been, crackling with icy winds and blowing snow and ice-tipped rain. The fog had lived all winter, creeping, crawling, curtaining sun and moon. Too often in that wind, in that fog, she'd heard her name called – a beckoning she refused to answer. Too often in that world of white and gray, she'd seen the dark.

She refused to truck with it.

Her man had begged her to take the children

and stay with his *fine* while he waged his battles over that endless winter.

As the wife of the *cennfine*, every door would open for her. And in her own right, for what and who she was, welcome would always be made.

But she needed her woods, her cabin, her place. She needed to be apart as much as she needed to breathe.

She would tend her own, always, her home and her hearth, her craft and her duties. And most of all, the precious children she and Daithi had made. She had no fear of the night.

She was known as the Dark Witch, and her power was great.

But just then she felt sorely a woman missing her man, yearning for the warmth of him, the fine, hard body pressed to hers in the cold and lonely dark.

What did she care for war? For the greed and ambitions of all the petty kings? She only wanted her man home safe and whole.

When he came home, they would make another baby, and she would feel that life inside her again. She mourned still the life she'd lost on a brutal black night when the first winter wind had blown through her woods like the sound of weeping.

How many had she healed? How many had she saved? And yet when the blood had poured from her, when that fragile life had flooded away, no magick, no offering, no bargain with the gods had saved it.

But then she knew, too well, healing others came more easily than healing self. And the gods as fickle as a giddy girl in May.

'Look! Look!' Brannaugh, her eldest at seven, danced off the hard path, with their big hound on her heels. 'The blackthorn's blooming! It's a sign.'

She saw it now, the hint of those creamy white blossoms among the black, tangled branches. Her first bitter thought was while Brighid, the fertility-bringing goddess, blessed the earth, her own womb lay empty inside her.

Then she watched her girl, her first pride, sharp-eyed, pink-cheeked, spinning through the snow. She'd been blessed, Sorcha reminded herself. Three times blessed.

'It's a sign, Ma.' Dark hair flying with every spin, Brannaugh lifted her face to the dimming light. 'Of coming spring.'

'Aye, it's that. A good sign.' As had been the gloomy day, as the old hag Cailleach couldn't find firewood without the bright sun. So spring would come early, so the legend went.

The blackthorn bloomed bright, tempting the flowers to follow.

She saw the hope in her child's eyes, as she'd seen it at the bonfire in other eyes, heard it in the voices. And Sorcha searched inside herself for that spark of hope.

But found only dread.

He would come again tonight – she could already sense him. Lurking, waiting, plotting. Inside, she thought, inside the cabin behind the bolted door, with her charms laid out to protect her babies. To protect herself.

She clucked to the pony to quicken his pace, whistled for the dog. 'Come along now, Brannaugh, your sister's all but asleep already.'

15

'Da comes home in the spring.'

Though her heart stayed heavy, Sorcha smiled and took Brannaugh's hand. 'He does that, home by Bealtaine, and we'll have a great feast.'

'Can I see him tonight, with you? In the fire?'

'There's much to do. The animals need tending before bed.'

'For a moment?' Brannaugh tipped her face back, her eyes, gray as smoke, pleading. 'Just to see him for a moment, then I can dream he's home again.'

As she would herself, Sorcha thought, and now her smile came from her heart. 'For a moment, *m'inion*, when the work's done.'

'And you take your medicine.'

Sorcha lifted her brows. 'Will I then? Do I look to you as if I'm in need of it?'

'You're still pale, Ma.' Brannaugh kept her voice beneath the wind.

'Just a wee bit tired, and you're not to worry. Here now, hold on to your sister, Eamon! Alastar smells home, and she's likely to fall off.'

'She rides better than Eamon, and me as well.'

'Aye, well, the horse is her talisman, but she's near sleeping on his back.'

The path turned; the pony's hooves rang on the frozen ground as he trotted toward the shed beside the cabin.

'Eamon, see to Alastar, an extra scoop of grain tonight. You had your fill, didn't you?' she said as her boy began to mutter.

He grinned at her, handsome as a summer morning, and though he could hop down as quick as a rabbit, he held out his arms.

He'd always been one for a cuddle, Sorcha thought, hugging him as she lifted him down.

She didn't have to tell Brannaugh to start her chores. The girl ran the house nearly as well as her mother. Sorcha took Teagan in her arms, murmuring, soothing, as she carried her into the cabin.

'It's dreaming time, my darling.'

'I'm a pony, and I gallop all day.'

'Oh aye, the prettiest of ponies, and the fastest of all.'

The fire, down to embers after the hours away, barely held back the cold. As she carried the baby to bed, Sorcha held out a hand to the hearth. The flames leapt up, simmered over the ashes.

She tucked Teagan into the bunk, smoothed her hair – bright as sunlight like her father's – and waited until her eyes – deep and dark like her mother's – closed.

'Sweet dreams only,' she murmured, touching the charm she'd hung over the beds of her babies. 'Safe and sound through all the night. All you are and all you see hold you through dark into light.'

She kissed the soft cheek, and as she straightened, winced at the pull in her belly. The ache came and went, but came more strongly as the winter held. So she would take her daughter's advice and make a potion.

'Brighid, on this your day, help me heal. I have three children who need me. I cannot leave them alone.'

She left Teagan sleeping, and went to help the older children with the chores.

When night fell, too fast, too soon, she secured the door before repeating her nighttime ritual with Eamon.

'I'm not tired, not a bit,' he claimed as his eyes drooped.

'Oh, I can see that. I see you're wide awake and raring. Will you fly again tonight, *mhic?*'

'I will, aye, high in the sky. Will you teach me more tomorrow? Can I take Roibeard out come morning?'

'That I will, and that you can. The hawk is yours, and you see him, you know him, and feel him. So rest now.' She ruffled his bark brown hair, kissed his eyes – wild and blue as his father's – closed.

When she came down from the loft, she found Brannaugh already by the fire, with the hound that was hers.

Glowing, Sorcha thought, with health – thank the goddess – and with the power she didn't yet fully hold or understand. There was time for that, she prayed there was time yet for that.

'I made the tea,' Brannaugh told her. 'Just as you taught me. You'll feel better, I think, after you drink it.'

'Do you tend me now, *mo chroi?*' Smiling, Sorcha picked up the tea, sniffed it, nodded. 'You have the touch, that you do. Healing is a strong gift. With it, you'll be welcome, and needed, wherever you go.'

'I don't want to go anywhere. I want to be here with you and Da, and Eamon and Teagan, always.'

'One day you may look beyond our wood. And there will be a man.'

Brannaugh snorted. 'I don't want a man. What would I do with a man?'

'Ah well, that's a story for another day.' She sat with her girl by the fire, wrapped a wide shawl around them both. And drank her tea. And when Brannaugh touched her hand, she turned hers over, linked fingers.

'All right then, but for only a moment. You need your bed.'

'Can I do it? Can I bring the vision?'

'See what you have, then. Do what you will. See him, Brannaugh, the man you came from. It's love that brings him.'

Sorcha watched the smoke swirl, the flames leap and then settle. Good, she thought, impressed. The girl learned so quickly.

The image tried to form, in the hollows and valleys of the flame. A fire within a fire. Silhouettes, movements, and, for a moment, the murmur of voices from so far away.

She saw the intensity on her daughter's face, the light sheen of sweat from the effort. Too much, she thought. Too much for one so young.

'Here now,' she said quietly. 'We'll do it together.'

She pushed her power out, merged it with Brannaugh's.

A fast roar, a spin of smoke, a dance of sparks. Then clear.

And he was there, the man they both longed for.

Sitting at another fire, within a circle of stones. His bright hair braided to fall over the dark cape wrapped around his broad shoulders. The *dealg* of his rank pinned to it glittered in the light of the flames.

The brooch she'd forged for him in fire and magick – the hound, the horse, the hawk.

'He looks weary,' Brannaugh said, and leaned her head against her mother's arm. 'But so handsome. The most handsome of men.'

'That he is. Handsome, and strong, and brave.' And oh, she longed for him.

'Can you see when he comes home?'

'Not all can be seen. Perhaps when he's closer, I'll have a sign. But tonight, we see he's safe and well, and that's enough.'

'He thinks of you.' Brannaugh looked over, into her mother's face. 'I can feel it. Can he feel us thinking of him?'

'He hasn't the gift, but he has the heart, the love. So perhaps he can. To bed now. I'll be up soon.'

'The blackthorn is blooming, and the old hag did not see the sun today. He comes home soon.' Rising, Brannaugh kissed her mother. The dog trotted up the ladder with her.

Alone, Sorcha watched her love in the fire. And alone, she wept.

Even as she dried her tears she heard it. The beckoning.

He would comfort her, he would warm her – such were his seductive lies. He would give her all she could want, and more. She had only to give herself to him.

'I will never be yours.'

You will. You are. Come now, and know all the pleasures, all the glory. All the power.

'You will never have me, or what I hold inside me.'

Now the image in the fire shifted. And he came

into the flames. Cabhan, whose power and purpose were darker than the winter night. Who wanted her – her body, her soul, her magick.

The sorcerer desired her, for she felt his lust like sweaty hands on her skin. But more, more, she knew, he coveted her gift. His greed for it hung heavy in the air.

In the flames he smiled, so handsome, so ruthless.

I will have you, Sorcha the Dark. You and all you are. We are meant. We are the same.

No, she thought, we are not the same, but as day to night, light to dark, where the only merging comes in shadows.

So alone you are, and burdened. Your man leaves you a cold bed. Come warm yourself in mine; feel the heat. Make that heat with me. Together, we rule all the world.

Her spirits sagged, the ache and pull inside her twisted toward pain.

So she rose, let the warm wind come to blow through her hair. Let the power pour in until she shone with it. And saw, even in the flames, the lust and greed in Cabhan's face.

Here is what he wanted, she knew, the glory that rushed through her blood. And this was what he would never have.

'Know my mind and feel my power, then and now and every hour. You offer me your dark desire, come to me in smoke and fire. Betray my blood, my babes, my man, to rule o'er all, only take your hand. So my answer to thee comes through wind and sea, rise maiden, mother, hag in trinity. As I will, so mote it be.'

21

She threw out her arms, released the fury, fully female, whirled in, flung it toward the beat of his heart.

An instant of pure, wild pleasure erupted inside her when she heard his cry of rage and pain, when she saw that rage and pain burst onto his face against the flames.

Then the fire was just a fire, simmering low for the night, bringing a bit of warmth against the bitter. Her cabin was just a cabin, quiet and dim. And she was just a woman alone with her children sleeping.

She slumped down in the chair, wrapping an arm around the tearing in her belly.

Cabhan was gone, for now. But her fear remained, of him, and that if no potion or prayer healed her body, she would leave her children motherless.

Defenseless.

She woke with her youngest curled with her, found comfort even as she shifted to rise for the day.

'Ma, Ma, stay.'

'There now, my sunbeam, I have work. And you should be in your own bed.'

'The bad man came. He killed my ponies.'

A fist of panic squeezed Sorcha's heart. Cabhan touching her children – their bodies, their minds, their souls? It brought her unspeakable fear, unspeakable rage.

'Just a dream, my baby.' She cuddled Teagan close, rocked and soothed. 'Just a dream.'

But dreams had power and risks.

'My ponies screamed, and I couldn't save them. He set them afire, and they screamed. Alastar came and knocked the bad man down. I rode away on Alastar, but I couldn't save the ponies. I'm afraid of the bad man in the dream.'

'He won't hurt you. I'll never let him hurt you. Only dream ponies.' Eyes tightly closed, she kissed Teagan's bright, tousled hair, her cheeks. 'We'll dream of more. Green ones, and blue ones.'

'Green ponies!'

'Oh aye, green as the hills.' Snuggling, Sorcha lifted a hand, circled her finger, twirled it, twirled it until ponies – blue ones, green ones, red ones, yellow ones – danced in the air above their heads. Listening to her youngest giggle, Sorcha stored up her fears, her anger, closed them in with determination.

He would never harm her children. She would see him dead, and herself with him, before she allowed it.

'All the ponies to their oats now. And you come with me then, and we'll break our fast as well.'

'Is there honey?'

'Aye.' The simple wish for a treat made Sorcha smile. 'There'll be honey for good girls.'

'I'm good!'

'You are the purest and sweetest of hearts.'

Sorcha gathered up Teagan, and her baby held tight, whispered in her ear. 'The bad man said he would take me first as I'm the youngest and weak.'

'He'll never take you, I swear it, on my life.' She eased Teagan back so her daughter could see the truth of it in her eyes. 'I swear it to you. And, my darling, weak you're not, and never will be.'

So she fed the fire, poured honey on the bread, and made the tea and oats. They'd all need their strength for what she would do that day. What she needed to do.

Her boy came down from the loft, his hair tousled and tangled from sleep. He rubbed his eyes, sniffed the air like a hound. 'I fought the black sorcerer. I didn't run.'

Inside her breast Sorcha's heart kicked to a gallop. 'You dreamed. Tell me.'

'I was at the turn of the river where we keep the boat, and he came, and I knew him for a sorcerer, a black one because his heart is black.'

'His heart.'

'I could see in his heart, though he smiled, friendly like, and offered me some honey cake. "Here, lad," says he, "I've a fine treat for you." But the cake was full of worms and black blood – inside it. I could tell it was poisoned.'

'You saw inside his heart, and inside the cake, in the dream.'

'I did, I promise.'

'I believe you.' So her little man had more than she'd known.

'I said to him, "Eat the cake yourself, for it's death in your hand." But he threw it aside, and the worms crawled out of it and burned to ashes. He thought he would drown me in the river, but I threw rocks at him. Then Roibeard came.'

'Did you call the hawk in your dream?'

'I wished for him, and he came, and he flashed out with his talons. The black sorcerer went away, like smoke in the wind. And I waked in my bed.'

Sorcha drew him close, stroked his hair.

She'd unleashed her fury at Cabhan, so he came after her children.

'You're brave and true, Eamon. Now, break your fast. We've the stock to tend.'

Sorcha moved closer to Brannaugh, who stood at the base of the ladder. 'And you as well.'

'He came into my dream. He said he would make me his bride. He ... tried to touch me. Here.' Pale with the telling, she covered her chest with her hands. 'And here.' Then between her legs.

Shaking, she pressed her face to her mother when Sorcha embraced her. 'I burned him. I don't know how, but I made his fingers burn. He cursed me, and made fists with his hands. Kathel came, leaping onto the bed, snarling, snapping. Then the man was gone. But he tried to touch me, and he said he'd make me his bride, but–'

Rage woke inside the fear. 'He never will. My oath on it. He'll never put his hands on you. Eat now, and eat all. There's much work to do.'

She sent them all out to feed and water the animals, clean the stalls, milk the fat cow.

Alone she prepared herself, gathered her tools. The bowl, the bells, the candles, the sacred knife, and the cauldron. She chose the herbs she'd grown and dried. And the three copper bracelets Daithi had bought her at a long-ago summer fair.

She went out, drew deep of the air, lifted her arms to stir the wind. And called the hawk.

He came on a cry that echoed over the trees and the hills beyond that, which caused servants in the castle by the river to cast their eyes up. His wings, spread wide, caught the glint of the winter

25

sun. She lifted her arm so those wicked talons clutched on her leather glove.

Her eyes looked into his, and his into hers.

'Swift and wise, strong and fearless. You are Eamon's, but mine as well. You will serve what comes from me. Mine will serve what comes from you. I have need of you, and ask this for my son, for your master and your servant.'

She showed him the knife, and his eyes never wavered.

'Roibeard, I ask of thee, a drop of blood from your breast times three. A single feather from your great wing, and for these gifts your praises I sing. To guard my son, this is done.'

She pricked him, held the small flask for the three drops. Plucked a single feather.

'My thanks,' she whispered. 'Stay close.'

He lifted from her hand, but soared only to the branch of a tree. And closing his wings, watched.

She whistled for the dog. Kathel watched her with love, with trust. 'You are Brannaugh's, but mine as well,' she began, and repeated the ritual, gathering the three drops of blood, and a bit of fur from his flank.

Last, she moved into the shed, into the sound of her children laughing as they worked. She took strength from that. And stroked her hand down the pony's face.

Teagan raced over when she saw the knife. 'Don't!'

'I do him no harm. He is yours, but mine as well. He will serve what comes from me, and you, as you will serve what comes from him. I have need of you, Alastar, and ask this for my daughter, for your mistress and your servant.'

'Don't cut him. Please!'

'Only a prick, only a scratch, and only if he consents. Alastar, I ask of thee, a drop of blood from your breast times three. A bit of hair from your pretty mane, and for these gifts, I praise your name. To guard my little one, this is done.

'Just three drops,' Sorcha said quietly as she pricked with the tip of the knife. 'Just a bit of his mane. And here now.' Though Alastar stood quiet, his eyes wise and calm, Sorcha laid her hands on the small, shallow cut, pushed her magick into it to heal. For her daughter's tender heart.

'Come with me now, all of you.' She lifted Teagan onto her hip, led the way back into the house. 'You know what I am. I have never hidden it. You know you carry the gift, each of you. I have always told you. Your magick is young and innocent. One day it will be strong and quick. You must honor it. You must use it to harm none, for the harm you do will come back on you threefold. Magick is a weapon, aye, but not one to be used against the innocent, the weak, the guiltless. It is a gift and a burden, and you will all carry both. You will all pass both to those who come from you. Today you learn more. Heed me and what I do. Watch, listen, know.'

She moved to Brannaugh first. 'Your blood, and mine, with the blood of the hound. Blood is life. Its loss is death. Three drops from thee, three drops from me, and with the hound's, the charm is bound.'

Brannaugh placed her hand in her mother's without hesitation, held steady as Sorcha pricked her with the knife.

'My boy,' she said to Eamon. 'Three drops from thee, three drops from me, and from the hawk's heart, to seal three parts.'

Though his lips trembled, Eamon held out his hand.

'And my baby. Don't fear.'

Her eyes shone with tears, but Teagan watched her mother solemnly as she held out her hand.

'Three drops from thee, three drops from me, with the horse as your guide, the magicks ride.'

She mixed the blood, kissed Teagan's little hand. 'There now, that's done.'

She lifted the cauldron, slid the vials into the pouch at her waist. 'Bring the rest. This is best done outside.'

She chose her spot, on the hard ground with snow lumped in the cool shadows of the trees.

'Should we get firewood?' Eamon asked her.

'Not for this. Stand here, together.' She moved beyond them, called on the goddess, on the earth, the wind, the water, and the fire. And cast the circle. The low flame bubbled over the ground, rounded until end met end. And inside, warmth rose like spring.

'This is protection and respect. Evil cannot come within, dark cannot defeat the light. And what is done within the circle is done for good, is done for love.

'First the water, of sea, of sky.' She cupped her hands, opened them over the cauldron, water blue as a sun-kissed lake poured out, poured in. 'And the earth, our land, our hearts.'

She flicked one hand, then the other, and rich

brown earth spilled into the cauldron. 'And the air, song of the wind, breath of body.' She opened her arms, and blew. And like music, the air swept in with earth and water.

'Now the fire, flame and heat, the beginning, the ending.'

She glowed, the air around her simmering, her eyes burning blue as she threw her arms up, cast her hands down.

Fire erupted in the cauldron, shooting flame, dancing sparks.

'These your father gave to me. They are a sign of his love, a sign of mine. You are, all three, of that love.'

She cast the three copper bracelets into the flame, and circling it, added fur and hair and feather, added blood.

'The goddess gifts to me the power so I stand in this place, in this hour. I cast the charm, protect from harm my children three and all that comes from them, from me. The horse, the hawk, the hound, by blood they are ever bound to shield to serve from life to life in joy, in sorrow, in health, in strife.

'In earth, in air, in flame, in sea. As I will, so mote it be.'

Sorcha lifted her arms high, turned her face to the sky.

The fire shot up in a tower, red and gold, wild blue in its core as it spun and twisted into the cold winter sky.

The earth shook. The icy water in the stream went to roaring. And the wind howled like a wolf on the hunt.

Then it stilled, it died, and there were just three children, hand gripping hand, watching their mother – pale as snow now – sway.

Sorcha shook her head as Brannaugh started toward her. 'Not yet. Magick is work. It gives, and it takes. It must be finished.' She reached in the cauldron, drew out three copper amulets. 'To Brannaugh the hound, to Eamon the hawk, to Teagan the horse.' She slipped an amulet over each child's head. 'These are your signs and your shields. They protect you. You must keep them with you always. Always. He cannot touch what you are if you have your shield, if you believe its power, believe in mine and your own. One day you will pass this to one who comes from you. You'll know which. You'll tell your children the story and sing the old songs. You'll take the gift, and give the gift.'

Teagan admired hers, smiled as she turned the small oval in the sunlight. 'It's pretty. It looks like Alastar.'

'It's of him, and of you, and of me and your father, of your brother and your sister. And why shouldn't it be pretty?' She lowered to kiss Teagan's cheek. 'I have such pretty children.'

She could barely stand, and had to bite back a moan as Brannaugh helped her to her feet. 'I must close the circle. We must take everything inside now.'

'We'll help you,' Eamon said, and took his mother's hand.

With her children, she closed the circle, let them carry the tools into the house.

'You need to rest, sit by the fire.' Brannaugh

pulled her mother to the chair. 'I'll fix you a potion.'

'Aye, and a strong one. Show your brother and sister how it's done.

She smiled when Teagan wrapped a shawl around her shoulders, when Eamon spread a blanket over her lap. But when she started to reach for the cup Brannaugh brought, her daughter held it back. Then squeezed at the flesh around the cut on her hand until three drops of blood plopped into the cup.

'Blood is life.'

Sorcha sighed. 'It is, aye. It is. Thank you.'

She drank the potion, and slept.

2

For a week, then two, she was strong, and her power held. Cabhan battered at it, he pushed, he slithered, but she held him back.

The blackthorn bloomed, and the snowdrops, and the light turned more toward spring than winter.

Each night Sorcha watched for Daithi in the fire. When she could, she spoke to him, risked sending her spirit to him to bring back his scent, his voice, his touch – and to leave hers with him.

So to strengthen them both.

She told him nothing of Cabhan. The magicks were her world. His sword, his fist, even his warrior's heart could not defeat such as Cabhan.

31

The cabin, hers before she'd taken Daithi as her man, was hers to defend. The children they'd made together, hers to protect.

And still she counted down the days to Beal-taine, to the day she would see him riding home again.

Her children thrived, and they learned. Some voice in her head urged her to teach them all she could as quickly as she could. She didn't question it.

She spent hours at night in the light of the tallow and the fire writing out her spells, her recipes, even her thoughts. And when she heard the howl of the wolf or the beat of the wind, she ignored it.

Twice she was called to the castle for a healing, and took her children so they could play with the other youths, so to keep them close, and to let them see the respect afforded the Dark Witch.

For the name and all it held would be their legacy.

But each time they journeyed home, she needed a potion to revive the strength sapped from the healing magicks she dispensed to those in need.

Though she yearned for her man, and for the health she feared would never be fully hers again, she schooled her children daily in the craft. She stood back when Eamon called to Roibeard – more his than hers now, as it should be. Watched with pride as her baby rode Alastar, as fierce as any warrior.

And knew, with both pride and sorrow, how often Brannaugh and her faithful Kathel patrolled the woods.

The gift was there, but so was childhood. She made certain there was music, and games, and as much innocence as she could preserve.

They had visitors, those who came for charms, for salves, who sought answers to questions, who hoped for love or fortune. She helped those she could, took their offerings. And watched the road, always watched the road – though she knew her love was still weeks from home.

She took them out on the river in the little boat their father had built on a day of easy winds when the sky held more blue than gray.

'They say witches can't travel over water,' Eamon announced.

'Is that what they say then?' Sorcha laughed, lifted her face to the breeze. 'Yet here we are, sailing fine and true.'

'It's Donal who says it – from the castle.'

'Saying it, even believing it, doesn't make it truth.'

'Eamon made a frog fly for Donal. It was like boasting.'

Eamon gave his younger sister a dark look, would've added a poke or pinch if his mother hadn't been watching.

'Flying frogs might be fun, but it isn't wise to spend your magick for amusements.'

'It was practice.'

'You might practice catching us some fish for supper. Not that way,' Sorcha warned as her son lifted his hands over the water. 'Magick isn't every answer. A body must know how to fend for himself without it as well. A gift should never be squandered on what you can do with your wit

33

and your hands or your back.'

'I like to fish.'

'I don't.' Brannaugh brooded as the little boat plied the river. 'You sit and sit and wait and wait. I'd rather hunt. Then you have the woods, and we could have rabbit for dinner.'

'Tomorrow's as good as today for that. We'll look for fish tonight if your brother has luck and skill. And perhaps a potato pie.'

Bored, Brannaugh handed her line to her sister, and gazed out over the water to the castle with its great stone walls.

'Did you not want to live there, Ma? I heard the women talking. They said we were all welcome.'

'We have our home, and though it was just a hut once, it's stood longer than those walls. It stood when the O'Connors ruled, before the House of Burke. Kings and princes come and go, *m'inion*, but home is always.'

'I like the look of it, so grand and tall, but I like our woods better.' She leaned her head on her mother's arm a moment. 'Could the Burkes have taken our home?'

'They could have tried, but they were wise to respect magick. We have no fight with them, nor they with us.'

'If they did, Da would fight them. And so would I.' She slid her gaze toward her mother. 'Dervla from the castle told me Cabhan was banished.'

'That you knew already.'

'Aye, but she said he comes back, and he lies with women. He whispers in their ear and they think he's their lawful husband. But in the morning, they know. They weep. She said you gave the

34

women charms to keep him away, but ... he lured one of the kitchen maids away, into the bog. No one can find her.'

She knew of it, just as she knew the kitchen maid would never be found. 'He toys with them, and preys on the weak to feed himself. His power is black and cold. The light and the fire will always defeat him.'

'But he comes back. He scratches at the windows and doors.'

'He can't enter.' But she felt a chill through her blood.

Just then Eamon let out a shout, and when he yanked up his line, a fish flashed silver in the sunlight.

'Luck and skill,' Sorcha said with a laugh as she grabbed the net.

'I want to catch one.' Teagan leaned eagerly over the water as if searching for a likely fish.

'We'll hope you do, as we'll need more than one, even such a fine one. It's good work, Eamon.'

They caught three more, and if she helped her baby a bit, the magick was for love.

She rowed them back with the sun sparkling, the breeze dancing, and the air full of her children's voices.

A good, fine day, she thought, and spring so close she could almost taste it.

'Run on home then, Eamon, and clean those fish. You can get the potatoes started, Brannaugh, and I'll see to the boat.'

'I'll stay with you.' Teagan snuck her hand into her mother's. 'I can help.'

'That you can, as we'll need to fetch some water

from the stream.'

'Do fish like us to catch and eat them?'

'I can't say they do, but it's their purpose.'

'Why?'

And *why*, Sorcha thought as she secured the boat, had been Teagan's first word. 'Didn't the powers put the fish in the water, and give us the wit to make the nets and lines?'

'But they must like swimming more than the fire.'

'I expect so. So we should be mindful and grateful when we eat.'

'What if we didn't catch and eat them?'

'We'd be hungry more often than not.'

'Do they talk under the water?'

'Well now, I've never had a conversation with a fish. Here now.' Sorcha pulled Teagan's cloak more closely around her. 'It's getting cold.' She glanced up, saw the clouds rolling over the sun. 'We may have a storm tonight. Best get home.'

As she straightened, came the fog. Gray and dirty, it slunk like a snake over the ground and smothered the sparkle of the day.

Not a storm coming, Sorcha realized. The threat was here already.

She pushed Teagan behind her as Cabhan rose out of the fog.

He wore black picked through with silver like stars against a midnight sky. His hair waved to his shoulders, an ebony frame for his hard and beautiful face. His eyes, dark as a gypsy's heart, held both power and pleasure as he scraped them over Sorcha.

She felt them, like bold hands on her skin.

Around his neck he wore a large silver pendant shaped like a sun with a fat jewel – a glinting red eye – in its center. And this was new, she thought, and sensed its black power.

'My lady,' he said, and bowed to her.

'You have no welcome here.'

'I walk where I will. And what do I see but a woman and her small, pretty child alone. Treats for brigands and wolves. You have no man to see you safe, Sorcha the Dark. I will escort you.'

'I see myself safe. Begone, Cabhan. You waste your time and powers here. I will never submit to such as you.'

'But you will submit. Joining with me is your destiny. I've seen it in the glass.'

'You see lies and desires, not truth or destiny.'

He only smiled, and like his voice, his smile held seduction. 'Together we'll rule this land, and any others we wish. You will wear fine cloth in bright colors and drape your skin in jewels.'

He swirled his hands. Teagan gasped when she saw her mother wearing the rich red of royalty, the sparkle of jewels, and a gold crown studded with them.

Just as quickly, Sorcha flicked a wrist and was once again draped in her simple black wool. 'I have no need, no wish for your colors and shine. Leave me and mine, or you will feel my wrath.'

But he laughed, the sound rolling from him in smooth and terrible delight. 'Is it a wonder, my heart, that I want none but you? Your fire, your beauty, your power, all meant to be mine.'

'I am Daithi's woman, and will ever be.'

With a grunt of disgust, Cabhan flicked his

fingers. 'Daithi cares more for his raids, his games, his petty little wars than for you or the whelps you bore him. How many times has the moon waxed and waned since he last shared your bed? You grow cold in the night, Sorcha. I feel it. I will show you pleasures you've never known. And I will make you more than you are. I will make you a goddess.'

Fear tried to crawl into her like the fog crawled over the ground. 'I would die by my own hand before being bedded by you. You only crave more power.'

'And you're a fool not to. Together we will crush all who stand against us, live as gods, be as gods. And for this I will give you what your heart most desires.'

'You don't know my heart.'

'A babe in your belly to replace the loss. My son, born of you. More powerful than any has known before or will again.'

Grief for the loss struck, and fear, a terrible fear for the tiny seed of want in her for what he offered. A life growing in her, strong and real.

Sensing that fear, Cabhan stepped closer. 'A son,' he murmured. 'Bright in your womb. Thriving there, born strong and glorious, like no other. Give me your hand, Sorcha, and I will give you your heart's desire.'

She trembled for a moment, a moment only, as oh, by all the gods, she craved that life.

And as she trembled, Teagan leaped out from behind her skirts. She hurled a rock, striking Cabhan on the temple. A thin line of blood, dark, dark red, trickled down his pale skin.

His eyes went fierce as he swung out. Before the blow could land, Sorcha shoved him back with sheer force of will.

She pulled Teagan up, into her arms.

Wind whipped around her now, one born of her own fury. 'I will kill you a thousand times, I will give you agony for ten thousand years if you lay hands on my child. I swear this on all I am.'

'You threaten me? You and your runt?' He fixed his eyes on Teagan's face, and his smile spread like death. 'Pretty little runt. Bright as a fish in the water. Shall I catch and eat you?'

Though she clung to Sorcha, though she shivered, Teagan didn't cower. 'Go away!'

In fury and fear, her young, untried power slapped out, struck as true as the stone. Now blood ran from Cabhan's mouth, and his smile became a snarl.

'First you, then your brother. Your sister ... a bit of ripening first for she, too, will bear me sons.' With a fingertip, he smeared the blood on his face, crossed it over the amulet. 'I would have spared them for you,' he told Sorcha. 'Now you will see their deaths.'

Sorcha pressed her lips to Teagan's ear. 'He can't hurt you,' she began in a whisper, then watched in horror as Cabhan changed.

His body shifted, twisted like the fog. The amulet glowed, the gem spun until his eyes sparked as red as the stone.

Black hair covered his body. Claws sprang from his fingers. And as he seemed to spill over onto the ground, he threw back his head. He howled.

Slowly, carefully, Sorcha set Teagan down again

behind her. 'He can't hurt you.' She prayed it was true, that the magick she'd imbued into the copper sign would hold even against this form.

For surely he'd bartered his soul for this dark art.

The wolf bared its teeth, and sprang.

She pushed back – thrusting out her hands, drawing up her strength so that pure white light shot from her palms. When it struck the wolf it screamed, almost like a man. But it came again, and again, leaping, snapping, its eyes feral and horribly human.

The claws lashed out, caught Sorcha's skirts, tore them. Then it was Teagan's scream that sliced the air.

'Go away, go away!' She pelted the wolf with rocks, rocks that turned to balls of fire as they struck, so the fog smelled of burning flesh and fur.

The wolf lunged again, howling still. Teagan tumbled back as Sorcha slashed down at it. The little girl's cloak fell open. From the copper sign she wore burst a blue flame, straight and sharp as an arrow. It struck the wolf's flank, scored a mark shaped like a pentagram.

On an agonized cry, the wolf flew back. As it pawed and snapped at the air, Sorcha gathered all she had, hurled her light, her hope, her power.

The world went white, blinding her. Desperate, she groped for Teagan's hand as she fell to her knees.

The fog vanished. All that remained of the wolf was scorched earth in its shape.

Weeping, Teagan clutched at her mother, burrowed into her – just a child now, frightened

40

of monsters all too real.

'There now, it's gone. You're safe. We need to go home. We need to be home, my baby.'

But she lacked the strength even to stand. She could have wept herself to be brought so low. Once she could have summoned the power to fly through the woods with her child in her arms. Now her limbs trembled, her breath burned, and her heart beat so fast and hard it pounded her temples.

If Cabhan gathered himself, came back...

'Run home. You know the way. Run home. I'll follow.'

'I stay with you.'

'Teagan, do as I say.'

'No. No.' Knuckling her eyes, Teagan stubbornly shook her head. 'You come. You come.'

Gritting her teeth, Sorcha managed to get to her feet. But after two steps, she simply sank to her knees again. 'I can't do it, my baby. My legs won't carry me.'

'Alastar can. I'll call him, and he'll carry us home.'

'Can you call him, from all this way?'

'He'll come very fast.'

Teagan rose on her sturdy legs, lifted her arms.

'Alastar, Alastar, brave and free, heed my call and come to me. Run swift, run true to find the one who needs you.'

Teagan bit her lip, turned to her mother. 'Brannaugh helped me with the words. Are they good?'

'They're very good.' Young, Sorcha thought. Simple and pure. 'Say it twice more. Three is strong magick.'

Teagan obeyed, then came back to stroke her mother's hair. 'You'll be well again when we're home. Brannaugh will make you tea.'

'Aye, that's what she'll do. I'll be fine again when I'm home.' She thought it was the first time she'd lied to her child. 'Find me a good, strong stick. I think I could lean on it and walk a ways.'

'Alastar will come.'

Though she doubted it, Sorcha nodded. 'We'll meet him. Find me a sturdy stick, Teagan. We have to be home before dark.'

Even as Teagan scrambled up, they heard the hoofbeats.

'He's coming! Alastar! We're here, we're here!'

She'd called her guide, Sorcha thought, and a sharp stab of pride pierced her fatigue. As Teagan ran forward to meet the horse, Sorcha gathered herself again, pushed painfully to her feet.

'There you are, a prince of horses.' Grateful, Sorcha pressed her face to Alastar as he nuzzled her. 'Can you help me mount?' she asked Teagan.

'He will. I taught him a trick. I was saving it for when Da comes home. Kneel, Alastar! Kneel.' Giggling now, Teagan swept a hand down.

The horse bowed his head, then bent his fore-legs, and knelt. 'Oh, my clever, clever girl.'

'It's a good trick?'

'A fine trick. A fine one, indeed.' Grasping the mane, Sorcha pulled herself onto the horse. Nimble as a cricket, Teagan leapt on in front of her.

'You hold on to me, Ma! Alastar and I will get us home.'

Sorcha gripped the little girl's waist, put her

trust in the child and the horse. Every stride of the gallop brought pain, but every stride brought them closer to home.

When they neared the clearing she saw her older children, Brannaugh dragging her grandfather's sword, Eamon holding a dagger, racing toward them.

So brave, too brave.

'Back to the house, back now! Run back!'

'The bad one came,' Teagan shouted. 'And he made himself into a wolf. I threw rocks at him, Eamon, like you did.'

The children's voices – the questions, the excitement, the licks of fear – circled like echoes in Sorcha's head. Sweat soaked her. Once again she grasped Alastar's mane, lowered herself to the ground. Swayed as the world went gray.

'Ma's sick. She needs her tea.'

'Inside,' Sorcha managed. 'Bolt the door.'

She heard Brannaugh giving orders, clipping them out like a chieftain – 'fetch water, stir the fire' – and felt as if she floated inside, into her chair, where her body collapsed.

A cool cloth on her head. Warm, potent liquid easing down her throat. A quieting of the pain, a clearing of the mists.

'Rest now.' Brannaugh stroked her hair.

'I'm better. You have a strong gift for healing.'

'Teagan said the wolf burned up.'

'No. We hurt him, aye, we hurt him, but it lives. He lives.'

'We'll kill it. We'll set a trap and kill it.'

'It may come to that, when I'm stronger. He has more than he did, this shifting of shapes. I

43

can't say what price he paid for the power, but it would be dear. Your sister marked him. Here.' Sorcha clutched a hand on her left shoulder. 'The shape of a pentagram. Watch for this, be wary of this, and any who bear that mark.'

'We will. You don't be fretting now. We'll make the supper, and you'll feel stronger for eating, and resting.'

'You'll make a charm for me. Exactly as I say. Make the charm, and bring it to me. Supper can wait until that's done.'

'Will it make you stronger?'

'Aye.'

Brannaugh made the charm, and Sorcha hung it around her neck, next to her heart. She sipped more potion, and though her appetite was small, forced herself to eat.

She slept, and dreamed, and woke to find Brannaugh keeping watch.

'Off to bed now. It's late.'

'We won't leave you. I can help you to bed.'

'I'll sit here, by the fire.'

'Then I'll sit with you. We're taking turns. I'll wake Eamon when it's his, and Teagan will bring you morning tea.'

Too weary to argue, too proud to scold, Sorcha only smiled. 'Is that the way of it?'

'Until you're all well again.'

'I'm better, I promise you. His magick was so strong, so black. It took all I had in me, and more, to stop it. Our Teagan, you'd be proud. So fierce and bright she was. And you, running toward us with your grandda's sword.'

'It's very heavy.'

44

The laugh felt good. 'He was a big man with a red beard as long as your arm.' On a sigh, she ran her hand over Brannaugh's head. 'If you won't go to your bed, make a pallet there on the floor. We'll both sleep awhile.'

When her child slept, Sorcha added a charm to make Brannaugh's dreams good and sweet.

And she turned to the fire. It was time, long past, to call Daithi home. She needed his sword, she needed his strength. She needed him.

So she opened her mind to the fire, opened her heart to her love.

Her spirit traveled over the hills and fields, through the night, through woods, over water where the moon swam. She flew across all the miles that separated them to the camp of their *clann*.

He slept near the fire with the moonlight like a blanket over him.

When she settled down beside him, his lips curved, and his arm curled around her.

'You smell of home fires and wooded glades.'

'It's home you must come.'

'Soon, *aghra*. Two weeks, no more.'

'Tomorrow you must ride with all haste. My heart, my warrior.' She cupped his face. 'We have need of you.'

'And I of you.' He rolled over onto the vision of her, lowered his mouth to hers.

'Not for the bed, though oh, I ache for you. Every day, every night. I need your sword, I need you by my side. Cabhan attacked today.'

Daithi sprang up, his hand on the hilt of his sword. 'Are you hurt? The children?'

'No, no. But nearly. He grows stronger, and I weaker. I fear I can't hold him.'

'There is none stronger than you. He will never touch the Dark Witch.'

Her heart broke at his faith in her, for she could no longer earn it. 'I'm not well.'

'What is this?'

'I didn't wish to burden you, and ... no, my pride. I valued it too much, but now I cast it away. I fear what comes, Daithi. I fear him. I cannot hold him without you. For our children, for our lives, come home.'

'I will ride tonight. I will bring men with me, and ride for home.'

'At first light. Wait for the light, for the dark is his. And be swift.'

'Two days. I will be home with you in two days. And Cabhan will know the bite of my sword. I swear it.'

'I will watch for you, and wait for you. I am yours in this life and all that come.'

'Heal, my witch.' He brought her hands to his lips. 'It's all I will ever ask of you.'

'Come home, and I will heal.'

'Two days.'

'Two days.' She kissed him, holding tight and close. And carried the kiss with her as she flew back over the mirror of the moon and the green hills.

She came back into her body, tired, so tired, but stronger as well. The magick between them flowed rich, flowed true.

Two days, she thought, and closed her eyes. While he rode to her she would rest, she would let the magick build again. Keep the children close, draw in the light.

She slept again; she dreamed again.

And saw in her dream he didn't wait for the light. He mounted in the moonlight, under the cold stars. His face was fierce as his horse danced over the hard ground.

His horse lunged forward, far outpacing the mounts of the three men who rode with him.

Using the moonlight and the stars, Daithi rode for home, for his family, for his woman. For the Dark Witch he loved more than his life.

When the wolf leaped out of the dark, he barely had time to clear his sword from its sheath. Daithi struck out, but cut through only air as the horse reared. Fog rose like gray walls, trapping him, blocking his men.

He fought, but the wolf sprang over the blade, time after time, snapping out with its jaws, swiping viciously with claws only to vanish into the fog. Only to charge out from it again.

She flew to reach him, soaring over those hills again, across the water.

She knew when those jaws tore, knew when the blood spilled from his heart – from hers. Her tears fell like rain, washing away the fog. Crying his name, she dropped to the ground beside him.

She tried her strongest spell, her most powerful charm, but his heart would not beat again.

As she clasped Daithi's hand in hers, cried to the goddess for mercy, she heard the wolf laugh in the dark.

Brannaugh shivered in sleep. Dreams stalked her,

full of blood and snarls and death. She struggled to outpace them, to break free. She wanted her mother, wanted her father, wanted the sun and warmth of spring.

But clouds and cold covered her. The wolf stepped out of the fog and into her path. And its fangs dripped red and wet.

On a muffled cry she shoved up on her pallet and clutched her amulet. Curling her knees up, she hugged them hard, swiped her teary face against her thighs to dry them. She wasn't a babe to weep over bad dreams.

It was past time to wake Eamon, and then hope to sleep more calmly in her own cot.

She turned her head first to check on her mother, and saw the chair empty. Knuckling her eyes, she called softly for her mother as she started to rise.

And she saw Sorcha lying on the floor between the fire and the loft ladder, still as death.

'Ma! Ma!' Terror seized her as she sprang over to drop at her mother's side. Hands shaking, she turned Sorcha over to cradle her mother's head in her lap. Saying her name over and over like a chant.

Too white, too still, too cold. Rocking, Brannaugh acted without thought or plan. When the heat surged through her, she poured it into her mother. Those shaking hands pressed hard, hard on Sorcha's heart as her own head fell back, as her eyes glazed and fixed. The black smoke of them pulled for the light and shot arrows of it into her mother.

The heat poured out, the cold poured in, until

shuddering, she slumped forward. Sky and sea revolved; light and dark swirled. Pain such as she'd never known sliced through her belly, stabbed into her heart.

Then was gone, leaving only exhaustion.

From somewhere far away, she heard her hound baying.

'No more, no more.' Sorcha's voice croaked out, harsh and weak. 'Stop. Brannaugh, you must stop.'

'You need more. I will find more.'

'No. Do as I say. Quiet breaths, quiet mind, quiet heart. Breath, mind, heart.'

'What's wrong? What happened?' Eamon came flying down the ladder. 'Ma!'

'I found her. Help me, help me get her to bed.'

'No, not bed. No time for it,' Sorcha said. 'Eamon, let Kathel in, and wake Teagan.'

'She's waked, she's here.'

'Ah, there's my baby. Not to fret.'

'There's blood. Your hands have blood.'

'Aye.' Burying her grief, Sorcha stared at her hands. ''Tisn't mine.'

'Fetch a cloth, Teagan, and we'll wash her.'

'No, not a cloth. The cauldron. Fetch my candles, and book, and the salt. All the salt we have. Build up the fire, Eamon, and Brannaugh make my tea – make it strong.'

'I will.'

'Teagan, be a good girl now and pack up what food we have.'

'Are we going on a journey?'

'A journey, aye. Feed the stock, Eamon – aye, it's early yet, but feed them and well, pack all the

49

oats you can for Alastar.'

She took the cup from Brannaugh, drank deep, drank all. 'Now, go pack your things, your clothes, blankets. You'll take the sword, the dagger, all the coin, the jewels my granny left me. All that she left me. All, Brannaugh. Leave nothing of value. Pack it all, and be quick. Quick!' she snapped, and had Brannaugh dashing away.

Time, the Dark Witch thought, it came, it went. And now she had so little left. But enough. She would make it enough.

She sat quiet while her children did her bidding. And built her strength, amassed her power.

When Brannaugh came down, Sorcha stood straight and tall. Her skin held warmth and color, her eyes focus and energy.

'You're well!'

'No, my darling, well I'm not, nor will be again.' She held up a hand before Brannaugh could speak. 'But strong is what I am, for this time and for this need. I will do what I must, and so will you.' She looked to her son, her baby girl. 'So will all of you. Before the sun rises, you will go. You will keep to the woods, go south. Do not use the road until you are well away. Find my cousin Ailish, the Clann O'Dwyer, and tell her the tale. She will do what she can.'

'We will all go.'

'No, Eamon. I will bide here. You must be strong and brave, protect your sisters, and they protect you. I would not survive the journey.'

'I will make you well,' Brannaugh insisted.

''Tis beyond you. 'Tis meant. But I do not leave you alone or helpless. What I am, what I

50

have will live in you. One day you will come back, for this is home, and home is the source. I cannot give you your innocence, but I will give you power.

'Stand with me, for you are my heart and soul, my blood and bone. You are my all. And now I cast the circle, and no dark shall enter.'

Flame circled the floor and, at the flick of her hand, leapt under the cauldron. Looking down at her hands again, she sighed once, then stepped forward.

'This is your father's blood.' She opened her hands over the cauldron, and the blood poured. 'And these are my tears, and yours. He rode to protect us, rode home as I asked him. A trap, set by Cabhan, using my fear, my weakness. He took your father's life, as he will take mine. The life, but not the spirit, not the power.'

She knelt, enfolded her weeping children. 'I would comfort you in every moment I have left, but there is no time for grieving. Remember him who made you, who loved you, and know I go to be with him, and watch over you.'

'Don't send us away.' Teagan sobbed on her mother's shoulder. 'I want to stay with you. I want Da.'

'You'll take the light in me with you. I will always be with you.' With hands now clean and white, Sorcha brushed tears from her daughter's cheek. 'You, my bright light, my hope. You, my brave son.' She kissed Eamon's fingers. 'My heart. And you, my steady, searching one.' She cupped Brannaugh's face. 'My strength. Carry me with you. And now, we work this spell together. Stand

51

with me! Say as I say, do as I do.'

She held out her hands.

'With blood and tears we spill our fears.' She waved a hand over the cauldron, and the liquid within began to stir. 'A pinch of salt times four to close and bolt the door. Weeds to bind, berries to blind. My children he will not see, and they will live safe and free. Pretty petals tinged with hate, scented sweet and so to bait. Boil it all in fire and smoke, and on this potion Cabhan chokes. When I call he comes to me, as I will, so mote it be.'

The light flashed so all in the circle burned with it.

She called on Hecate, on Brighid, on Morrigan and Babd Catha, summoning the strength and power of the goddesses. The air quaked, seemed to split and crack. It rang with voices as Sorcha stood, arms high in both prayer and demand.

The smoke turned red as blood, fogged the room. Then, as if in a whirlpool, sucked back into the cauldron.

Eyes bright, Sorcha poured the potion into a vessel, sealed it, slid it into her pocket.

'Mother,' Brannaugh breathed.

'I am, and will be. Don't fear me, or what I give you now. My baby.' She took Teagan's hands. 'It will grow in you, as you grow. You will ever be kind, ever ask why. You will ever stand for those who cannot stand. Take this.'

'It's hot,' Teagan said as her hands glowed in her mother's.

'It will cool again, until you need it. My son. You will fly, and you will fight. You will ever be loyal and true. Take this.'

'I would take you. I would guard you.'

'Guard your sisters. Brannaugh, my first. So much to ask of you. Your gift is strong already, and now I give you more. More than Teagan and Eamon, as I must. You will build and you will make. When you love, you will never stop. You will ever be the one they look to first, and will ever bear the burden. Forgive me, and take this.'

Brannaugh gasped. 'It burns!'

'Only for a moment.' And in that moment Sorcha grieved a thousand years. 'Open. Take. Live.'

She kept only enough, just enough, then let herself slide to the floor when it was done. She was the Dark Witch no more.

'You are the Dark Witch, one by three. This is my gift, and my curse. Each of you is strong, and stronger together. One day you'll return. Go now, and quickly. Day comes. Know my heart goes with you.'

But Teagan clung to her, kicked, cried when Eamon pulled her away.

'Take her outside, onto Alastar,' Brannaugh said quietly.

But first Eamon knelt to his mother. 'I will avenge my father, and you, my mother. I will protect my sisters with my life. I swear this.'

'I am proud of my son. I will see you again. My baby,' she said to Teagan. 'You will return. I promise you.'

Brannaugh turned to her sister, passed a hand over her head. And Teagan nodded to sleep.

'Take her, Eamon, and the packs you can carry.

I'll bring the rest.'

'I'll help you. I'm strong enough,' Sorcha insisted. And she didn't intend to allow Cabhan into her house.

As they loaded the horse, Brannaugh looked into her mother's eyes. 'I understand.'

'I know—'

'I'll let no harm come to them. If you cannot destroy Cabhan, your blood will. If it takes a thousand years, your blood will.'

'Night's fleeting, go quickly. Alastar will carry the three of you far enough into day.' Sorcha's lips trembled before she found the will to firm them. 'She is tender of heart, our baby.'

'I will always care for her. I promise you.'

'Then that's enough. Go, go, or all is for naught.'

Brannaugh pulled herself up behind her brother and her spell-struck sister. 'If I am your strength, Mother, you are mine. All that come from us will know of Sorcha. All will honor the Dark Witch.'

Through the blur of tears, she looked ahead, and kicked the horse into a gallop.

Sorcha watched them, kept them in her mind's eye as they rode through the dark of the woods, away from her. Toward life.

And as day broke, she took the potion from her pocket, drank. Waited for the dark one to come.

He brought the fog, but came as a man, drawn to her scent, to the shimmer of her skin. To her power, false now, but potent.

'My man is dead,' she said flatly.

'Your man stands before you.'

'But you are not a man like other men.'

54

'More than others. You called me, Sorcha the Dark.'

'I am not a woman like other women, but more. Needs must be met. Power calls to power. Will you make me a goddess, Cabhan?'

Greed and lust darkened his eyes and, Sorcha thought, blinded him.

'I will show you more than you can imagine. Together we will have all, be all. You have only to join with me.'

'What of my children?'

'What of them?' His gaze shifted to the house. 'Where are they?' he demanded, and would have pushed by her.

'They sleep. I am their mother, and I would have your word on their safety. You cannot enter until it's given. I cannot join with you until you swear your oath.'

'They will come to no harm from me.' He smiled again. 'So I swear to you.'

Liar, she thought. I can still see your mind, and the dark pit of your heart.

'Then come and kiss me. Make me yours as I make you mine.'

He pulled her hard against him, twisted her hair cruelly in his hand to drag her head back. And crushed his lips to hers.

She opened those lips, and with death in her heart allowed his tongue to sweep into her mouth. Allowed the poison to do its work.

He stumbled back, clutching at his throat. 'What have you done?'

'I have beaten you. I have destroyed you. And with my last breaths, I curse you. On this day and in this hour, I call upon what holds of my power. You will burn and die in pain, and know the Dark Witch has you slain. So my blood curses your blood for all eternity. As I will, so mote it be.'

He threw his power at her, even as his skin began to smoke, to blacken. She fell, in blood, in agony, but clung to life. Clung only to watch his death.

'All that come from you be damned,' she managed as flames burst from him, as his screams tore the world.

'My death for his,' she whispered when the black ashes of the sorcerer smoldered on the ground. 'It is right. It is just. It is done.'

She let go, released her spirit and left her body by the cabin in the deep green woods.

And as the fog swirled, something shifted in the black ashes.

3

County Mayo, 2013

The cold carved bone deep, fueled by the lash of the wind, iced by the drowning rain gushing from a bruised, bloated sky.

Such was Iona Sheehan's welcome to Ireland.

She loved it.

How could she not? she asked herself as she hugged her arms to her chest and drank in the wild, soggy view from her window. She was standing in a castle. She'd sleep in a castle that night. An honest-to-God Irish castle in the heart of the west.

Some of her ancestors had worked there, probably slept there. Everything she knew verified that her people, on her mother's side in any case, had sprung from this gorgeous part of the world, this magical part of this magical country.

She'd gambled, well, pretty much everything to come here, to find her roots, to – she hoped – connect with them. And most of all, to finally understand them.

Burnt bridges, left them smoldering behind her in the hopes of building new ones, stronger ones. Ones that led somewhere she wanted to go.

She'd left her mother mildly annoyed. But then her mother never rose to serious anger, or sorrow, or joy or passion. How difficult had it been to find herself saddled with a daughter who rode emotions like a wild stallion? Her father had just patted her head in his absent way, and wished her luck as casually as he might some passing acquaintance.

She suspected she'd never been any more than that to him. Her paternal grandparents considered the trip a grand adventure, and had given her the very welcome gift of a check.

She was grateful, even knowing they belonged to the out-of-sight-out-of-mind school and probably wouldn't give her another thought.

But her maternal grandmother, her treasured Nan, had given her a gift with so many questions.

She was here in this lovely corner of Mayo, ringed by water, shadowed by ancient trees, to find the answers.

She should wait until tomorrow, settle in, take a nap, as she'd barely slept on the flight from

Baltimore. At least she should unpack. She had a week in Ashford Castle, a foolish expense on the practical scale. But she wanted, so wanted that connection, that once-in-a-lifetime treat.

She opened her bags, began to take out clothes.

She was a woman who'd once wished she'd grow taller than her scant five three, and curvier than the slim, teenage boy body the fates had granted her. Then she'd stopped wishing and compensated by using bright colors in her wardrobe, and wearing high, high heels whenever she could manage it.

Illusion, Nan would say, was as good as reality.

She'd once wished she could be beautiful, like her mother, but worked with what she had – cute. The only time she'd seen her mother close to genuinely horrified had been just the week before when Iona had chopped off her long blond hair to a pixie cap.

Far from used to it herself, she raked her fingers through it. It suited her, didn't it? Didn't it bring out her cheekbones a little?

It didn't matter if she regretted the impulse; she'd regretted others. Trying new things, taking new risks – those were her current goals. No more wait-and-see, the mantra of her parents as long as she could remember. Now was now.

And with that in mind, she thought, the hell with unpacking, the hell with waiting until tomorrow. What if she died in her sleep?

She dug out boots, a scarf, the new raincoat – candy pink – she'd bought for Ireland. She dragged a pink-and-white-striped cap over her hair, slung her oversized purse on cross-body.

Don't think, just do, she told herself, and left her warm, pretty room.

She made a wrong turn almost immediately, but it only gave her time to wander the corridors. She'd asked for a room in the oldest section when she'd booked, and liked to imagine servants scurrying with fresh rushes, or ladies sitting at their spindles. Or warriors in bloody mail returning from battle.

She had days to explore the castle, the grounds, the nearby village of Cong, and she meant to make use of all of it.

But her primary goal remained to seek out and make contact with the Dark Witch.

When she stepped outside into the whistling wind and drenching rain, she told herself it was a perfect day for witches.

The little map Nan had drawn was in her bag, but she'd etched it on her memory. She turned away from the great stone walls, took the path toward the deep woods. Passed winter-quiet gardens, spreads of soaked green. Belatedly she remembered the umbrella in her bag, dragged it out, pushing her way forward into the evocative gloom of the rain-struck woods.

She hadn't imagined the trees so big, with their wide, wide trunks, crazily gnarled branches. A storybook wood, she thought, thrilled with it even as the rain splashed over her boots.

Through its drumming she heard the wind sigh and moan, then the rumble of what must be the river.

Paths speared, forked, but she kept the map in her head.

She thought she heard something cry overhead, and for a moment imagined she saw the sweep of wings. Then despite the drumming, the rumbling, the sighs and the moans, everything suddenly seemed still. As the path narrowed, roughened, her heartbeat pounded in her ears, too quick, too loud.

To the right an upended tree exposed a base taller than a man, wider than her arm span. Vines thick as her wrist tangled together like a wall. She found herself drawn toward them, struck by the urge to pull at them, to fight her way through them to see what lay beyond. The concept of getting lost flitted through her mind, then out again.

She just wanted to see.

She took a step forward, then another. She smelled smoke and horses, and both pulled her closer to that tangled wall. Even as she reached out, something burst through. The massive black blur had her stumbling back. She thought, instinctively: Bear!

Since the umbrella had flown out of her hand, she looked around frantically for a weapon – a stick, a rock – then saw as it eyed her, the biggest dog ever to stand on four massive paws.

Not a bear, she thought, but as potentially deadly if he wasn't somebody's cheerful pet.

'Hello ... doggie.'

He continued to watch her out of eyes more gold than brown. He stepped forward to sniff her, which she hoped wasn't the prelude to taking a good, hard bite. Then let out two cannon-shot barks before loping away.

'Okay.' She bent over from the waist until she caught her breath. 'All right.'

Exploring would definitely wait for a bright, sunny day. Or at least a brighter, dryer one. She picked up her soaked and muddy umbrella and pressed on.

She should've waited on the whole thing, she told herself. Now she was wet and flustered and, she realized, more travel weary than she'd expected. She should be napping in her warm hotel bed, snuggled in listening to the rain instead of trudging through it.

And now – perfect – fog rolled in, surfing over the ground like waves on the shore. Mists thickened like those vines, and the rain sounded like voices muttering.

Or there were voices muttering, she thought. In a language she shouldn't understand, but almost did. She quickened her pace, as anxious to get out of the woods as she'd been to get into them.

The cold turned brutal until she saw her breath hazing out. Now the voices sounded in her head: Turn back. Turn back.

It was stubbornness as much as anxiety that had her pushing ahead until she nearly ran along the slippery path.

And like the dog, burst into the clear.

The rain was just the rain, the wind just the wind. The path opened into a road, with a few houses, smoke puffing out of chimneys. And beyond, the beauty of the mist-shrouded hills.

'Too much imagination, not enough sleep,' she told herself.

She saw dooryard gardens resting their bright

blooms for spring, cars parked on the roadside or in short drives.

Not far now, according to Nan's map, so she walked along the road, counting houses.

It sat farther off the road than the others, farther apart as if it needed breathing room. The pretty thatched-roofed cottage with its deep blue walls and bright red door transmitted that same storybook vibe – yet a shiny silver Mini sat in the little driveway. The cottage itself jogged into an L, fronted by curved glass. Even in the winter, pots of bright pansies sat on the stoops, their exotic faces turned upward to drink in the rain.

A sign of aged wood hung above the curve of glass. Its deeply carved letters read:

THE DARK WITCH

'I found her.' For a moment Iona just stood in the rain, closed her eyes. Every decision she'd made in the last six weeks – perhaps every one she'd made in her life – had led to this.

She wasn't sure whether to go to the L – the workshop, Nan had told her – or the cottage entrance. But as she walked closer she saw the gleam of light on the glass. And closer still, the shelves holding bottles full of color – bright or soft – hanks of hanging herbs. Mortars and pestles, bowls and ... cauldrons?

Steam puffed from one on a stove top, and a woman stood at a work counter, grinding something.

Iona's first thought was how unfair it seemed that some women could look like that even without fussing. The dark hair bundled up, sexily messy, the rosy flush from the work and the steam. The fine bones that said beauty from birth to death, and the deeply sculpted mouth just slightly curved in a contented smile.

Was it genes or magick? she wondered. But then, for some, one was the same as the other.

She gathered her courage and, setting her umbrella aside, reached for the door handle.

She barely touched it when the woman looked up, over. The smile deepened, polite welcome, so Iona opened the door, stepped in.

And the smile faded. Eyes of smoke gray held so intensely on her face that Iona stopped where she was, just over the threshold.

'Can I come in?'

'It's in you are.'

'I ... I guess I am. I should've knocked. I'm sorry, I... God, it smells amazing in here. Rosemary and basil and lavender, and ... everything. I'm sorry,' she said again. 'Are you Branna O'Dwyer?'

'I am, yes.' As she answered, she took a towel from under the counter, crossed to Iona. 'You're soaked through.'

'Oh, sorry. I'm dripping on the floor. I walked over from the castle. From the hotel. I'm staying at Ashford Castle.'

'Lucky you, it's a grand place.'

'It's like a dream, at least what I've seen of it. I just got here. I mean, a couple hours ago, and I wanted to come to see you right away. I came to meet you.'

'Why?'

'Oh, I'm sorry, I—'

'You're sorry for a lot it seems, in such a short time.'

'Ha.' Iona twisted the towel in her hands. 'Yeah, it sounds like it. I'm Iona. Iona Sheehan. We're cousins. I mean, my grandmother Mary Kate O'Connor is cousins with your grandmother Ailish, um ... Ailish Flannery. So that makes us ... I get confused if it's fourth or third or whatever.'

'A cousin's a cousin for all that. Well then, take off those muddy boots, and we'll have some tea.'

'Thanks. I know I should've written or called or something. But I was afraid you'd tell me not to come.'

'Were you?' Branna murmured as she set the kettle on.

'It's just once I'd decided to come, I needed to push through with it.' She left her muddy boots by the door, hung her coat on the peg. 'I always wanted to visit Ireland – that roots thing – but it was always eventually. Then ... well, it was now. Right now.'

'Go have a seat at the table back there, by the fire. It's a cold wind today.'

'God, tell me! I swear it got colder the deeper I went into the woods, then... Oh Jesus, it's the bear!'

She stopped as the massive dog lifted his head from his place at the little hearth, and gave her the same steady stare he had in the woods. 'I mean the dog. I thought he was a bear for a minute when he came bursting through the woods. But he's a really big dog. He's your dog.'

'He's mine, yes, and I'm his. He's Kathel, and he won't harm you. Have you a fear of dogs, cousin?'

'No. But he's *huge*. What is he?'

'Breeding, you mean. His father is an Irish wolfhound, and his mother a mix of Irish Dane and Scottish deerhound.'

'He looks fierce and dignified at the same time. Can I pet him?'

'That would be up to you and him,' Branna said as she brought tea and sugar biscuits to the table. She said nothing more as Iona crouched, held out the back of her hand for the dog to sniff, then stroked it gently over his head.

'Hello, Kathel. I didn't have time to introduce myself before. You scared the crap out of me.'

She rose, smiled at Branna. 'I'm so happy to meet you, to be here. Everything's been so crazy, and it's all running around in my head. I can hardly believe I'm standing here.'

'Sit then, and have your tea.'

'I barely knew about you,' Iona began as she sat, warmed her chilled hands on the cup. 'I mean, Nan had told me about the cousins. You and your brother.'

'Connor.'

'Yes, Connor, and the others who live in Galway or Clare. She wanted to bring me over years ago, but it didn't work out. My parents – well, mostly my mother – didn't really want it, and she and my father split up, and then, well, you're just bouncing around between them. Then they both remarried, and that was weird because my mother insisted on an annulment. They say how that doesn't really make you a bastard, but it sure feels like it.'

Branna barely lifted her eyebrows. 'I imagine it

does, yes.'

'Then there was school and work, and I was involved with someone for a while. One day I looked at him and thought, Why? I mean, we didn't have anything for each other but habit and convenience, and people need more, don't they?'

'I'd say they do.'

'I want more, sometime anyway. Mostly, I never felt like I fit. Where I was, something always felt a little skewed, not quite right. Then I started having the dreams – or I started remembering them, and I went to visit Nan. Everything she told me should've sounded crazy. It shouldn't have made sense, but it did. It made everything make sense.

'I'm babbling. I'm so nervous.' She picked up a cookie, stuffed it in her mouth. 'These are good. I'm–'

'Don't be saying you're sorry again. It's coming on pitiful. Tell me about the dreams.'

'He wants to kill me.'

'Who?'

'I don't know. Or I didn't. Nan says his name is – was – is Cabhan, and he's a sorcerer. Evil. Centuries ago our ancestor, the first dark witch, destroyed him. Except some part of him survived it. He still wants to kill me. Us. I know that sounds insane.'

Placidly, Branna sipped her tea. 'Do I look shocked by all this?'

'No. You look really calm. I wish I could be really calm. And you're beautiful. I always wanted to be beautiful, too. And taller. You're taller. Babbling. Can't stop it.'

Rising, Branna opened a cupboard, took out a

bottle of whiskey. 'It's a good day for a little whiskey in your tea. So you heard this story about Cabhan and Sorcha, the first dark witch, and decided to come to Ireland to meet me.'

'Basically. I quit my job, I sold my stuff.'

'You...' For the first time Branna looked genuinely surprised. 'You sold your things?'

'Including twenty-eight pairs of designer shoes – bought at discount, but still. That stung some, but I wanted the break clean. And I needed the money to come here. To stay here. I have a work visa. I'll get a job, find a place to live.'

She picked up another cookie, hoping it would stop the flood of words, but they just kept pouring out. 'I know it's crazy spending so much to stay at Ashford, but I just wanted it. I've got nothing back there but Nan, not really. And she'll come if I ask her. I feel like I might fit here. Like things might balance here. I'm tired of not knowing why I don't belong.'

'What was your work?'

'I was a riding instructor. Trail guide, stable hand. I'd hoped to be a jockey once, but I love them too much, and didn't have the passion for racing and training.'

Watching her, Branna only nodded. 'It's horses, of course.'

'Yeah, I'm good with them.'

'I've no doubt of that. I know one of the owners of the stables here, the hotel uses them for guests. They do trail rides, and riding lessons and the like. I think Boyle might find a place for you.'

'You're kidding? I never figured to get stable work right off. I figured waitress, shop clerk. It would be fabulous if I could work there.'

Some would say too good to be true, but Iona had never believed that. Good should be true.

'Look, I'll muck out stalls, groom. Whatever he needs or wants.'

'I'll have a word with him.'

'I can't thank you enough,' Iona said, reaching for Branna's hand. As they touched, gripped, heat and light flashed.

Though Iona's hand trembled, she didn't pull away, didn't look away.

'What does it mean?'

'It means it may be time at last. Did cousin Mary Kate give you a gift?'

'Yes. When I went to see her, when she told me.' With her free hand, Iona reached for the chain under her sweater, took out the copper amulet with the sign of the horse.

'It was made by Sorcha for her youngest child, her daughter–'

'Teagan,' Iona supplied. 'To shield her from Cabhan. For Brannaugh it was the hound – I should have realized that when I saw the dog. And for Eamon, the hawk. She told me the stories as long as I can remember, but I thought they were stories. My mother insisted they were. And she didn't like Nan telling them to me. So I stopped telling her – my mother – about them. My mother prefers to just sort of glide along.'

'That's why it is the amulet wasn't passed to her, but to you. She wasn't the one. You are. Cousin Mary Kate would come, but we knew she wasn't the one, but like a guardian for the amulet, for the legacy. It was passed to her by others who guarded and waited. Now it comes to you.'

And you, Branna thought, have come to me.

'Did she tell you what you are?' Branna asked.

'She said...' Iona let out a long breath. 'She said I'm the Dark Witch. But you—'

'There are three. Three is good magick. So now we're three. You and I, and Connor. But each must accept the whole, and themselves, and the legacy. Do you?'

Hoping for calm, Iona took a gulp of whiskey-laced tea. 'I'm working on it.'

'What can you do? She wouldn't have passed this to you unless she was sure. Show me what you can do.'

'What?' Iona wiped suddenly damp palms on her jeans. 'Like an audition?'

'I've practiced all my life; you haven't. But you are the blood.' Branna tilted her head, her beautiful face skeptical. 'Have you no skills as yet?'

'I've got some skills. It's just I've never ... except with Nan.' Annoyed, uneasy, Iona drew the candle on the table closer. 'Now I'm nervous,' she muttered. 'I feel like I'm trying out for the school play. I bombed that one.'

'Clear your mind. Let it come.'

She breathed again, slow and steady, put her focus, her energy on the candlewick. Felt the warmth rise in her, and light seep through. And she blew gently.

The flame flickered, swayed, then burned true.

'It's so cool,' Iona whispered. 'I'll never get used to it. I'm just ... magick.'

'It's power. It must be trained, disciplined, and respected. And honored.'

'You sound like Nan. She showed me when I was little, and I believed. Then I thought they were just magick tricks, because my parents said they were. And I think – I know – my mother told her to stop or she wouldn't let her see me.'

'Your mother's mind is closed. She's like a lot of others. You shouldn't be angry with her.'

'She kept me from this. From what I am.'

'Now you know. Can you do more?'

'A few things. I can levitate things – not big things, and it's fifty-fifty. Horses. I understand what they're feeling. I always have. I tried a glamour, but that was a terrible bust. My eyes went purple – even the whites, and my teeth glowed like neon. I had to call in sick for two days before it wore off.'

Amused, Branna added more tea and whiskey to the cups.

'What can you do?' Iona demanded. 'I showed mine. You show yours.'

'Fair enough then.' Branna flicked out a hand, and held a ball of white fire in her palm.

'Holy shit. That's...' Warily Iona reached out, brought her fingertips close enough to feel the heat. 'I want to do that.'

'Then you'll practice, and you'll learn.'

'You'll teach me?'

'I'll guide you. It's already in you, but needs the route, the signs, the ... finesse. I'll give you some books to read and study. Take your week at the castle, and think about what you want, Iona Sheehan. Think carefully, for once it begins, you can't go back.'

'I don't want to go back.'

'I don't mean to America, or your life there. I mean from the path we'll walk.' She flicked her hand again and, with it empty, picked up her tea. 'Cabhan, what is left of him, may be worse than what was. And what is left wants what you have, what we have. And he wants our blood. Your power and your life, you'll risk both, so think carefully, for it's not a game we'd be playing.'

'Nan said it had to be a choice, my choice. She told me he – Cabhan – would want what I have, what I am, and do whatever he could to get it. She cried when I said I was going to come, but she was proud, too. As soon as I got here, I knew it was the right choice. I don't want to ignore what I am. I just want to understand it.'

'Staying is still a choice. And if you decide to stay, you'll stay here, with me and Connor.'

'Here?'

'It's best we stay together. There's room enough.'

Nothing had prepared her for this. Nothing in her life measured as amazing a gift. 'You'd let me live here, with you?'

'We're cousins, after all. Take your week. Connor and I have committed, have taken an oath if the third came, we'd accept. But you haven't had a lifetime, so think it through, and be sure. The decision has to be yours.'

Whatever it was, Branna thought, would change all.

4

The rain soaked her again on her trek back, but it didn't dampen her mood. After warming her bones in the shower, Iona dug out flannel pants, a thermal T-shirt, then, dumping her suitcase on the floor – she'd unpack properly later – she crawled into bed.

And slept like the dead for four solid hours.

She woke in the dark, completely disoriented and starving.

Though her thoroughly disorganized possessions taunted her, she rooted through for jeans, a sweater, warm socks, boots. Armed with her guidebook and one of the books Branna had lent her, she took herself off to the hotel's cottage restaurant for the food, the company.

A fire snapped in the hearth while she dug into a bowl of roasted vegetable soup and pored over her books. She liked the comfort of the mix of voices around her, Irish, American, German – and, she thought, possibly Swedish. She dined on fish and chips, and since it was her first night, treated herself to a glass of champagne.

The waitress had a smile as brilliant as her bright red hair, and gifted Iona with it as she refilled the water glass. 'Are you enjoying your meal then?'

'It's wonderful.' Drawing her shoulders up and in, in a self-hug, Iona beamed a smile back. 'Everything's just wonderful.'

'Would it be your first time at Ashford?'

'Yes. It's amazing. It still feels like a dream.'

'Well, they say we should have better weather tomorrow if you're after rambling about.'

'I'd like to.' Should she rent a car? Iona wondered. Try her luck on the roads? Maybe just a walk to the village, for now. 'Actually, I took a walk through the grounds, the woods this afternoon.'

'In all that drench?'

'I couldn't resist. I wanted to see my cousin. She lives nearby.'

'Is that the truth? Sure it's nice to have family while you're visiting. Who is she, if you don't mind me asking?'

'They, really, though I only met Branna today. Branna O'Dwyer.'

The girl's smile didn't dim, but her eyes showed new focus. 'A cousin to the O'Dwyers, are you now?'

'Yes. Do you know them?'

'Everyone knows Branna and Connor O'Dwyer. He's a falconer. The hotel will book hawk walks through the falconry school, and that Connor manages. It's a very popular activity with the guests here. And Branna ... she has a shop in Cong. She makes soaps and lotions and tonics and the like. The Dark Witch, it's called, after a local legend.'

'I saw her workshop today. I'll have to check out the shop and the falconry school.'

'Both are pleasant walks right from the hotel. Well then, enjoy your meal.'

The waitress left her to it, but Iona noticed she stopped by another server for a quick word. And both of them glanced back to Iona's table.

So, she thought, the O'Dwyers were local interests. Hardly surprising. But it was weird sitting there eating her fish and chips knowing she'd become an object of speculation.

Did they all know Branna wasn't merely the owner of the Dark Witch, but was one?

And so am I, Iona thought. Now I have to learn just what that means. Determined to do just that, she opened another book, and read her way through the rest of the meal.

The rain eased, but the night wind blew fierce, urging her to hurry back to the main hotel rather than strolling along the river Cong as she'd hoped.

She got 'good evenings' and 'welcome backs' from the staff as she stepped in, crossed through the lobby. Curious, she took brochures on the falconry school and the stables, then – what the hell, she was sort of on vacation – asked for tea to be sent to her room.

Once inside, she made herself set the brochures and books aside to deal, finally, with the unpacking.

After the brutal purge of her wardrobe, the selling of whatever she'd put aside, she still had more than enough. And she'd brought all she thought she'd need for her new life.

By the time she'd filled the wardrobe, the drawers, repacked items she decided could wait, the tea arrived, along with a plate of pretty cookies. Satisfied she'd done her chores, she changed back into her sleep pants, piled up the pillows and, sitting in bed, composed the email on her notebook to let her grandmother know she'd arrived safe, had met with Branna.

Ireland's all you said and more, even just the little I've seen. So is Branna. It's so generous of her to let me stay with her. The castle's just awesome, and I'm going to enjoy every minute I'm here, but I'm already looking forward to moving in with Branna – and Connor. I hope I meet him soon. If I get the job at the stables, it'll just be perfect. So think good thoughts.

Nan, I'm sitting in this wonderful bed in a castle in Ireland, drinking tea and thinking of all that's yet to come. I know you said it could be a hard road, hard choices, and Branna sure as hell made that clear. But I'm so excited, I'm so happy.

I think, maybe, I've finally found where I fit.

Tomorrow I'll check out the stables, the falconry school, the village – and Branna's shop. I'll let you know how it all goes. I love you!

Iona

She sent dutiful emails to her mother, her father. A few cheerful ones to friends and coworkers. And reminded herself to take some pictures to send next time.

She set the notebook aside to charge, retrieved the books, the brochures. This time she got into the bed, wiggled her shoulders back against the pillows.

Blissfully happy, she scanned the brochures,

75

studied the photos. The school sounded absolutely fascinating. And the stables perfect. One of her mother's favorite warnings was: Don't get your hopes up.

But Iona's were, high, high up.

She slipped the stable brochure under her pillow. She'd sleep on it for luck. Then she opened Branna's book again.

Within twenty minutes, with the lights on, the tea tray still on the bed beside her, she'd dropped back into sleep.

And this time dreamed of hawks and horses, of the black hound. Of the deep green woods where a stone cabin nestled with fog crawling at its feet.

After dismounting a horse as gray as the fog, she walked through the mists, the hood of her cloak drawn up to cover her hair. She carried roses, for love, to the stone polished smooth and carved deep by magick and grief. There she laid the roses, white as the innocence she'd lost.

'I am home, Mother. We are home.' Dabbing the tears on her cheeks with her fingers, she traced the name.

SORCHA
The Dark Witch

And the words bled against the stone.
I am waiting for you.
Not her mother's voice, but his. With all that had been done, all that had been sacrificed, he survived.

She had known it. They had all known it. And hadn't she come here, alone, for this as much as to visit her mother's grave?

'You will wait longer yet. You will wait a day, a moon, a thousand years, but you will never have what you covet.'

You come alone, in the starlight. You look for love. I would give it to you.

'I am not alone.' She spun around. Her hood fell back and her bright hair caught the light. 'I am never alone.'

The fog swirled, spun up, spun out, coalesced into the form of a man. Or what had been a man.

She'd faced him before, as a child. But she had more than rocks now.

A shadow he was, she thought. A shadow to haunt dreams and smother light.

Such a pretty thing. A woman now, ripe for plucking. Do you still throw stones?

Even as she stared into his eyes, she watched the red stone he wore around his neck gleam.

'My aim is as true as it was ever.'

He laughed, weaved closer. She caught his scent, the hint of sulphur. Only a devil's bargain could have given him the power to exist.

Your mother is gone, no skirts to hide behind now. I defeated her, took her life, rent her power with my hands.

'You lie. Do you think we cannot see? Do you think we do not know?' His amulet pulsed red – his heart, she thought. His center, his power. She meant to take it, at any cost. 'With a kiss she burned you. And I marked you. You bear it still.'

She held up her hands, fingers curled toward him so the mark on his shoulder burned like a flame.

On his scream she leapt forward, snatching at the stone he wore. But he lashed out, fingers going to claws, and scored their grooves in the back of her hand.

Damned to you and all your blood. I will crush you in my fists, wring what you are out into a silver cup. And drink.

'My blood will send you to hell.' She struck out with her bleeding hand, driving her power through it.

But the fog collapsed so she struck only air. The red stone pulsed, pulsed, then vanished.

'My blood will send you to hell,' she repeated.

And in the dream he seemed to stare at Iona, into her eyes. Into her spirit.

'It is not for me, in this time, in this place. But for you in yours. Remember.'

And cradling her wounded hand, called to her horse.

She mounted. She turned once to look at the stone, the flowers, the home she'd once known.

'On my oath, on my love, we will not fail though it takes a thousand lifetimes.' She laid her hand on her belly, on the gentle bulge. 'There is already another coming.'

She rode away, through the woods, toward the castle where she and her family were housed.

Iona woke trembling. Her right hand throbbing with pain, she groped for the light with her left. In its flash she saw the raw gashes, the run of blood. On a shocked cry, she scrambled up, dashed toward the bath, snatching a towel as she lurched toward the sink.

Before she could wrap the wound, it began to

change. She watched in fascinated horror as the gashes in her skin closed, the blood dried, then faded, like the pain. Within seconds she examined her unmarked hand.

A dream, but not, she thought. A vision? One where she'd been an observer, and somehow a participant.

She'd *felt* the pain – and the rage, the grief. She'd felt the power, more than she'd ever experienced, more than she'd ever known.

Teagan's power?

Lifting her gaze, Iona studied herself in the mirror, called back the images from the dream. But it *had* been her face ... hadn't it? Her build, her coloring.

But not, she thought now, her voice. Not even her language, though she'd understood every word. Old Gaelic, she assumed.

She needed to know more, to learn more. To find a way to understand how events that had happened hundreds of years before could draw her in so absolutely that she actually felt genuine pain.

Leaning over the sink, she splashed cold water on her face, caught the time on her watch. Still shy of four A.M., but she was done with sleep. Her body clock would adjust eventually, and for now she might as well just go with it. Maybe she'd read until sunrise.

She walked back into the bedroom, started to lift the tea tray she'd ended up sleeping with. And she saw on the lovely white sheets three drops of red. Of blood. Hers, she realized.

The dream – vision – experience – hadn't just

given her pain. She'd bled in it.

What kind of power could drag her into her own dreams and cause her to bleed from an ancestor's wound?

Leaving the tray where it was, she sat on the side of the bed, brushed her fingers over her throat.

What if those claws had struck there, slashed her jugular? Would she have died? Could dreams kill?

No, she didn't want books, she decided. She wanted answers, and she knew who had them.

By six, fueled with coffee, she headed out once again past the fountains and flowers and green lawns to the thick woods. This time the light held soft and luminous to drip palely through branches as the wide path narrowed. And this time she saw the signposts for the falconry school, the stables.

Later that morning, she promised herself, she'd visit both, then top it off with a hike to Cong. But she wouldn't be put off with a stack of books and a bit of tabletop magick.

The dream stayed with her so closely she caught herself checking her hand for claw marks.

A long, high note had her head snapping up, her gaze shooting skyward. The hawk soared across the pale blue, a gorgeous golden brown sweep that circled, then swooped. She swore she heard the wind of its wings as it danced through the trees, and landed on a branch overhead.

'Oh my God, look at you! You're just gorgeous.'

He stared down at her, golden eyes steady, unblinking, his wings regally folded. She wondered fancifully if he'd left his crown at home.

Slowly, she dug into her back pocket for her

phone, holding her breath as she hit camera mode. 'I hope you don't mind. It's not every day a woman meets a hawk. Or a falcon. I'm not sure which you are. Just let me...' She framed him in, took the shot, then a second.

'Are you hunting, or just out for your version of a morning stroll? I guess you're from the school, but–'

She stopped when the hawk turned its head. She thought she caught it, too, a faint whistle. In response, the hawk lifted off the branch, swooped and dodged its way through the trees and was gone.

'I'm definitely booking a falcon walk,' she decided, and checked her photos before she stuffed the phone away to hike on.

She reached the upended tree, the wall of vines. Though the pull returned, she pushed it back. Not now, not today when the emotion of the dreams swam so close to the surface.

Answers first.

The dog waited at the edge of the woods as if he'd been expecting her. He swished his tail by way of greeting, accepted the stroke on his head.

'Good morning. It's nice to know I'm not the only one out and about early. I hope Branna's not pissed when I come knocking, but I really need to talk to her.'

Kathel led the way to the pretty blue cottage, straight to the bright red door. 'Here goes.' She used the knocker shaped like a trinity knot, considered how best to approach her cousin.

But the one she hadn't yet met answered the door.

He looked like some rumpled, sleepy warrior prince with his mass of waving hair, a burnished brown that spilled around a face as elegantly boned as his sister's. Eyes green as the hills blinked at her.

He stood tall and lean in gray flannel pants and a white pullover unraveling at the hem.

'I'm sorry,' she began, and thought those words appeared to be her default when she came to this house.

'Good morning to you. You must be cousin Iona from the States.'

'Yes, I–'

'Welcome home.'

She found herself enfolded in a big, hard hug that lifted her up to the toes of her boots. The cheerful gesture made her eyes sting, and her nerves vanish.

'I'd be Connor, if you're wondering. Did Kathel find you and bring you 'round?'

'No, that is, yes. I was already coming here, but he found me.'

'Well then, come in out of the cold. Winter's still got its teeth in us.'

'Thanks. I know it's early.'

'That it is. The day will insist on starting that way.' In a gesture she found both casual and miraculous, he flicked a hand at the living room hearth. Flames leaped up to curl around the stacked peat. 'We'll have some breakfast,' he continued, 'and you can tell me everything there is to know about Iona Sheehan.'

'That won't take long.'

'Oh, I'll wager there's plenty to tell.' He

grabbed her hand and pulled her through the house.

She had a quick impression of color and jumble and light, the scents of vanilla and smoke. And space, more of it than she'd expected.

Then they were in the kitchen with a pretty stone hearth, long counters the color of slate, walls of lake blue. Pots of herbs thrived on wide window-sills, copper pots hung over a center island. Cabinets of dark gray showed colorful glassware, dishes behind their glass fronts. In a jut ringed with windows stood a beautiful old table and charmingly mismatched chairs.

The combination of farmhouse casual and the modern efficiency of glossy white appliances worked like magick.

'This is really beautiful. Like something out of a really smart magazine.'

'Is it? Well, it's Branna who has very definite ideas, and this is one of them.' Tilting his head in study, he gave her another quick, charming smile. 'Can you cook?'

'Ah ... sort of. I mean, I can, I just suck at it.'

'Well now, that's a real pity. I'm on duty then. Will it be coffee or tea for you?'

'Oh, coffee, thanks. You don't have to cook.'

'I do if I want to eat, and I do. In general, around here Branna's the cook and I'm the bottle washer, but I can manage breakfast well enough.'

He punched controls on a very intimidating-looking coffeemaker as he spoke, pulled a basket of eggs, a hunk of butter, a pack of bacon from the fridge.

'Take off your coat and be at home,' he told her.

'Branna says you're living the life at Ashford for a few days before you're coming here. How are you finding Ashford?'

'Like a dream. I slept too much of the day away yesterday. Obviously, I'm making up for it. You don't mind me moving in?'

'Why would I? We'll be taking turns as bottle washers, so that's one for me.'

He got down a skillet, set it on the stove top. 'Cups up there, and fresh cream if you're wanting it, and sugar as well.' He gestured here and there before he tossed bacon into the skillet.

All of it, and all of him, she thought, seemed as casual and miraculous as his wrist-flick fire-starting.

'I hear you're after working at the stables.'

'I'm hoping.'

'Branna had a word with Boyle. He'll be talking to you about that today.'

'Really?' Her heart actually leapt at the prospect. 'That's great. That's fantastic. A lot of people thought I'd lost my mind, just packing up, coming here without a serious plan, without a ready job or a place to stay.'

'What's an adventure if you know all the steps before you take them?'

'I know!' She grinned at him. 'Now I've got a job interview, and family to live with. And this morning – certainly it wasn't my plan last night to walk over at six A.M. – I saw a hawk in the woods. It flew right down, sat on a branch and watched me. I took pictures.'

She dug out her phone to show him. 'I guess you'd know what kind of hawk – falcon – he is.'

As he lifted the bacon out of the skillet, Connor angled his head to study the image. 'A Harris's hawk – the same we use for our hawk walks. That's Fin's Merlin, and a fine bird he is. Finbar Burke,' he added. 'He owns the stables with Boyle, and he started the falconry school here at Ashford. He owns quite a bit of this and that, does Fin.'

'Will I interview with him, too?'

'Oh, he'd likely leave that to Boyle. Plenty of cream and two sugars in my coffee, if you will.'

'Same as me.'

'Branna, she's one for just a dollop of the cream. Go ahead and fix her up. She's on her way down, and she'll need it.'

'She is? How do you... Oh.'

He only smiled. 'She sends out fierce vibrations of a morning before her coffee, and it's a bit on the early side for her so she may bite.'

Iona grabbed another cup, hurriedly poured the coffee. She was stirring in that dollop of cream when Branna walked in, dark hair tumbled nearly to her waist, eyes blurry and annoyed.

She took the cup Iona held out, took two deep swallows as she watched Iona over the rim. 'All right then, what happened?'

'Ah now, don't poke at her,' Connor said. 'She's had a rough go. Give her a chance to get some food into her.'

'I doubt she's come here at dawn for breakfast. You're going to overcook those eggs, Connor, as always.'

'I'm not. Slice up some bread for toasting why don't you, and she'll tell us once she's settled.'

'She's standing right here,' Iona reminded them.

'At half-six in the bloody morning,' Branna finished, but she picked up a bread knife, took a cloth off a loaf on a cutting board on the counter.

'I'm sorry, but–'

'Every second sentence she utters starts with those two words.' Branna sliced bread, tossed it into the toaster.

'Jesus, finish your coffee before your black mood ruins my appetite. Let's have some plates, Iona, there's a girl.' His tone shifted from sharp to gentle as his sister leaned back against the counter and sulkily drank her coffee.

Saying nothing, Iona got down plates and, at his direction, located the flatware, set the table.

She sat with her cousins, looked at the platter heaped with bacon and eggs, the plate of toasted bread, listened to the two of them bicker about how the eggs were cooked, whose turn it was to go to the market and why the laundry hadn't been folded.

'My coming here like this put you at odds, so you're fighting, but I–'

'We're not fighting.' Connor scooped up a forkful of eggs. 'Are we fighting, Branna?'

'We're not. We're communicating.' Then she laughed, tossed her magnificent hair, and bit into her toast. 'If we were fighting, more than these eggs would be scorched.'

'They're not scorched,' Connor insisted. 'They're ... firm.'

'They're good.'

Branna rolled her eyes at Iona. 'You'd have eaten better at the hotel, be sure of it. The chef there is brilliant.'

'I wasn't thinking about food this morning. I can't just read books, and stumble around trying to... I don't know what to do unless I *know*.'

'She's a bit of food in her now,' Branna said to Connor. 'So, what happened?'

'I had a dream, that wasn't a dream.'

She told all of it, every detail she could remember as carefully as she could manage.

'Let me see your hand,' Branna interrupted. 'The one that bled.'

She took it, held it fast while she traced fingertips over the back. The skin split, filled with blood. 'Be still!' Branna snapped when Iona gasped and tried to pull free. 'It's but a memory now. There's no pain. This is just the mirror of what was.'

'It was real. It hurt, burned. And there was blood on the sheet.'

'Then, yes, it was real. This is only a reflection.' She traced her fingertips over it again, and the wound vanished.

'I was pregnant. I mean, she was pregnant. In the vision, or dream. He didn't know. He couldn't see it, or feel it? I don't know which.' Agitated, Iona shoved at her hair with both hands. 'I have to know, Branna. You said I needed to think carefully, but how can I when I don't have all the information?'

'It's twined close,' Branna said, and got Connor's nod. 'And you're more open than I understood. I'll give you something to filter the visions; it may help you keep yourself a step back we'll say. We'll guide you, Connor and I, best that we can. But we can't tell you what we don't know. If Teagan went alone back to the cabin, back to the woods, was confronted, you're the one telling us.'

'We know pieces, Branna and I, and now you'll know more. We've both gone back, had glimpses, felt as you feel now.'

'But we were only two,' Branna added. 'There must be three.'

'He was bolder with you, as you're more vulnerable. You won't stay that way,' Connor assured her.

It sounded ridiculous, but she had to say aloud what churned through her mind. 'Can he kill me? If I go back, when I sleep, could he kill me?'

'He could try and likely will try.' Branna answered the ridiculous with bald simplicity. 'You'll stop him.'

'How?'

'With your will, with your power. With the amulet you wear, and must always wear, and with what I'll give you.'

Branna stopped pushing her eggs around her plate, picked up her coffee. And once again watched Iona over the rim.

'But understand, if you stay, if you mean to be with us, and be what you are, he will come for you. You must stay freely, and knowing that, or go and live your life.'

It was all too fantastic. And yet. She'd lived that dream. She'd felt the pain.

And she knew the draw and pull of what lived inside her.

Bridges burned, Iona reminded herself, for the chance to build new ones. Wherever they led – and they'd already brought her closer to what and who she was than any of the ones before.

'I'm not leaving.'

'You've had little time to think or understand,' Branna began, but Iona only shook her head.

'I *know* I've never belonged anywhere before. And I think I understand this is why. Because I belong here. I come from her, from Teagan. I understand, too, she wanted me to see she hurt him that night, and he was afraid. Doesn't that– Couldn't that mean I can hurt him?'

'If it's here you belong, and I believe it is, then here you are. But don't rush your fences,' Connor warned her, and patted her hand. 'You've only begun.'

'I'm an excellent rider with a damn good seat. And I'll learn. Teach me.' She leaned closer as the urgency rose in her. 'Show me.'

Branna sat back. 'You haven't much patience.'

'It depends. No,' Iona admitted. 'Not a lot.'

'You'll need to find some, but we'll take some steps. Small ones.'

'Tell me about the cabin. They lived there, Sorcha died there. Is it still there? There's a big tree, uprooted, and these thick vines, and–'

'Don't go there,' Branna said quickly. 'Not yet and not alone.'

'She's right. You have to wait for that. You have to promise not to go through on your own.' Connor gripped her hand, and she felt the heat pump against her palm. 'Your word on it, and I'll know if you mean to keep it.'

'All right. I promise. But you'll take me.'

'Not today,' Branna told her. 'I have things I have to do, and Connor needs to go to work. And you need to go see Boyle.'

'Now?'

'After breakfast's soon enough, and after you've washed up as payment for getting me out of my bed at this ungodly hour. Come back later. I should be done and ready by about three.'

'I'll be here.' Settled, confident again, Iona helped herself to another piece of toast.

5

As she followed the path, Iona tried working on her interview skills. What to say, how to say it. She hoped she'd dressed appropriately, as she hadn't expected an immediate job interview when she'd left her hotel room that morning in jeans and her favorite red sweater. Still, she was aiming for a stable job, so she'd hardly need a business suit and a briefcase.

Neither of which she had anyway, she mused, or had ever wanted.

What she did have was the résumé she'd put together, the recommendation by her previous employers, all the references from her students or their parents.

She didn't care what they paid her, not to start. She just needed a riding boot in the door. Then she could, and would, prove herself. And while she proved herself she'd not only have work, she'd have the work she loved.

Her stomach knotted, as it did when she wanted

something too much, so she ordered herself not to babble when she met the man who could hire her or just send her on her way.

The minute she turned into the clearing, saw the building, the nerves dropped away. Here was the familiar, a kind of home. The shape of the stables and its weather-faded red paint, the two horses with their heads poking out of the half doors, the trucks, the trailers scattered around the graveled lot.

The scents of hay, horses, manure, leather, oil, grain caught at her heart. It all flooded over her as her boots crunched on the gravel.

She couldn't help herself. She went straight to the horses.

The chestnut held her gaze steadily, watching her approach. He snorted at her, shifted his weight. He bent his head when she stroked his cheek, then gave her an easy push with his nose.

'It's nice to meet you, too. Look how handsome you are.'

Clear eyes, clean, glossy coat, well-brushed mane, and a look of the easygoer about him, she noted. Healthy, well-tended horses boosted the as-yet-unmet Boyle McGrath and Finbar Burke in her estimation.

'I'm hoping we'll be seeing a lot of each other. And who's your friend?' She turned to the second horse, a sturdy-looking bay who rubbed his neck on the window frame as if he wasn't the least bit interested in her.

When she stepped toward him, he laid his ears back. Iona just angled her head, sent him soothing thoughts until they perked up again. 'That's better. No need to be nervous. I'm just here to say hello.'

She gave him a quick rub.

'That's Caesar taking your measure there.'

Iona turned, saw the Amazon in riding boots behind her. The woman's curvy body filled out snug riding pants and a rough plaid jacket. Her hair, worn in a long, messy braid, reminded Iona of her grandmother's prized mink coat – rich and luxurious brown. Though Ireland sang in her voice, her golden skin and deep brown eyes spoke of sunny climes and gypsy campfires.

'He generally likes to act fierce on first acquaintance. And can be shy about being touched – usually,' she added when Iona continued to stroke him.

'He's just careful around strangers. Are they both trail horses?'

'We save Caesar for experienced riders, but they both have a job here, yes.'

'I'm hoping I will, too. I'm Iona Sheehan. I've come to talk to Boyle McGrath.

'Ah, you'd be the Yank, a cousin of Connor's and Branna's. I'm Meara Quinn.' She stepped forward, shook Iona's hand firmly, gave her a quick, no-nonsense appraisal. 'You've come early today.'

'I'm still adjusting to the time change. I can come back if it's not a good time.'

'Oh, one time's as good as another. Boyle's not here, but will be soon enough. I can show you about if you'd like.'

'I would, thanks.' Like Caesar's, Iona's nerves dropped away. 'Have you worked here long?'

'Oh, about eight years. Closer to nine, I'm

thinking. Well, who's counting, yeah?'

She led the way in, long strides on long legs that had Iona quickening her pace to keep up. Iona saw a room off to the side, jumbled and crowded with riding hats, leg protectors, some boots. A lean tabby sidled out, gave Iona a look as measuring as Meara's had been, then strolled outside.

'That was Darby, who graces us with his presence. A fierce mouser is Darby, so we put up with his sullen moods. He earns his kibble, and comes and goes as he pleases.'

'Nice work if you can get it.'

Meara grinned. 'That's the truth. And so, we take bookings for rides, guide the customers between the Lough Corrib and Mask. Usually an hour, but we'll do longer if they ask and pay for it. And we have the training ring here.'

Iona walked in to watch a woman in her thirties on the back of a compact chestnut, and the fireplug of a man in work jeans putting horse and rider through the paces.

'That's our Mick. A jockey he was in his youth, and has unlimited stories to tell about those days.'

'I'd like to hear them.'

'Be sure you will if you're here above five minutes.' Meara set her hands on her hips, watched Mick a moment, letting Iona do the same. 'Took a bad fall, Mick did, in a race at Roscommon, and so ended that portion of his career. Now he teaches and trains, and his students collect blue ribbons.'

'Sounds like you're lucky to have him.'

'That we are. We've another area at the big

stables, not far from here, for jumping practice and instruction. We cater to locals as well for lessons, and the occasional guided ride. We tend to run a bit slow this time of year, but there's plenty needs doing. We've twenty-two horses between what we keep here and what's at the other stable. The tack room's this way.'

She glanced over at Iona. 'We ride English, so if you're used to a Western saddle, you'd have to adjust.'

'I ride both.'

'That's handy for you. Boyle's fierce about keeping the tack in good order,' she continued as she gestured Iona into the room. 'Those of us who work here do whatever comes to hand. Deal with the tack, take bookings, muck out, groom, feed – there's a board with each horse's feed schedule and diet hung outside their stalls. Have you done any guided rides?'

'Back home, sure.'

'Then you know it's more than plodding along with the clients. You need to judge how they handle the ride, the mount, and most who book here want some color, if you understand me, some talk of the area, the history, even flora and fauna.'

'I'll study up. Actually, I've already done some. I like knowing where I am.'

'Hard to know where you're going unless you do.'

'I'm open to surprises there.'

Familiar scents surrounded her – leather and saddle soap. To most eyes, she imagined, the tack room would strike as cluttered and disorganized, but she saw the basic pattern, the day-to-day use, repair, maintain.

Bridles hung on one wall, the saddles on their racks on another. Harness racks on the third, with hooks and racks for bits and saddle pads, shelves for this and that, rags and brushes and saddle soaps and oils. And a kind of alcove for brooms, pitchforks, the curry combs, hoof picks, hooks again for buckets. She spotted an old refrigerator.

'Medicine's in there,' Meara told her. 'Close and handy when there's need. We do what we can to keep it all reasonably tidy, and a time or two a year when we're slow, we put some elbow grease into it. Would you have your own gear?'

'I sold it.' That had been painful. 'Except for my riding boots, my muck boots, riding helmet. I didn't know if I'd have any place to keep it, or even if I'd be able to use it, at least for a while. Do I need my own?'

'You don't, no. Well then, you'll want to see the horses we have here. We board as well, but at the big stable. Here we keep the riding hacks, and switch them out between here and there as needed.'

Meara walked and talked, more long strides in battered boots as she led Iona through to the stalls.

'We've a booking for four later this morning, and two more this afternoon, a party of two and another of six. Lessons booked through the day so we've a full house here.'

She stopped to rub the head of a sturdy chestnut with a white blaze. 'This is Maggie, as sweet as they come. She's good with children or the skittish. She's patient, is Maggie, and likes the quiet life. Don't you, darling?'

The mare nuzzled at Meara's shoulder, then dipped her head at Iona.

'Such a pretty face.' After a rub and a scratch, Maggie bumped at Iona's pocket, made her laugh. 'I don't have any with me today. I'll be sure to bring along an apple next time. She's...' Iona trailed off as she caught Meara's questioning look. 'What?'

'Odd, is all. Maggie has a particular fondness for apples.' Leaving it at that, Meara gestured. 'And that's our Jack. He's a big boy, and likes his naps, and will try to graze his way through the ride if he's able. Needs a firm hand.'

'Like to eat and sleep, do you? Who doesn't? I bet a big, strong boy like you can carry three hundred without blinking an eye.'

'He will that. And here we have Spud. He's young and feisty but goes well.'

'A dark horse.' Iona moved over to run a hand down his black mane. 'With a weakness for potatoes.' She caught the look again, used a smile. 'His name. Spud.'

'We'll use that one if you like. And here's Queen Bee, as she thinks she is. She bosses the others every opportunity, but she likes a good ride.'

'I wouldn't mind one myself. She's had some trouble with her right foreleg?'

'A bit of a strain a week or so back. Healed up nicely. If she told you different, she's just looking for sympathy.'

Unsure, Iona took a step back, slid her hands into her pockets.

'I'm not likely to get the jitters if someone shares

a communion with horses,' Meara commented. 'Especially someone blood kin to the O'Dwyers.'

'I'm good with them. Horses,' Iona qualified as she stroked the regal-eyed Queen Bee. 'I'm hoping to work on getting good with the O'Dwyers.'

'Connor's an easygoer, with a weakness for a pretty face. You've got one. Branna's fair, and that's enough.'

'You're friends.'

'We are, and have been since we were in nappies, so I know Branna, being fair, wouldn't have sent you to us if you weren't suited.'

'I'm good at this. It's what I'm good at.' All, she thought, she was certain she was good at.

'You'll need to be. All my life,' Meara said at Iona's questioning look. 'So I know it's the one who communes with horses who makes the three.'

Iona thought of the looks from the wait staff over dinner the night before. 'Does everyone know?'

'What people know, what they believe, what they accept? Those are all different matters, aren't they? Well then, since Boyle's running behind, we can–' She broke off, pulled out her phone when it jingled in her pocket, checked the text. 'Ah, good, he's on his way. We'll just go out, if that's good for you, and meet him.'

Her potential new boss, Iona thought. 'Any tips?'

'You could remember Boyle's fair as well, though he's often short on words and temper.'

Meara gestured Iona along as she shoved her phone away again. 'He's riding Fin's latest acquisition over. Fin's Boyle's partner, and travels about when he's a mind to buying horses and hawks or whatever strikes his fancy.'

'But Boyle – Mr. McGrath – runs the stables.'

'He does – or they both do, but it's Boyle who deals more with the day-to-day. Fin found this stallion in Donegal, and had him sent, as Fin himself's still rambling. He plans to stud him out later in the year, and Boyle's just as determined to teach him manners.'

'Fin or the stallion?'

Meara let out a big, brassy laugh as they stepped back outside. 'That's a question, and it may be both, though I'd wager he'll have better luck with the horse than Finbar Burke.'

She nodded toward the end of the road. 'He's a fine-looking bastard for all that, with a devil's temper.'

Iona turned. She couldn't say if Meara spoke of the horse or the man astride him. Her first impression was of magnificence and hotheads on both counts.

The horse, big and beautiful at easily sixteen hands, tested his rider with the occasional buck and dance, and even with the distance, she could see the fierce gleam in his eyes. His smoke gray coat showed some sweat, though the morning stayed cool – and his ears stayed stubbornly back.

But the man, big and beautiful as well, had his measure. Iona heard his voice, the challenge in it if not the words, as he kept the horse at a trot.

And something in her, just at the sound of his voice, stirred. Nerves, excitement, she told herself, because the man held her happiness in his hands.

But as they drew closer, the stir grew to a flutter. Attraction struck her double blows – heart and belly as, oh, he really was as magnificent as the horse. And every single bit as appealing to her.

His hair, a kind of rich caramel that wasn't altogether brown, wasn't quite red, blew everywhere in the breeze. He wore a rough jacket, faded jeans, scarred boots, all suiting the tough, rawboned face. The strong jaw and a mouth that struck her as stubborn as the horse he rode just echoed the hard lines of temper barely leashed when the horse bucked again.

A thin scar, like a lightning bolt, cut through his left eyebrow. For reasons she couldn't quite comprehend, it stirred up a delicious little storm of lust inside her.

Cowboy, pirate, wild tribal horseman. How could he be three of her biggest fantasy weaknesses all rolled into one big, bold package?

Boyle McGrath. She said his name in her head, and thought: You could be trouble for me, and I'm so *interested* when it comes to trouble.

'Oh, he's in a mood, our Boyle is. Well, you'd best get used to it if you come to work here, for God knows he has them.'

Meara stepped forward, raised her voice. 'Giving you a run for it, is he then?'

'Tried to take a chunk out of me. Twice. The right bastard. Tries it again I may geld him myself with a bleeding butter knife.'

When Boyle pulled up, the horse shook, pranced, tried to rear.

Big hands, scarred at the knuckles like the eyebrow, the boots, fought the horse down. 'I may murder Fin for this one.'

As if daring his rider, the horse tried to rear yet

again. Instinctively Iona stepped up, gripped the bridle.

'Stay back there,' Boyle snapped. 'He bites.'

'I've been bitten before.' She spoke directly to the horse, her eyes on his. 'But I'd rather not be again, so just stop it. You're gorgeous,' she crooned. 'And so pissed off. But you might as well cut it out and see what happens next.'

She flicked a glance up at Boyle. He wouldn't bite, she thought, but suspected he had other ways to take a chunk out of a foe.

'I bet you'd get testy, too, if somebody packed you up and took you away from home, then dumped you with a bunch of strangers.'

'Testy? He kicked a stable hand and bit a groom, and that was just this morning.'

'Stop it,' Iona repeated when the horse tried to jerk his head free. 'Nobody likes a bully.' Using her free hand, she stroked his neck. 'Even beautiful ones like you. He's pissed off, that's all, and making sure we all know it,' she said to Boyle.

'Oh, is that all? Well then, no harm done.' He dismounted, shortened the reins. 'You'd be the American cousin then, the one Branna sent.'

'Iona Sheehan, and I'm probably as inconvenient to you as this stallion. But I know horses, and this one didn't like being taken away from all he knew. Everything's different here. I know what that's like,' she said to the horse. 'What's his name?'

'Fin's calling him Alastar.'

'Alastar. You'll make your place here.' She released the bridle, and the horse flicked his ears. But if he considered trying for a nip, he changed his mind, looked carelessly away.

'I brought my résumé,' Iona began. Business, business, business, she reminded herself. And stay out of trouble. And pulled out the flash drive she'd stuck in her pocket that morning.

'I've ridden since I was three, and worked with horses – grooming, mucking, trail and guided rides. I've given instruction, private and group. I know horses,' she repeated. 'And I'm willing to do whatever you need for a chance to work here.'

'I've shown her around and about,' Meara began, then took the flash drive from Iona. 'I'll put this on your desk.'

Boyle kept the reins firm in his hand, and his eyes, a burnished gold with hints of green, direct on Iona. 'Résumés are just words on paper, aren't they? They're not doing. I can give you work, mucking out. We'll see if you know your way around a horse for grooming before I set you on that. But there's always tack to clean.'

Riding boot in the door, she reminded herself. 'Then I'll muck and clean.'

'You'd make more walking over to the castle and seeing about work there. Waitresses, house-keeping, clerking.'

'It's not about making more. It's about doing what I love, and what I'm meant to do. That's here. I'm fine with mucking out.'

'Then Meara can get you started on it.' He took the flash drive from Meara, stuck it in his own pocket. 'I'll see to the paperwork once I get this one settled.'

'You're going to put him in a stall?'

'I'm not after checking him into the hotel.'

'He'd like... Couldn't he use a little more exercise? He's gotten warmed up.'

Boyle arched his brows, drawing her gaze to the scarred one – the sexy one. 'He's given me near an hour's fight already this morning.'

'He's used to being the alpha, aren't you, Alastar? Now you come along and you're ... a challenge. You said a résumé's not doing. Let me do. I can take him around your paddock.'

'What are you? Seven stones soaking wet?'

He was giving her a job, she reminded herself. And compared to him – even compared to Meara – she probably did come off as small and weak. 'I don't know how much seven stones is, but I'm strong, and I'm experienced.'

'He'd rip your arms out, and that's before he tossed you off his back like a bad mood.'

'I don't think so. But then, if he did, you'd be right.' She glanced back at the horse. 'Think about that,' she told Alastar.

Boyle considered it. The pretty little faerie queen had something to prove, so he'd let her try. And she could nurse her sore arse – or head, depending on which hit the ground first.

'Once around the ring. Inside,' Boyle said, pointing. 'If you manage to stay on him that long. Get her a helmet, will you, Meara. It might help her from breaking her head when she lands on it.'

'He's not the only one who's pissed off.' Confident now, Iona offered Boyle a smile. 'I need to shorten the stirrups.'

'Inside,' he repeated, and led the horse in. 'I hope you know how to fall.'

'I do. But I won't.'

She shortened the stirrups quickly, competently. She knew Boyle watched her, and that was fine, that was good. She *would* settle, and gratefully, for a job doing no more than mucking out stalls and cleaning tack.

But God, she wanted to ride again. And she wanted, keenly, to ride this horse. To feel him under her, to share that power.

'Thanks.' She strapped on the helmet Meara brought her, and since Meara had carried one over, Iona used the mounting block.

Alastar quivered under her. She tightened her knees, held out a hand for the reins.

Now he reconsidered – she could see it in those tawny eyes.

'Branna won't be pleased with me if you end up in the hospital.'

'You're not afraid of Branna.'

She took the reins. Maybe she'd never been sure where she belonged, but she'd always, from the first moment, felt at home in the saddle.

Leaning forward, Iona whispered in Alastar's ear. 'Don't make a fool out of me, okay? Let's show off, and show him up.'

He walked cooperatively for four steps. Then kicked up his hind legs, dropped down, reared up.

Stop it. We can play that game another time.

She circled him, changed leads, circled back, changed again before nudging him into a trot.

When the horse danced to the side, tried another kick, she laughed.

'I may not weigh as much as the big guy, but I'm sticking.'

She took him up to a pretty canter – God, he had beautiful lines – back to a trot.

And felt alive.

'She's more than words on paper,' Meara murmured.

'Maybe so. Good seat, good hands – and for some reason that devil seems to like her.'

He thought she looked as if she'd been born on a horse, as if she could ride through wind and wood and all but fly over the hills.

Then he shifted his feet, annoyed with his own fanciful thoughts.

'You can take her out with you – *not* on that devil – see how she does on a guide.'

'He'll breed well, you know. Fin's got the right of that.'

'Fin's rarely wrong. But when he is, it's massive. Still, she'll do. Until she doesn't. Have her put Alastar in the paddock. We'll see if he stays there.'

'And you?'

'I'll see to her paperwork.'

'When do you want her to start?'

Boyle watched her slide into a fluid lope. 'I'm thinking she already has.'

She didn't get to the village. Her plans changed in the best possible way as she spent the rest of her morning mucking out, grooming, signing papers, learning the basics of the rules and rhythms from Meara.

And best of all, she tagged along on a guided ride. The pace might have been easy to the point of lazy, but it was still a ride on the cheerful Spud. She tried to remember landmarks as they rode placidly along the hard path, through the deep green woods, along the dark hum of the river.

An old shed, a scarred pine, a tumble of rocks.

She listened to the rise and fall of Meara's voice as she entertained the clients – a German couple on a brief getaway – and enjoyed the mix of accents.

Here she was, Iona Sheehan, riding through the forests of Mayo (employed!), listening to German and Irish, feeling the cool, damp breeze on her cheeks and watching the fitful sunlight sprinkle through clouds and trees.

She was here. It was real. And she realized with a sudden, utter certainty she was never going back.

From this day forward, she thought, this was home. One she'd make herself, for herself. This was her life, one she'd live as she wanted.

If that wasn't magick, what was?

She heard other voices, a quick rolling laugh so appealing it made her smile.

'That would be Connor,' Meara told her. 'Out on a falcon walk.'

When they came around a curve she saw him down the path, standing with another couple. A hawk perched on the woman's gloved arm while the man with her snapped pictures.

'Oh, that's amazing!' Dazzling, Iona thought. And somehow out of time. 'Isn't it amazing?'

'Otto and I have booked for tomorrow,' the German woman told her. 'I look forward, very much.'

'You'll have so much fun. I have to try it. That's my cousin,' she added, unabashedly proud. 'The falconer.'

'He's very handsome. You have your cousin, but you have not done a falcon walk?'

'I just got here yesterday.' She beamed as Connor lifted a hand, sent her or Meara, probably both, a cheeky wink.

''Tis a Harris's hawk you see there,' Meara said. 'As you've booked a walk for tomorrow, you should be sure to take the time to tour the school. I'm wagering the falcon walk will be one of the highlights of your visit to Ashford, and it's more complete if you see the other hawks and falcons, and learn a bit about them.'

The hawk took wing, glided up to a branch. The two groups gave room to each other.

'Good day to you, Connor,' Meara said as they passed.

'And to you. Out for a ride, cousin?'

'I'm working.'

'Well, that's brilliant, and you can buy me a pint to celebrate later.'

'You're on.'

And now, Iona thought, she'd have a beer with her cousin after work. It really *was* magick.

'I'm sorry. My English is sometimes not good.'

'It's excellent,' Iona disagreed as she shifted to look at the woman rider.

'This is your cousin. But you're not Irish.'

'American, Irish descent. I've just moved here. Literally.'

'You came only yesterday? Not before?'

'No, never before. I'm actually staying at the castle for a few days.'

'Ah, so you are visiting.'

'No, I live here now. I came yesterday, got this

job today, and I'm moving in with my cousins next week. It's all kind of wonderful.'

'You just came, from America to live here? I think you're very brave.'

'I think I'm more lucky. It's beautiful here, isn't it?'

'Very beautiful. We live in Berlin, and work there. It's very busy. This is quiet and ... not busy. A good holiday.'

'Yes.' And an even better home, Iona thought. Her home.

By the time she'd rubbed down Spud, put away her tack, met the other staff on duty that day – Mick with his ready grin, whose oldest daughter turned out to be the waitress who'd served her dinner the night before – and helped feed and water the horses, Iona deemed it too late to visit Cong or the falconry school.

She approached Meara.

'I'm not really sure what my hours are.'

'Oh well.' Meara took a long drink from a bottle of orange Fanta. 'I expect you didn't plan to be working a full day, which you nearly have. Are you up for working tomorrow?'

'Sure. Absolutely.'

'I'd say eight's good enough, but you'd best be checking with Boyle to be certain, as he may have put a schedule together. I'd think you could go on now, as Mick and Patty have things handled here, and I've got a private over at the big stables.'

'I'll find him and see. Thanks, Meara, for everything.'

Going with the joy of the day, she wrapped her

arms around Meara in a hug.

'I'm sure you're welcome but I didn't do anything, less than usual as it happens, as you did most of my sweaty work.'

'It felt good. It feels good here. I'll see you tomorrow.'

'Have a good one, and my best to Branna and Connor when you see them.'

Iona checked the ring, then what Boyle called his office, backtracked, circled, and found him outside in the paddock having a stare-down with Alastar.

'He doesn't think you like him.'

Boyle glanced back. 'Then he's an intuitive bastard.'

'But you do.' She boosted herself up to sit on the fence. 'You like his looks and his spirit, and wonder how you can smooth his temper without breaking that spirit.'

She smiled when Boyle walked toward her. 'You're a horseman. There's not a horseman alive who wouldn't look at that magnificent animal and think just what I said. You irritate each other, but that's because you're both big and gorgeous and strong-willed.'

Feet planted, Boyle hooked his thumbs in his front pockets. 'And that's your conclusion after this brief acquaintance, is it?'

'Yeah.' The sheer joy of her day sat on her like sunlight. She thought she could sit there for hours, in the cool, damp air, with the man and the horse. 'You challenge each other, so there's respect – and strategies brewing on both sides to work out how to come out on top.'

108

'As I'll be riding him rather than the other way around, that's already a conclusion.'

'Not altogether.' She sighed as she studied Alastar. 'When I was little, I used to dream about having a horse like that – a big, bold stallion all of my own, one only I could ride. I guess most girls go through that equine fantasy stage. I never grew out of mine.'

'You ride well.'

'Thanks.' She glanced down at him, and realized it was a good thing she sat on the fence or she might have given him a hug as she had Meara. 'It got me a job.'

'It did that.'

He said nothing as Alastar wandered over, oh so casually, and ignoring him, went all but nose to nose with Iona. The horse, Boyle thought, looked at the woman as if she knew every answer.

'We had a good day, didn't we?' She stroked the smooth cheek, down the strong line of throat. 'It's a good place here. Just takes some getting used to.'

Then, the horse, who only that morning had left a welt the size of a man's fist on his veteran groom's biceps, seemed to sigh as well. And stepped in, all but laying his head on Iona's shoulder so she could glide her hands over his long neck.

I'll look out for you, she told him. *And you'll look out for me.*

'Sure, you're one of them,' Boyle murmured. 'An O'Dwyer, through and through.'

Caught up with the horse, Iona answered absently. 'My grandmother, mother's side.'

'It's not a matter of sides, but blood and bone. I should've figured it the way you handled this one, first time up.'

He leaned back against the fence to give Iona a long, careful study. 'You don't have the look of them, of Branna or Connor, being a bright-haired little thing, but it's blood and bone.'

Because she thought she understood him, nerves came back. 'I hope they think so, since they're giving me a place to live. And because Branna helped me land this job so I don't have to scramble to find one I'd probably be terrible at. Anyway, I–'

'Legend has it the younger daughter of the first dark witch talked to horses, and they to her. And even as a babe could ride the fiercest of war-horses. And some nights, in the dark of the moon, when the mood was on her, she took one to flying over the trees and hills.'

'I ... should probably study up on the local legends, for the guided rides.'

'Oh sure, I'm thinking you know that one well enough. The one of Cabhan, who lusted for and craved Sorcha, for her beauty and her power. And the three who came from her, and took the power she passed to them, and all the burdens with it. Blood and bone,' he said again.

It made her throat dry, the way he looked at her, as if he could see something in her she'd yet to fully comprehend. Sensing her distress, Alastar quivered, laid his ears back as he turned his head to Boyle.

Cautious, Iona slid her fingers under the bridle to calm him.

110

My own fault, she told Alastar. *I don't know what to say, how to react yet.*

'My grandmother told me a lot of stories.' Evading, she knew, but until she knew *him*, that seemed best all around. 'Anyway, unless you need me to do something else, I should go. I'm supposed to meet Branna, and I'm late. Meara said I should be clear for the day, and come in tomorrow at eight?'

'That's fine then.'

'Thanks for the job.' She gave Alastar a last stroke before getting off the fence. 'I'll work hard.'

'Oh, I'll see that you do, be sure of it.'

'Well.' Now her hands felt sweaty enough to rub against her jeans. 'I'll see you tomorrow.'

'My best to your cousins.'

'Okay.'

He watched her walk away, moving fast, as if getting clear of something boggy in the ground.

Pretty thing, he thought, though he'd be wise to ignore that. Pretty and sunny and a bloody faerie goddess astride a horse.

Ignore all that for certain. Harder, he figured, to ignore the fact that he'd just hired a witch.

'A dark one, the last of the three. All here together now, with hound and hawk, and by God horse.' He gave Alastar a scowl. 'You'd be Fin's doing then, no doubt of it. And what in hell's name will that mean?'

He wondered, too, what Fin – friend, partner, next to brother – had in his mind, in his heart.

As if expressing his opinion on Fin, and Boyle for that matter, Alastar raised his tail and shat.

Boyle managed to jump aside before the opinion hit his boots. Then, after one fulminating stare, he threw back his head and laughed.

6

Sure of her way, Iona hurried through the woods. She saw a young couple, strolling along, hand in hand, and thought hotel guests, maybe honeymooners. Tourists, taking advantage of a dry day and patchy sunlight.

She'd be a guest of the hotel for a few more days, but no longer qualified as a tourist. She was an expat.

It sounded strange and glamorous even if she smelled of horses, and maybe just a slight whiff of manure. But as she was already a little late, she didn't want to take the time to go back to her room, shower, and change.

She'd have to work out some sort of loose schedule, she thought, which included that visit to the falconry school and a trip to Cong. Maybe she could work the visit into her break tomorrow, assuming she had one. If Connor was up for it, she'd buy him that pint in the village after her lesson with Branna, maybe have dinner.

And she could hardly wait to email Nan, tell her about the job, about her day, about whatever she learned from Branna. Her life, so scattered and unsatisfying only days before, now brimmed with possibilities.

This was her walk now, to work, to home. No more commuting in traffic to and from her tiny apartment. No more wishing for just a little adventure because now she was living one.

No more wondering what she lacked that made it so easy for people to walk away from her. This time she'd done the walking. No, she corrected, she'd done the arriving. That mattered so much more.

Now it was up to her to make it all matter.

As she came to the downed tree she felt that pull, that yearning, and heard the seductive whisper of her name. Pausing, she looked around, saw no one.

And yet, it came again, that soft, almost sweet whisper of her name.

She hesitated – was there a light, faint, and distant flickering through that wall of vines? Like a light in a window, a welcoming home?

Though she reminded herself she was late, that Branna had told her not to linger there, to explore there, she took a step closer.

It would only take a minute, just to look.

Another step, and it all became so dreamy. The light growing stronger, the whispers deeper, and a sleepy warmth, creeping out, creeping into her.

Home, she thought again. She'd wanted one for so long. And this...

As her fingers touched the vines, the air pulsed like a heartbeat; the light dimmed softly to twilight.

Behind her, the dog barked sharply, jolting her back.

She trembled, like a woman teetering on a cliff,

and took several steps back until she stood with the dog, one hand braced on his handsome head.

Her own breath sounded so loudly in her ears she barely heard her thoughts through it.

'I was going through. It felt like I had to, and wanted it more than anything else. I almost broke my word, and I never do. What is this place?' She rubbed her chilled hands together, gave one last shudder. 'I'm glad you came, and I bet it wasn't just happenstance. We'll go. I imagine she's waiting for both of us.'

The wind lifted as they walked away. Before she came to the edge of the woods, rain pattered down, from a single cloud as far as Iona could tell, as the sun continued to send out pearly light.

She and Kathel quickened their pace. Though she'd aimed for the cottage door, she caught a glimpse of Branna in the workshop, and changed course.

As before, the workshop smelled glorious – smoke and herbs and candle wax. Branna stood, her hair bundled up, a sweater the color of plums skimming her hips. She set a white flowerpot on the work counter, arranging it with a white bowl, a fat white candle and a white feather.

'I'm late. I'm sorry, but–'

'You said you might be on the message you left on my phone. It's not a matter.' She studied Iona as Kathel walked over to rub against her leg. 'Congratulations to you. Your first day went well?'

'Amazing. Fabulous. Thank you. Thank you so much.' As she spoke, Iona rushed across the room to throw her arms around Branna in a hard hug.

'All right then.' Branna gave Iona a little pat on

the back. 'Still it's Boyle who did the hiring.'

'You got my foot in the door.' After another squeeze Iona stepped back. 'It's everything I could want. It felt ... right from the first second. Do you know what I mean? Everything just clicked. And Meara – you know Meara.'

'I do indeed.' In her smooth way, Branna turned to put the kettle on. 'She's a good friend to me, and one you can count on.'

'I liked her right away, another click, I guess. She showed me around before Boyle got there, and I met Mick – you probably know him, too.'

'I do, yes.'

'He's so funny and full of stories. I already have a little crush on him.'

'He's a wife and four children, with the first grandbaby on the way.'

'Oh, I didn't mean... You're teasing. Anyway, it was great, just so great. Even though Boyle was in a bad mood.'

'He's known to have them.' Branna put cookies on a plate, chocolate ones today.

'He came riding in, like something out of a movie, him on that magnificent horse. Both of them so pissy and handsome and, well, tough. And he's cursing the horse. I'm pretty sure the horse was cursing him right back. His partner – Fin, right? – bought him, and had him sent to Boyle. And he's just spectacular.'

'The horse, you're meaning.'

'Yeah. Well, Boyle's not too shabby. In fact, I had a couple minutes of...' She drummed her hand against her heart. 'Just looking at him. Too bad about the moods, because, really.' She grinned, rolled her eyes, fanned her hand. Then her eyes widened. 'Oh God, you aren't– You and Boyle aren't a thing?'

'Romantically? No.' With an easy laugh Branna began to brew the tea. 'He and Connor have been mates since boyhood, and for that matter, we've been friends longer than I can remember. He's a fine man with a hot temper, but like Meara, one you can count on, thick and thin.'

'Good to know, and I guess he had reason for the mood today. Alastar was giving him a bad time, and he'd bitten one of the stable hands. Kicked one, too, I think, and–'

'Wait.' Branna gripped Iona's arm to stop the flood of words. 'You said Alastar? The horse is Alastar?'

'Yes. What is it? What's wrong?'

'And Fin, he bought the horse, had it sent?'

'Yes. Meara said Fin was still traveling, but sent the horse ahead a couple days ago.'

'So.' She took a long breath, laid her hands on the counter for a moment. 'He knows.'

'Who, and what? You're freaking me out, Branna.'

'Fin. He knows you're here. Or he knows the three are here, together. That it's to begin. Alastar, it's said, was the name of Teagan's horse. He was her first guide.'

'Alastar. I didn't know, but ... it was like we recognized each other. There was something there, but I thought, I guess I thought it was just he needed me, needed someone who understood him. Alastar. Teagan's horse. You don't think it's coincidence.'

'That you would come, and so would this horse? And Boyle all but bringing him to you this morning? I bloody well don't, and add in Finbar Burke and there's no mistaking it.'

'How would he know about me, or the name of Teagan's horse?'

Branna set teacups down with a clatter. 'He has power.'

'He's like us? Fin?'

'He's like no one but himself, but he comes from the blood, as we do. He springs from Cabhan, the black sorcerer.'

'Wait a minute. Wait.' She tried to take it in, even pressed her hands to the sides of her head as if to hold it all in. 'The evil guy, the one that Sorcha killed – or mostly killed? This Fin is descended from him?'

'He is.' Eyes flashing, face grim, Branna shoved impatiently at a loosened pin in her hair. 'He bears the mark, and it was Teagan who marked Cabhan. He has power, and the blood.'

'He's evil?'

In an impatient gesture, Branna waved a hand in the air, then poured the tea. 'Sure there's no simple answer to a question like that. He's harmed no one, and I would know. But he's of Cabhan, and the time's coming 'round. He sent the horse so we'd know.'

'But isn't having Alastar an advantage, for me? For us? For our side of this?'

'We'll see what we see.'

'I don't understand.' Because they were there, Iona took a cookie, gestured with it. 'He's Boyle's partner, and his friend, I got that. I don't see how

117

he could be dangerous if–'

'An easier question to answer. Dangerous Fin is, and always has been.'

'But if Boyle's such a stand-up guy, how can they be friends?'

'Life's a puzzle.'

'One thing, it explains how Boyle knew I was … you know.'

On a sigh, Branna lifted her teacup. '*Witch* isn't a bad word, Iona. It's who and what you are.'

'It hasn't exactly been cocktail-party conversation in my life. I'm getting used to it, a little. I should've told you before, right away. He knew. I didn't tell him – why would I? – but he knew. He didn't seem very weirded out by it, but since he's friends with a sorcerer–'

'Fin's a witch, just as we are.'

'Right. It just sounds a little girly.'

'You've much to learn, cousin.' She handed Iona her tea.

'I should tell you something else first. I don't break my word. It's important. But today, walking back from the stables, I started to go through those vines. I didn't mean to, but I thought I saw a light, and I heard my name, over and over. It was almost like the dream I had. I felt out of myself, pulled in. Like I needed to go through, to whatever waited. Kathel stopped me – again. I don't break promises, Branna. I don't lie.'

'Ever?' Branna sipped her own tea.

'Ever. I'm crap at it anyway, so why bother? But I'd have gone back there if Kathel hadn't come. I couldn't have stopped myself.'

'He's testing you.'

'Who?'

'Cabhan, or what remains of him. You'll have to be stronger, and smarter. Once you're both, Connor and I will take you back, as we promised. Well then, let's see what we have to work with.'

Too delighted to drink, Iona set the tea aside. 'Are you going to teach me a spell?'

On another laugh, Branna shook her head. 'Did you gallop the first time you sat a horse?'

'I wanted to.'

'Today you walk, and on a lead. Tell me what your granny said was the most important thing about your power, about the craft?'

'To harm no one.'

'Good. An it harm none. What you have is as much a part of you as the color of your eyes, the shape of your mouth. What you do with it is a choice. Choose well.'

'I made the choice to come here, to you.'

'And I'm hoping you won't regret it. Now then, the elements are four.' She gestured to the worktable. 'Earth, air, water, fire. We call on them, use them, with respect. It's not our power over them, but the merging of our power with theirs. Fire, almost always the first learned.'

'And the last lost,' Iona put in. 'Nan said.'

'True enough. Light the candle.'

Pleased to have something to show, Iona stepped forward. She schooled her breathing, focused her mind, imagined drawing up the power in her, then releasing it on a long, quiet breath.

The candlewick sparked, then burned.

'Very good. Water. We need it to live. It runs through our physical bodies, it dominates the

119

world we live in.'

She gestured to the white bowl, filled with water. 'Clear and calm now. Still. But it moves, like the sea, rises like a geyser, spills like a fountain. Its power, and mine.'

Iona watched the water stir, form little waves inside the bowl that lapped at the side. She let out a muffled gasp when it shot up to the ceiling, rippled, a liquid spear, then opened almost like a flower, and spilled back into the bowl without a drop lost.

'That was beautiful.'

'A pretty bit of magick, but an important skill. Stir the water, Iona. Feel it, see it, ask it.'

Like the candle flame, she thought. It would be focus, and that drawing up. She steadied her breath again, tried to do the same with her mind, her pulse. She stared at the water, tried to form an image of those little waves rocking its quiet surface.

And didn't manage a ripple.

'I'm doing something wrong.'

'No. You lack patience.'

'It's a problem. Okay, again.'

She stared at the water, pushed herself at it until her eyes ached.

'It takes longer for some. Where is your center of power. Where do you feel it rise?' Branna asked.

'Here.' Iona pressed a hand on her belly.

'For Connor it's here.' Branna tapped her heart. 'Pull it up, send it out. Use your hand for a guide. Up, out. Imagine, focus, ask.'

'Okay. Okay.' She loosened her shoulders, shoved at her hair, took a new stance. She wanted to move the damn water, she thought. She wanted to learn how to send it up like a spear. Maybe she'd been too timid. So...

She drew in a breath, pulled, drawing her hand up from her belly, flinging it out toward the bowl.

And barely choked back the scream when the water flew up toward the ceiling.

'Holy shit! I just – oops!'

It fell again, like a small flood. Stopped, went still just above the counter.

'I'd prefer to avoid the mess,' Branna said, and with a flick of her finger, had the water spilling back into the bowl.

'Oh, you did it. I thought I had.'

'You sent it up, lost your focus. I spared you the mopping.'

'I did that?' Thrilled, she did a quick dance in place. 'Go me. Wow, it's just so cool. Not respectful,' she said with a wince.

'No reason there can't be joy and wonder. It's magick after all. Do it again. But slow. Smooth. Control, always.'

'Like riding a horse,' Iona murmured.

She took it up, only inches this time, and imagining a small fountain, created it. Slowly, slowly, she turned the fountain so it circled just above the bowl. The dance of the water filled her with that joy and with that wonder.

'You have a lot sleeping inside you,' Branna told her.

Delighted, proud, dazzled at herself, Iona let the water slide back into the bowl. 'Let's wake it up.'

When Connor walked in, she floated a feather.

121

Not in the graceful dance Branna demonstrated, but it floated.

He sent her a wink, then, twirling a finger, had the feather spinning up to tickle her under the chin.

'Show-off,' she said, but laughed, and did a twirl of her own. 'I'm in witch kindergarten. I've made flame, moved water, floated the feather, and I did that.'

She gestured toward the white flowerpot, and the pretty painted daisy blooming in it.

'That's well done.' Impressed, he walked to the worktable.

'I did that,' she corrected, showing him the little seedling beside the bloom. 'Branna did the flower.'

'Still well done. It's quite the day you've had, cousin.' He draped an arm around her shoulders for a quick hug. 'And I'm here to collect on my pint. School's out, don't you think, Branna? It's half-six, and I'm next to starving.'

'The magick's in his heart, but our Connor thinks with his belly. Or what's just below it.'

'And shamed I am of neither. Let's go to the pub. Iona buys my pint, I buy the meal. That's a good deal on any table.'

'Why not?' Branna decided. 'We've things to talk about, and I could do with a pint and some food while we're doing it.'

She pulled the clips from her hair, shook it, and had Iona sighing with envy. 'Come on, Kathel. I'll be five minutes,' she said.

'She'll be twenty,' Connor corrected. 'We'll meet you there,' he called out, and reached for Iona's hand.

'I don't mind waiting.'

'She's going to decide to change her clothes, then having done that, to fuss with her face. I could have my pint by the time she's finished, and you can be telling me about your day.'

'Possibly the best day ever. It'll take a while.'

'I've nothing but time – as long as we're heading for that pint and my supper.'

Maybe it was the residual energy from the power she'd practiced, combined with the excitement of a new job, but Iona felt she could have sprinted all the way to the village.

Connor had other ideas and set a meandering pace on the winding road. She knew she chattered, but he'd asked, after all. And he listened, laughed, tossed in comments.

When she told him of Alastar, Connor lifted his eyebrows, angled his head. His eyes, so full of fun, seemed to sharpen with a quick, canny focus.

'Well now, that's an interesting sort of development, isn't it then?'

'It upset Branna.'

'Well, Fin tends to most days of the week, and him sending back this particular horse? That's a message from him, to her particularly.'

'A warning?'

He gave Iona a quiet smile. 'She might take it as one.'

'It doesn't upset you.'

'It's coming, isn't it – whatever it will be. We knew that when you showed up on the doorstep.'

He looked away, toward the woods, and his eyes, she thought, looked beyond anything she could see.

'This is just the next of it,' he told her, 'and I'd say having a good horse is a positive thing.'

'But he's Fin's, and if Fin's part of the – I don't know – opposing force–'

'He's not.'

'But ... Branna said–'

'Blood ties, curses, and devil's marks.' Connor shrugged them off like an old jacket.

'Is he Cabhan's descendant?'

'That he is. I'd like to know who doesn't have a twisted branch on his family tree. Coming from something doesn't make it what you are. You've choices, don't you? You've made your own. Fin makes his own, that's God's truth, as does our Branna. She's my sister, and as important to me as my next breath. And Fin's my friend, as he's been all of my life. So I walk that line, and it's fortunate I've good balance.'

'You don't think he's evil.'

Connor paused long enough to draw her to his side, brush his lips on the top of her head with an easy affection that warmed her to the bone. 'I think evil comes in too many forms to count. Fin's not one of them. As for Alastar being his? Buying something doesn't make it yours as you can keep it, lose it, give it away. It's you who connected with the horse, isn't it?'

'I guess that's true. You trust him, I can see that. But Branna doesn't.'

'She's conflicted, you could say, which she is on little else. He'll be back when he's a mind to, then you can decide for yourself where you stand on it.'

'You were boys together? You and Fin and Boyle.'

'Still are.'

She laughed, but felt a little pang with it. 'I don't have any lifelong friends. We moved when I was about six, then my parents split up when I was ten, so another move, and a lot of back and forth, and other moves when each of them re-married. It's nice, I think, to have friends you grew up with.'

'Friends are friends whenever you make them.'

'You're right. I like that.'

He took her hand again, gestured with the other as they came into the village. 'There you have the ruins of Cong Abbey. It's a fine ruin for all that, and the tourists come to wander around it, though most come to Cong for the Quiet Man.'

'Nan loves that movie. I watched it again myself before I came.'

'We've a festival in September to commemorate the film. It's grand. Maureen O'Hara herself came two years back. She's still a rare beauty. Regal and real all at once.'

'Did you get to meet her?'

'For a moment I did. Sure it was a fine moment. You didn't get your village tour today?'

'No, but there's plenty of time. I feel like I've been here. From everything Nan's told me,' she explained. 'And her photos, the guidebook. It's just like I imagined.'

The pretty shops and pubs and restaurants, the little hotel, the flowers in pots and window boxes tipped down the road in the shadow of the ruined abbey. Though the shops were closed, the pubs were open, and a scatter of people strolled along the narrow sidewalks.

'Where's Branna's shop?'

'Around the corner, there, down a bit next to the tea shop. She'll be closed now, but I've a key if you want to see it.'

'That's all right. I'll have a day off, I assume.'

'Sure you'll have your day off. Boyle, he'll work you hard enough, but not to the bone.'

They walked down, against the rise of the road, and she lifted her face, happy to feel the cool air on her skin. 'Is that... Is it peat I smell?'

'Sure it is. Nothing like a peat fire on an evening, and a pint to go with it. And here, we'll have both.'

He opened a door, nudged her in.

The yeasty smell of beer pouring from the tap, the earthy scent of peat simmering in the hearth – yes, Iona thought, there was nothing like it. People claimed stools at the hub of the bar, or sat at tables already into their meal. Their voices hummed over the clink of glassware.

A half dozen patrons hailed Connor the minute he stepped in the door. He called out greetings, sent out a wave, and steered Iona to the bar.

'Good evening to you, Sean. This is my cousin Iona Sheehan, from America. She's grand-daughter to Mary Kate O'Connor.'

'Welcome.' He had a shock of white hair shaggy around a ruddy face, and sent her a quick beam out of cheerful blue eyes. 'And how's Mary Kate faring?'

'She's very well, thanks.'

'Iona's working for Boyle at the stables. Had her first day.'

'Is that a fact? A horsewoman are you then?'

'I am.'

'She's buying me a pint to celebrate. I'll have a Guinness. What's your pleasure, Iona?'

'Make it two.'

'Branna's on her way, so it's to be three. We'll just find us a table. Well, it's Franny.' Connor gave a pretty blonde a peck on the cheek. 'Meet my cousin Iona from America.'

So it began. Iona calculated she met more people in ten minutes within feet of the bar than she normally did in a month. By the time they moved away she carried a blur of faces and names in her head.

'Do you know everybody?'

'Hereabouts, most. And there's two you know yourself.'

She spotted Boyle and Meara at a table crowded with pints and plates. Connor snagged one beside them. 'How's it all going then?'

'Well enough. Taking in the local nightlife are you, Iona?' Meara asked her.

'Celebrating my new job. Thanks again,' she said to Boyle.

'It happens we're working out schedules,' Meara told her, 'and you've Thursday off if you've a mind to make plans.'

'I'm nothing but plans right now.'

'Iona tells me Fin sent you a new horse. Alastar, is it – and temperamental.'

'My arse.' Boyle hefted what was left of his pint. 'Tried making a meal out of Kevin Leery's arm this morning after he kicked the shit out of Mooney.'

'Take any piece of you?'

'Not yet, and not for lack of trying. Behaved like a gentleman for your cousin.'

Iona smiled into her beer. 'He's just misunderstood.'

'I understand him fine.'

'We wonder what Fin's about with this one.' Meara spooned up some soup, kept her eyes on Connor. 'Alastar's no riding hack, that's for certain. It may be he'll breed well, but he never said he was after acquiring a stallion for that when off he went.'

Connor gave his easy shrug. 'No one knows what's in Fin's mind save Fin, and plenty's the time he doesn't know either. And speaking of that, there's our Branna.'

He lifted a hand, caught her eye.

'Well now, it's a party,' she said when she walked to the table. Her hand lowered to rub on Meara's shoulder as she sent Boyle a smile. 'Are you working my girl then, right through her supper?'

'More the other way around,' Boyle claimed. 'She's relentless. I was coming to see you tomorrow. The salve you made for us is about gone.'

'I've more on hand. I'll send it along with Iona in the morning.' She sat, picked up her beer. 'So, here's to Iona and her new position, and to you for having the good sense to hire her.'

She felt nearly giddy, sitting there. Cousins, boss, coworker – and ordering, at Connor's suggestion, the beef and barley stew.

As her first working day in Ireland, it couldn't get better.

And then it did.

Connor slid away from the table. He came back a few moments later with a violin.

'Connor,' Branna began.

'I'm buying, so the least you can do is play for your supper.'

'You play the violin?'

Branna glanced at Iona, gave a shrug much like her brother's. 'When the mood comes.'

'I always wanted to play something, but I'm hopeless. Please, won't you?'

'How can you say no?' Connor handed his sister the violin and bow. 'Give us a song, Meara darling. Something cheerful to match the mood.'

'You didn't pay for my supper.'

He sent her a wink, both cheeky and wicked. 'There's always a sweet to come, if you've the appetite.'

'One.' Branna tested the bow. He'd rosined it, she noted, confident he'd coax her into it. 'You know he won't leave off till we do.'

She angled her chair, tested again, tweaked the tuning. Voices around them quieted as Branna smiled, tapped her foot in time.

Music danced out, cheerful as Connor had asked, lively and quick. Branna's gaze laughed toward Meara, and Iona saw the friendship, the ease and depth of it even as Meara laughed and nodded.

'I'll tell me ma when I go home, the boys won't leave the girls alone.'

More magick, Iona thought. The bright, happy music, Meara's rich, flirtatious voice, the humor on Branna's face as she played. Her heart, already high, lifted as she imprinted everything –

the sound, the look, even the air on her memory.

She'd never forget this moment, and how it made her feel.

She caught Boyle watching her, a bemused smile on his face. She imagined she looked like a starstruck idiot, and didn't care.

When applause rang out, she found herself bouncing on her seat. 'Oh, that was great! You're both amazing.'

'Won us a prize once, didn't we, Branna?'

'That we did. First prize, Hannigan's Talent Show. A short-lived enterprise to match our short-lived career.'

'You were grand, both of you, then and now, but we're grateful Meara didn't run off to be a singing star.' Boyle gave her hand a pat. 'We need her at the stables.'

'I'd rather sing for the fun than my supper.'

'Don't you want to have more fun?' Iona gave Meara a poke on the arm. 'Give us another.'

'Look what you started,' Branna said to her brother.

'You don't play for fun often enough. I always wish you would.' And when he laid a hand on Branna's cheek, she sighed.

'You have a way, you do, and you know it.'

'Iona's not the only Yank in here tonight. I've spotted a few others. Give them "Wild Rover," and send them back with the memory of the two beauties in the pub in Cong.'

'Such a way, you do,' she said and laughed. And shaking her hair back, lifted the fiddle.

Iona saw the smile fade, all the humor fade out of the smoky eyes. Something else came into them, so quick there, then gone, she couldn't be sure. Longing? Temper? Some combination of both.

But she lowered the instrument again.

'Your partner's back,' Branna said to Boyle.

7

Everything about him was sharp. The cheekbones, the jaw, even the bold green of his eyes – and the glint in them.

He'd come in on a kick of wind that had the simmering peat fire giving a quick snap.

As they had with Connor, several people hailed him. But Connor had been greeted with easy and affectionate warmth. Finbar Burke's welcome was edged with respect and, Iona thought, a little caution and wariness.

He wore a black leather coat that skimmed to his knees. Rain, which must have started while she'd been cozy and warm, beaded on it, and on his sweep of black hair.

Cautious herself, Iona skimmed her gaze toward Branna. Nothing showed on her cousin's face now, as if that momentary swirl of emotion had been nothing more than illusion.

Fin wound through the crowd and, as Branna had with Meara, laid a hand on Boyle's shoulder, and on Connor's. But his gaze, Iona noted, fixed on Branna.

'Don't let me interrupt.'

'And there he is, home from the wars at last.' Connor sent him a cheeky grin. 'And just in time to stand the next round.'

'Some of us have to work tomorrow,' Branna reminded her brother.

'Sure it's fortunate my boss is an understanding and generous sort of man. Unlike yours,' Connor added with a wink for Branna, 'who's a tyrant for certain.'

'I'll stand the round,' Fin said. 'Good evening to you, Meara, and how's your mother faring? I got word she was feeling poorly,' he said when she blinked at him.

'She's better, thanks. Just a bout of bronchitis that lingered awhile. The doctor dosed her with medicine, and Branna with soup, so she's well again.'

'It's good to hear it.'

'You brought the rain,' Boyle commented.

'Apparently. And Branna. You look more than well.'

'I'm well enough. You cut your travels short then?'

'Six weeks was long enough. Did you miss me?'

'No. Not a bit.'

He smiled at her, quick and again sharp, then turned those vivid eyes on Iona. 'You'd be the American cousin. Iona, is it?'

'Yes.'

'Fin Burke,' he said and extended a hand over the table. 'As this lot doesn't have the manners for introductions.'

She took his hand automatically, and felt the heat, a quick zip of power. Still smiling, he cocked an eyebrow as if to say: What were you expecting?

'Another Guinness for you?' he asked.

'Oh, no. Despite understanding and generous bosses, this is my limit. Thanks anyway.'

'I wouldn't mind some tea before I head out in the rain,' Meara said. 'Thanks, Fin.'

'Tea then. Another pint, Boyle?'

'I'm in my truck, so this will have to do me.'

'I'm on my feet,' Connor said, 'so I'll have another.'

'Sure I'll join you.' Fin had barely glanced around when their waitress hurried up. 'Hello there, Clare. The ladies, they'll have tea. Connor and I will have a pint. Guinness tonight.'

He found a chair, pulled it up. 'We won't bring business into the party,' he said to Boyle. 'We'll talk later in that area, though I think we've kept each other up to date. And you as well, Connor.'

'Suits me. I took Merlin out a few times while you were rambling, as did Meara,' Connor told him. 'And he took himself out when he wanted. Will you be coming by the school tomorrow?'

'I'll make a point of it, and the stables.'

'Make sure you have a kind word for Kevin and Mooney.' Boyle lifted his beer. 'As your newest acquisition battered both of them.'

'Got spirit, he does, and an iron will. Has he battered you as well?'

'Not for lack of trying. He likes this one.' Boyle nodded toward Iona.

Locking eyes with Iona again, Fin tapped his fingers on the table as if to an inner tune. 'Does he now.'

'After doing his damnedest to buck me across

133

to Galway, the Yank here mounts him and takes him around the ring like a show horse.'

Fin smiled slowly. 'Is that a fact? Are you a horsewoman then, Iona?'

'It is, and she is,' Boyle answered. 'She's now in our employ, which I'm keeping you up to date with in person.'

'Happy to have you. A working holiday for you, is it?'

'I ... I'm going to live here. That is, I'm living here now.'

'Well then, welcome home. Your grandmother's well, I hope. Mrs. O'Connor?'

'Very. Thanks.' To keep them still, Iona clutched her hands together under the table. 'I needed a job, so Branna asked Boyle to meet with me. I worked at Laurel Riding Academy in Maryland. I have references, and my résumé. That is, Boyle has them now, if you need to see them.'

Shut up, shut up, she ordered herself, but nerves overwhelmed her. 'You have a wonderful operation. Meara showed me around. And you're right. Alastar has spirit, and a strong will, but he's not mean. Not innately. He's just mad and un-settled, finding himself in a strange place, with people and horses he's not used to. Now he has something to prove, especially to Boyle.

'Thank God,' she breathed when the tea ar-rived. She could use it to stop her mouth.

'You make her nervous.' Amused now, Branna spoke to Fin. 'She tends to chatter on when she's nervous.'

'I do. Sorry.'

'And apologizes continually. That really has to

134

stop, Iona.'

'It does. Why did you buy him – Alastar?' she began. Then held up a hand. 'Sorry. None of my business. Plus you said you didn't want to talk business.'

'He's beautiful. I have a weakness for beauty, and strength, and … power.'

'He's all that,' Meara agreed. 'And anyone who knows bloody anything about horses knows he's not meant to plod around with tourists on his back every day.'

'No, he's meant for other things.' He looked at Branna. 'Needed for other things.'

'What are you about?' she murmured.

'He spoke to me. You understand me,' he said to Iona.

'Yes. Yes.'

'So, he's here, and on her way is the prettiest filly in the West Counties. Spirited, too, a two-year-old, fine as a princess. She's Aine, for the faerie queen. We'll be playing matchmaker there, Boyle, when she's mature enough. Until she is, she'll do well on the jump course, even, I think, with novices.'

'You've more than breeding on your mind.' Branna nudged her tea aside.

'Ah, darling, breeding's ever on it.'

'You knew she'd come, and what it would mean. It's already begun.'

'We'll talk about it.' Fin laid a hand over Branna's on the table. 'But not in the pub.'

'No, not in the pub.' She drew her hand from under his. 'You know more than you say, and I'll want the truth of it.'

135

Irritation simmered in his eyes. 'I've never lied to you, *mo chroi*. Not in all our lives, and you know it. Even when a lie could have given me what I wanted most.'

'Leaving gaps is no different from a bold lie.' She pushed to her feet. 'I've work yet. Boyle, use your truck to see Iona back to the hotel, would you? I won't have her walking through the wood at night.'

'Oh, but—'

'I'll see to it.' Boyle interrupted Iona's protest smoothly. 'Not to worry.'

'I'll get that salve to you in the morning. And see you, Iona, tomorrow, after work. We've much more to do.'

'Well and hell.' Connor sighed, started to rise as Branna left.

'No, stay and finish your pint.' Meara rubbed at Connor's arm as if to soothe even as she pushed back her chair. 'I'll go with her. It's time I started home anyway. Thanks for the tea, Fin, and welcome back. I expect I'll see the lot of you tomorrow.'

Grabbing her jacket, Meara dragged it on as she hurried out of the pub.

Connor patted Iona's arm. 'You'll need to get used to that.'

'That's God's truth,' Fin muttered, then very deliberately eased back, smiled. 'I tend to put our Branna in difficult moods. So tell us, Iona from America, what is it you've seen and done in Ireland?'

'I...' How could they just pick up the small talk when the air actively pulsed with temper and heartbreak? 'Ah... not very much. And a lot, I guess. I came to meet Branna and Connor, and to find a place, to find work. Now I have. But I haven't had time, yet, to see anything but here. It's so beautiful, it's enough.'

'We'll have to get you out and about more than that. You say you found a place, to live you mean? That's quick work.'

'I'm staying at Ashford for a few more days.'

'Now there's a rare treat.'

'It really is. Then I'm going to live with Branna and Connor.' She saw his eyes flicker, narrow, shift quickly to Connor. 'Is that a problem?'

In answer, Fin leaned over the table, kept those eyes focused on her face. 'She knew you. She reaches out to many, but holds precious few. Home is sanctuary. If hers is yours, she knew you. Have a care with them,' he murmured to Connor. 'By all the gods.'

'Don't doubt it.'

'Speaking of gaps.' Frustrated, Iona looked from one man to the other, and to Boyle who sat, saying nothing at all. She'd get nothing out of any of them, not there and then. 'I should go. Thanks for dinner, Connor, and for the tea, Fin. You don't have to drive me back to the hotel, Boyle.'

'She'll skin my arse if I don't, and it could be literal. I'll see you back at home,' he said to Fin.

'I'll be coming along shortly.'

Stuck, Iona walked to the door. She took one glance back, caught a glimpse of Fin brooding into his pint, and Connor leaning over the table, talking quick and low.

She stepped out into windy rain, and found

herself grateful after all for the ride.

'You and Fin live together?'

'I keep my place over the garage, and make use of his house when I've a mind to, as he's out as much as in. It's handy for both of us, living there near the big stables.'

He opened the door of an old truck with faded red paint, and reaching in, shoved at the clutter on the seat. 'Sorry about that. I wasn't expecting a passenger.'

'Don't worry about it. It's a relief to see someone's as messy as I am.'

'If that's the way of it, take a warning. Hide and confine your debris. Branna's orderly, and she'll hound you like a dog if you leave things flung about.'

'So noted.'

She boosted up, slid in among clipboards, wrappers, an old towel, rags, and a shallow cardboard box holding hoof picks, bridle rings, a couple of batteries, and a screwdriver.

He got in the opposite door, shoved a key in the ignition.

'You didn't say much in there.'

'Being friends with all parties, I find it best to stay out of it altogether.'

The truck rattled, the rain pattered, and Iona settled back.

'They're a thing.'

'Who's a thing?'

'Branna and Fin. They either are, or were, involved. The sexual buzz was so loud my ears are still ringing.'

He shifted, frowned out at the road. 'I'm not

after gossiping about friends.'

'It's not gossip. It's an observation. It must be complicated, for both of them. And it's clear I need to know what's going on. You know more about any of it than I do, and I'm in it.'

'Put yourself there from what I can see.'

'Maybe I did. So what? How did you know I'm like them?'

'I've known them most of my life, been a part of theirs. I saw it in you, with the horse.'

Brows knit, she shifted to face him. 'Most people wouldn't be so casual about it. Why are you?'

'I've known them most of my life,' he repeated.

'I don't see how it can be that simple. I can do this.' She held out her palm and, focusing hard, managed to flick a small flame in its center.

It was pitiful compared to Branna, but she'd been working on it off and on.

He barely glanced her way. 'Convenient if you're backpacking and misplace the matches.'

'You're a cool customer.' She had to admire it. 'If I'd pulled that on the guy I'd been dating, he'd have gone through the door, leaving a cartoon-guy hole in it.'

'Must not have been much for backpacking.'

She started to laugh, then caught her breath when fog rose up on the road ahead like a wall. Her hands balled into fists as the truck punched through it, tightened as the fog blanketed over them.

'Do you hear that? Can you hear that?'

'Hear what?'

'My name. He keeps saying my name.'

Though he was forced to slow to a crawl, Boyle kept his hands steady on the wheel. 'Who's saying your name?'

'Cabhan. He's in the fog. Maybe he *is* the fog. Can't you hear him?'

'I can't.' And so far, never had. He wouldn't mind keeping it that way. 'I'm thinking you'll work with Meara again tomorrow.'

'What? What?'

'I'll want her go-ahead before you take any guests out on your own.' He spoke easily, drove slowly. He could navigate this road blindfolded, and thought he damn nearly was. 'And I'll want to see how you handle instruction. We'll have you work with Mick there, or with me from time to time. Do you do any jumping?'

He knew she did, and had the blue ribbons and trophies to prove it, the certification to teach it. He'd read her résumé.

'Yes. Competitively since I was eight. I wanted to try for the Olympic team, but…'

'Too much commitment?'

'No. I mean, yes. In a way. You need a lot of family support for that kind of training. And the financial backing.' While her eyes tracked right and left, she rubbed a hand from between her breasts up to her throat, back again. 'Did you hear that? God, can't you hear that?'

'That I did.' The wild howl shot cold fingers up his spine. And that, he thought, was new, at least to him. 'I expect he doesn't like us talking over him.'

'Why aren't you afraid?'

'I'm riding with a witch, aren't I? What have I

140

got to worry about?'

She choked out a laugh, struggled to steady her pulse. 'I learned to levitate a feather today. I don't think that's going to do a lot of good.'

And he thought he had his two fists, and the utility knife in his pocket, if needed. 'It's more than I can do. See now, the fog's thinning, and there's Ashford up ahead.'

So it was, the glamorous fairy-tale spread of it, windows lighted pale gold.

'They went there. The first three. They came back, years after their mother sent them away to save them. They stayed in the castle, walked the woods. I dreamed of the youngest coming back, riding back as she'd ridden away as a child. On a horse named Alastar.'

'Ah, well then. I didn't know the name of the horse. That explains it, doesn't it?'

'I don't know what it explains. I don't know what I'm supposed to do.'

'What you must.'

'What I must,' she murmured as he stopped at the hotel's entrance. 'Okay. Okay. Thanks for the ride, and for talking me through the weird.'

'Not a problem. I'll see you in.'

She started to object. She was only steps from the door. And thinking of the voice in the fog, changed her mind. It was just fine to have a big, strong man walk her in. No shame in it.

With him she walked into the warmth, into the rich colors, the flowers. And the smile of the woman on duty at the lobby table.

'Good evening to you, Ms. Sheehan. And Boyle, it's good seeing you.'

'Working late, Bridget?'

'I am. A good night for it, as it's gone wet again. I've your key right here, miss. I hope you enjoyed your day.'

'I did, very much. Thanks again, Boyle.'

'I'll see you to your door.'

'Oh, but–'

He just took the key from her, glanced at the number. 'This is in the old part, isn't it?' So saying, he took Iona's arm, pulled her along and down the corridor.

'It's that way now.' Iona made the turn.

'The place is a rambling maze.'

'Part of its charm.' She tried not to worry about the desk clerk likely thinking she and Boyle were a thing.

He stopped at the door, unlocked it. After pushing the door open, he took a long, careful look.

'Well, you are messy.'

'As advertised.' Her eyes widened when he walked right in. He couldn't possibly think–

He picked up the hotel pen on the nightstand, scrawled something on the pad.

'That's my mobile. If you get nervous, ring me up. Better you ring Branna, but I'm just minutes away if it comes to that.'

'That's... That's so kind.'

'Don't get watery about it. I've just hired you, haven't I, and done the bloody paperwork. I can't have you running back to America. Lock the door and go to bed. Switch on the telly if you need the noise.'

He walked to the door, opened it. 'And remember,' he said, looking back at her. 'You can hold a flame of your own making in the palm of your hand.'

He shut the door. Even as she started to smile, he rapped hard enough to make her jump.

'Lock the bloody door!'

She dashed to it, locked it. And listened to his boot steps fading away.

She made a bargain with herself. At work, she'd focus on work. She couldn't and wouldn't let whatever she might have to face interfere with making a living.

When work was done, she'd take whatever time Branna was willing to give. She'd learn, she'd practice, she'd study.

But she would also demand and get answers.

So she mucked, cleaned, brushed, hauled, fed, and watered. And did her best to stay out of Boyle's way. Remembering the ride home, and her panic, left a thin layer of embarrassment. She was the one with power, however unrefined, and she'd gone weak and trembly, and let him look after her.

Worse, for just a second – maybe two or three seconds – when he'd come into her room, she'd been the one with the wrong idea. A sad fact she'd been forced to admit when she'd pulled out of a dream. Not of evil sorcerers and shadows, she thought as she brushed Spud's mane.

But of a sex dream, and a damn good one, involving her and Boyle and a *Wizard of Oz* field of poppies.

But it sure as hell hadn't put them to sleep.

That subconscious revelation added a lot of thicker layers to the embarrassment.

Meara poked her head in the stall. She wore a kelly green cap today, with her hair streaming through the back opening in a long tail. 'You braided Queen Bee's mane.'

'Oh, yeah. I just... I'll take it out.'

'No, indeed. It looks charming, and she's fairly preening with her new do. Just don't do the fancy work with any of the geldings. Boyle'll huff about, say we're making them into dandies when they're good plain hacks. He's such a man, is Boyle.'

'I noticed. You're good together.'

'Well, I should hope. It's going clear, so the ride's on for the afternoon. They shifted to three, hoping for better weather, and it looks like we may get it. It's a party of four – two couples, friends from America, so that should be nice for you. Boyle's sent off for Rufus, he's a big, playful gelding. One of our guests is near to two meters tall.'

'Which is what?'

'Oh, in Yank?' With a frown, she pushed at her cap, scratched her head. 'About six and a half feet, I'm thinking. Otherwise, we'll saddle up Spud there, and Bee, and Jack. You can take your pick from the rest.'

'Maybe Caesar, unless you want him.'

'Go ahead.' Meara made a little note on her clipboard. 'They asked for ninety minutes, so you'll see more than yesterday.'

'I want to see it all. And, Meara?' The guilt over the dream wouldn't allow her to just let it go. 'I just wanted to say thanks for lending me Boyle last night for the ride home.'

'I'm not in the habit of lending him, but you're welcome to keep him if you like.'

'Oh, did you have a fight?'

'About what?' The puzzled frown gave way to wide eyes, then a roll of wicked laughter. 'Oh! You're thinking me and Boyle are tangled. No, no, no! I love the man to distraction, but I don't want him in my bed. It would be like shagging my brother. And that thought's just put me off my lunch.'

'You're not...' Embarrassment kicked up several notches. 'I just assumed.'

'Look like lovebirds, do we?'

'There's just something, I guess, intimate, between you, so I thought you were together. That way.'

'We're family.'

'Got it. Good. I guess it's good. Maybe it's a problem.'

Now Meara leaned on the side of the stall opening. 'You're a fascination to me, Iona. A problem?'

'It's just that when I assumed, I had a good reason to ignore the...' She wiggled her fingers over her stomach.

'You've got' – Meara mimicked the gesture – 'for Boyle.'

'He looks really good, on a horse and off. The first minute I saw him, I just ... whew.' She laid one hand on her heart, the other on her belly, patted both.

'Is that the truth?'

'He's all tough and cranky. Then there's the big hands, the scar,' she said, tapping her eyebrow. 'And those liony eyes.'

'Liony.' Meara tried out the words. 'Well now, I suppose they are. Boyle McGrath, King of the

Beasts.' She let out another of her barroom laughs.

'That's just looks, but they're really impressive. On top of it, he was really kind to me. Then there was the sex. Dream,' Iona said quickly when Meara's mouth fell open. 'Sex dream. I had one last night, and I felt so guilty because I really like you. And you don't want to hear any of this.'

'You're mistaken, entirely. I want to hear all of this, in the greatest of detail.'

On a laughing moan, Iona covered her face with her hands. 'You're Boyle's friend. If you tell him the Yank's got this slow simmer going on, he'll either laugh himself into a coma or fire me.'

'He'd do neither, but why would I tell him any such thing? There's a sisterhood that covers such matters. That's a universal sort of thing to my mind.'

'Of course there is. Anyway, I think I'm just jet-lagged, and turned around, and coming to grips. It's nothing. It'll pass.'

'Maybe you should take him on a ride before you–'

She broke off at the sound of raised voices. 'Ah, Christ.'

Turning on her heel, Meara strode out, and as the voices – male, extremely pissed – escalated, Iona followed her.

Boyle faced off with a hard-packed bull of a man in a red cap and plaid jacket. The bull, his face nearly as red as his cap, jabbed out with a finger. 'I come here being reasonable, though you're a cheat and a liar for all that.'

'And I'm telling you, Riley, what business we had is done and over. Get off my property, and

146

keep clear of it.'

'I'll get off your bleeding property when you give me back the horse you next to stole from me, or hand over fair payment. You think you can steal from me. Bloody thief.' He shoved Boyle back two steps.

'Oh Jesus,' Meara muttered. 'Now he's done it.'

'Don't put your hands on me again,' Boyle warned, very quietly.

'Oh, I'll put more than my hands on you, you fucking shite.'

Riley threw a punch. Boyle shifted his weight, angled his head, and the fist breezed by his ear.

'We should call the police. The guard, whatever it's called.'

Meara barely glanced at Iona. 'No need.'

'You get one more.' With his arms still down by his sides, Boyle spread his hands. 'Take it, if you've a mind to, and know you won't be walking away from this if you do.'

'I'll beat ya bloody.' Riley charged, fists up, head down.

Dancing to the side, Boyle turned, jabbed two short punches.

Kidney punches? Iona wondered as her eyes went wide. Oh God!

Riley stumbled, but stayed on his feet, punched out again. The blow grazed Boyle's shoulder as Boyle slapped it away with a forearm.

Then he followed up. A right to the jaw, left to the nose. Jab, uppercut – Iona thought – a left cross. Two punches to the middle.

Fast, so fast. Light and quick on his feet, barely showing a reaction when Riley managed to land

147

a blow. Bare knuckles slapped and crunched into flesh and bone. Riley, his nose pouring blood, his mouth dripping it, made a staggering charge. On a pivot, Boyle swept up his fist – definitely an uppercut – hitting the jaw like an arrow in a bull's-eye.

He started to follow up, pulled back. 'Fuck it,' she heard him mutter as he simply put a boot on Riley's ass and shoved him facedown on the ground.

'Oh God. My God.'

'There now.' Meara patted her shoulder. 'It's just a bit of a dustup.'

'No. It's...' She fluttered her fingers over her belly.

Meara snorted out a laugh. 'Aye, a fascination to me you are.'

A few feet away, Fin sat astride a restless Alastar. 'Again?' he said mildly.

'Fucker wouldn't walk away.' Boyle sucked at his raw knuckles. 'And I gave him every chance.'

'I saw you giving him those chances as I rode up, and how could he be walking away with your fist in his face?'

Boyle only grinned. 'That was after the chances.'

'Well, let's make sure you haven't killed him, as I've no desire to help you hide a body this morning.' As he dismounted, he crooked a finger at Iona. 'Yes, you. Be a darling and tie Alastar to the post. Don't unsaddle him.'

When he held out the reins, she hurried over to take them.

Using his boot again, Boyle rolled Riley onto his back. 'Broke his nose, that's for certain, and loosened some teeth, but he'll live through it.'

Fin stood, hands in his pockets as they both studied the unconscious Riley. 'This goes back to that horse you won off him, I take it.'

'It does.'

'Bloody git.'

Whistling cheerfully through his teeth, Mick strolled out carrying a bucket of water. 'Thought you could be using this.'

Fin took it. 'Stand clear then,' he advised, then tossed the water in Riley's face.

The man sputtered, coughed. His eyes opened and rolled in his head.

'Good enough.' Boyle crouched down, took one arm. On a sigh, Fin took the other.

Absently stroking Alastar, Iona watched them haul the man to his truck, shove him up and in. She couldn't hear what words were exchanged, but in moments, the truck drove away, weaving a bit.

As she did, the men watched it. Then Fin said something that had Boyle letting out a laugh before he slung an arm around Fin's shoulders and turned to walk back.

She saw it then, the ease between them. More than partners, she realized. More still than friends. Brothers.

'Performance is over for the day,' Boyle called out. 'There's work needs doing.'

At his words, the staff that had gathered, scattered.

Iona cleared her throat. 'You should put something on those knuckles.'

Boyle merely glanced at them, sucked at them

149

again. And shrugging, continued inside. Fin stopped by Iona.

'He's a brawler, is Boyle.'

'The other guy started it.'

Now Fin laughed. 'No doubt. Maturity's given Boyle the sense to wait until he's well provoked, and rare is it for him to throw the first punch. Otherwise, he'd have given Riley the hammering he deserved weeks ago instead of making the wager.'

She should mind her own business. She should... 'What was the wager?'

'Riley's a horse trader of the lowest sort. He had in his possession a mare he'd neglected. I'm told she was skin and bones and sick and lame. He planned to sell her off for dog food.'

Eyes fired, lips peeled back in a snarl. 'I'd like to punch him myself.'

'You don't have the hands for it.' Fin watched Alastar nuzzle at Iona's shoulder, and the way she leaned her head to his. 'Best to use your feet for such matters, and aim for the balls.'

'I'd be happy to, in this case.'

'I'll tell you, as Boyle likely won't, as he's a man of few words – or none at all if he can manage it. He offered Riley what he'd have gotten for selling her off, and more besides, but Riley doesn't care much for Boyle, or for me, and he demanded double that. So being a cannier businessman than you might think, Boyle wagered him on who could drink the most whiskey and stay on his feet. If Riley won, Boyle would pay the asking price. If Boyle won, Riley turned over the mare for what was offered. The publican wrote it in the book,

150

and considerable money changed hands, I'm told.'

As he spoke, Fin unlooped the reins from the post. 'And at the end of the long night, it was Boyle still on his feet. Though I'd wager he had the devil's own head the next morning, he had the mare as well.'

'A drinking bet.'

'As I said, our Boyle's matured. Now then.' Fin handed the reins to Iona, made a hammock with his hands. 'Up you go.'

Her mind full of questions, impressions, she put her boot in Fin's hands, mounted Alastar smoothly. 'Where do you want him?'

'I want both of you in the ring. Let's see what you can do.'

8

At the end of the workday, she let herself think of magick. What would Branna teach her today? What new wonder would she see, feel, do? She said good-bye to the horses, to her coworkers before starting out.

And saw Boyle in his little office, all beetled brow and swollen knuckles as he hacked away at paperwork.

Definitely a flutter going on, she thought. Not that she intended to flirt with her boss. Plus, for all she knew, he had a parade of girlfriends. Or maybe even more daunting, didn't find her attractive.

Besides, she wasn't looking for a relationship,

or an entanglement. She needed to get her feet firmly planted in her new life, learn more about her awakening powers – and hone them if she intended to be a real help to her cousins.

When a woman planned to go up against ancient evil, she shouldn't allow herself to become distracted by sexy eyebrows or broad shoulders or–

'In or out,' Boyle ordered, and kept pecking at his keyboard. 'Stop the bleeding hovering.'

'Sorry. I, ah, wasn't sure if... I'm finished for the day,' she told him.

He glanced up, held her eyes for a beat. Grunted and looked back down at his work.

His hands had to hurt, she thought. She could practically see them throbbing. 'You really should ice down those knuckles.'

'They'll be all right. I've had worse.'

'Probably, but if they're swollen and stiff – or worse, get infected – you won't be much good around here.'

'Don't need a nurse, thanks.'

Stubborn, she thought. But so was she. She went back in, got the first-aid kit, a couple of ice packs. Marched back to his office.

'Some would say you're being stoic and manly,' she began as she dragged over a chair. 'But my take is sulky baby because your hands hurt.'

'I enjoyed the getting of them, so I'm not sulky. Put that away.'

'When I'm done with it.' She got out the antiseptic, gripped his wrist. 'This is going to sting.'

'Don't be– Shit! Bloody fucking hell.'

'Baby,' she said with some satisfaction, but

152

blew on the sting. 'If you're going to punch somebody in the face with bare knuckles, you're going to pay the price.'

'If you disapprove of fighting, you're in the wrong place. Likely the wrong country.'

'I don't – that is situationally, and that jerk deserved it. Just let this lie while I clean this one up.' She set the ice pack on one hand while she doctored the other. 'You knew what you were doing. Did you box in college?'

'In a manner of speaking.' Resigned – and in any case the ice pack felt just grand – he sat back a little. 'Are you trying to set my hand on fire to purify it?'

'It'll only sting for a minute. What manner of speaking?'

The look he gave her could only be described as a glower. She'd always wondered what a glower actually looked like.

'You're full of questions.'

'It's only one,' she pointed out. 'And talking will distract you. What manner of speaking?'

'Jesus. I worked my way through university fighting. Bare-knuckle matches, so this current situation isn't new to me. I know how to tend to myself.'

'Then you should have done it. That's a hard way to earn tuition.'

'Not if you like it, and not if you win.'

'And you did both.'

'I liked it better when I won, and I won my share.'

'Good for you. Is that how you got that scar through your eyebrow?'

'That's another question. A different kind of fight – pub fight, and a broken bottle. As I'd been drinking myself, my reflexes were a bit slow.'

'You're lucky you have the eye.'

Surprised by her response, and the matter-of-fact tone, he cocked that scarred brow. 'Not that slow.'

She only smiled. 'Switch hands.'

He had big ones, she thought. Strong, with blunt fingers and wide palms. The rough hands of a man who worked with them, and she respected that.

'Fin told me about the mare, and the bet.'

He didn't glower this time, but shifted a little on the chair. 'Fin loves a story, and the telling of one.'

'I'd like to meet her.'

'We keep her at the big stables. She's skittish around strangers yet, and needs more time and pampering.'

'What do you call her?'

He shifted again, as she knew now he did when uncomfortable or mildly embarrassed. 'She's Darling. It fits her. Haven't you done with that yet?'

'Nearly. I like that you drank him under the table for the horse that needed you. And I like that you knocked the crap out of him today. I probably shouldn't. My parents tried to raise me to be someone who wouldn't. But they failed.'

She glanced up to find his eyes on her again. 'You can't be what you aren't.'

'No, you really can't. I'm a mild disappoint-ment to them, which is worse somehow than being a serious disappointment. So I'm working hard not to be any kind of disappointment to myself.'

She eased back. 'There.' And took his hands gently by the fingers to examine the knuckles. 'Better.'

Oh yeah, she thought as their eyes met yet again. Flutters and tingles, and a quick churning to top it off. She'd be in serious trouble if she didn't watch herself.

But it was Boyle who drew away. 'Thanks. You'd better get on. You'll have things to do.'

'I do.' She started to reach for the kit, but he brushed her away.

'I'll deal with it. Eight tomorrow.'

'I'll be here.'

When she left, he brooded down at his hands. He could still feel her touch on them. A different kind of sting. He looked up when Fin eased into the doorway, leaned on the jamb. Smiled.

'Don't start with me.'

'She's a pretty thing. Bright, eager. And if she'd been flirting any harder, I'd have been forced to shut the door for privacy.'

'She was doing no such thing. She'd had it stuck in her head to tend to my hands, that's all.'

'Not nearly all, and I know you, *mo dearthair*. You think of her, even as you tell yourself you shouldn't think of her.'

Sure if he had, he was human, wasn't he? But he was also not a stupid, irrational sort of man.

'She's Connor's cousin, and she works for us. I've no business thinking of her beyond that.'

'Bollocks. She's a pretty woman, and smart and

155

strong enough to make her choices – as she's already proved. The power now, that worries you some.'

Now Boyle sat back, gave a slow nod with his eyes on Fin's. 'What it means, and what all of you, and me besides, as I'm with you, may be doing concerns me. And should be your priority as well. It's no time for flirtations.'

'If not now, when? For this could be the end of all of us and I'd sooner die after bedding a woman than before.'

'I'd rather live, and bed the woman after the battle's won.'

Fin's mood lightened with his smile. 'Eat your pudding first. You can always have seconds. I'll be taking Alastar for a ride, see how he does.'

'Toward Branna's?'

'Not yet, no. She's not ready. I'm not either.'

Alone, Boyle went back to brooding. They needed to get ready, he thought, remembering the howl in the fog. Every blessed one of them.

At the end of the week, Iona sat in bed at just before six in the morning. She'd spent her last night in the castle. She wanted so much to make her home with her cousins, but to do that, she had to leave this indulgent dream.

No more cheerful maids to tidy her room and bring her tea and biscuits. No more dazzling breakfast buffets. No more snuggling in at night, listening to the wind or the rain or both and imagining herself in the thirteenth century.

But she was trading all that for family. A much better deal.

She'd done most of the packing the night before, but rose now to finish, to calculate the tip for housekeeping. To take her last castle shower.

With a half hour to spare before Connor – at his insistence – picked her up, she practiced her craft.

The feathers seemed safest, considering. Branna had refused to teach her anything new until she'd mastered the four elements. And mastered them to Branna's high watermark.

No amount of wheedling, bribery, cajoling had moved her cousin one inch.

So master them, she would.

At least she'd progressed to a small pile of feathers rather than a single one.

In the dim light she quieted her mind, reached down for the power. Reaching out her hands, she thought of air lifting, warm gentle breeze, a stir, a whisper.

Fluttering, the white feathers rose, separated, swayed, and turned in the air. She sent them higher, little climbs, gentle tumbles. Easy, easy, she told herself. A light touch.

She held her arms high, circled herself, watched them circle with her. And joyful, quickened just a bit.

A turn, a twirl, pretty white feathers mirroring her moves. Up, down, lazy swirls, perfect rings, then a slim white tower.

'I feel it,' she murmured. 'I do. And it's lovely.'

On a laugh, she spun, again, again. Spread her arms so feathers followed each one, formed two whirling circles. Serpentine, figure eights, then again into one downy cloud.

'A plus. Even Branna has to give me the mastery check mark on this one.'

At the hard and rapid knock on the door, she let out a yelp. The feathers fell, tumbling over her.

'Damn it!'

She brushed them off her shoulders. Blew them out of her face as she walked to the door.

'You broke my hold,' she began. 'I was just– Oh. Boyle.'

'There's feathers everywhere. Did you rip the pillow?'

'No. They're my feathers. What are you doing here?' Irritation cleared into worry. 'Is something wrong? Is someone hurt?'

'Nothing's wrong. No one's hurt. Connor got called in to the falconry school. A plumbing thing, and he's the handy one. I'm drafted to fetch you. Are you packed?'

'Yes. I'm sorry. I could've gotten someone from the hotel to take me.'

'I'm here, so let's get your things.'

'All right. Thanks. I've just got to clean this up. The feathers.'

'Hmm.' He reached out, surprising her with the skim of his fingers over her hair. 'Here's a couple more,' he said, and handed them to her.

'Oh. Okay.' She got on her hands and knees, started scooping feathers.

'Are they valuable feathers you have scattered everywhere?'

'They're just feathers.'

'Well then, leave them. The housekeeper will deal with them. It'll take you an hour to pluck them off the floor.'

'I'm not leaving this mess for Sinead.' She plucked a few more, then sat back on her heels. 'I'm an idiot.'

'I'll not comment on that.'

'Wait. Just wait.' She got to her feet, took a breath. Quiet the mind first, she reminded herself.

And floated the feathers up. On a pleased little laugh, she gathered them, then cupped her hands, let them fall into her palms.

'Did you see that?' Glowing, she held her cupped hands out. 'Did you see?'

'I've eyes, don't I?'

'It's just so wonderful. It's feels so *right*. Watch this.'

She threw her hands up, sent the feathers flying, sent them swirling again, dipping, rising, then once again cupped her hands to gather them.

'It's so pretty. I've been practicing for days, and I've finally got it. Really got it.'

Still beaming, she looked up at him. Stopped. Everything stopped.

He looked at her, in that straight way he had – dead eye to eye. It wasn't wonder she saw there, or amusement, or irritation.

It was heat.

'Oh.' She sighed it, and following her heart, leaned toward him.

He stepped back, a quick and complete evasion. 'You've got your feathers.' Moving past her, he dragged the two suitcases off the bed. 'Grab something. If there's more, I'll come back for it.'

'Just my jacket, and my laptop. I'll get them. I'm sorry.' Mortified, she dumped the feathers in their bag, secured it. 'I guess I was caught up, and I misread. I thought you ... but obviously not.'

'Get a move on, will you?' The words snapped out of him; she felt them like hard finger flicks on her cheeks. 'We've all of us got work.'

He carried the cases as if they weighed nothing, and breezed right by her.

'Fine. Fine! I get it. And again, I'm an idiot. You're not attracted to me, message received. But you don't have to be rude about it.'

She shoved the bag of feathers in her laptop case. 'I've been rejected before, and somehow I survived. Believe me, I'm not planning on jumping you, so you don't have to add the slap and kick. I'm a big girl,' she added, snatching up her jacket and scarf. 'And I'm responsible for my own–'

He dropped the cases with a bang that made her jump. 'You talk too bloody much.' With that, he gave her a yank. Off guard, she plowed into him, and managed no more than a quick *oof* before he shoved her chin up. And took her mouth like a man starving for it.

Rough and hard, the kind of kiss that gave her no choice but to hang on. Blasts and booms of that heat assaulted her. She'd have staggered from them if he hadn't hauled her right off her feet.

Dazzled, done for, she wrapped her arms around his neck and rode that high, hot wave.

And seconds later he dropped her unceremoniously back on her feet.

'That shut you up at least.'

'Ah– '

He hefted the cases again. 'You want the ride, get yourself moving.'

'What?' She shoved her hands through her hair. 'What *was* that?'

'You are an idiot. Of course I'm attracted to you. Any man with blood in him would be. That's not the issue.'

'It's not the issue. What is?'

'I'm not interested in doing anything about it. And if you ask one more question, I'm dumping these bags, and you can find your own way to Branna's.'

'All I did was move in a little,' she said as she dragged on her jacket. 'You're the one who did the grabbing.' She snatched up her laptop case, and sailed out of the room.

'That I did,' he muttered. 'And that's made me an idiot as well.'

She kept her mouth firmly shut on the short drive. She wouldn't say a word. It took bitter will-power, as she had plenty to say, but she refused to give him the satisfaction.

Better to ignore him. More mature to say nothing.

No, she decided, more *powerful* to keep silent.

Even as she thought it, the truck jolted, as if it hit an invisible bump on the smooth road.

Boyle spared her one brief, hot look.

Had she done that? Iona gripped her hands together, fighting against a leap of glee. Had she actually lifted an entire truck? Unintentionally, but still a big jump from a pile of feathers.

She considered trying it again, just to see, but fortunately for all involved Boyle pulled up at Branna's cottage.

She shoved out of the truck, started around to

the bed to drag out her suitcases. Then thought the hell with it. He'd carted them out, so he could cart them in. She reversed, strode straight for the cottage door.

A sleepy-eyed Branna opened it before she knocked. 'You're timely.'

'He was early. Thanks again for letting me stay.'

'See if you're thanking me after a week or two. Good morning to you, Boyle. If you're after hauling those all the way, it's the second on the left. I'll show you your room,' Branna continued, and led the way up the narrow stairs. 'Mine's at the back, and Connor's the front. I've my own bath, as when we added on, that was priority. Sharing a bath with him was a trial, and one you'll now experience for yourself.'

'I don't mind, not at all.'

'And if you're saying the same after that week or two, you're a liar. But that's how it has to be.'

The bed with its simple headboard of iron slats painted creamy white faced a window where the view of the woods was framed in lace. The ceiling followed the slant of the roof and formed a cozy nook for a little desk and chair with a needle-pointed seat.

The dresser, small scale again, bloomed with painted flowers against the same creamy white as the headboard. A little pot of shamrocks with their pretty white bells blooming sat on the dresser. The same rich green covered the walls and served as a backdrop for colorful prints of the hills, of the woods and gardens.

'Oh, Branna, it's wonderful. It's so pretty.' Iona brushed her fingers over the cloud-soft throw, an energetic pop of plums and purples and lavenders, folded at the foot of the bed. 'I love it. I'm so grateful.'

This time Branna was a bit more prepared for the enthusiasm of the embrace, if not the quick bounce.

'You're very welcome of course, and if you've a mind to change anything–'

'I wouldn't change a thing. It's perfect.'

'Where do you want these?' Boyle demanded from the doorway in a tone that took no trouble to hide aggravation.

Iona turned, and eyes that had gone misty dried cool. 'Anywhere. Thank you.'

Taking her at her word, he dropped them just over the threshold, and kept the toes of his boots firmly on the other side. 'Well, I'll be off then.'

'You've time yet, don't you?' Branna's mind might have leapt with questions at the temper, the hot and cold of it, running in the room like open taps, but she kept her smile and tone easy. 'I'll fix you breakfast for your trouble.'

'Thanks for that, but I've things to do. Nine's soon enough to come in this morning. Take time to settle.'

He left quickly, and with a clomp of boots on the stairs.

'So, what's all this about?' Branna wondered, then noting the fire in Iona's eyes, held up a hand. 'Hold that in until we're down in the kitchen. I've a feeling I'll be wanting more coffee for this.'

She led the way, then poured two mugs. 'Go on then, cut it loose.'

'He comes banging on the door. I'd been floating feathers. I've got it, Branna. I'll show you. But he broke my focus, and there's feathers everywhere, but I pulled it back, and I showed him. I was excited and happy, who wouldn't be? But I'm not blind or stupid.'

She stomped around the kitchen as she spoke, one hand gesturing wildly. Branna kept her eye on the coffee in the mug in case it threatened to lap over.

'I know when a man's thinking about making a move. I know that look. You know that look,' she said, pointing at Branna.

'I do indeed, and it's a fine one under most circumstances.'

'Exactly, and since it felt fine, I went with it, or would have. I mean, for God's sake, all I did was lean in a little, and he pulls back like I'd jabbed him with a burning stick.'

'Hmm,' Branna said and got down a skillet.

'I felt like an idiot. You know how that kind of thing makes you feel. Well, you probably don't,' Iona reconsidered. 'What man would pull back from you? But I felt hot, not in the good way. Embarrassed. So I apologized. Just read it wrong, that's all, sorry about that. Okay, so maybe I babbled a little, but I felt awful and stupid, and completely flustered because I'd thought he and Meara were a thing, but she said no, so I let myself open that door, which I hadn't because of Meara, and you don't poach. Besides, he's the boss, and you don't want to step in it. And then I did, so it was worse. And I'm apologizing and trying to make it like no big thing, and he grabs me.'

Branna paused for a moment in her task of

frying bacon and eggs. 'Is that the truth of it?'

'He yanked me in, and kissed me until my brains leaked out of my ears and the top of my head blew clean off.' She made an exploding noise, threw her hands up, fountained them down. 'And in like five seconds he just drops me, and makes some nasty comment about shutting me up, and says let's get going.'

'A poet Boyle McGrath will never be.'

'Screw poetry. He didn't have to slap me down that way.'

'He didn't, no.' Sympathy twined around amusement. 'He's brusque, is Boyle, and sometimes that can be taken for unkindness, but he's not unkind as a rule.'

'I guess he broke the rule with me.'

'I'd say he did, by kissing the brains from your ears. You work for him, so it's an awkward sort of situation. He'd take that to heart, Boyle would.'

'But I–'

'Here, have this at the table.' She offered Iona a plate with the bacon and egg on a thick piece of toasted bread. 'Morning drama stirs my appetite.' Branna carried her own, and her coffee, took a seat. 'I'll tell you, he's a man of rules. You don't cheat, steal, or lie. You don't misuse animals or take advantage of those weaker than you. You don't spoil for a fight – which is a rule come to be in the last few years – but you don't walk away from one. You stand for your friends and for your round in the pub. You never touch a woman who belongs to another, and you don't give your word unless you intend to keep it.'

'I wasn't spoiling for a fight, and I don't belong

165

to anyone. I'm not weaker than he is. Physically, sure, but I have something more. I think I lifted his truck – lorry – just a little, like a good-sized bump in the road. On the way over here.'

More amused now, Branna enjoyed her breakfast. 'Temper can spark power. You'll want to learn how to control that. You said yourself, he's your boss. He'd think of that, Iona. It would count with him, and yes, even though you could say you made the first move. So if he kissed the brains out of your ears, you can be sure he wanted to enough. It – like the bump of the lorry – wasn't controlled.'

Thoughtfully now, Iona cut into the open-faced sandwich. 'You don't think he did it to teach me a lesson?'

'Oh no, not Boyle. No, he'd not think of such a thing. I'm saying – and it's just my thought hearing only from you – he said what he did after only because he was mad at his own self. He gave you a look or two the other night at the pub.'

'He... Really?'

'Ah, what a position this is. My cousin and dark sister on one hand, and the man I've been friends with most of my life.'

'You're right. I shouldn't put you in the middle.'

'Don't be daft. Sisters weigh the scale. I'd say he's had a thought about it, decided it's against the rules. And now he's pissed and frustrated, as he's muddied the waters more than they were.'

'Good.' Iona cut another bite, decisively. 'Then we can both be pissed and frustrated. But I feel better, talking to you. I know I throw most everything out there, and you ... well, you don't. But I want to say if you ever need to talk to anyone, I know when to shut up and listen.'

'We'll have plenty to talk about. Now that you're living here, we'll need to put our time to good use. You've much yet to learn, and I don't know how long you have to learn it. I can't see it, and that worries me not a little.'

'I know it's a small thing, but I floated all the feathers at once. I could direct them, change the speed, turn them. And it was like I didn't have to think how once I understood. I just felt it.'

'It's not a small thing. You've done well so far. If it was only a matter of bringing out what's in you, we could take all the time, and there'd be more joy in it for both of us.' Branna looked out the windows toward the hills. 'But I don't know how or when he'll come. I don't know how it's possible he can, as he was burned to ash by powerful magicks. But he will, cousin, when he believes he's strong enough to defeat us all. We have to make certain he's wrong.'

'There are four of us, so–'

'Three,' Branna said sharply. 'We're three. Fin isn't part of the circle.'

'All right.' Dark territory, Iona thought. She'd try to steer clear of that until she had more light. 'We're three, he's one. That's a big advantage.'

'He can and will bring harm to all and any to win. We're bound by our blood, by our art, by everything we are to harm none. He may not understand it, but he knows it.'

She rose, went to the back door. When she opened it, the dog padded in. Iona hadn't heard a thing. 'Kathel will walk with you to the stables when you're ready.'

'My guard dog?'

'He enjoys the ramble. Cabhan will pay more mind to you as your power lights, so be aware of it.'

'I will. When will you take me to the place in the woods?'

'Soon enough. I need to get ready. I've work. Go on and get unpacked before you head out.'

'I'll clear up here. You don't have to make me breakfast.'

'Be sure I won't unless I'm in the mood to,' Branna said in such an easy way it made Iona feel only more welcome. 'And you'll not clear today, but you and Connor will work that out between you from tonight. If I do the cooking, one or both of you does the clearing.'

'More than fair.'

'There's a little washer and dryer – though in good weather, we hang out the wash – right in there. And we'll be working out the marketing and the other chores. Come the spring, there'll be gardening, and you won't touch a blade of grass until I'm sure you know what you're about.'

'Nan taught me. I'm pretty good.'

'We'll see. You'll want to go hawking with Connor.'

'I'd love to.'

'You'll enjoy it, but it's for more than that. We each of us have our guide, but we're stronger when we connect with each, and they with all of us.'

'All right. Will you come see Alastar?'

'I will, soon enough. This is your home now,

and ever will be.'

'You've always known where you belong. I don't know if you can understand what it means to me to finally feel that.'

'Then go, put your things away. And when you come home, we'll work. And for you.' Branna lifted a hand, closed it into a fist, then opened it again. A silver key lay in her palm. 'We don't always lock the doors, but in case, this will open them for you.'

'You have to show me how to do that,' Iona murmured, and took the key, still warm from Branna's magick. 'Thank you.'

'Sure, you're welcome. I'll be in my workshop when you're done at the stables for the day. Come there, and come ready to learn.'

'I will.' Thrilled at the prospect, Iona all but danced out and up the stairs.

Her home now, Branna thought again. She'd tend to it, work for it, and one day, she'd have no choice but to fight for it.

9

Iona led her first group solo, mounted on Alastar. She couldn't be sure if she'd earned the responsibility, or if Boyle had tossed it at her to get her out of the way.

It didn't matter.

She enjoyed the hour with the horse, and though she knew he'd have preferred a good gallop, sensed his pleasure in her companionship. Just as she gained pleasure from the easy conversation with the couple from Maine, and the pride of being confident on the paths, the directions, and most of the answers.

We're earning our keep, she thought, giving Alastar a pat on the neck.

When she returned, Meara came out to greet her and her group. 'I'll take it from here, if you don't mind. Iona's needed at the big stables.'

'I am?'

'And Alastar. Can you find your way?'

'Sure. You showed me, and I marked it on the map. But–'

'Fin's orders, so you'd best go on. And how was your ride?' she asked the couple.

At a loss, Iona turned her mount, headed back the way she'd come.

Had Boyle complained about her? Was she about to be fired?

Her unsettled thoughts had Alastar turning his head to stare at her.

'I'm being stupid. Just overreacting, that's all. Boyle's pissy, but not petty.' Plus, she thought Fin liked her, at least a little.

She'd know when she got there. And thinking that, gave herself the pleasure of letting Alastar have his head.

'Let's go,' she decided, and even before she could give him a light kick with heels, he flew. 'Oh God, yes!' On a laugh, she lifted her face to the sky as Alastar thundered down the path.

Her thrill, his thrill – the same. Glorious and entwined. Power, she realized, his and hers, spurred them both so that for an instant, just an instant more, she felt them both lift above the ground. Flying truly now, the wind whipping her hair, his mane.

As she laughed, Alastar bugled in triumph.

He'd been born for this, she realized. So had she.

'Easy,' she murmured. 'We should stick to the ground. For now.'

The moment of flight, and now the joy of the gallop with a gorgeous horse under her blew away any worries. She let him set the speed – the stallion could move – turned with the river, then away, down a narrow path through the thick trees, and into the clearing where the stables spread behind a big jumping paddock.

Slowed him now – easy, easy – so she could catch her breath and look.

The house rose, gray stone with two fanciful turrets and many glinting windows. A pretty stone courtyard backed by a garden wall separated it from the garage and the rooms – Boyle's – over it.

A second paddock cocked to the right. A trio of horses stood at the fence, gazing toward the trees as if in deep contemplation.

She saw men, trailers, trucks – lorries, damn it – a husky black four-wheeler.

It all looked, she thought, prosperous, practical, and fanciful at the same time. Slowing Alastar to a dignified trot, she aimed for the stables, then him pulled up when she heard her name called.

She spotted Fin – jeans, boots, that enviable leather jacket – wave her over toward the jumping paddock as he walked to it himself.

He opened the gate, gestured her in.

'Meara said you wanted to see me.'

'That I do.' He cocked his head, studied her with those sharp green eyes. 'You've had some fun.'

'I... What?'

'You're glowing a bit, as is our boy here.'

'Oh. Well. We had a good gallop over.'

'I'll wager you did, and likely more, but in any case,' he continued before she could think how to respond, 'I want to see how you and Alastar handle the course here.'

Little could have surprised her more. 'You want me to take him over the course?'

'As I said.' He shut the gate, slid his hands into his pockets. 'Take it as you please.'

She sat for a moment, studying the course. She'd have called the current layout inter-mediate. A couple of doubles, nothing tricky, and plenty of room for the approach.

'You're the boss.' She nudged Alastar forward, circled him around, kicked him up to an easy lope.

She never doubted him – after all, they'd flown together. She felt him gather for the first jump. They sailed over it, approached the next, glided up and over.

'What are you about?' Boyle muttered to Fin as he came out. His hands were in his pockets as well, but his fingers curled.

Fin barely glanced over as Boyle stepped up behind him. 'I told you I wanted to see what she's about. I need to know. Reverse it, take him around again,' he called out.

He skimmed his gaze toward the woods. No

shadows now but trees, but that would change. So he needed to know.

'You don't need me here for this,' Boyle began.

'I've business over in Galway, as you know. One of us has to stay with her until we're sure she can handle the lesson.'

'No need to use her for it.'

'No need not to, is there? Jesus, they're silk, the pair of them. That horse is already hers. I find I'm jealous of that. He likes me well enough, but he'll never love me as he does her. Sure, another crack for my heart.'

He gave Boyle a slap on the shoulder. 'Meet me at the pub, I should be well done and back by eight. We'll have a pint and a meal, and you'll tell me how she fared. And we'll have a second pint where your tongue might loosen enough for you to tell me what happened between you and the blond witch to put that brood in your eyes.'

'Two pints doesn't loosen my tongue, mate.'

'We'll go for three then. Well done, Iona. You're a picture, the pair of you.'

'He was born for it.' She rubbed Alastar's neck as she walked him over. 'I'm just ballast.'

'You're a unit. We've a new student due in a few minutes. She's eleven, and she's a steady rider, but she's decided she wants to learn to jump. You'll take her.'

'Take her where?'

'On. As instructor. You'll earn part of the fee for the lesson. If it works well for both of you. Boyle will stay on to supervise this first lesson out, as I've business elsewhere.'

Fin watched her eyes track over to Boyle, then

173

flick away again. 'All right. What's her name, and what mount do you want for her?'

'She's Sarah Hannigan, and her mother will be along as well ... that's Molly. They'll be saddling up Winifred, Winnie we call her. She's a veteran. It's thirty minutes today, the lesson. We'll see how she likes it. If it's on, you'll work out times and days among you.'

'Sounds good. This is fine for now, but I'd prefer a jumping saddle next time I instruct.'

'Sure, we'll fix you up. I'm off then. At the pub, Boyle.'

As Fin strode off, Iona glanced down at Boyle, watched him shift his weight. 'So?'

'I'll see Winnie's saddled.'

When he turned toward the stables, Alastar butted Boyle hard with his head.

'Alastar! Sorry,' she said immediately, and bit down hard on the gurgle of laughter that wanted to escape. 'Don't be rude,' she told the horse, and leaning over to his ear added, 'even if it's funny.'

She dismounted, looped the reins around the fence. 'Wait here. Can I see your Darling?' she asked Boyle.

'My what?'

'The horse, Darling. The one you got from that asshole.'

'Ah.' He scowled a moment, then shrugged. 'She's inside.'

'You can just point the way. I should take a look at Winnie, to see what I'm working with.'

'All right then.'

He strode off, and after rolling her eyes at Alastar, she followed. With her mouth firmly shut.

He didn't introduce her to the stable hands, or the black-and-white mutt with the wagging tail, so she introduced herself. And, ignoring Boyle's obvious impatience, she shook hands with Kevin and Mooney, and scratched Bugs (because he ate them) between the ears.

She judged the operation to be at least half again the size of the other stable, but the smells, the sounds, the look felt the same.

He paused outside a stall and the good-looking bay mare. 'This is Winnie.'

'She's clever, isn't she? You're a smart girl, aren't you, Winnie?' Compact, Iona judged as she stroked Winnie's cheek. A good size for a young girl, and the steady look in her eyes boded well for a novice on the jump course.

'I can saddle her for the lesson if you show me the tack room.'

'Kevin will handle it. Kevin! We've young Sarah coming in for her first jumps. It's Winnie for her.'

'I'll get her ready then.'

Iona turned. And saw the white filly.

'Oh my God, look at you.'

Nearly pure white, sleek, regal – young, Iona thought as she approached – the filly watched her with eyes of gilded brown. 'That's–'

'Aine,' Iona finished. 'Fin's faerie queen. Still a princess yet, but one day.' When Iona lifted a hand, Aine bent her head as if granting a great favor.

'She's astonishingly beautiful, and knows it very well. She's proud, and only waiting for her time to come. And it will.'

'We'll wait, another year, I think, before breeding her.'

Not that time to come, Iona thought, but only nodded.

You'll fly, she thought. And you'll love.

'Fin knows his horses,' Iona commented as she stepped back.

'He does.'

She paused to greet other horses on the walk down the sloped concrete. Good, healthy animals, she judged, and some real beauties – though none reached the level of Alastar and Aine – housed in clean, roomy stalls. Then she came to the roan mare with the big, poignant eyes, the long white blaze down her nose, and knew without being told.

'You're Darling, and that's just what you are.'

Even before Boyle stepped up beside her, the mare turned her head, big eyes warming, body quivering. Not in fear, Iona thought, but simple delight.

She'd smelled him, sensed him, before he came into view. And it was love twined with utter devotion that had the mare stretching her neck so her head could bump his shoulder, light as a kiss.

'That's the girl.' He all but crooned it, and Darling whickered, turned her head for his hand.

He opened the stall door, eased in. 'I'll just check the foreleg while I'm here.'

'It's better,' Iona said. 'But she remembers how much it hurt. She remembers being hungry. Being afraid. Until you.'

Saying nothing, he crouched to run his hands up the foreleg, down again as Darling nibbled playfully at his hair.

'Do you have an apple in your coat pocket?

176

She's pretty sure you do.'

It was ... disconcerting, to have his horse's thoughts translated to him, but he rose again, slid his hands along Darling's flank.

Iona thought if a horse could purr, she would have.

While Aine had astonished her, so much beauty and grace, Darling tugged her heart with her simple, unabashed devotion.

They knew, she and Darling, what it was to yearn for love, or at least genuine understanding and acceptance. To wish so hard and deep for a place, for a purpose.

It seemed they'd both gotten that wish.

Then Boyle reached in his pocket for the apple, into another for his pocketknife. Iona felt Darling's pleasure in the treat, and more, that it would be offered.

'You're filling out well, my girl, but what's a bit of an apple, after all?' She took it neatly, eyed the second half as she ate.

'This one's for Winnie, if she behaves with her student.'

'You saved her.' Iona waited while he stepped out, closed the stall door. 'She'll never be anything but yours.'

Iona reached up to stroke; Darling stretched out her neck again.

'She's not skittish with you,' Boyle noted. 'That's progress. She's still a bit nervy with strangers.'

'We understand each other.'

When Darling angled her head so her cheek pressed to Boyle's, and when he took the half apple out of his pocket, and fed it to her, Iona knew she was done.

'I'll get another for Winnie. You haven't had enough of them in your life.'

'That's done it,' Iona muttered. 'I'm good at getting mad, mostly when it's justified. At least I think so. But I suck at staying mad. I just can't hold on to it, it's so heavy. Then add in me standing here watching this mutual love affair, and I can't do it. So I'm finished being mad at you, if that matters.'

Boyle eyed her with some cautious speculation. 'The day and the work go easier without having the mad weighing it down.'

'Agreed. So.' She held out a hand. 'Peace?'

He frowned at her hand a moment, but he took it. He meant to let it go, right away. But he didn't.

'You work for me.'

Iona nodded. 'That's true.'

'You're cousin to one of my closest mates.'

Her pulse skipped lightly, but she nodded again. 'I am.'

'And it's barely a week since I first set eyes on you.'

'I can't argue.'

'And what you are is ... a matter.'

Now she frowned. 'A matter of what?'

'A matter of, well, fact. And something you yourself are just getting acquainted with.'

'Okay. Is it the fact that's a problem for you?'

'I wasn't saying it was a problem.'

'Are you a witch bigot?'

Insult flew across his face so the green shimmered deeper over the tawny gold of his eyes. 'That's a softheaded thing to say, seeing as I'm friends with three of them, and one of those stands as my partner as well.'

'Then why did you bring it up as one of the reasons you're not or shouldn't be – I'm not sure which – interested in me?'

'Because it's there. It is. And I'd like to know one single bloody man,' he continued with some heat, 'who wouldn't give it some considerable thought.'

'Maybe I should get mad again.' She mulled it over. 'But it's hard to work that up when Darling's standing there watching you with adoring eyes. Plus, everything you said is true, can't be denied. And if all of that is an issue for you, it is. None of it's an issue for me.'

'But you're not standing where I'm standing.'

'No, I'm not. Peace holds.' And so, if you factored in her hand, did he. 'Are we good?'

'Some of it should be an issue for you.'

'Why? People get involved with bosses and employees all the time, and it's fine – from my point of view – as long as the power structure isn't used as a lever. People date friends' relatives all the time, too. And I can't, and wouldn't, change what I am.'

'Being logical doesn't change a thing.'

She had to laugh. 'Being illogical does?'

'It's not– Bloody hell.'

He gave her his second yank of the day, as frustrated as the first. And since she was still laughing, he put the stop to it by crushing his mouth to hers.

She tasted as he imagined light would, warm and bright with a snap of energy. It pulled at him, that taste, made him want more of it, and more still. She befuddled him, that's all it was, all that warm and bright there in the dim, closed in by the familiar scent of horses. His world, and now she was in it.

And she wrapped her arms around him as if she always would be.

If that didn't jolt a man, what would?

He jerked back. 'This isn't wise.'

'I wasn't thinking about wise or unwise. Kiss me again and I will.'

She had to boost up on her toes, pull his head down, but she met his mouth with hers. She thought it was like clinging to a volcano just before it erupted, or flying on a cloud about to swirl into a tornado.

What would it be like when the fire spewed and the storm broke?

She wanted, very much, to find out.

But again, he drew back. 'You're not thinking.'

'You're right, I forgot. Let's try it again.'

He laughed himself, and though there was a little pain in it, he might have taken her up on it. Except for the exaggerated throat-clearing behind him.

'Begging your pardon, but Sarah and her mother are here.' Kevin gave a wide smile. 'Winnie's saddled and ready – that is, whenever you are.'

'I'm on my way.' She looked at Boyle. 'Is there paperwork?'

'Just a form for her mother to sign. I'll take care of that.'

'All right. I'll go get her started.'

As Iona strode out, Darling gave another whicker that might have been an equine chuckle.

Kevin slid his hands in his pockets, whistled a tune.

'Not a bloody word,' Boyle muttered. 'From either of you.'

Pleased with her day on every level, Iona walked home through the green shadows. It felt good to step into her instructor's boots again, and with such a promising student. Maybe, with that door cracked, Fin or Boyle would trust her with another student or two.

And speaking of doors cracking, the unexpected and thoroughly satisfying interlude in the stables gave both her ego and her mood a big, lofty boost.

Plus, she could see some very interesting possibilities through that crack.

Boyle McGrath, she thought. Tough, taciturn, temperamental. And a marshmallow when it came to the pretty, traumatized mare who adored him. She really wanted to get to know him better, to find out if all this fluttering and stirring equaled basic physical attraction, or something more.

She'd hoped for something more most of her life.

Plus, it boosted everything higher because he was reluctant, conflicted, and a little pissed off. He just couldn't help himself, and that was so sexy.

Maybe she should ask him out, just something casual. A drink at the pub? A movie? First she'd have to find out where people went to movies around here.

If she could cook, she'd invite herself to his place to make him dinner. But there lay disaster waiting to happen. Maybe instead, she could...

She paused, baffled as she glanced around. She hadn't veered from the path, had she? Maybe she hadn't paid strict attention, but after taking this walk back and forth for days, it was instinct.

Yet, something was wrong, the direction seemed off.

She did a circle, rubbing arms that had gone suddenly cold.

And watched the fog crawl across the ground. 'Uh-oh.'

Iona took a step back, struggled to orient herself. On impulse she turned right, started down the narrow track at a jog. It took only seconds to realize she'd chosen wrong, and was moving deeper into the woods.

When she turned around to backtrack, trees wide as her arm span blocked the way. Fog oozed between their rugged trunks.

She ran. Better to run in any direction than become trapped. But to the right, trees pushed out of the ground, crackling, snapping as they broke through the turf. And forcing her to angle away.

The light changed, going gray like the fog. Wind, ice-edged, whistled through limbs as they knotted and tangled together to close out the sun.

Air, she thought frantically, trees through the earth, water in the form of fog.

He used the elements against her.

She forced herself to stop, pulled for power though fear rose with it. Throwing out her hands, she held twin balls of fire.

The chuckle sounded low, pricked over her skin like the legs of a spider. She shivered at the whisper of her name. Then every muscle quivered at the rustle, at the growl.

'Kathel.'

But what stepped out of the gray light was the wolf of her nightmare.

Not a dream this time. As real as her terror, as the wild beat of her heart.

As he padded closer, slinking toward her, she caught a glimpse of the jewel glowing red at his throat.

'Keep back,' she warned, and the wolf showed his fangs.

She'd never outrun it, she thought even as she took a step back. And the look in its glinting eyes told her it knew.

She hurled the fire, one ball, then the other, only to watch them burst into smoke inches from the wolf that stalked her. Desperate, she struggled to conjure another, but her hands shook, and her mind clogged with terror.

Quiet mind, she ordered, but it wanted to scream.

All real, she thought. It had all seemed so fanciful, so otherworldly – sorcerers, curses, fighting an evil that lived in shadows.

But it was all very, very real. And it meant to kill her.

She saw the wolf poised, ready to spring. Then on a feral scream, the hawk dived out of the sky. Its talons scored the wolf's flank, drawing blood as black as the hide before the hawk soared up again.

A moment's hot relief doused when a second growl sounded behind her. When she whirled, relief poured back. Kathel stood snarling. Iona sidestepped to him, laid a hand on his head, and felt a ribbon of calm wind through her fear even as Connor, then Branna, stepped through the fog.

Connor lifted one gloved arm so the hawk glided down to land, wings outstretched.

'Take my hand,' he told Iona, keeping his eyes calm and cold on the wolf.

'And mine.'

Connor and Branna flanked her, and when hands joined it wasn't calm she felt, but the hot rise of power filling her like life.

'Will you test us here?' Branna challenged. 'Will you try it here and now?' A bolt of light, jagged as lightning, flew from her outstretched hand, arrowed into the ground a bare whisper from the wolf's forelegs. It retreated. The red jewel glowed, fiercely red; its snarl sounded like thunder, but it retreated.

Fog gathered in on itself, boiled into a smaller and smaller mass. Connor lifted Iona's hand with his. Light glowed from it, spread and strengthened until the fog tore and vanished.

And with it, the wolf was gone.

'I... God, I was just–'

'Not here,' Branna snapped out at Iona. 'We'll not be talking here.'

'Take her back to the cottage. Roibeard and I will have a look around, then we'll be home.'

Branna nodded at Connor. 'Have a care.'

'I always do. Go on now with Branna.' He gave Iona's hand a steadying squeeze. 'You'll have a tot of whiskey, and you'll do fine enough.'

With Iona's hand clasped in hers, that power still humming at the edges, Branna strode briskly through the woods. Wanting nothing more than to get inside, Iona let herself be pulled along despite her shaking knees.

'I couldn't–'

'Not until we're inside. Not a bloody word about it.'

The dog led the way, always in sight. As she saw the cottage through the trees – at last – Iona watched the hawk circle through the heavy sky.

The minute they were inside, Iona's teeth began to chatter. As gray teased the edges of her vision, she pressed her hands to her knees, lowered her head between them.

'Sorry. Dizzy.'

'Hold your guts a moment.' Though her voice rang with impatience, the hand Branna laid on the back of Iona's head stayed gentle, and the dizziness passed as quickly as it had come.

'Sit,' she ordered, giving Iona a shove into the living room, flicking her fingers toward the smoldering fire to have the flames leap up and spread more heat. 'You're having a bit of shock, that's all. So sit, breathe.'

Briskly she walked to a decanter, poured two fingers of whiskey in a short glass. 'And drink.'

Iona drank, hissed a little, drank again. 'Just a little...' She sighed. 'Scared shitless.'

'Why were you off the path, and so deep?'

'I don't know. It just happened. I didn't turn off, or don't remember turning off. I was just walking home, and thinking about stuff. Boyle,' she admitted. 'We made up.'

'Oh well, that's fine then.' With two jerks, Branna pulled pins from her hair, tossed them on the table as it tumbled free. 'All's well.'

'I didn't go off the path, not knowingly. And when I realized I wasn't where I was supposed to be, should've been, I started back. But ... the fog came first.'

Iona looked down at the empty glass, set it down. 'I knew what it meant.'

'And didn't call us, or your guide? Called to none of us.'

'It all happened so fast. The trees – they moved, the fog closed in. Then the wolf was there. How did you come? How did you know?'

'Connor was out with Roibeard, and the hawk saw, from above. You can thank him for calling Connor, and me.'

'I will. I do. Branna–' She broke off as the door opened and Connor walked in.

'There's nothing now. He's gone to whatever hole he uses.' He walked to the whiskey, poured his own. 'And how are you doing now, cousin?'

'Okay. All right. Thank you. I'm sorry I–'

'I don't want apologies,' Branna snapped. 'I want sense. Where's your amulet?'

'I–' Iona reached for it, then remembered. 'I left it in my room this morning. I forgot–'

'Don't forget, and don't take it off.'

'Ease back a bit there.' Connor touched Branna's arm as he walked over to Iona. 'You gave us all a fright.' Now his hand stroked Iona's arm, and the calm seeped into her. 'It's not your fault. It's not her fault,' he said to Branna before she could snap back. 'She's barely a week under her feet. We've a lifetime.'

'She won't have time or opportunity for more if

186

she doesn't have the good sense to wear what protection she has, and to call out for her guide and for us when she needs more.'

'And who's been educating her if not you?' Connor tossed back.

'Oh, so it's my fault now she's no more sense than a babe in a pram.'

'Don't fight about me, and don't talk over me. It was my fault.' Steadier, Iona rose to go stand nearer the fire, and the warmth. 'I took off the amulet, and I wasn't paying attention. Neither will happen again. I'm sorry I–'

'By all that's holy, I swear I'll sew your lips shut a week on the next apology.'

Iona just threw up her hands at Branna's threat. 'I don't know what else to say.'

'Just tell us what happened, in detail, before we got to you,' Branna told her. 'No, back in the kitchen. I'll make the tea.'

Iona followed her back, then crouched to pet Kathel, to thank him. 'I was walking home, from the big stables.'

'Why were you there?'

'Oh, Fin sent for me. They gave me a student, for jumping instruction. I rode over on Alastar. We flew a little.'

'Sweet Brighid.'

'I didn't mean to, exactly, and I stopped. Then Fin had to leave, but Boyle stayed to supervise, to make sure I didn't screw it up, I'd say. I asked to meet Darling, but first I met Aine, and oh my God, she's miraculous.'

'I'm not interested in a report on the horses,' Branna reminded her.

'I know, but I'm trying to explain. Then I met Darling, and watched her and Boyle, and I couldn't stay mad at him. Then one thing led to another because I wasn't mad at him.'

'Why were you?' Connor wondered.

'Oh, we had kind of a thing this morning when he picked me up.'

'He kissed the brains out of her ears,' Branna supplied, and Connor's grin broke out.

'Boyle? Did he indeed?'

'Then he was rude and nasty, and that pissed me off. But then, watching him and Darling, I just couldn't stay mad, so I told him I wasn't mad anymore, and then it was the one thing leading to another and he just grabbed me and did it again. I've probably lost at least twenty percent of my brain cells now. And the lesson went really well, it felt so good to have a student again, so I was feeling good, and distracted,' she admitted, 'and thinking that maybe I should ask Boyle out – for a drink or the movies, or some-thing. It was such a good day, after a rocky start, and I was just full of all of it. Then I wasn't where I should've been.'

She told them the details she remembered.

'You didn't focus,' Branna said. 'If you're to use fire as defense or offense, you have to *mean* it.'

'She's never used it against anything or anyone,' Connor pointed out. 'But she had the wit and the power to bring the fire. Next time she'll burn his arse. Won't you, Iona darling?'

'Damn right.' Because she'd never feel that helpless and terrorized again. 'I was going to try again, and okay, I was terrified. Then Roibeard

188

dived out of the sky. He's the most beautiful thing I've ever seen.'

'He makes a picture,' Connor said with a smile.

'Then Kathel was there, then both of you. I did freeze,' she admitted. 'It was like being caught in a dream. The fog, the black wolf, the red gem glowing at its throat.'

'Feeding his power. The stone,' Branna explained, 'and your fear. We'll work harder. You'll wear the amulet. Connor will walk you to the stables in the mornings, and we'll see someone brings you home at the end of the day.'

'Oh, but—'

'Branna's right. A week and he's come at you in dreams, and in the here and now. We'll be more careful, is all. Until we decide what's to be done. Go get the amulet now, and we'll get to work.'

Iona rose. 'Thanks for being there.'

'You're ours,' Connor said simply. 'We're yours.'

The words, and the quiet loyalty in them, made Iona's eyes sting as she hurried through the back toward the kitchen and the cottage.

'She's taken on a great deal in no time at all,' Connor began.

'I know it. I know it perfectly well.'

'And you were sharp with her, as you were frightened for her.'

Branna said nothing a moment, just went about the soothing process of making the tea. 'I'm the one who's teaching her.'

'It's not your fault any more than it's hers. And this was, for all of us, a lesson learned. He's grown bold since she's come here.'

'With the three of us together, he knows, as we do, the time's coming. If he can harm her, or turn her–'

'She won't turn.'

'She won't, no, not willingly. She's got your loyalty, I think, and far too much gratitude for too little given.'

'When you've had less than little in some things, you're grateful for even a spoonful of more. We've always had each other. And we've always been loved. She wants love, the giving and the having of it. I didn't pry,' he added. 'It's so much a part of her, I can't not see it.'

'I see it myself. Well, she has us now, like it or not.'

Connor took the tea his sister gave him. 'So, it's Boyle, is it? Grabbing our cousin and kissing her stupid from the sounds of it. She's barely landed on our doorstep, and my mate's jumping her like a rabbit.'

'Oh, leave off being such a child.'

He laughed, drank tea. 'Why would I leave off, when it's such a grand time?'

10

Focus. Branna harped on it relentlessly. Iona struggled to find it, then hold it. She'd improved – Branna gave her frustratingly faint praise for that – but she'd yet to reach the skill her exacting mentor judged strong enough.

She wondered how the hell anyone could focus soaking wet and half frozen.

Rain poured out of thick gray skies as it had, without pause, for two solid days and nights. That equaled, for the most part, inside work for both her job and her craft. She didn't mind it, not really. She enjoyed reorganizing the tack room with Meara, and working with Mick on instructing one young rider, and one feisty octogenarian in the ring.

She loved having extra time to groom and bond with the horses. She'd braided the manes of all the mares, delighted by the way they preened at the added attention. And though she sensed the geldings would have liked that style and attention just as much, she knew Boyle would object. So she'd worked a small, single braid into each, to please the horse and satisfy the boss.

And she learned. Inside Branna's workshop with the fire simmering, the scents of herbs and candle wax sweetening the air, she'd learned to expand her own understanding, embrace her power, and begin to polish those raw edges. At night, she read, she studied while the wind blew that steady rain against the windowpanes.

But how the hell was she supposed to think, much less focus, with rain splatting on her head, and the raw chill of it shivering straight to her bones.

Worse, Branna stood there, absolutely dry, her hair a gorgeous black sweep, and her eyes merciless.

'It's water,' Branna reminded her. She stood in the quiet sunlight she'd created, smiling coolly through the curtain of rain that fell outside her boundary.

'I know it's water,' Iona muttered. 'It's running down the back of my neck, into my eyes.'

'Control it. Do you think you'll be warm and dry and happy every time you need what you are, what you have? Will Cabhan wait for fine, fair weather to come for you?'

'All right, all right, all right!' Flickers of fire sizzled from Iona's fingertips, and a stream of rain went to steam.

'Not that way. You're not after changing it, though well done enough there. Move it.' Smoothly, effortlessly, Branna widened her sunny spot a few inches.

'Show-off,' Iona muttered.

'It's in you as much as me. Slide the rain away from you.'

She liked the feel of the fire snapping through her, from her, but drew it back. And used the frustration and annoyance that helped her call it to nudge, to slide, to open.

An inch, then two – and she saw it, felt it. It *was* just water. Like the water in the bowl. Thrilled, she pushed, and pushed hard enough to have that streaming rain leap away, gather. And splat with some force against Branna's borders.

'I didn't mean to – I mean I wasn't trying to splash you. Exactly.'

'It wouldn't have hurt your feelings if you'd managed to,' Branna said easily. 'So well done as well there. You'll work on subtlety, and finesse – and absolute control – but you managed it, and that's a start.'

Iona blinked, swiped at her wet face, and saw she'd opened a narrow but effective swath of dry. No pretty pale gold sunlight in her little corner, but no rain either.

'Woo to the hoo!'

'Don't lose it. Don't spread it. It's only for you.'

'The rest of the county would probably appreciate some dry, but I get it. Stop rain here, maybe cause a flood there.'

'We can't know, so we don't risk it. Move with it,' Branna demonstrated, walking in a wide circle, always within the dry.

On her attempt, the edges of Iona's circle turned soggy, but she kept control.

'Well done. As it's Ireland, you'll have no lack of rain to practice on as we go, but well done for today. We'll go inside, have a go at a simple potion.'

As Branna headed back toward the workshop, Iona struggled to keep up – and maintain her dry area. 'I could help on the bottling and packaging of your stock, for your shop. I'd like to help somewhere,' she continued. 'You do almost all the cooking, and you're spending a lot of your time – Connor, too – teaching me. I'm pretty good at following directions.'

'You are.'

Branna had always preferred the solitude of her workshop. It was one matter to hire clerks and such for the shop in Cong, to have them deal with customers, shipping, and so on. But her workshop was her quiet place. Usually.

And still, she thought, the lessons, and the need for them, did cut into her time.

'It would be a help,' she decided. 'We'll see

about it.'

Branna stepped into the workshop, and Iona nipped in behind her dripping on the floor.

'I was about to leave you a note,' Meara said from behind the work counter. 'The both of you.'

'Now you'll have some tea, and a visit. I've missed seeing you. Iona, don't track up the floor.'

'Easy for you to say. You're dry, I'm soaked. I must look like a wet cat.'

'More a drowned one,' Meara commented.

Branna walked straight to the kettle. 'Do a glamour.'

Saying nothing, Iona glanced at Meara.

'Meara knows all there's to know, and likely more besides. Fix yourself up.'

'I'm no good at glamours. I told you I tried one once, and it was a disaster.'

'Sure it's why it's called practice. For usual, it's my thinking glamours or drying your clothes instead of changing them is lazy and vain, but for now, it's good practice. If you end up with warts or boils, I'll fix it for you.' With a wicked smile, Branna glanced back. 'Eventually.'

'You did one for me, do you remember, Branna, when we were fifteen, I think, and I desperately wanted to go blond, as Seamus Lattimer, my heart's desire at that time, preferred them.'

At home, Meara took off her jacket, hung it on a peg, unwrapped her scarf to do the same, then her cap. 'I was about to do the deed – had the hair product I'd saved two weeks to buy, and Branna came along, did the glamour, and changed it for me.'

Considering, Iona studied Meara. 'I can't picture you as a blond, not with your coloring.'

'It was a rare disaster. I looked as if I'd developed the jaundice.'

'And you were too stubborn to admit it,' Branna reminded her.

'Oh, I was, so I lived with it near to a week before I begged her to turn it back. Do you remember what you said to me?'

'Something about changing for yourself was one matter, changing for a man was weak and foolish.'

'Wise, even so young,' Meara said with her bawdy laugh. 'And Seamus spent his time snogging with Catherine Kelly, as blond as a daffodil. But I lived through the disappointment.'

'A lesson learned, of some sort,' Branna said. 'But in this case, we're considering it practice. Fix yourself up there, Iona, and we'll have some tea.'

'Okay. Here goes.' She released a breath, sincerely hoping she didn't set herself on fire as she concentrated on her jacket, sweater, and jeans first.

Steam puffed, but no flames snapped. She began to feel her toes thaw out, her skin warm, and, smiling, ran a hand over the dry sleeve of her jacket.

'It worked.'

'Think of the time I'd save on laundry if I had a trick like that,' Meara commented.

Grinning, Iona ran a hand over her wet, dripping hair, turned it to a sunny, dry cap. On a quick laugh, she covered her face with her hands, closed her eyes briefly. When she lowered them, her face glowed, the color of her lips deepened to a rosy pink, her eyelashes darkened, lengthened.

'How do I look?'

'Ready to head to the pub and flirt with all the handsome men,' Meara told her.

'Really?' Delighted, Iona rushed to the mirror. 'I look good! I really do.'

'Smoothly done, and with a bit of finesse as well. You've come along well.'

'Stick around,' Iona said to Meara. 'She never says things like that to me.'

'So when I do, you know I mean them. I've shortbread biscuits, Meara, and the jasmine tea you're fond of.'

'I won't say no to either.' She made herself at home at the table, taking a moment to rub Kathel when he laid his big head in her lap. 'The weather's dampening our business, and they're saying we're in for more of the same tomorrow. Boyle's arranged for classes from the school to come in, see the horses. We'll give the young ones rides on leads around the ring.'

'That's a good idea.'

'Oh, he has them, our Boyle does.' Meara smiled at Iona as she helped herself to a cookie. 'And as for you, I had a thought for my sister's birthday next month. Maureen. She lives down in Kerry, as she and her husband work there,' she added for Iona. 'You know the sets you do – the soap, the candle, the lotion, and such – the special ones you make with that particular person's traits and personality in mind.'

'I do. You'd like one done for Maureen?'

'I would, yes. She's the oldest of us, as you know, and about to turn thirty-five. For some reason, she's gone half mad over it, as if her youth is done and over, and she's nothing but the miseries of age left to her.'

'Bless her, Maureen was always one for drama.'

'Oh, that she is. She married her Sean when she was just nineteen, so she's had sixteen years of his plodding. He's a sweet man under it,' she continued, 'but a plodder for all that. She's two teenagers driving her to the edge of insanity, or beyond it, and another coming up behind them. She's taken to texting me, our other sister, or our ma all day and half the night to keep us abreast of her trials and tribulations. I'm thinking the gift, being it's created for her, and it speaks to pampering and female things, might perk her up enough to have her leave off hounding me until I want to thrash her.'

'So it's about you,' Branna said with a laugh.

'I'm saving her life, and that makes me a fine sister.'

'I'll have it for you next week.'

'I always wanted a sister,' Iona mused.

'Would you like one of mine? Either of them's up for the grabbing. I'll keep my brothers, as they're not gits most of the time.'

'Being an only child is lonely and you never get to bitch about your siblings.'

'I would miss the bitching,' Meara admitted. 'It makes me feel so superior and smart.'

'I had imaginary siblings.'

Amused, Meara sat back with her tea. 'Did you now? What did you call them?'

'Katie, Alice, and Brian. Katie was the oldest, and patient, smart, comforting. Alice was the baby, and always made us laugh. Brian and I were the closest in age. He was always getting into trouble, and I was always trying to get him out of it. Sometimes I could see them, as clear as I see you.'

'The power of your wishes,' Branna told her. Lonely child, she thought. So not tended, so not understood or cherished.

'I guess. I didn't understand that kind of thing, not really, but they were more real to me, a lot of the time, than anyone else. Between them and horses, I kept pretty busy.'

She stopped, laughed. 'Am I the only one who had imaginary people in her life?'

'Connor was more than enough for me.'

'He's more than enough, indeed,' Meara echoed.

'And we both knew, Connor and I, much younger than you, what we were about.'

'And even with that, you both forged other really strong things. Your work here, the shop, his falconry – and his handy hands. And you, Meara. You're not one of the owners, but you're an essential element in the business.'

'I like to think so.'

'It's clear you are. Both Boyle and Fin respect your skills and your opinion, and depend on both. I don't think either of them give that sort of thing lightly. It's what I want. To forge something, and to earn respect, to have people who matter know they can depend on me. Do either of you want more than that?'

'It's good to have what you say,' Meara considered. 'I wouldn't mind a pot of money to go with it.'

'What would you do with it?'

'Well now, that's a thought. I think first a fine house. Doesn't need the fancy, just a good house, with a bit of land and a little barn so I could have my own horse or two.'

'No man?'

'For what?' Meara laughed. 'For the keeping or for the fun?'

'Either or both.'

'I'd take the fun, there's been a lack of that sort of amusement in my life in recent months. Keeping though, that's not what I'm after. Men come and go,' she added as she settled back with her fragrant tea. 'Except for sweet and plodding Sean, as far as I've seen. Best not to expect or want them to stay, then it's less fraught.'

'But fraught means you're living,' Iona said. 'And I want one to keep, one who wants me just as much. I want wild, crazy love, the sort that never goes away. And kids – not just one – a dog, a horse, a house. A big, sloppy family. What about you?' she asked Branna.

'What do I want? To live my life. To end this curse that hangs over all of us, and crush what remains of Cabhan.'

'That's not just for you. Just you, Branna,' Iona insisted. 'Money, travel, sex? Home, family?'

'Enough money to travel to exotic places and have reckless sex with exotic men.' She smiled as she poured more tea. 'That should cover the lot.'

'I'll travel with you.' Meara laid a hand over Branna's. 'We'll break hearts the world over. You're welcome to join us,' she told Iona. 'We'll see all the wonders, and take our pleasures where we find them. Then you can come back, pick the one you'll keep, and make the babies. I'll build my house and barn, and Branna will live her life exactly as she pleases, curse-free.'

'Agreed.' Branna lifted her teacup to toast. 'We've only to vanquish ancient evil and earn great wealth, and the rest is but details.'

'Both of you could have all that exotic sex now,' Iona protested. 'It's not hard to have your pick of men when you look like Celtic goddesses.'

'We're keeping her,' Meara told Branna. 'She's a wonder for my ego.'

'It's true. Branna looks like something out of a fairy tale without even trying, and you're this image of a warrior princess. Men should be falling at your feet.'

The door opened, bringing in the rain, along with Connor, Boyle, and Fin.

'Not all of them,' Meara murmured.

'Look what I've dragged in.' Connor shook rain from his hair like a dog as Kathel bounded over to greet the newcomers. 'It was haul them in or build a bleeding ark. Have you tea and biscuits to spare?'

'Of course. Don't track up my floor. Has the business world shut its doors then?'

'For the day,' Boyle told Branna. 'We were nudging Fin along to buy us dinner, but damn near drowned considering the where.'

'And here's better.' Connor walked over to hold his hands out to the fire. 'Especially if someone could be cajoled into making a vat of soup.'

'Someone?'

Connor merely smiled at Branna. 'And I

thought of my own darling sister.'

'You think of me in the kitchen entirely too often.'

'But you're brilliant in it.' He leaned down to kiss her.

'I'll peel and chop whatever you need.' It was, Iona calculated, sort of like asking Boyle to dinner. 'You can peel and chop, can't you, Boyle?'

'I can, especially if it gets me dinner.'

'I'm willing to be a kitchen slave for a hot meal on a night like this,' Meara added. 'What of you, Fin?'

He continued to unwind the scarf from around his neck. 'Whatever Branna needs or wants tonight.'

'Then I'd best go see what there is to put together for this famous vat of soup.' She rose, and moved through the rear doorway. The dog left Fin's side to follow her.

'She'd be easier if I went on,' Fin said.

'You'll not.' A rare edge of anger laced Connor's voice. 'It can't be that way, and she knows it as well as you do. We need you. I've told Fin and Boyle what happened a few days ago,' he told Iona.

'What happened?' Meara demanded.

'I'll tell you as well, in a moment. But it stands, Fin. We need you, and she understands that. In the end she won't let what's tangled between you get in the way of it.'

'Maybe someone should tell me about the tangle.' Iona shoved her tea away. 'It might help to know all the details instead of trying to figure everything out with pieces of them.'

Fin walked over to the table, then tugged down

the neck of his sweater. 'This is his mark, the mark your blood put on mine. I bear it, and Branna won't see past it to what she is to me or what I am to her.'

Iona rose to study it closely. A pentagram, as the legend claimed, and as clear and defined as a tattoo. 'It doesn't look like a birthmark, but more like a scar or a tattoo. Were you born with it?'

'No. It ... manifested much later than that. I was more than eighteen.'

'Did you always know?'

'Not where the power had come from, no, but only that I had it.' He adjusted his sweater. 'You're a steady one, Iona.'

'Not really, or not enough. Yet.'

'I think you're wrong there.' He tipped her head up with a hand on her chin. 'You'll hold when it counts most, I think. She'll need that steadiness from you, and that open mind.'

'Connor says we need you, and I trust him. I'm going to go help Branna get started.'

'I'm with you.' Meara rose. 'Give her a few minutes to settle into it, but don't gorge on the biscuits. She'll do whatever needs be, Fin, whatever the cost.'

'As will I.'

Iona went with Meara through the back, in and out of the storeroom, and into the house.

'Wait, before we go into Branna.' Iona stopped. 'What happened between Fin and Branna? I'm not asking you to gossip, or betray the sisterhood, and one that's so obviously close and intimate between you and Branna. I think you know that. I hope you know that.'

'I do, and still it's not easy to say to you what she hasn't. I'll tell you they were in love. Young and wild for each other. Happy in it, though they scraped and squabbled. She was going onto seventeen when they came together the first time. It was after they'd been together the mark came on him. He didn't tell her. I don't know whether to blame him for that, but he didn't tell her. And when she found out, she was angry, but more, she was devastated. He was defensive and the same. So it's been an open wound between them ever since. A dozen years of wanting and turmoil and too much distrust.'

'They still love each other.'

'Love hasn't been enough, for either of them.'

It should be, Iona thought. She'd always believed it would be. But she went with Meara toward the kitchen to do what she could to help.

It might have been an ordinary gathering of friends and family on a rainy night. The little fire simmering in the kitchen hearth, with the big dog snoring in front of it. The wine Connor pulled out, uncorked, and poured generously into glasses. Volunteers dutifully peeling and chopping small mountains of potatoes and carrots, mincing garlic and onions while the hostess busied herself dredging chunks of beef in flour, browning it in a big, sturdy pot on the stove. The scents rising up, teasing of what was to come, and the mix of voices all talking to or over one another.

It might have been just a gathering, Iona thought while she chopped carrots, and the parts that were warmed her, gave her so much of what she'd come to understand she'd yearned for her whole life. But it wasn't just a friendly gathering, and the undercurrents tugging and pulling beneath the surface were deadly.

Still, she didn't want to spoil the moment, send ripples over that surface. After all, she stood hip to hip with Boyle – who unquestionably had a more competent hand than she with the kitchen knife – and he seemed more relaxed here than when they worked together at the stables.

And he smelled wonderful, of rain and horses.

Better to say nothing, she decided, than say the wrong thing. So she watched and listened instead. She watched Connor reach over to flick a tear from Meara's cheek as she minced onions, and caught the easy flirtation in the gesture in his eyes.

'If you were mine, Meara my love,' he said, 'I'd ban onions from the house so you'd never shed a tear.'

'If I were yours,' she shot back, 'I'd be shedding them over more than onions.'

He laughed, but Iona wondered. Just as she wondered when Fin topped off Branna's wineglass and, at her request, handed her oil for a skillet. Their polite tone remained as stiff as their body language, but under it – oh yeah, undercurrents everywhere – there boiled such passions, such wild emotion she'd have had to have been both blind and heartless not to feel it.

It was Connor, she thought, who kept it all going, tossing out comments, questions, knitting the group together with relentless cheer and encompassing affection.

The man struck her as next to irresistible. So

why did Meara–

'You study everything and everyone,' Boyle put in, 'as if there's to be an exam within the hour. And your brain's full of questions and conclusions.'

'It feels like family.' She spoke the first thought that popped from the tangle of them in her mind. 'It's something I always wanted to feel, be part of.'

'Sure it is family,' Connor told her. 'And yours.'

'You're generous with people. It's your nature. Not everyone is, or at least they're more cautious before opening the door. I'm the newest here, on a lot of levels. Observing gives me a better sense of that family. Even just observing Boyle peel and chop a lot faster and better than I do.'

'Well now, he's no Branna O'Dwyer,' Fin told her, 'but he's a passable cook. It's just one reason Connor and I tolerate him.'

'If a man can't toss a few things in a pan, he's too often hungry. Here, put the palm of your hand on the tip, fingers up, out of range.' Boyle took Iona's hand, to show her. 'And the other on the hilt so you can use that to steer the blade.'

She let him guide her hands to produce nice, neat rounds of carrot, and appreciated the light press of his body to hers.

'I'll have to practice,' she decided. 'And figure out what to do with them after I chop them. It's probably just as well I didn't get the chance to ask you to dinner.'

She glanced up and around at him, caught the surprise on his face, and the hint of embarrassment as the room went quiet.

'You're better off with Branna doing the cooking,' Iona continued. 'I'll have to figure out some other way to get you on a date.'

When Connor failed to disguise a chuckle with a cough, she shrugged.

'Family,' she said again. 'And more, family with the kind of problem and mutual goal that means we could all get our asses kicked, or worse, tomorrow or anytime after. So I figure there's not a bunch of time to waste or circle around what might make us happy. Speaking as someone who's lived her life with half the happy, I'd like to finish it out – especially considering potential ass kickings – with a great big armload of it.'

From where he stood, leaning against the counter, Fin smiled at her. 'I believe I'm already half in love with you myself.'

'You don't have half to spare.' Then she sighed. 'Now, let's see. Who else can I embarrass?'

'You haven't me,' Fin told her. 'And as for love, *deirfiúr bheag*, there are no limits to it.'

'I've always hoped that. What does that mean, what you called me?'

'Little sister.'

'I like it. I should learn Irish. Do all of you speak it?'

'Branna, Connor, and Fin.' Finished with her mincing, Meara walked over to rinse her hands. 'Boyle and I have enough to get by, wouldn't you say, Boyle?'

'Enough.'

'Is magick more powerful, do you think, with it? Sorry,' Iona said immediately. 'I shouldn't keep bringing that up and screwing with the mood. And I shouldn't have put you on the spot like that,' she said to Boyle.

'You just disconcerted him, as he wouldn't be accustomed to a woman who speaks her mind and feelings right out, without filtering. Connor,' Branna continued, 'I need a Guinness for the pot, and I'd say another bottle of wine for the rest of us. And you're right as well, Iona, to speak of the rest of it. We can't know if we've a day or a year before we'll face what's coming, but logic says a day's the closer to it. And all that said, I'm damned if any one of us will have our ass kicked. So we'll get this stew on the simmer, have more wine, and we'll talk of it.'

She turned, face flushed from the steam, eyes glittering with a determination so fierce Iona couldn't believe it could be defeated.

'Well then, let's have those vegetables. They won't cook themselves.'

11

It still might have been any gathering of friends and family – all crowded around the kitchen table with glasses of wine, and the dog still sprawled at the hearth.

But Iona recognized it for what it truly was.

A power summit.

'I'd like to say something first,' Branna began, 'to Meara and to Boyle. 'Tisn't your blood mixed into this, and you've neither power of your own as weapon or shield.'

'To begin with insulting us doesn't make a

strong first step,' Boyle told her.

'Sure it's not meant like that, but to acknowledge what it means to the rest of us to know you're with us. In truth, I don't know how Connor or myself would have fared without you. You're the truest friends I've ever had, or ever will. I don't know if, as Fin claims, love has no limits, but I know I've yet to reach the limit of mine for either of you. And there, that's said.'

'We don't have power, but we're not helpless. Far from it.' Meara looked to Boyle, got his nod.

'We have our brains, our fists. He's never shown interest in us, and that's his mistake.'

'That may be, and we should find a way to use it. But he's taken a strong interest in Iona.' Connor gestured toward her. 'Branna and I agree he's hoped to do her harm – and worse – and by doing that, take her power, increase his own. It cost him, we think, to set the trap for her a few days ago, then fail.'

'What trap?' Boyle demanded. 'Were you hurt?' he grabbed Iona's arm. 'Why didn't you tell me?'

'It isn't easy to talk about this kind of thing at the stables. And I wasn't hurt. Branna and Connor saw to that.'

Fin spoke quietly. 'What happened? Be specific. Iona, you tend to be just that. Tell the rest of us.'

'It was the day I gave Sarah her first lesson. When I was walking home.'

She told them, specifically, and didn't gloss over her fear.

As she spoke, Fin rose, strode to the window looking out over the back gardens. On the table, Boyle's hands balled into fists.

'You'll not walk to work or home alone from now on.'

Iona gaped at Boyle. 'That's ridiculous. I have to–'

'You'll not. And that's the end of it.'

Before Iona could speak again, she caught Meara's eye, and her friend's subtle shake of the head.

'Connor can walk with her to the stables.' Branna spoke smoothly. 'They go the same way, and you and Fin have only to see their schedules mesh close enough.'

'It's done,' Boyle said definitely. 'And I'll see her home. It's done,' he repeated.

'I appreciate the concern. Is someone going to be with me every time I take a step out of the house, or want to go into the village? And you'd better start sleeping with me, too,' she told Boyle. 'Because he's poking around in my dreams. I'm allowed to be afraid, but I'm not allowed to be helpless. And no one else is allowed to think I am.'

'Far from helpless,' Connor soothed. 'But precious. And necessary. We need you, so a few precautions, at least for now, will ease our minds.'

'Precious. Necessary.' Fin turned, his face cool. 'I agree with that. And yet you didn't call me when the precious and necessary was threatened.'

'It was quick,' Connor told him. 'And in truth I only thought to get to Iona, and to bring Branna as fast as we both could. So you're right, the fault's mine there.'

'Could you have done more?' Branna asked Fin.

'We can't know, can we? But you have to decide,

all of you, if I'm to be a part of this, or if you'll hold me outside.'

Rather than answer, Branna changed angles. 'Can you read him? Sense his thoughts?'

'I can't, no. He's blocked me out. He knows I've chosen my side. Sure he believes I can be turned still, and he'll pull at me. In dreams, and in waking ones.'

'You don't block him.'

Fin bit off a curse. 'I've a life to live, don't I? Other thoughts in my head. He's got only the one purpose for his whole existence, and I've more than that. And if I block him altogether, if I could, there's no chance then, is there, none at all that I might learn something that could help us end this. If you don't believe I want that, to end it, to see even the thought of him destroyed, I've nothing left to convince you.'

'I don't doubt that. I don't.' Branna rose to go over, stir the soup. 'She needs the horse. Iona needs her guide.'

Sheer frustration flicked over Fin's face. 'He's been hers since the first I saw him. You've no place to keep Alastar here, so he's with Boyle and me. If you don't trust that, I'll sign his papers over to her tomorrow.'

'No!' Appalled, Iona pushed to her feet. 'That's not right.'

'Nor is it what I was saying or meaning. It's you who have to tell her he's hers. You and Boyle, as you brought him here, and you're keeping him for her. I only meant that.'

'Even without any magick to it, the horse was hers the minute they set eyes on each other.'

Boyle lifted his hands, let them fall. 'And Fin's the right of it. You've no place here to keep him as he needs to be. We spoke of it the very night Fin came home again.'

'I'm grateful to you, both.' Branna's tone softened. 'And I'm sorry, truly, if it seemed I wasn't.'

'I've never wanted your gratitude or your apologies,' Fin told her.

'You have them, wanted or not, and can do what you please with them.' Setting the spoon aside, Branna came back to the table.

Iona, like Fin, remained standing.

'Thank you.'

'You're entirely welcome,' Fin told her.

'And thank you,' she said to Boyle. 'Since he's mine, I'll pay for his food and lodging. And that's the end of it,' she said as Boyle opened his mouth in obvious protest. 'I haven't had much that was mine that mattered, but I take care of what belongs to me.'

'Fine then. We'll work it out.'

'Good. I also know what it's like to be held outside. There's no colder place than right outside the warmth. None of you know what that's like but me, and Fin. All of you have always been a part of something, even the center of it,' she added, looking at Branna. 'So you don't know what it is to feel you're not wanted or accepted or understood. I think what's between you and Fin, and what stands between you is personal. But there's a lot more here to consider. You said I'm part of this, that this is family and it's mine. So I want to say that Fin's my family, too.'

On impulse she picked up the wine, and though

211

he'd barely touched his, added a few drops to his glass. 'You should come sit down,' she told him.

He murmured something in Irish before he came back, took his seat. And lifted his wine to drink.

'He said his heart and hand are yours,' Branna told her.

'Oh. Back at you, and that's why we'll win.'

'You've shamed me in my own house.'

'Oh, oh, Branna, I didn't mean to—'

'And it's good you did. I earned it, and it seems needed, the same sort of unfiltered thoughts and feelings you gave Boyle. We're a circle or we're not, and a circle with chinks in it is easily breached. So a circle we are, from here till it's done.' She lifted her glass, held it toward Fin. After a moment, he tapped his to it.

'*Sláinte.*' Connor tapped his own to Fin's, then his sister's, then around the table. 'Or better yet, may all the gods who ever were bless us, and help us send the bloody bastard to hell.'

'I'm good with that.' A little exhausted from the emotion, Iona sat again. Under the table Boyle took her hand in his. Surprised, she looked at him, met his quiet, steady gaze.

She all but felt something spill into her heart, something full of warmth and light, and hope.

'Well,' Meara said from across the table, 'now that we've settled all that, what the hell do we do next?'

Plenty of ideas shot around the table with arguments for and against. At some point Meara got up and, obviously at home, put together a plate of crackers and cheese and olives to keep hunger

212

at bay as the stew simmered.

'We're not ready to confront.' Connor popped an olive as he ticked off reasons against Boyle's push for a frontal attack. 'We don't have a solid plan, with the contingencies we'd surely need as yet, and more, Iona isn't as well armed as she needs to be.'

'I'm not going to be responsible for holding anyone back.'

'Then study and practice more,' Branna ordered.

'Nag, nag. Didn't I stop the rain?'

Brows lifted, Boyle pointed to the window where it lashed in wet whips.

'Temporarily and in a limited location. I'm better with fire.'

'It controls you more than you controlling it,' Branna corrected.

'Harsh, but true. Still, I'm better. And...' She focused, managed to levitate the table a few inches, then cautiously set it down again. 'Getting air pretty well, and I've done the flowers in the workshop, so earth's coming along. If I could try a couple spells...'

'You've not worked with her on spells?' Fin asked.

'She's barely getting her grip on the elements.'

'Caution has its place, Branna, but as you've said yourself, we don't know how much time we have.'

'Push me,' Iona begged. 'At least a little.'

'You might regret the asking of it, but that's what I'll do.'

'I think if there's any of this prodding into

dreams, you should all write them down.' Meara spread a cracker with cheese, handed it to Branna. 'They stay clearer that way, and you could compare them. There might be something there.'

'That's a sensible thing,' Connor agreed.

'What about the place in the woods?' Iona asked. 'Where the first dark witch lived. When can I see it?'

In the beat of silence that followed, Iona felt tension, fury, grief. Once again, Boyle took her hand under the table.

'You're not ready,' Branna said simply. 'You need to trust me there.'

'If I'm not ready to go there, why can't you tell me why?'

'It's a place between.' Fin spoke slowly, frowning at his wine. 'Sometimes it's simply a place with the ruins of an old cabin, and the echoes of the life lived there, the power wielded there. A gravestone where that power lies under the earth. It's the trees and the quiet.'

'And other times,' Connor said, 'it slips away, and it's alone. It's not tightly bound to the world, to the here. Without the knowing, a person might be caught there, in that other, that alone. And it's there he might come, stronger for it, and take what you are.'

'But you go there, have gone there. I have to know how to go, and how to stay.'

'It'll come,' Branna promised.

'He took me there in a dream.'

'Not him, I think, but her. Teagan. To show you, and still keep you safe. Be patient here, Iona.'

'He marked me there.'

Silence fell again after Fin's words. 'I knew of him, but not that I'd come from him. And there, in a place that had been a kind of sanctuary, at a time when there was joy and promise, he laid his mark on me, and the burn of it seemed to sear down to my bones. He slipped the bounds, took it all adrift, and marked me. And he came in the form of a man, and I could see myself in this man. He told me he would give me more power than I could imagine, that I would have all and more anyone could dream of. I was his blood, and all this I would have. I had only to do one thing for it.'

'What?'

'Only to kill Branna as she slept beside me. Just that.'

A shudder wanted to rise out of her, but Iona fought it back, kept her gaze on Fin's, quiet and steady. 'But you didn't.'

'It's him I'd've killed had I known how. One day I will, know how and get it done and finished. Or die trying. So it's best you wait a bit longer before we take you there. And all of us will take her when that time comes. That's a firm line, Branna. I'll not be shut out of it.'

'When the time comes,' she agreed. 'For now, we wait and watch. We learn, and we plan.'

'And talk more than we have,' Connor added. 'We'll be stronger for that.'

'You're right. We close no one out.' Branna touched a hand, briefly, to Fin's arm. 'I was wrong. Will we say Fin and Connor will use their hawks to patrol – if that's the word – the woods? We've Meara and Iona leading the guided rides most days, and keeping their eyes and ears open there. Boyle's seeing Iona home, so I'll make a charm for you, Boyle, for protection.'

'I'll see to it,' Fin told her.

'Fair enough. I'll work with Iona, and there I may call on all of you from time to time for help. If we dream, we write it down, all the details of it.'

'There'll come a time it'll take more than protecting ourselves,' Boyle said.

'I know it. What I don't know is what it will take, and how to get it.'

'It's time to find it.'

Branna nodded. 'We can hope with six of us looking, we will. Now, as has been said, we've lives to live. We can start that by setting the table while I see to the stew.'

'And I say we live it well.' Connor pulled his sister up, kissed her. 'For that's surely a boot up his fucking arse.'

'All right then, well it is. Put on some music, Connor, and we'll start living well right now.'

They set the dark aside, for the moment, with Connor and Meara arguing over the music until Connor tapped in some sort of fast jig with lots of fiddles and drums, and pulled her into a dance.

'Wow,' was Iona's reaction. 'They're really good.'

'They've both of them wings on their feet.' Boyle took the bowls Iona held, set them around the table. 'Always have.'

'Can you do that?'

'I haven't got the wings, but I don't have lead either.'

'Ask the lady to dance then, you git.' Fin dropped napkins on the table.

Iona only shook her head. 'I don't know how to do that.'

'Then it's past time you learned,' Connor proclaimed and, snatching her hand, pulled her in.

'You're slow, brother,' Fin murmured to Boyle.

'I move at the pace that suits me.'

'Slow,' Fin repeated. 'As a snail on a turtle's back.'

But Boyle shrugged it off. He liked watching Iona try to keep up with Connor's fast and clever feet. More, he liked the way she laughed as she spun around.

And who could argue with the laughter, he thought when Fin twirled Meara in three fast circles, and at the stove Branna clapped her hands in time.

The light and the laughter felt good, felt needed. So he'd take it.

Neither he nor any of the others in the bright kitchen with the warm smells, the quick music, the rolling laughter saw the shadow outside the rain-splashed window that watched. That hated.

With the meal behind them, the kitchen put to rights, and the hour growing late, Boyle readied to go.

'We'll see you home, Meara. I've my lorry. Branna, I meant to ask if you've any of the tonic you make for head colds. Mick's been blowing and sneezing for the last two days, and I've a mind to pour some of it down his throat.'

'I do, of course.' She started to rise.

'I'll get it for him,' Iona said. 'In the blue bottle, right, on the shelves nearest the front window.'

'That's the one. You can settle up with me here or at the shop, Boyle, at the end of the month.'

'I'll do that, and thanks for dinner. I'll meet you and Meara out front,' he told Fin.

He walked back with Iona, made the turn into the workshop. She hit the lights.

'I've been trying to get a good sense of her stock and what she keeps here, what she sells in the village. She won't let me make anything yet – not unsupervised – but at least I'm learning some of what goes into what.'

She reached for the bottle, clearly marked with Branna's Dark Witch label. 'I hope this helps Mick. He's been miserable the last couple days.'

'Less if he'd taken his medicine sooner.'

'I guess swallowing witch potions makes some people nervous.'

'He'll swallow this, if I have to personally hold his nose.' Boyle slipped the bottle in his pocket. 'I wanted to say, while there's a moment, it meant something before, the way you stood up for Fin.'

'Being excluded hurts, just like being blamed for what you are hurts. I can understand Branna's feelings, but my instincts are to trust him, and I get tripped up when I go against my instincts. Sometimes when I go with them, too.'

'Speaking out as you did, it mattered. So...' He shifted his feet. 'We'll go have dinner sometime.'

'Oh?' Her heart grinned like an idiot, but she did her best to keep her smile polite. 'All right.'

'I prefer doing the asking. Whether or not that's old-fashioned, it's how it is.'

'Good to know. My social calendar's pretty clear.'

'Then we'll book something. I'll see you in the morning.'

He started out, got halfway to the door, turned back.

This time Iona was ready for the grab, and grabbed him back.

She loved the way he hauled her to her toes. It didn't make her feel small. It made her feel wanted. The reluctance in it only added a sexy edge. Everything about the kiss, the heat of his lips, the strong grip of his hands made her feel irresistible.

And that was a heady sensation, a powerful thrill.

He kept meaning to take it slow with her, if at all. He'd taught himself control, learned – for the most part – to balance heat and temper with cool-headed thinking and logical steps.

Yet here he was again, wrapped around her, wrapped up in her. And it was God's own truth, he just wanted to sink there, be there, and draw all that natural sweetness, that cheerful energy in.

And with it, he wanted his hands on all those pretty curves and dips, his mouth on that smooth skin. That surprisingly tough little body moving, moving, moving under his.

She clung another moment when he would've pulled back, and nearly undid him.

'Well then,' he managed, and ordered his hands back down by his sides. Then, safer yet, into his pockets.

She just stood there, her pretty eyes heavy, her lips curved and so soft. So soft he wanted to–

'You could come back, after you take Meara

219

home. You could drop Fin off and come back. Then you could take me to work in the morning.'

'I...' The idea of it, a night with her, had every need inside him threatening to boil over. 'I'm thinking with Branna and Connor in the house that would be awkward at best. And there's the matter of rushing the fences.'

'You want dinner first.' Her smile perked up when she clearly saw he didn't get the joke. 'That's fine. I think it's simpler to be clear, from my side, that when it's not awkward or rushed, I want to be with you. It's not that I take sex lightly, it's that I don't.'

'You're a puzzle, Iona. I'd like to figure more of you out.'

'That's nice. I don't think I've ever been a puzzle to anyone before. I think I like it.' She rose on her toes again, brushed his lips lightly with hers. 'I'll help you fit some of those pieces together if I can.'

'I'll work on it in my own time. In the morning then.'

'Okay. Good night.'

She locked up behind him, watched through the rain as he strode to his truck. And did a little dance in place as she watched the lights sweep, then move away through the dark.

She puzzled him, and wasn't that wonderful? Iona heart-on-her-sleeve Sheehan, the girl who too often blurted out her thoughts before they'd fully formed, puzzled Boyle McGrath.

Talk about power. Talk about wonder.

The delight of it carried her out of the workshop and into the kitchen, where she threw her arms around Branna for a spin.

'Well then, I see groping with Boyle's given you a fine burst of energy.'

'It was really good groping. He asked me out, in his Boyle way. 'We'll go have dinner sometime.'

'Christ Jesus!' Eyes wide, hand flying to her heart, Branna goggled. 'It's all but a proposal of marriage.'

Too happy to be dampened, Iona laughed. 'It's a big step up from grunting at me. He thinks I'm a puzzle, can you imagine? I mean, seriously, who couldn't figure me out? I'm as simple as they come.'

'Do you think so?'

'I sure don't run deep. I'm going to have some tea. Do you want tea? God, I'm crazy about him.'

'It's early days for crazy, isn't it?'

'I don't get that, never have.' Iona put the kettle on, contemplated Branna's collection of home-made teas. 'Don't you know when you know? Five minutes, five years – how does that change what you know? I wanted to know with the man I was with before. I tried to know. I liked him, and I was comfortable with him. I told myself, give it more time. But time didn't change anything. Not for either of us as it turned out.'

Branna thought of what Connor had said. 'You want to give love, and to be given it.'

'It's what I've always wanted most. I'm going for your lavender blend, not only because it smells wonderful, but it's for relaxation.' She glanced back. 'For a restful night's sleep. I'm so up I need to come down some to get one. Right?'

'It's a good choice, and yes, you're learning.

Which brings me to this. It's a bit late, but I think we've both got another hour in us. We'll work a spell. Something very, very simple,' she said as Iona's face burst with joy. 'A toe in the water.'

'I'm a jump-in-feet-first fan, but I'll take the toe. Thanks, Branna.'

'Thank me in an hour, and if you've managed to master the spell. Here.'

'A broom. Am I going to fly on it?'

'You are not. You'll learn a protection spell, and with this, you'll learn to sweep away the negative energies, the films and dusts of dark forces and lay in the strong, the positive. Our home is always to be protected. It's the first you should learn, and I should've taught you before this.'

Iona took the broom. 'Teach me now.'

She slept deep and dreamless, and faced the day – rain, but slower and thinner – with enthusiasm. As she beat both her cousins to the kitchen, she put on the coffee and considered trying her hand at breakfast for three. Her talents there might be limited, but she thought she could handle scrambled eggs. And if she cooked ham and cheese in them, they'd be a sort of lazy-woman's omelet.

Organization, she told herself. Line up ingredients and tools first. She got down a skillet, a mixing bowl and whisk, a grater for the cheese, a knife and board for the ham.

So far so good.

Eggs, ham, cheese from the fridge – oh, and butter for the skillet.

Break eggs in bowl, she instructed herself, then

open the cupboard under the sink to toss the shells in the bin Branna used for compost waste. She noted then in the confusion of cleanup the night before they'd neglected to take out the trash.

Determined to be organized, she pulled out the filled liner, tied it, and hauled it to the door to take out to the big bin.

Inches beyond the little stoop lay a pile of dead rats. Black as midnight, coated with blood and gore, they lay in a circle of scorched earth.

The bag slipped out of her hand, hit the stoop with a hard splat. Revulsion urged her to step back in, close and bolt the door. Indeed her hand shook as she groped back for the knob to do just that.

Can't run, she reminded herself. Can't hide. There would be a shovel in the garden shed, she thought. She only had to get it, dig a hole, bury the ugliness. Sprinkle the ground with salt.

She started to step out, around the horrible circle.

'What's it then, in or out?'

Connor's sleepy voice behind her had Iona jumping back, barely muffling a scream.

'Didn't mean to give you a start. Is this breakfast to be? Here, I'll take that out when we leave for work, then–'

He stepped over, reached for the bag. Stopped when he saw the rats.

'So, he's sent us a gift.' The sleepy cheer in his voice turned to flint on the words. 'Here now.' And still his hand as he took Iona's arm to draw her back held warmth, comfort. 'I'll deal with it.'

'I was going to. Get a shovel from the shed.'

'That's what big, strong cousins are for.' He touched his lips to her forehead.

'And just what are they for other than waking a body up singing in the shower like he's on the bleeding *X Factor*?' The annoyance Branna led with faded as she got a clear look at Iona's face, then her brother's. 'What is it?'

'See for yourself.' He moved back to the door, opened it.

'He's bold,' she said coldly, as she looked out. 'Leaving such a thing on our doorstep.'

'I didn't do the spell right. Last night, the protection spell. I–'

'Is that ugly mess *in* the house?' Branna demanded. 'Are they living and scampering about in here?'

'No.'

'Then you did it fine and well. Do you think he wanted them dead, and outside if he could've had them in and swarming over us?'

The image had Iona shuddering. 'No. Good point.' She let out a long breath as at least the guilt she felt fell away. 'I was going to bury them.'

'No, it's not burying we do with them, not at first. We burn them.' Branna turned to Iona. 'All of us, but the first fire is yours. Strong, white, and hot.'

She took Iona's hand, stepped outside, with Connor behind them.

'Say the words I say, then send the fire.

'White to dark, power I call. On evil's stench my fire will fall. Destroy this threat to mine and me. As I will, so mote it be.

'Say it,' Branna demanded. 'Feel it. Do it.'

Iona repeated the words, her voice growing stronger, her rage keener. And her power at the end of them full and white.

Flames snapped, shot to the center of the circle, spread.

'Again,' Branna told her, as she and Connor joined her on the words.

Fire, white as lightning, burned. When it banked, only black ash remained.

'We bury the ash?' Iona's body tingled, as if from an electric shock. Even her blood felt hot.

'We do.'

'And salt the earth.'

'I've better than that, but that would do as well. Fetch the dustpan and broom,' she told Iona, 'and Connor the shovel. I've the spot for this.'

She waited a moment as they moved off to obey. 'Oh aye, just the spot for this.'

She led them around, to the far front corner of the workshop.

'Here?' Iona stared at her. 'So close to the house, to where you work. I don't–'

'She's a plan, make no mistake.' And trusting it, Connor shoved the blade of the shovel into the rain-softened ground. 'Just what I wanted to be about this morning. Digging a hole for rat ashes in the bleeding rain.'

'I can help with that.' Calling on her lesson from the day before, Iona slid the rain back so the three of them stood in the warm, the dry.

'Very well done.' Branna shook back her damp hair, laid her hands on her hips as Connor dug. 'That'll do well enough. Dump them in, Iona. We've all three taken part in this, and the work's stronger for it.'

'Then you can shovel the dirt back over them,' Connor suggested when Iona dumped the black ashes into the hole.

'You're doing such a fine job, and I've my own to do when you're done with it.'

'He's watching,' Connor said quietly as he tossed dirt back into the hole. 'I can just feel it.'

'I thought he might be. So much the better. Now this is mine.'

In her flannel pants, bare feet, her hair wet from the rain, Branna lifted her hands, palms up.

'Fire of white to purify, power of light to beautify. From Cabhan's dark grasp I set you free. As I will, so mote it be.'

From the freshly turned earth flowers burst, bloomed, spread. A deep rainbow of colors shimmered in the gloom of morning, pretty shapes dancing in the light wind.

'It's beautiful. It's brilliant.' Iona clasped her hands together as the defiant palette glowed. 'You're brilliant.'

With a satisfied nod, Branna tucked her hair back. 'I can't say I disagree.'

'And there's a fragrant stick up the arse for him.' Connor set the shovel on his shoulder. 'I'm hungry.'

Beaming happy, Iona hooked arms with her cousins. 'I'm cooking breakfast.'

'God help us, but I'm hungry enough myself I'll risk it.'

Branna walked back with them, glancing back once. Right up the arse, she thought.

12

She enjoyed the new routine, walking with Connor in the mornings, riding Alastar on the guideds, juggling in a few students, then having Boyle walk or drive her home again.

Late afternoons meant work and practice, and an additional hour at night for refining her skills.

The sun came out again, so the river sparkled with it. The loughs went to gleaming mirrors, and the green of the fields and hills only deepened under its shine through the puffs and layers of clouds streaming across the sky.

She could forget – almost – all that lay on the line, all yet to be faced. After all, she was having a romance.

Not one that included poetry and flowers, and her romantic sensibilities would have relished just that. But when your heart aimed toward a man like Boyle, you had to learn to find poetry in brief words and long silences, and flowers in an unexpected mug of tea pushed into your hands or a quick nod of approval.

And who needed flowers when the man could kiss the breath out of her? Which he did in the green shadows of the woods, or in the disordered cab of his lorry.

Romance, a home, a steady paycheck, a magnificent horse she could call her own, and the new and brilliant understanding of her craft. If she just eliminated the threat of ancient evil, her life struck the top of the bell.

She finished her lesson with Sarah, both of them pleased with the progress.

'Your form's really improving. We're going to work more on changing leads, smoothing that out.'

'But when can we add another bar? I'm ready, Iona, I know it.'

'We'll see how it goes next lesson.' Looking up into Sarah's pleading eyes, Iona patted her mount's neck. And remembered herself at that age. 'I'll tell you what. One bar up, one jump before you take Winnie in and tend to her.'

'You mean it! Oh, thanks! Thanks! This is brilliant.'

'One bar, one jump,' Iona repeated, and glanced at Sarah's mother as she started to the bars. She hefted one, maneuvered it in place.

Just three feet, she thought, and believed her student could handle it. If not, the horse would know.

She looked back at the horse now.

She wants to fly, wants to feel you fly with her. Keep it steady.

Iona stepped back, noted Sarah's mother twisted the ends of the scarf she wore around her neck.

'All right, Sarah. It's only one bar, but you have to let Winnie know you're in it together. Trust her, and let her know she can trust you. Eyes open, let's have a good, steady pace, and remember your form.'

Her heart was pounding, Iona knew. With such excitement, and some nerves. Still a beginner's course, even with the single additional bar, but a new challenge, a new hope.

'Good, that's good,' she called out, circling as Sarah took Winnie around the course. 'Posture, Sarah, light hands. You both know what to do.'

Set, she thought, steady and smooth. Gather. And go.

She flew a little herself as she watched her student soar cleanly over the bar, land well, adjust. Then wave one hand over her head in triumph. 'Oh, it's like magick, it is! Can't I do it again, Iona? Just once more?'

'Once more around, then Winnie needs her rubdown.'

She watched now with a critical eye, noting little things they'd work on.

'I feel I could do it forever, and jump twice as high.'

'One bar at a time,' Iona told her.

'Did you see, Ma! Did you see me?'

'I did. You were beautiful. Go on now, see to your horse, and we'll go home and tell your da. Could I have a word?' she said to Iona.

'Sure. I'll be right in, Sarah. And tell Mooney Winnie earned an apple.'

'I nearly made you stop,' Mrs. Hannigan told her. 'I nearly called out to you, no, not yet. All I could see in my mind's eye was Sarah flying off, lying on the ground with something broken.'

'It's hard to let her push new boundaries.'

'Oh, it is indeed, and you'll know yourself one day when you've children. But I knew, under it, you wouldn't let her do something she wasn't ready for. She's doing so well with you, is so happy with you. I wanted you to know that.'

'She's a joy to teach.'

'I think it shows in both of you. I took a picture with my phone when she did the jump.' She pulled the phone out, turned the screen to Iona. 'My hand shook, I'm afraid, so it's a bit blurry, but I knew I'd want to have that moment.'

Iona studied the screen, the flight – the young girl on the back of the sturdy horse, and the bar and air under them. She gave the slightest push, then turned the screen back.

'It's a wonderful shot, and it's clear and sharp. You can see the joy and the concentration on her face.'

Lips pursed, Mrs. Hannigan studied the photo again, then those lips curved. 'Oh, it is good. It must've been my eyes blurry when I first looked at it.'

'You stay for every lesson.' Her mother hadn't, Iona remembered. 'I think it makes her strive to do better, knowing you're here for her, that you support her.'

'Well of course I do. I'm her ma. I'm going to call her father right now, and tell him to pick up some strawberry ice cream. It's her favorite. We'll have a little celebration after dinner. I won't keep you, but I wanted to thank you for building her confidence, and my own. They're lucky to have you here.'

Iona wasn't sure her boots touched the ground all the way into the stables. She stopped when her eyes adjusted to the change of light and she spotted Boyle.

'I didn't know you were here.'

'Only just, and I've gotten an earful from Sarah. She's floating three feet off the ground.'

'We both are. I wish you could've seen her. I should make sure she's tending Winnie.'

'She is, and well, as she's now fully in love. And Mooney's keeping an eye. I thought you might want to take Alastar out. I'm going to give Darling a try, just see how she goes. He'd be good company for her. And you for me,' he added after a moment.

'I'd love it, but I've still got about a half hour on the clock.'

'You'll be helping exercise the horses, so you can consider it a job if it eases your conscience.'

'Works for me.'

In fact she couldn't think of a better way to end her workday than with a ride with the man who made her heart flutter.

She watched Darling as Boyle mounted, caught the quiver along her flanks, the expression in her eyes.

'She's nervous.'

'I can feel that for myself.' To soothe, he bent over, murmuring and stroking.

'Do you know why?'

'She's more weight on her than she's used to, and hasn't had a rider on her back in weeks.'

'That's not it.' Iona turned Alastar so Boyle and Darling fell into step beside her. 'She trusts you, and loves you. She's nervous she won't do well, and you won't want to ride her again.'

'Then she's foolish. It's a fine day for a ride. We'll head to the lough, and around a bit if it's all right with you.'

'More than all right.'

'You'll tell me if she hurts, and I don't notice.'

'I will, but she's feeling very sound. She likes the look of Alastar,' she added, sotto voce. 'Thinks he's very handsome.'

'He is that.'

'He's pretending not to notice her, but he's peacocking a little.'

'Now you're hunting up a romance for the horses?'

'I know he's for Aine, but a stallion like Alastar's meant to sire foals, and she's made for breeding. Plus, I don't have to hunt up anything. I just have to pay attention to say they like the look of each other.'

'I hadn't thought of breeding her.'

'Aine will make the regal and the magnificent,' Iona said. 'Darling? She'll make the sweet and the dependable. In my opinion,' she added.

'Well, Alastar's yours, so you'll have a say in it.'

'I think he has the most to say, as do the ladies. It's almost spring.' She lifted her face, looked at the sky through the boughs. 'You can feel it coming.'

'Still cold as February.'

'That may be, but it's coming. The air's softer.'

'That would be the rain moving in tonight.'

She only laughed. 'And I saw a pair of magpies flirting out by Branna's feeder this morning.'

'Just how does a magpie flirt?'

'They fly to and away, to and away, then chatter at each other and do it again. I asked Connor why the hawks don't go after them, and he said they have an arrangement. I like that.'

They moved into single file when the path narrowed, and wound by the river where the water thrashed under a broken rope bridge.

'Will they ever fix that?' she wondered.

'I'm doubting it, as people would be foolish enough to walk on it, and end up falling in. You'd be one of them.'

'Who says I'd fall in? And if I did, I'm a strong swimmer.' Because she enjoyed flirting, she sent him a long, under-the-lashes look. 'Are you?'

'I live on an isthmus on an island. I'd be a bleeding git not to swim and well.'

'We'll have to take a dip sometime.' She glanced back again, and remembered her first sight of him, and how striking, how compelling he'd looked – the big, tough man on the big, tough horse.

But she realized he only looked more striking now, seated on the mare he'd brought back to health, his hands light on the reins, her eyes glowing with pride.

'She's not nervous anymore.'

'I know it. She's doing fine and well.' He moved up beside Iona as the path allowed.

'I talked to my grandmother last night,' she began. 'I couldn't settle for email anymore, just wanted to hear her voice. She sends you her best.'

'And mine goes back to her.'

'She's planning to come for a few weeks either this summer or fall. I want her to, but at the same time...'

'You worry if we've still battles to fight. You want her safe.'

'She's everything to me. I thought when... I talk too much.'

'No doubt of it, but you might as well speak your mind.'

'I was just going to say how Sarah's mother's always there for her lessons and her father's come by twice to watch her. My mother would just drop me off, or more often I'd catch a ride to and from with one of the other students. My father never came. Never once. Rarely to a competition either. But Nan did, whenever she could. She'd drive to wherever they were, whenever she could. Sometimes she'd just be there, and I wouldn't know she'd planned to come. She paid for the lessons, and the entry fees. I didn't know that until I was staying with her once, and heard a message on her machine about renewing the contract with the stables.'

'She gave you what you loved.'

'I want her to be proud of me. I guess it's a lot like Darling. I want to do well, so she can see she didn't waste the time and effort.'

'Then you're foolish as well.'

'I know. Can't seem to help it.'

She looked out over the lake, away to the elegant rise of the castle, its gardens still caught in the last of winter's bite. People strolled around, here to see and do and experience from wherever they'd traveled.

She understood it was like the photo of Sarah, a moment she wanted to have. So as they walked the horses along the water, she let everything else go, and took a page from Boyle's book.

She embraced the silence.

'We should start back,' he said at length. 'I don't want to overwork her.'

'No, and Branna will be expecting me for *my* lesson.'

'Going well enough then?'

'Yes. Branna might have some quibbles, but I think it's going just … grand.'

She glanced to him with a grin, saw him looking past her with a frown. 'What's wrong?'

'Nothing's wrong. I was … noticing the cottage there. They've a fine menu. Maybe after your lesson, you'd like to have some dinner there.'

She lifted her eyebrows. 'With you?'

His frown only deepened. 'Well, of course, with me. Who else?'

'There's no one else,' she said simply. 'I'd love to. I could be ready by seven or seven thirty.'

'Half-seven's good. I'll book it, and fetch you.'

'That sounds grand, too.'

As they slipped into the woods, into the dimmer light, she began a mental inventory of her wardrobe. What should she wear? Nothing too fancy, but not jeans or trousers. Maybe Branna could help her out there, as her options were limited.

Something simple, but pretty. Heels, not boots. Her legs were damn good if she said so herself. She'd like to dazzle him, at least a little, so—

Alastar shied; Darling reared.

And the wolf stepped across the path.

Her thoughts centered on the safety of the horses, Iona didn't think, just acted. She streamed a line of fire across the path between them.

'It won't hurt you. I won't let it hurt you.'

Boyle drew a knife from a sheath on his belt she hadn't noticed. 'He bloody well won't.'

'Don't dismount!' Iona shouted, anticipating.

'She's terrified. She'll bolt, and it might get to her. You have to hold her, Boyle.'

'Take her reins, talk her down, and get them safe. I'll hold it off.'

'Separating us makes us easier prey.' It's what it wanted, hoped for – she could *feel* it. 'Trust me, please. Please.'

And struggling to focus, she murmured, her voice quiet, steady, an incantation she learned from the books. One still untried.

The wolf lunged at the line of fire, looking for an opening. With its fierce charge the flames dimmed, lowered.

Gripping the reins in one hand, Iona lifted the other high.

'From north and south, from east and west, bring on the wind for this contest. Strike up the power, bring on the fire until the tower whirls higher and higher. Blow strong, blow fierce, blow wild and free. As I will, so mote it be.

'You think I don't have it,' she said between her teeth. 'You're wrong.'

Above, the sky churned, and with her lifted hand she balled a fist, as if pulling the flame-edged whirlwind that formed into her fingers.

She flung out her arm, sent a raging funnel of wind through the fire.

It lifted the wolf off its feet, threw it up as it screamed in rage. And she hoped, in fear. It spun, claws lashing air as it bore him up and away.

Iona fought to control what she'd conjured, felt it building beyond her. A tree snapped, collapsed into jagged splinters.

'Take it down.' Boyle's voice came steady in her

ear. 'It's more than you need, and too much. Take it down again now, Iona, as only you can. Let it calm. Let it go.'

A line of sweat beaded down her back as she fought to do just that. The roar of the wind began to fade, the impossible swirl of it to slow.

'All the way down now, Iona.'

'I'm trying. It's so strong.'

'It's you who made it. It's you who's strong.'

She'd made it, she thought. She'd control it. She'd end it.

'Still now,' she said. 'And soft. Calm and sweet. Disperse.'

The wolf dropped like a stone in the light breeze. Then sprang up, fangs dripping. Did the red jewel seem dimmer? she wondered.

Then it leapt into the woods, pulsing out a curtain of smoky fog. After one distant howl, silence fell again.

'It could come back.' All calm deserted her as her hands shook, as her voice jumped. 'It could come back. We need to get the horses in. I need to make sure the stables are safe. It–'

'That's what we'll do. Breathe a minute. You've gone dead pale.'

'I'm all right.' Under her Alastar pawed the ground. He'd pursue, she realized – longed to. To calm him, she had to calm herself. 'We've done enough,' she said softly. 'It's enough for now. I need to tell Branna, Connor. But the horses–'

'We're going now, easy.'

'Easy.' She took those breaths, then laid her hand on Alastar's neck, and over on Darling's. 'Easy,' she repeated. 'It won't hurt you. I ... didn't know you had a knife. A really big knife.'

'A pity I didn't get to use it.' Those gilded eyes hard, he sheathed the blade again. 'But worth it for the show I suppose. And you need more lessons on this business.'

'Absolutely. That one wasn't even on the lesson plan.'

'What do you mean?'

'I read it in a book. I guess you could say I added a bar to the jump. It seemed like the time.'

'In a book. She read it in a book. Christ Jesus.'

'I could really use a drink.'

'You're not alone there.'

She didn't say more, needed to steady herself. Needed to tell her cousins, she thought again. Needed, really, to sit down on something that didn't move.

They were nearly back to the stables before she could think clearly, or almost clearly again. 'Darling was so scared. For herself, but for you, too. My fire scared her, too. I wish I'd thought of something else.'

'She did just fine. Wanted to bolt, but didn't. You may not know it, but that one? He was a rock under you. He never, from that first start, flinched a muscle. I'm thinking he would have done whatever you asked, even up to charging through the fire and taking the beast by the scruff.'

'I didn't have to think. I didn't have to tell him. He just knew. I need to call Branna.'

'I'll see to that.'

When they reached the stables, he dismounted, then stepped over to her. 'Come on down then.'

'I'm not sure I can.'

'That's what these are for.' He lifted his hands, took hold of her, helped her down. 'Go sit on the bench there for a minute or two.'

'The horses.'

'They'll be seen to, and well, what do you think?' The sizzle of impatience had her obeying. And her shaky legs carried her to the bench, almost wept with gratitude as she sat.

When Boyle came out, she managed to get to her feet. 'I need to do a protection spell, for the stables.'

'Do you think Fin hasn't already seen to that?' Boyle simply took her arm, pulled her along. 'He's not due home for a few hours, but I think he knows what he's about in these matters. Branna knows where you are. She'll tell Connor.'

'Where am I going?'

'Up to mine, where you'll have that drink and sit a bit more.'

'I could really use both.'

She climbed the stairs with him. Not exactly the circumstances she'd imagined for her first invitation into his place, but she'd take it.

He opened the door off a narrow porch. 'Company wasn't expected.'

She peeked in first, then smiled. 'Thank God it's not all neat and tidy or I'd feel intimidated. But it's nice.' She stepped in, looked around.

It smelled like him – horses, leather, man. The room, a kind of combination living/sitting/ kitchen, let in the early evening light. A mug sat next to the sink, a newspaper lay spread on the short counter that separated the kitchen from the rest.

A couple of books and some magazines were scattered around – mystery novels, she noted, and horsey magazines. A tumble of boots in a wooden box, a clutter of old jackets on pegs. A sofa with a little sag in the middle, two big chairs, and, to her surprise, a big flat screen on the wall.

He noticed her speculative look. 'I like it for watching matches and such. You'll have some whiskey.'

'I absolutely will, and a chair. I get shaky after it's all done.'

'You were steady enough while it counted.'

'I almost lost it.' She spoke as he went to the kitchen, opened cupboards. 'You helped me hold on.'

Since she was here, and safe, and it was done, he could speak of it. Or try. 'You were glowing like a flame. Your eyes so deep it seemed like worlds could be swallowed up by them. You reached up, and you pulled a storm from the sky with your hand. I've seen things.'

He poured whiskey for both of them, brought the glasses back to where she sat, dwarfed in one of the big chairs. 'I've run tame with Fin most of my life, and Connor, and Branna. I've seen things. But never have I seen the like of that.'

'I've never felt anything like it. A storm in my hand.' She looked down at it now, turned it, amazed to recognize it, to find it so ordinary. 'And a storm inside me. I don't know how to explain it, but it was inside me, so *huge* and full. And absolutely right.

'I broke a tree, didn't I?'

He'd watched it shatter like brittle glass, into

shards and splinters. 'It could've been worse, entirely.'

'Yeah, it could've been. But I need more lessons, more practice.' More control, she thought, and more of the famous focus Branna continually harped on.

Then she looked at Boyle. The hard, handsome face, the scarred eyebrow, the tawny eyes with temper still simmering in them. 'You were going to fight it with a knife, with your hands.'

'It bleeds, doesn't it?'

'I think so. Yes.' She let out one more cleansing breath. 'It bleeds. It wasn't expecting what I did, or could do. Neither was I.'

'I think neither of you will underestimate that again. Drink your whiskey. You're pale yet.'

'Right.' She sipped at it.

'I think it's not the night for dinner out with people.'

'Maybe not. But I'm starving. I think it's something to do with expending all that energy.'

'I'll throw you together something. I've a couple of chops, I think, and I'll fry up some chips.'

'Are you taking care of me?'

'You could use it at the moment. Drink your whiskey,' he said again, then walked back to the kitchen.

Rattling pans, a thwack of a knife on wood, the sizzle of oil. Something about the sounds eased her frayed nerves. She sipped more whiskey, rose, and walked back to where he stood at the stove, frying pork chops in one skillet, chipped potatoes in another.

She wasn't sure she'd ever had a fried chop, but

241

wasn't complaining.

'I can help. Keep my hands and head busy.'

'I've a couple of tomatoes in there Mick's wife gave me from her little greenhouse. You could slice them up.'

So she worked beside him, and felt better for that, too.

He made some sort of thin gravy from the drippings, tossed some herbs in it, then poured it over the chops.

Seated at the counter, Iona sampled a bite. 'It's good.'

'What were you expecting?'

'I didn't have a clue, but it's good. And, God, I'm seriously starving.'

Her color came up well as she ate, he noted, and that slightly dazed look faded from her eyes.

She'd gone from glowing and fierce to pale and shaky in the blink of an eye. And now, it relieved him to see her slide back to just normal. Just Iona.

'He didn't use the fog,' she said abruptly. 'I just realized, he just – it just walked out of the trees. I don't know what that means, but I have to remember to tell Branna and Connor – and Fin. And the jewel, the red jewel around its neck. It wasn't as bright at the end. I don't think. Was it?'

'I couldn't say. I was more about its teeth, and the way you'd gone so white. I wondered if you'd slide right out of the saddle.'

'Never going to happen.' She laughed a little, closed her hand over his. And stilled when his turned under hers, gripped hard.

'You scared the life out of me. The fucking life.'

242

'I'm sorry.'

'What in hell are you apologizing for? It's an irritating habit.'

'I'm ... working on it.'

'One minute we're riding along, easy as you please, and I'm thinking, well then, we'll have dinner and see how that goes. The next, you're reaping a bloody whirlwind.'

He shoved up, snatched his plate and hers. Which was too bad, she thought, as she'd had a couple more chips, and would've eaten them.

'If you don't want me to apologize, don't yell at me.'

'I'm not yelling at you.'

'Who then?'

'No one. I'm just yelling. A man can express himself as he pleases in his own house.'

'Nobody ever yelled in my house.'

'What?' He looked genuinely astonished. 'Were you reared in a church?'

She laughed again. 'I think, maybe – if I go by your gauge – nobody cared enough to yell. Do you care, Boyle?'

'I care you're not lying on the ground out there with your throat torn out.' He cursed himself as her color slid away. 'Now I'm sorry. Truly. I've the devil's own tongue when I'm in a temper. I'm sorry,' he repeated, and put his hands gently on her face to cup it. 'You were so fierce. I don't know what turned me more around. The wolf or you.'

'We came through it. That means a lot.' She put her hands over his. 'And you made me dinner, you let me settle before you let it rip. That means a lot, too.'

'Then we're all right, all right enough for now.'

He touched his lips to hers, gentle this time. And her hands slid to his wrists, tightened.

'I should take you home now.' He eased back, but she kept her hands on his wrists.

'I don't want you to take me home. I want to stay with you.'

'You're still turned around.'

'Do I look turned around?'

He managed to step back, a foot away. 'Maybe I'm turned around.'

'I don't mind that.' She rose. 'I might even like it. We won a battle, Boyle, together. I want to be with you, to hold on to you, to go to bed with you.'

'I think ... the sensible thing is to take some time, to talk about that before ... that.'

'I thought I was the one who talked too much.' She took a step toward him, then another.

'You do, Jesus, you do. But I think, under the circumstances... We'll talk later,' he said, and grabbed her.

'Perfect,' she said, and grabbed him back.

13

Her feet left the floor again, a giddy sensation with her mouth pressed to his. He had a hand fisted on the back of her sweater as if he might rip it away at any second, which would have suited her just fine. If she could have managed it, she'd have wiggled right out of the sweater – and everything else.

'We need to–' Whatever he'd meant to say slid away as her mouth came back, avidly, to his.

'Where's the bedroom?' It had to be close, and if not, the saggy couch looked more than adequate.

'It's...' He tried to think through the hot haze in his brain, then just gripped her ass, gave her a boost. She hooked her legs around his waist as her arms chained around his neck.

Everything tilted and sizzled. She had a vague impression of a dimly lit room, some clutter, some of which he kicked away as he carted her to a bed with dark wooden spindles and cool white sheets.

Then she might have been anywhere – the forest, the ocean, a city sidewalk, a country meadow. There was nothing but him, the weight of him pressed down on her, the big hands roaming, the urgent mouth seeking, taking. Nothing but those cool white sheets growing warmer, warmer as he tugged the sweater over her head, tossed it aside.

Everything about her was so small and exquisite. The breasts that fit so perfectly into his palms, the hands that dived under his shirt to glide over his skin. He wasn't a clumsy man, but feared he would be with her, and tried to slow his pace, smooth out his rhythm.

But her hips arched up, her fingers dug into bunched muscles, urging him on.

He wanted her naked, as simple and basic as that. He wanted that pretty little body uncovered for him, stripped bare for his hands, for his mouth.

He reached down, tugged at the buckle of her

belt. She spoke, the words muffled against his lips.

'What? What?' If she'd said stop, he'd kill himself.

'Boots.' Her lips roamed over his face, then her teeth nipped at his jaw. 'Boots first.'

'Boots. Right. Right.' Already winded, and a bit disconcerted by it, he slid down, knelt at the foot of the bed, yanked at her right boot. He tossed it; it landed with an abrupt thump. As he tugged on the left, she levered up, got a grip on his hair and yanked his head back to hers.

'You look– It's all shadowy, and I can just hear the rain starting, and my heart's pounding so hard.' She punctuated the words with wild kisses. This time when he threw the boot, something crashed and shattered.

'Yours, let me get yours.' She wiggled back for his boot. 'They have to go, have to go because I have to get you naked or I'll go out of my mind.'

'I was thinking the same of you.'

'Good, good.' Her laugh, shaky with nerves and excitement, raced up his spine. 'Same page, same station.' She shoved the first boot to the floor. 'Put your hands on me, would you? Anywhere, everywhere. I've almost got this.'

She couldn't know it, but she'd gotten her wish. She'd dazzled him. 'Will it shut you up?'

'Maybe. Probably. There!' She pried off the boot, dropped it.

And flew at him.

She nearly upended them both off the bed, but he managed to wrap around her and roll. Even as he sank into the next kiss, her hands got busy on his shirt. 'You've got such great shoulders. I just want to–' She dragged it off, pulled the thermal beneath it up and away.

She made a sound like a woman licking melted chocolate from a spoon as her hands ran over his pecs, up to his shoulders, down to squeeze his biceps.

'You're so strong.'

'I won't hurt you.'

She laughed again, no nerves this time. 'I'm not going to promise the same.'

Agile and quick, she reached back, unclipped the clasp of her bra. 'Made it easy for you.'

'I'm up for difficult work.' He drew the bra aside. 'Now be quiet, so I can concentrate on it.'

In a moment she couldn't think, much less speak. So many sensations rushed over her like his hands that thrilled, that took, that tortured. Those rough, workingman palms, the prickly stubble of a daylong beard – thrill over thrill on her quivering skin.

Boys, she realized. Every one who'd ever touched her had been a boy compared to him. All too smooth, too easy, too practiced. Now she had a man who wanted her.

He wasted no time peeling her out of the jeans, exploring her body, feasting on it.

She'd brought the whirlwind in the woods. Now he stirred one inside her just as reckless and wild.

She gave to him, with no hint of restraint or shyness – a bounty of delights and demands that aroused him beyond reason. Her gasp or groan fired more needs, her willful hands sparked nerves over and under his skin. And her mouth, restless and hungry, stirred in his blood like a drug.

Mad for her, he took her hands, drew her arms back until they both gripped the spindles.

When he drove into her, he thought, for a moment, the world exploded. It shook him, the force of it, blinded him, the brilliance of it. Left him, for that breath of time, utterly weak.

Then she rose up to him, taking him deeper on the sigh of his name.

And he was strong as a god, randy as a stallion, mad as a hatter.

He thrust into her, again, again, again, crazed for all that heat, all that softness. She matched his frantic pace, her fingers twining with his, her hips slick pistons – driving and driven.

He felt himself flying – an arrow from a bow – the helpless glory of it. Heard her, dimly, let out a sobbing cry as she flew with him.

He collapsed, mindless of his weight on her. His mind still whirled; his lungs still labored. And something in his speeding heart pulsed like an ache.

She quivered beneath him, trembling limbs, pinging muscles. She wanted, badly, to wrap around him, to stroke and nuzzle. But she didn't have the strength.

He'd just hulled her out.

She could only lie there, washed in heat, listening to his rapid breathing and the slow patter of rain.

'I'm smothering you.'

'Maybe.'

His own muscles shook as he pushed himself off, then just flopped over on his back. He'd never been so ... caught up, he decided.

What did it mean?

She took a couple of deep drinks of air, then curled over to nestle her head on his chest. There was a simple sweetness in that he couldn't resist, and he found himself drawing her in a bit closer.

'Are you cold then?'

'Are you kidding? We generated enough heat to melt the Arctic. I feel amazing.'

'You're stronger than you look.'

She tipped her head up to smile at him. 'Small but mighty.'

'I can't argue.'

It would be easy, he realized, to just stay as they were, to just drift off into sleep awhile. Then take each other again. And what did it mean that he was thinking about it again when he'd barely gotten his breath back?

It meant, perhaps, easy was a mistake.

'I should take you home.'

She didn't speak for a moment, and the hand lazily stroking his chest stilled.

'Branna'd be waiting, I'd think.'

'Oh.' He felt her breath go in, go out. 'You're right. She'll want to know exactly what happened before. I forgot about all that for a minute. It seems like something outside all this. It's a good thing one of us is practical.'

Turning her head, she brushed her lips over his skin, then sat up.

When he looked at her in that shadowed light, a glow against the coming dark, he wanted to draw her close again, close, and just hold on.

'We'd better get dressed,' she said.

Branna was waiting, and trying not to pace and fret. She *hated* only having bits and pieces. Though Boyle had assured her no one was hurt, and he'd look after Iona until she was well settled again, it had been two hours now.

More, she realized.

Worse, Connor had told her not to be such a mother hen, and had taken himself off to the pub rather than – in his words – have his brain assaulted with all her fussing.

Fine for him, she thought with some bitterness. Off he goes to flirt with available women, have a pint or two, and she was left to brood alone.

If Iona didn't walk in the door within another ten minutes, she'd–

'At last,' she muttered when she heard the front door open. Striding out, half a lecture already in mind, she stopped both her forward progress and her nagging words the minute she saw both of them.

A woman didn't have to be a witch to realize how the pair of them had spent a portion of the last two hours.

'So.' She laid her hands on her hips as Kathel padded over to greet them both. 'We'll have some tea, and you'll tell me what happened. You as well,' she said to Boyle, anticipating him. 'I want to hear it all, so don't think about scooting out the door again.'

'Is Connor about?'

'He's not, no. Took himself off to the pub to flirt

with whoever's about, so you've no cover there. Have you had anything to eat?' she asked as she walked into the kitchen.

'Boyle fixed dinner,' Iona told her.

'Did he now?' Brow lifted, Branna sent him a sidelong look as she put the kettle on.

'I was starving after. I was hungry after the spell with the rats, but this was like eat or pass out.'

'It won't always be so keen. You're new at it. And you're looking fit and fine and more than well tended to now. Oh, stop shuffling about, Boyle. A blind monkey could see the two of you have been at each other. I've no problem with that except instead of a good shag, I've been twiddling about waiting for you to come talk to me.'

'I should've come home sooner, instead of worrying you.'

Branna shrugged, then softened. 'If I'd had a man willing to make me dinner and give me a good roll after a fright like that, I'd have taken it as well. I trust he did a good job with both.'

Iona grinned. 'Exceptional.'

Heat rose up Boyle's back like a fever. 'Would you mind not batting around my sex life, at least while I'm sitting here?'

'We'll bat it around when you're not then.' Branna poured his tea, kissed the top of his head.

'Have you eaten?' Iona asked her.

'Not yet. I will once I hear what you have to say. From the start, Iona. And if she leaves anything out, Boyle, however slight, you fill it in.'

Iona began, trying to speak in full detail, and with calm.

Branna gripped her hand. 'You're saying you

called a whirlwind? How did you know the way?'

'It's in the books. I know it's advanced, and it's risky, but it was... I don't know why or how, but I knew it was what I needed to do. I knew I could.'

'Why didn't you call me, or Connor? Both?'

'It was so fast. When I play it back, it's like it was hours, stage by stage, but it was so fast. I don't think it was more than a couple minutes.'

'If that,' Boyle confirmed.

'All right, but it's best if you call for me and Connor.'

'Or Fin,' Boyle put in.

'I'm not shutting him out.' Or only a little, Branna admitted. 'But blood calls to blood, Boyle. We've the same blood, Connor, Iona, and I. And this is blood magicks at work. You weren't so afraid. Connor would have sensed that, as he did before. You weren't so afraid as before, in the woods alone.'

'A little, but no, not like before, maybe because I wasn't alone. I could only think he'd hurt Boyle and the horses, to get to me. It helped me focus, I think.'

Branna nodded, but pushed at her hair. 'I'm jumping you around. You said he didn't bring the fog.'

'No.'

'More to catch you off guard than to rattle your nerves then. And it may be he pulls some power from the fog as well, and wasn't as strong.'

'Didn't think he'd need to be?' Boyle nodded. 'He learned different. She turned a tree to tooth-picks.'

'I had some trouble with control.'

'Calling a whirlwind with no practice? I'm not surprised, and it's a wonder if a tree's all the damage done.'

'All that I saw,' Boyle said. 'Unless you count the bastard spinning around in the air.'

'If I could've held it, focused it better, I might have destroyed it.'

Branna dismissed that with a shrug. 'If it was that easy, I'd have done it myself before this. You did well. Finish it out now.'

Listening, nodding, Branna didn't interrupt again.

'Yes, you did well indeed. I'd tell you it was a big risk, but I can't question your instincts. They told you this was the way, and you followed them. You're safe and well. I think you took Cabhan off guard, and you cost him. It may be you hurt him a bit as well, if his power source – the jewel is that, I think – lessened. How did it feel?'

'Enormous. Like I could feel every cell in my body burning. Like nothing could stop me.'

At that, Branna's brows drew together. 'There's the danger as true as the wolf.'

'I think I know. Part of feeling that invincibility was why I couldn't control it, or started to lose it, and let it control me.'

'It's a vital lesson learned. It's that being en-gulfed by the power, the thirst for more of it that made Cabhan.'

Iona thought she understood how that could be, how the temptation, the seduction of such great power could overwhelm. 'Boyle talked me down. He helped me hold it, calm it, and finally stop it.'

Now those eyebrows rose. 'Is that the way of it?

That's no small feat, to rein in a witch who's not only reaping a whirlwind but riding one. Otherwise, the pair of you would be roaming about Oz looking for ruby slippers.'

'But I'd be the good witch.'

'Hmm. I'm relieved you weren't hurt, either of you. And I'm thinking we might have a space of time, before he makes another lunge at us, to smooth out more rough edges. I'm proud of you,' she added, then rose.

Simple words, simply spoken, but they poured into Iona like fine wine. 'Thanks.'

'I've a thing or two to see to in the workshop now that my head's clear,' Branna continued. 'I'll tell Connor all of this, and as he came at you when you were with Boyle, it's best if we tell Meara the whole of it as well. And Fin,' she added before Boyle could. 'We'll meet again, would you say, in a day or two, once I've – once we've all had time to think it all through.'

'I think that's the right thing,' Iona said. 'We're stronger together, right, than separately?'

'I'll hope. See you at breakfast, Boyle,' Branna said with a wink, then left them.

'Oh well, I don't know as I should–'

'You should.' Now Iona got to her feet, held out a hand. 'You really should. Come upstairs with me, Boyle.'

The wanting was so steep he couldn't climb out of it. He stood, took her hand, and went upstairs with her.

Under strict orders to report to Branna's workshop directly from the stables, and with Boyle busy in a meeting with Fin, Iona tapped Meara for a ride home.

'I have to get a car.' She frowned at the winding, narrow road Meara zoomed along as if it were a six-lane highway. 'A cheap car. A cheap, reliable car.'

'I can put the word out on that.'

'Yeah, that'd be good. Then I have to learn how to drive on the wrong side of the road.'

'It's you Yanks who drive on the wrong side, and can put the fear of God into a person just driving out to do the weekly marketing.'

'I bet. But why do you guys drive on the left? I read it was about having the right hand free for the sword, but it's been a really long time since people needed to battle it out on horseback with swords.'

'You never know, do you? Most don't battle it out on horseback with whirlwinds as a rule.'

'You got me there. Maybe I can talk Boyle into letting me drive some tomorrow. He's going to take me around to some sites. I've been so buried in work and lessons I haven't seen anything outside of that, and the village. Not really.'

'A day off's good for the soul. But it'll take considerable talk of the very sweetest of nature, and very likely promises of exotic sexual favors to convince Boyle to let anyone behind the wheel but himself.'

'I'm a good driver,' she insisted. 'Or was when the steering wheel was on this side. And does everyone know I'm in the position to offer Boyle sex?'

'Anyone with eyes. If there'd been more opportunity today, I'd've pulled more out of you about the whirlwind business, and the sex. But we had too many people about for it.'

'You could come in,' Iona said as Meara pulled up at the workshop. 'Then Branna couldn't dump me right into more work, and I could give you lots and lots of details.'

'Why is it so entertaining to have a window into others' sexual adventures? Maybe so we don't have to deal with the upheaval of them in our own lives. In any case,' Meara continued before Iona could think of an answer, 'I'd be all ears, that's for certain. But I've errands need doing. Now, I could meet you at the pub later, with my ears, unless you're already planning more adventures with Boyle.'

'I could squeeze in time for a drink with a friend. Do you believe in reincarnation?'

'Sure that's a question.' Meara shoved back her cap. 'Where did it come from?'

'I was wondering why some connections seem so easy, so natural, as if they'd already been made and are just getting picked up again. It's the way it worked for me with you, with Branna and Connor. With Boyle. Even Fin.'

'I guess I don't discount anything. You don't when your best friend in the world's a witch. But I think a big part of that is you're open to those connections. You reach for them, you do. It's hard not to reach back, even when you're not the reaching type in general.'

'You're not?'

'Not as a rule, no. I keep my circle tight. Less upheavals, so to speak.'

'Then I'm glad you widened it for me. See you at the pub? A couple hours?'

'That'll do fine.'

'Thanks for the lift.' Iona jumped out, shot back a wave. She liked the idea of being open to connections, and the prospect of meeting a friend for a drink. Maybe she could talk Branna into joining them – a kind of impulsive girls' night out.

Then maybe she'd get lucky and top it off with a little adventure with Boyle.

Pleased with the plan, she swung through the door.

'Let the lesson begin, then we can– Oh, sorry. I didn't see you had company – a customer.'

She hesitated at the doorway, not quite sure if she should go in or out, then recognized the woman standing at the work counter with her cousin.

'Oh, hi. I met you my first night at Ashford, at the Cottage. You're Mick's daughter. Iona,' she added when the woman simply stood there, flushed and staring.

'I remember, yes. My father speaks well of you.'

'He's terrific. Just one more reason I love my job. Sorry to interrupt. I'll just go–'

'No, no, it's not a problem a'tall. I've just finished. And thanks, Branna, I'll be on my way then. Best to Connor.'

She hurried out, pushing a little bottle into her coat pocket.

'Sorry. I know you do some business here, even though most of it's through the shop in the village.'

'A bit here, a bit there.' Branna tucked some euros into a drawer. 'Those who come here are

257

often looking for what I don't sell in the village.'

'Oh.'

'I'm not a doctor, but I'm discreet. Still, in this case I'll tell you, as it's hardly the secret Kayleen thinks it is, and there may come a time you'll be asked for the same.'

She lifted a ladle, poured a pale gold cream from bowl to bottle through a funnel, and touched the air with the scent of honey and almonds.

'There's a fine-looking Italian come over to work at his uncle's restaurant in Galway City. Our Kayleen met him a few weeks ago at a party, and they've been seeing each other a bit. I met him myself when they came into the shop, and he's charming as a prince and twice as handsome.' She continued to work as she spoke, filling her bottles, then wiping them clean before sealing them with the stoppers.

'Kayleen's mad in lust for him, and who could blame her for it? I'd have a go at him myself if I was in the market. Others feel the same, and it appears he's fine with that situation. And who could blame him?' she added, tying a thin gold ribbon around the bottle's neck.

'But Kayleen doesn't want to share, and feels the handsome Italian only requires a bit of a boost to pledge to her alone. She had in mind I'd give her the boost.'

'I'm not following.'

Branna set the finished bottle in a box for transporting. 'A love spell was her request, and she was willing to pay a hundred hard-earned for it.'

'A love spell? Can you do that?'

'Can and will are different matters entirely.

258

There are ways, of course. There are always ways, and there's nothing more dangerous or filled with pain and regret as spells that involve the heart.'

'You told her no. Because it's taking someone's choice away. And because you're not supposed to use magick for gain.'

Hands quick and clever, Branna tied the next ribbon. 'Every spell's for gain, one way or the other. You want something or believe in something, want to protect or block or vanquish. This cream here, it'll make the skin smooth and fragrant, and it can lift the ego of the one wearing it, as well as draw a response from the one catching its scent. I create it, someone buys it, and I'm paid. That's gain as well.'

'I guess that's a way to think about it.'

'It is. As for choice, there are times we do that as well, however well-intentioned. And so we have to be willing to pay the price, for magick's not free.' She looked up then, met Iona's eyes with her smoky ones. 'Not for us, not for any.'

'Then why did you say no?'

'Emotions are magick of their own, aren't they? Love and hate the strongest and most powerful. It's my philosophy that you don't tamper with feelings, don't push them in one direction or the other, not with power. The risk is great. What if the love is already there, about to bloom? You push it along, maybe it opens to obsession. Or the one who paid for the spell has a change of mind or heart. Or there's another who loves and would be loved and is now shunted aside by magickal means. So many ors and ifs there. I don't play with love spells or their kin. You'll make up your own mind where you stand on it, but it's, to me, an unethical and risky line to cross.'

'Unethical, yes. And even more it just wouldn't be fair.' For Iona, that was even more important. 'And yeah, I get what you're saying. A lot of magick isn't fair. But love should be, I don't know, sacred. People have to be able to love who they love.'

'And not love when they don't. So I said no, and always will.'

'What did you sell her instead?'

'Truth. She'll decide if she makes use of it. If she does, they'll both be able to say what they feel, and want and expect. If not, she can go along enjoying what is for as long as it lasts. I think she won't use it. She has a fear of magick, and she's not ready for truth.'

'If she loved him, she'd want the truth.'

Branna smiled, slipped the next bottle into the box. 'Ah, and there you have it. She's a bit besotted and wildly in lust, but not anywhere near the borders of love. She only wishes to be. Love doesn't break under the truth, even when you want it to.'

The door opened. Kathel trotted in, and Fin followed.

'Ladies.' He pushed back his wind-tossed hair. 'I heard we had a bit of trouble. You're all right, darling?' he said to Iona.

'Yes. Fine.'

'I'm glad of it. And still, I'd like the details of it all, and what's being planned in the certainty there'll be another attack.'

'Boyle didn't come with you?'

'He's dealing with the farrier, and Connor's out on a hawk walk, so it's left to the two of you to deal with me on this.'

'Boyle was there as well.' Branna carried the box to a shelf in the back. 'He'll have as many details as Iona.'

'He sees it from his eyes. I want hers.'

'We've work, Fin. She needs more knowledge, more practice.'

'Then I'll help you with it.' As if it was already accepted, he shrugged out of his coat.

'We have different ... techniques, you and I.'

'So we do, and Iona would only benefit from seeing, and trying the differences.'

'This habit of talking about me in the third person when I'm right here is getting really old,' Iona decided.

'And rude,' Fin said with a nod. 'You're right. I'd like to help, and once we're done with the work, I'd very much like if you'd tell me exactly what happened, and how you left it – from your eyes, Iona. If you will.'

'I ... I'm supposed to meet Meara later. But...' Iona glanced back at Branna, watched her cousin sigh, shrug. 'We could ask her to come here, and Boyle, too. It would be smart, I think, to have us all here, go through it once and for all, and talk about what comes next.'

'All right then. I can have dinner brought in. You've no need to cook for a horde again, Branna.'

'I've sauce I put on an hour ago for pasta. It'll stretch easily enough.'

'I'll ring up the others then.' He drew out his phone. 'Then we'll get started.'

14

It felt good, And it felt right to have everyone together again. Everyone tucked into the roomy kitchen with good cooking smells, voices carrying over voices, the dog sprawled at the hearth.

It made the normal, to Iona's mind, despite the dark and light of the paranormal.

She tossed a big salad, kind of her specialty. She did pretty well in the kitchen as long as it didn't involve actually cooking.

So she felt good and right and, with the increased push on her lessons with Branna, strong. Even the recounting of the altercation with the wolf, once again, reminded her of the power in the blood, at her fingertips. And made her feel confident.

'It's bold, isn't it?' Meara commented as she slathered herbed butter over thick slices of baguette. 'To come at the pair of you that way, in the daylight and so close to Ashford.'

'I'm thinking it wasn't planned.' Connor nipped a slice of bread from the baking tray before Meara could slide it in the oven to toast. 'But more he saw an opportunity and took it, without the planning.'

'Maybe to frighten more than harm,' Fin suggested. 'To harm certainly if that opportunity opened. You were having a nice, easy ride, relaxed.'

'And not on guard.' Boyle nodded. 'A mistake

we won't be making again.'

'It's a kind of terrorism, isn't it?' Fin carried the big bowl of salad to the table. 'The constant threat, the not knowing when or where it may come. And the disruption of the normal rhythm of things.'

'Sure he's the one who bore the brunt of it.' Branna dumped drained pasta in a cheerful blue-and-white bowl. 'And got his arse kicked by a witch barely out of the cupboard.'

'Satisfying.'

But as Fin spoke, Iona caught the quick look he shared with Branna.

'But? But what?'

'He's come after you twice. Here, sit now, get started,' Branna ordered. 'And both times he's been sent off with his tail between his legs.'

'He underestimated her,' Boyle said as he took his seat.

'No doubt of that, and little that he'll do so again.' Branna handed the salad set to Meara. 'Dish it up. I'll turn the bread.'

She could follow the dots, Iona thought, especially when they were so clearly marked. 'You think he'll come after me again? Specifically?'

'It's you coming here that's set things in motion that held for hundreds of years. There's apples in here,' Connor discovered as he sampled the salad. 'It's nice.'

'So if he scares her off – at least – and back to America?' Meara frowned. 'What does that do?'

'I'm not sure it matters now. She's the third.' Branna brought the bread to the table, sat to have her salad. 'And he knows it, as we do now.

Her power has opened, and wider and faster than he – or I for that matter – had anticipated. The cork's not going back in that bottle.'

While she appreciated the compliment, Iona continued to follow the dots, into a very uneasy place. 'But if he kills me, or either of you?'

'Pain's better.' Connor ate with obvious enjoyment, and spoke with something kin to cheer. 'Or seduction. Those lead to turning, and by turning any of us, he gains more power. Killing outright, he'd get some, but far from all. Still he might try it out of frustration or spite.'

'There's a happy thought,' Meara muttered.

'If that's true, why hasn't he gone for either of you long before I got here?'

'Oh, he's made a few swipes from time to time, but no scars.' As soon as the words were out of his mouth, Connor winced. 'I'm sorry for that, Fin.'

'It's no matter. He couldn't know, as none of us could know, the three of you *were* the three. Not until you came, Iona, and the links clicked together.'

'And the amulets help to shield,' Branna added. 'And if he did away with me or Connor, there'd be another. There's O'Dwyers a plenty.'

'Not like you.' Boyle spoke quietly. 'Nor like Connor. Or you,' he said to Iona. 'You knew, Fin, it would be this three and this time.'

'Only for certain when I saw the horse. I saw you on him,' Fin said to Iona. 'Astride the stallion under a moon so full and white it seemed to pulse against the black sky like a bright heart. I saw fire in your hands, and power in your eyes.'

'You said nothing of this before.'

Fin glanced at Branna. 'I bought the horse because I knew it was hers. I didn't know when you'd come, not for certain,' he said to Iona. 'Only that you would, and you'd have need of Alastar. And he of you.'

'What else have you seen?' Branna demanded.

His face shuttered. 'Too much, and not enough.'

'I'm not looking for riddles, Finbar.'

'You're looking for answers, as always you do, and I don't have them. I've seen the fog spread, as you have, seen him watching from the shadows, a shadow himself. I've seen you under that same bright moon, glowing like a thousand stars. With the wind flying through your hair, and blood on your hands. I've wondered if it was mine.'

Saying nothing, Branna rose to go to the stove, to pour the simmering sauce in a bowl.

'I don't know what it means,' Fin continued, 'or how much is real and true, how much is wondering.'

'When the time comes, it'll be his blood spilled.' The cheer left Connor's voice. Now there was only a hard edge, a lick of temper.

'Brother. I am his blood.'

'He doesn't own you.' With her shoulders very straight, her eyes very direct, Iona looked at Fin. 'And feeling sorry for yourself isn't helping. He's been around, waiting for hundreds of years,' she continued in a practical tone as Branna shot her a quietly approving look over her shoulder. 'What the hell has he been doing for centuries?'

'Fin thinks he goes back and forth, when he's a mind to, between times, or worlds. Or both,'

Boyle added.

'How does he– Oh, the cabin, the ruins. The place behind the vines. If he can do that, why doesn't he kill Sorcha before she burns him to ashes?'

'He can't change what was. Her magick was as powerful as his, maybe more,' Fin speculated, 'before she took ill, before he killed her man. It's her, I think, who spellbound the place, protects it still. What was, was, and can't be altered. I've tried myself.'

'Well now, you're full of secrets, aren't you then.' Branna dropped the bowls on the table, snatched up the salad to put it aside.

'If I could've finished what she started, and ended him, it would be done.'

'But so would you,' Iona pointed out. 'Maybe: I think. Time paradoxes are ... paradoxical.'

'In any case, I couldn't change it. My power was there, I felt it, but it made no matter. And I couldn't hold my place, if you take my meaning. It all wavered, and brought me back where I'd started.'

'You could've been lost,' Connor reminded him. 'Taken somewhere, or some time else entirely.'

'I wasn't. I think it's like a string of wire, from then to now, and there's no veering off from the wire.'

'But there's a lot of years on the wire,' Iona mused. 'Maybe it's a matter of finding the right spot.'

'Change one thing that was, it all changes. And you should know better,' Branna said to Fin.

'I was young, and foolish.' He sent Iona a quick

smile. 'And feeling sorry for myself. Now that I'm older and wiser, I see it's not any one of us who'll end him or the curse he carries, but all of us.'

'What if we all went back?'

Connor paused in ladling sauce over his pasta to study Boyle. 'All of us, together?'

'Maybe it would change things, but we don't know when he'll try to harm any one of us, or what else he might do. I don't know why you can't change what was, or why you shouldn't try when what was is something evil.'

'It's a slippery hill to climb, Boyle.' Branna twirled pasta, untwirled, twirled it again. 'Some ask if you had the way and means, wouldn't you go back and kill Hitler? Oh, the thousands of lives saved, and so many innocent. But one of those lives saved might be worse and more powerful than Hitler ever dreamed.'

'But don't you try all the same? A lot of years on the wire, as Iona said. Can't we find the time, the place, take the battle to him? A time and place we know won't wink Fin out of existence.'

'Thanks for that.'

'I'm used to you,' Boyle shot back to Fin. 'And have no desire to run the businesses on my own. Is there not some magick the four of you can devise to give us the best chance of it?'

'We may not come back to the world we left, if we come back at all,' Branna insisted.

'Maybe we'd come back to better. He's a shadow in this time, as Fin said.'

'Shadows fade in the light.' Meara lifted her wine. 'That's something to consider. I may not be able to conjure a spell, but I know basic physics. Is it physics? Ah, well, action, reaction, yes? And I know it's always better to take the enemy by surprise, on ground of your choosing.'

'You'd go?' Iona asked. 'I mean if we could, and would.'

'Well now, unless I had a hot date lined up.'

'It's not a joke, Meara.'

Meara reached over, rubbed a hand on Branna's arm. 'You've carried the weight long enough. Time to spread it around. Saying we're a circle and really meaning it are different matters, Branna. You can't protect us all, so let's protect each other.'

'We could think on it. On how to find that time and place, and block him from knowing it. And how to make the time and place here and now – or here and when we've found the answer to destroying him once and for good.'

'She'll study and think and work,' Iona said quietly to Boyle as they cleared the table. 'And worry. I wonder sometimes if there'd be less work and worry all around if I hadn't come.'

'It's been an axe dangling over their heads long before that. And you did come. I don't think much about what's meant, but it seems you were meant to come. It needs to end sometime, doesn't it? Why not now? And with us?'

'I'm not a big fan of procrastination.' She thought it over as she wiped the table clean, kept her voice down under the clatter of dishes being loaded into the washer. 'I just like plowing through to whatever's next. But I think I could happily push all this into a box in a corner for a couple hundred years.'

'Someone's got to shovel the shit.'

'And we've got the shovels. Yeah,' Iona conceded. 'Might as well put our backs into it. I'm looking forward to tomorrow, and not just to get out and see the world beyond a two-mile radius of Ashford.'

'It's kilometers here.'

'I've a feeling I'll master Irish easier than the metric system. I think getting a better sense of the area beyond our little core of it might be helpful. Plus, I have an exceptional guide.'

'We'll be seeing about that.'

Take the moments, she thought. Every moment of normal, of happiness and ease. 'I want ruins and old cemeteries and green hills. And sheep.'

'You don't have to ramble far for any of that.'

'But I'll be rambling with you.' Turning, she wrapped her arms around his waist.

She felt him shift, that subtle move of embarrassment, though the clatter and chatter continued around them. And because she found it endearing, she added to it by raising to her toes and giving him a quick kiss. 'I could drive for a while. Practice the on-the-left thing before I buy a car.'

'I think no, most firmly.'

'I know how to drive a truck.'

'You know how to drive a truck on the right when you're counting the miles. But you don't know how to drive a lorry on the left when you're clicking off kilometers.'

He had her there. 'That's the point. You could teach me.'

'Best you try that with someone less ... volatile,'

Branna suggested.

'She means someone less likely to shout blue murder if you clip a hedgerow or veer off the wrong direction on a roundabout,' Meara explained. 'You're better off with Connor, as he's long on patience.'

'I'd need be no longer than a thumbnail to have more patience than Boyle. I'll take you out on the road, cousin, first chance we have for it.'

'Thanks.'

'And if you're after buying a car, I've a friend in Hollymount in the trade who'd make you a fair deal.'

'Connor's friends everywhere.'

He merely smiled at Meara. 'Sure I'm a friendly sort.'

'And all the girls attest to it. I should be off. You'll text me if you devise some grand scheme,' she said to Branna.

'I've some thoughts to put together. I'll let you know when I have them sorted out.'

'Have a care.' Meara added a hug.

'I could use a care as well.'

Lifting her eyebrows at Connor, Meara tapped his cheek. 'Enjoy your rambling, Iona, and you and Boyle have a care as well. And you, Fin.'

'I'll walk out with you. I've some thoughts of my own to put together,' he said to Branna. 'We might consider Litha.'

She nodded. 'I am.'

'Isn't that – yes, that's the summer solstice,' Iona remembered. 'Not till June?'

'A bit of time yet. Light smothers dark – and it's the longest day, which we may use to our advantage. I've to think about it.'

'Would you rather I stay here tomorrow? Work with you?'

'No, go rambling. You're right that it's good for you to have a better sense of the world around this core of it. And I need that time to think.'

'Why don't we give you some peace then,' Boyle suggested. 'I'll come fetch you, Iona, about nine.'

'You could. Or I could go with you now, and we can leave from your place whenever you're ready.' She smiled at him. He didn't shift, but she sensed he wanted to. 'They all know we're sleeping together.'

'Is that a fact?' Connor feigned surprise. 'And here I thought you've been having a chess tournament and discussing world events.'

'You're a rare one,' Boyle muttered. 'We can leave from my house if you'd rather. Just don't take half the night getting together what you need, as we'll just be tramping around rubble and gravestones.'

'I packed a bag already, just in case. Call me,' she told Branna, 'if you need me for anything.'

'Just have a good time of it.' She moved them along, friends and family, up to waving them away from the front door of the cottage.

And stood there a moment longer in the chilly dark.

'All right then, it's just you and me as you wanted.' Connor laid a hand on her shoulder. 'What is it?'

He wouldn't look, Branna thought. Though she knew how to block him, he wouldn't draw on her

271

heart or mind. He'd consider it an intrusion.

'I don't mean to cut Iona out, and she's proven herself, God knows.'

'But you're still getting used to her and used to the others, all being part of it. Makes you feel tight in your skin, doesn't it, all these people crowding you?'

How he knew her, she thought, and thank all the gods for it, and him. 'It does, yes. How we ever came from the same parents is a wonder. Nothing suits you more than a crowd, and nothing suits me less.'

'Keeps us balanced.'

'Seems it does, and I'm thinking balance might be the thing.'

'Ostara, the equinox, the balance of day to night? Rather than the solstice?'

'I've thought of it – as obviously you have as well – but the time's just too short to prepare it all, as it's nearly on us.'

'I didn't think her ready, our Iona,' he admitted, 'but I wonder if I was wrong about that.'

'She needs more seasoning, to my mind. And deserves it as well. The solstice is close enough, and that's a kind of balance as well. That tipping point of the year. It may be a chance. If you'd work with me a bit now. Just putting our heads together.'

He touched his forehead to hers. 'A ritual, a spell of balancing – and banishing at the moment day holds longest – then slides into its ebbing.'

'There, you see. I don't have to explain to you, so it goes easier.'

'What you're thinking won't come within a

league of easy, but it might work. We'll see what we can put together. Just us two for now, and the rest soon enough.'

They went to the workshop together, with Branna trying not to feel guilty over the relief that it was just the two of them, at least for now.

'I embarrassed you?' Iona said while they made the short drive to Boyle's.

'What? No. I'm not embarrassed.'

'A little. I probably should've said something about staying with you tonight when there weren't other people around. I never think about things like that. And it occurred to me too late to consider you might not have wanted company.'

'You've stopped being company.'

What did it say about her that she found the careless comment romantic? Oh well.

'Then it occurred to me you'd have had no problem saying no, and you'd pick me up in the morning.'

'Do I look thickheaded to you?'

'Not a bit.'

'I'd have to be not to want to spend the night with you, wouldn't I?'

More romance, she thought, Boyle McGrath-style. 'But I shouldn't have announced it like the minutes of the next meeting. If we took minutes.'

'It's a private thing.'

'I get that, and it would be. Or I'd try harder there. But it seems to me, the way things are, privacy's not really on the table. That's harder for you than it is for me.'

'It may be, but you're right. There are more

immediate things to worry about.'

He pulled in right behind Fin, jiggled his keys as he got out.

'Good night then,' Fin called out, 'and enjoy tomorrow.'

'I'll have my mobile if there's a need.'

Iona bumped against Boyle as they climbed the stairs to his rooms. 'It *is* harder on you. But Fin's got to be used to you bringing a date back with you now and then, and you with him doing the same.'

'I don't bring women here. As a rule,' he said after a moment.

'Oh.' Privacy, she thought, and more. 'If you go to their place, you can leave when you want.'

'There's that.' He stepped inside.

'You need to tell me when you want me to go. I'd rather be told than tolerated.'

'I don't tolerate much.' He tossed his keys in a bowl. 'I'm not tolerating you.'

It made her smile. 'Good. Don't. It's miserable to be tolerated.'

He set her little bag on a chair. 'If I didn't want you here, you'd be somewhere else. Do you want something to drink?'

'I thought I wasn't company anymore.'

'You're right.'

He grabbed her the way she liked, pulled her through to the bedroom. 'You can get your own drink after.'

'I'll get you one, too.' She yanked his jacket off his shoulders and away. 'Boots,' she said and made him laugh.

'I'm aware of the order of things.'

And still they dived toward the bed. Pulling, tugging, then tossing boots.

'We broke something last time,' she remembered as she rushed to unbutton his shirt. 'What was it?'

'My grandmother's crystal vase.'

Her fingers stilled, her eyes widened in distress. Then he grinned.

'Oh! Liar!' She threw a leg over him, shoved him onto his back. 'You're going to pay for that.' Crossing her arms, she grabbed the hem of her sweater, pulled it over her head, winged it over her shoulder.

'I'll pay more,' he told her. He slid his hands up her sides, over her breasts as she fought open the last buttons.

'You bet you will, buddy.' She lowered her head, catching his mouth in a crushing kiss before scraping her teeth over his bottom lip, ending with a nip.

He retaliated by flipping her over, doing the same.

They wrestled off clothes, wrestled each other in a rush of give-and-take.

So much the same, she thought, wonderfully the same, but now she *knew* what they could bring to each other. All heat and demand and speed, like flying through fire – simmers and flashes and bursts.

She reveled in the thrill of skin sliding against skin – his to hers, hers to his – the heady friction of it. His mouth, dark with hunger, his hands, rough with greed, raced over her.

How had she lived without knowing what it was

to be wanted so completely, so urgently, so thoroughly?

She needed to give him the same, to show him how the want for him flooded through her.

He couldn't get enough of her. Whatever he took only sparked a bright hot need for more. When he had her like this, moving, moving in the dark, he couldn't think, could only feel.

And she made him feel drunk, half-mad with it. Made him feel strong as a god, reckless as a cornered wolf.

The world outside dissolved; time spun away.

Just her body, the shape of her, those sleek muscles under smooth skin. The sound of her – breath and sigh and soft, soft moan. And her taste, so hot and sweet.

She struggled up, fast hands, quick legs, to straddle him, and starlight caught in the crown of her hair like diamonds.

She took him in, fast and deep, her hands pressed to her own breasts as the first wave of ecstasy swamped her.

Then she rode, free and wild, starlight on her skin, dark triumph in her eyes.

He gripped her hips, clinging to her and some last thread of sanity.

And she lifted her arms high, crying out in that same dark triumph.

Flames shimmered at her fingertips, tiny pinpoints of light that flashed, bright and blinding as the sun. Stunned by them, bewitched by her, he held on – and he let go.

In the dark, in the dream, she reached for him.

276

'Do you hear that? Do you hear that?'

'It's just the wind.'

'No.' The woods were so thick, the night so black. Where was the moon? Why was there no moon, no stars?

And with a shudder, she understood. 'It's *in* the wind.'

Her name, the seductive pull of the whisper. A stroke of silk on bare skin.

'You need to sleep.'

'But I am. Aren't I?'

When she shivered again, he rubbed her chilled hands between his. 'We should have a fire.'

'It's so dark. It's too dark, too cold.'

'I know the way home. Don't fret now.'

He began to guide her, through the trees, away from the little licks of fog that flicked, sly as the tongue of a snake, along the ground.

'Don't let go,' she said as the whisper slid and stroked over her skin.

'The way's blocked, do you see?' He gestured to the thick branches blocking the path. 'I'll need to move them before we can get through.'

'No!' On a spur of panic, she gripped his hand tighter. 'It's what he wants. Just like before, to separate us. We have to stay together. We have to hold on.'

'The way's blocked, Iona.' He turned her now, looked into her eyes. His were dark gold, intense, unwavering. 'We should have a fire.'

'The fog's closer. Can you hear it?'

The wolf now, just the faintest growl through the black, through the fog.

'I hear it. Fire, Iona. It's what we need.'

277

Fire, she thought. Against the dark, against the cold.

Fire. Of course.

She threw her arms out, out, lifted her face up. And called it.

Strong, bright, with a whip-snap that lashed through the creeping fog, made it boil, made it steam and die to thin black ash.

'To the dark I bring the light. Against the black I forge the white. From my blood I call the fire to burn, to flame high and higher. Awake or in dreams, my power runs free. As I will, so mote it be.'

A curl of fog snuck out, slithered close. Boyle lunged in front of Iona, threw out a fist.

He felt a quick pain across his knuckles. Then both fog and ash vanished, and there was only fire and light.

She saw blood well up across Boyle's hand.

And woke with a jolt.

Morning, she saw now, the pearly promise of it glowing against the window.

A dream, just a dream, and she took a breath to steady herself. When Boyle sat up beside her, she reached for his hand.

And saw the blood.

'Oh God.'

'In the woods, together.' His fingers curled tight over hers. 'Is that how it was?'

She nodded. 'It's a kind of astral projection, I think. We're here, but we were there. I must have pulled you in with me. You... You hit out at the fog.'

'It worked, and felt fine as well, though your

fire did more.'

'No, yes. I don't know. You struck out, and it was like you punched a hole, for a moment. I... But you're bleeding.'

'Sure it's but a scratch.'

'No, it's from him. I don't know if it's just a scratch.' She could call on Connor or Branna, but she *felt*, somehow, this was for her to do.

'I need to fix it.'

'Just needs a quick wash, and ointment if you're going to fuss about it.'

'Not that way.' Her heart beat so fast now, faster, she realized, than it had, even through the fear of the dream.

He bled, and it was Cabhan who'd drawn that blood.

'It's an unnatural wound. I've studied it, if you'll trust me.'

She laid her hand over the shallow gash, closed her eyes. She saw his hand – strong, broad, the fascinating scarred knuckles from his boxing days. The blood, and deeper, looking deeper, the thin black line of Cabhan's poison.

Just as she'd feared.

Draw it out, she told herself. Out and away. White against black again. Light against dark. Out and away before it sank deeper, before it could spread.

She felt it go, little by little, felt it burn away. She knew by the way his hand stiffened, it caused him pain. But now the wound ran clean. Slowly, carefully, she set to the healing of the shallow gash. Now the pain – small, sharp stings were hers. But they faded, faded.

Just a scratch, as he'd said, once the poison had been drawn out.

She opened her eyes, found his on her.

'You've gone pale.'

'It took some doing. My first try at this kind of thing.' Her head spun a little, and her stomach did a couple of slow rolls.

But the wound was clean, and it was closed. She studied his hand, satisfied. 'He used poison. I don't know if it would've done anything, but it might have spread. It wasn't much, but it's gone now. You could have Connor take a look.'

Boyle continued to study her as he flexed his fingers. 'I'd say you did well enough.'

'I don't know if he expected me to pull you with me. And I don't know how I did. But you told me what needed to be done. The fire. You told me, and it worked.'

'Burned him to ashes.'

'Well, wouldn't be the first time, and I really don't think it's the last.'

'No, not the last of it.'

'I'd say I'm sorry I dragged you into that, but I'm awfully glad you were with me.'

'It was an experience for certain.'

One that left him shaken, and more, puzzled him. During it he'd felt such calm, and such absolute faith she would do what needed to be done.

'It seemed like a dream,' he continued, 'the way your mind can be a bit slow, and you don't question the oddities.'

'I'll do a charm for the bed, or better, have Branna do one. It should help.'

'I hurt him.' Again, Boyle flexed his fingers. 'He wasn't expecting a punch, I'm thinking. I know when one lands well, and it did. I'm thinking as well, the poison was for you. Could I have pulled you back out, as you did me? Do you know that? And if I did that, could I have gotten you to Connor in time to deal with the poison, if I'd thought to?'

'You knew what to do.' Instinctively, she lifted her hands to rub at his shoulders, found them knotted. 'You knew we needed fire, and you stayed so calm. I needed you to stay calm. I'm going to believe you'd know what to do if and when he comes at us again.'

She let out a long breath. 'I'm starving. I'll go fix breakfast.'

'I'll do it. You're a terrible cook.'

'That's so entirely true. Fine, you cook. I'll give Branna a call, tell her, just in case. Are we still on for that rambling?'

'I don't see what this changes about it.'

'Great. I'll grab a shower, then call Branna. It's early, and she'll be less cranky with another fifteen minutes' sleep.'

'I'll put the kettle on.'

But he picked up his phone first and, while she ran the shower, punched in Fin's number. He'd sooner know what Fin had to say before he fried up the bacon.

15

It was the country of her blood, and as she watched it rise and fall and spread outside the truck window, Iona understood it was the country of her heart.

It settled into her like a sip of whiskey on a cold night, warm and comforting. Green hills rolled under a sky layered with clouds, stacked like sheets of linen. The sun shimmered through them, making intermittent swirls of blue luminous as opals. Fat cows and woolly sheep dotted emerald fields bisected with rough hedgerows or silvery gray rock walls.

Farmhouses, barns, pretty little cottages scattered over the land with postcard charm as the road twisted and curved. Dooryard gardens reached for spring, with brave blooms opening in wild blues, sassy oranges, delicate whites, topped here and there by the heralding trumpets of daffodils.

She would have spring in Ireland, Iona thought, the first of a lifetime. And like those brave flowers, she determined to bloom.

The road might turn, curve out like a tunnel with high, high hedgerows of wild fuchsia hugging the sides of the twists, the turns with their blooms dripping like drops of blood. Then the world opened again to the hills, the fields, and, thrillingly, the shadows of mountains.

'How do you stand it?' Iona wondered. 'Doesn't it constantly dazzle your eyes, take your breath, make your heart ache?'

'It's home,' Boyle said simply. 'There's nowhere I'd rather be. It suits me.'

'Oh, me, too.' And finally, she thought, she felt she suited it.

The wind kicked, and a splatter of rain struck the windshield. Then the sun ran behind it to turn the drops into tiny rainbows.

Magick, Iona thought, simple and mysterious.

As was Ballintubber Abbey.

Its clean lines lent a quiet dignity to the old gray stone. It made its home on pretty grounds backed with fields of sheep spread before the green hills, the loom of mountains.

Simple grandeur, she thought, finding the oxymoron the perfect description of the ancient and the life going quietly on around it. She climbed out of the truck to study the pathways, the gardens defying winter's last shivers, and smiled as the breeze carried the baaing of sheep.

She thought she could sit on the grass and spend an entire day happily just looking, just listening.

'I suppose you'll be wanting the history of the place.'

She'd read some of it in her guide, but enjoyed the idea of Boyle giving her his take.

'I wouldn't mind.'

'Well, it was Conchobair who built it – Cathal Mor of the wine-red hand, of the O'Connor clan, so he'd be one of yours.'

'Oh. Of course.' How deep her blood ran here, she thought. And how marvelous was that? 'Like

Ashford, before the Burkes won it.'

'There you are. Back in 1216 it was. I know the date, as they're after restoring the east wing, I think it is, for its eight-hundred-year celebration. And so the legend – or one of them – says while Cathal was the son of King Turloch, he was forced to flee from Turloch's queen, and spend some time laboring and in hiding before he took the throne. And there was a man who treated him kindly, and Cathal, now king, asked him what he could do to repay him. It was a church that the man, now old, wanted, in Ballintubber, and so Cathal ordered it built.'

They walked the path as he told the tale, with his voice rising and falling on the words, the sheep baaing their chorus. Ridiculously happy, Iona took Boyle's hand to link them, to seal the moments.

'After some years, the king saw the old man again, and was scolded for not keeping his word. It seems the church had been built right enough, but in Roscommon.'

Laughing, Iona looked up at him. 'Oops.'

'So you could say. But Cathal ordered another church built, and it came to be Ballintubber Abbey.'

'A man of his word.'

'So it's said.'

'I like knowing I have a grateful and honest king in my ancestry.'

'And it's a lasting legacy, as it's said to be the only church in Ireland founded by an Irish king and still in use.'

'I think that's wonderful. People too often knock down the old for the new instead of understanding

284

that legacy.'

'What comes before now matters,' he said simply. 'Pierce Brosnan was married here a few years back, and that's been a newer claim to fame. Older it's the start of Tórchar Phádraig.'

'The pilgrimage route to Saint Patrick's mountain. I've read about that.'

'It's also said Seán na Sagart, who was a nefarious priest hunter, is buried in the cemetery here. There.' Boyle lifted his hand to point to a large tree. 'So it's said.'

'It's a good place. Clean, powerful. And I feel this recognition somewhere deep, this connection. Is that weird?'

He only shrugged. 'Your blood built it.'

'So you made it our first stop.' Smiling, she leaned her head against his arm. 'Thanks.' She glanced down at an old, pitted stone and its carving. 'The Crowning?'

'Oh well, they've more than the abbey, and the graves and such. That's part of the Stations. They've added that, a Rosary Walk, and over there, a little cave that's fashioned as a stable, for the Nativity. It's a bit odd.'

'It's wonderful.' Tugging his hand she followed the path, finding other stones and markers among the trim and pretty gardens. 'It's so abstract, so contemporary, and a really creative contrast against the antiquity.'

She paused at a little stream, its bank blanketed with low, spreading bushes as it rose to rough stones. Three crosses topped it to represent the Crucifixion.

'It should be sad, and I know it should be

reverent. It is, but it's more ... compelling. And then this.' She stepped into the cave to look over the statues of Mary, Joseph, the Baby Jesus. 'It's wonderful, too – sweet and a little kitschy. I think Cathal would like what's been done.'

'He's made no objections that I know of.'

They went inside, and there she found hushed reverence.

'The Cromwellians set fire to the place,' Boyle told her. 'You can see from the ruins outside the monastery that the quarters and such fell. But the church stood, and still does. The baptismal area there, they say, is a thousand years old.'

'It's comforting, isn't it, to know the things we build can survive. It's beautiful. The stained glass, the stone.'

The way her footsteps echoed in the quiet only added to the atmosphere.

'You know a lot about it,' she commented. 'Did you study up?'

'Didn't have to. I had an uncle worked here on some of the repairs and improvements.'

'So my blood built it, and yours helped keep it. That's another connection.'

'True enough. And I've had two cousins and a couple of mates married here, so I've been around and about it a few times.'

'It's a good place for a wedding. The continuity, the care, the respect. And the romance – tales of kings and priest hunters, Cromwellians and James Bond.'

He laughed at that, but she only smiled. She felt something here. A kinship, a recognition, and now a kind of knowing.

She'd come here before, she realized, or her blood had come.

To sit, perhaps, in that quiet reverence.

'Candles and flowers, light and scent. And music. Women in pretty dresses and handsome men.' She wandered again, painting it in her mind. 'A fretful baby being soothed, a shuffle of feet. Joy, anticipation, and love making a promise. Yes, it's a good place for a wedding.'

She wanted it for hers, this place of age and contrast and endurance.

She went back to him, took his hand again. 'Promises made here would matter, and they'd hold, if the ones making them believed it.'

Back outside she wandered the ruins, brushing her fingers over old stone, moved through the cemetery where the long dead rested.

She took pictures to mark the day and, though he grumbled about it, persuaded Boyle to pose with her as she took a self-portrait with her cell phone.

'I'll send it to my Nan,' she told him. 'She'll get a kick out of seeing...'

'What is it?'

'I... The light. Do you see it?' She held out the phone to him.

On the screen they posed with her head tipped to his shoulder. She smiled, easy, and Boyle more soberly.

And light, white as candle wax, surrounded them.

'The angle maybe. A flash from the sun.'

'You know it's not.'

'It's not, no,' he admitted.

'It's this place,' she murmured. 'Founded by my blood, kept by yours – that's part of it. It's a good place, a strong place. A safe one. I think they came here, the three. And others that came from them. Now me. I feel … welcome here. It's a good light, Boyle. It's good magick.'

She took his hand, studying the back of it where dark magick had spilled blood.

'Connor said it was clean,' he reminded her.

'Yeah. Light banishes shadows. Meara was right about that.' Still holding his hand, she looked into his eyes. 'But like promises made, the light has to believe it.'

'And do you?'

'I do.' She lifted her free hand to his face, rose on her toes to brush her lips to his.

She believed it. Deep down in her belly she carried faith and resolve. And her heart came to accept what she understood as she'd walked with him along the paths and tidy gardens that opened for spring, among the spirits and the legends, into the promise kept by one of hers.

She loved. At last. Loved as she'd always hoped. He was her once in a lifetime. And with him she had to learn patience, and hold only to that faith as well. The faith that he would love as she loved.

She put on her best smile. 'What's next?'

'Well there's the Ross Abbey. Actually, it's a friary. Ross Errilly. It's not far, and you'd probably like to poke about in it.'

'Bring it on.'

She glanced around as they walked to the truck, and knew she'd come back. Maybe to walk the Stations or just stand in the breeze and look out at the fields.

She'd come back, as her blood had come.

But now, as he drove away, she looked forward.

She saw it from the road, the foreboding mass of it, its peaks and tower and rambling walls. Under the thick sky it looked like something out of an old movie where creatures who shuffled in the dark hid and plotted.

She couldn't wait to get a closer look.

The truck bumped down a skinny track with pretty little houses on one side, laced with gardens with blooms testing the chill. The other side of the track spread with fields loaded with cows and sheep.

Ahead, beyond the tidy and pastoral, loomed the ruins.

'I didn't study up,' he told her. 'But I know it's old, of course – not as old as the abbey, but old for all that.'

She walked toward it, heard the whistle of the wind through the peaks and jut of stone, and the flapping of wings from birds, the lowing of cattle.

The central tower speared up above the roofless walls.

She stepped inside a doorway, and now her feet crunched on gravel.

Vaults for the dead, or stones for them fixed flat into the ground.

'I think the Brits kicked out the monks, as they were wont, then, as *they* were wont, the Cromwellians did the rest and sacked the place. Pillaged and burned.'

'It's massive.' She stepped through an arch, looking up at the tower and the black birds that circled it.

The air felt heavy – rain to come, she decided. Wind blew through the arched windows, whistled down the narrow curve of stone steps.

'This must've been the kitchen.' She didn't like the way her voice echoed, but moved closer to look down in what seemed to be some sort of dry well. 'Stand over there.' She gestured to the ox-roasting fireplace.

He shuffled his feet, gave her a pained look. 'I'm not much for pictures.'

'Indulge me. It's a big fireplace. You're a big guy.'

She snapped her pictures. 'They'd butcher their own meat, grow their own vegetables, mill flour. Keep fish in the well there. The Franciscans.' She wandered out, even at her height ducking under archways, to an open area.

A line of archways, gravestones, grass. 'The cloister. Quiet thoughts, robes, and folded hands. They looked so pious, but some had humor, others ambition. Envy, greed, lust, even here.'

'Iona.'

But she moved on, stopped at the base of steps where a Christ figure had been carved in the arch. 'Symbols are important. The Christians followed the pagans there, carving and painting their one God as the old ones carved and painted the many. Neither understand that the one is part of the many, the many part of the one.'

Wind fluttered through her hair as she stepped out on a narrow balustrade. Boyle took her arm in a firm grip.

'I died here, or my blood did. It feels the same.

Breaking the journey home, too old, too ill to continue on. Some would burn the witch, such is the time, but her power's gone quiet, and they take her in. She wears the symbol, but they don't know what it means. The copper horse.'

Iona's hand closed over her amulet. 'But he knows. He smells her weakness. He waits, but must come to her. She can't finish the journey. And she feels him nearing, greedy for what she has left. He has less than he did, but enough. Still enough. She has no choice now, it can't be done in the place of her power, at the source. He's whispering. Can you hear him?'

'Come away now.'

She turned. Her eyes had gone nearly black. 'It's not done, and it must be done. She has her granddaughter – such love between them, and the power simmers in the young. She passes what she has, as the first did, as her own father had done with her, and with the power, she passes on the symbol. A burden, a stone in the heart. It's always been that for her, never with joy to balance it. So she passes power and symbol with grief.

'And the rooks flap their wings. The wolf howls on the hill. The fog creeps along the ground. She speaks her last words.'

Iona's voice rose, carried over the wind – in Irish. Above the layered clouds something rumbled that might have been thunder, might have been power waking. The circling birds swooped away with frightened calls, leaving only sky and stone.

'The bells tolled as if they knew,' she continued. 'Though the girl wept, she felt the power rise up – hot and white. Strong, young, vital, and fierce. So he was denied what he craved yet again. And again, and again, he waits.'

Iona's eyes rolled back. When she swayed, Boyle dragged her in close.

'I have to leave here,' she said weakly.

'Bloody right.' He plucked her off her feet, carried her down the narrow, curving stairs, through archways where he nearly bent double to pass through, and out again into the air and the patter of rain.

The wet felt like heaven on her cheeks. 'I'm okay. Just a little dizzy. I don't know what happened.'

'A vision. I've seen Connor caught in one.'

'I could see them, the old woman, the girl, bathing her grandmother's face. Fever, she was so hot, like she was burning from the inside out. I could hear them, and him. I could hear him trying to get to her, trying to draw her out. I felt her pain, physical and emotional. She wished, so much, she could spare the girl she loved from the risk and responsibility. But there wasn't a choice, and there wasn't time.'

He shifted her to open the truck door, maneuvered her inside, amazed his hands didn't shake to mimic his heart.

'You spoke in Irish.'

'I did?' Iona shoved at her hair. 'I can't remember, not exactly. What did I say?'

'I'm not sure of it all. "You're the one, but there must be three." And I think...' He struggled with the translation. '"It ends here for me, begins for you." Something like that, and more I couldn't understand. Your eyes went black as a raven's, and your skin pale as death.'

'My eyes.'

'They're back,' he assured her, stroked her cheek. 'Blue as summer.'

'I need more training. It's like trying to compete in the Olympics when you're still learning how to change leads and gaits. And that's a potent place, full of energy and power.'

He'd been there before, felt nothing but some curiosity. But this time, with her...

'It hooked to you,' he decided. 'Or you to it.'

'Or she did, the old woman. She's buried in there. One day we should come back, one day when this is finished, and leave flowers on her grave.'

At the moment he wasn't inclined to bring her back ever. But as he walked around to get in the truck, the rain stopped.

'Look.' She took his hand, pointed with the other at the rainbow that glimmered behind the ruins. 'Light wins.'

She smiled and meant it and, thinking rainbows, leaned over to kiss him.

'I'm starving.'

He didn't think at all, but pulled her in again to kiss her until the image of her swaying on the ledge faded away. 'I know a place not far that does a fine fish and chips. And Christ knows I could do with a pint.'

'That's what I'm talking about. Thanks,' she added.

'For what?'

'For showing me two amazing places, and for catching me before I fell.'

She looked back at the friary, at the black birds, at the rainbow. Her life had forever changed, she thought. But unlike her ancestor, she considered it a gift.

In the cozy kitchen with the hound at her feet and a fire in the hearth, Iona told her cousins everything.

'A busy day for you,' Connor commented.

'And then some.'

'That would be three events, we'll call them, in a single day.' Branna, her hair still bundled up from her workday, contemplated her tea. 'But only the first involving Cabhan.'

'The last one, too,' Iona reminded her. 'She felt him coming.'

'A vision of the past. Whether yours or another's, still the past. I doubt he'd venture so far now.' Branna looked at Connor.

'Not now, no, and why should he? Tell me what you were feeling – before, during, after the vision came on you.'

'Before I'm not sure. I felt I'd been there before, like the abbey, but not ... bright, not happy like that. It was dark and, well, sorrowful. I knew the layout, what things were, but I realize now it was her, our ancestor. I was thinking her thoughts, and some were pretty damn bitter. She knew she was dying, but more than death she hated passing the amulet, the power, the responsibility on to her granddaughter.

'I don't remember going up the steps. It seemed I was just there. The old woman in bed, gray hair streaked with white. Her face gray, too, and shiny with fever. And the girl sitting beside her, bathing her face. Long red hair. Eimear – I think she called the young girl Eimear.'

'You don't remember the Irish you spoke,' Connor prompted her.

'No, just what Boyle thought it meant, or what he understood of it. I remember sorrow and fear, then the light just bursting into the room. For an instant, a sense of power – just wild, huge. Like a, well, like a really excellent orgasm. Then it all went gray, and spinning. Dizzy, weak, disoriented, and when that passed, hungry.'

'The dizziness will ease after a time,' Connor told her. 'It's good you weren't alone when you had your first. You weren't expecting this then?' he asked Branna.

'Not yet, no. Not yet. I want to say she's – you're,' she corrected, and addressed Iona directly, 'accelerating. I think it's where you are, and who you're with. We're three together, so what you have is coming ripe more quickly than it might otherwise. It's a good thing, this. You'll be stronger, less vulnerable.'

'Should I expect any more surprises?'

'You'll take them as they come.'

'Let's backtrack a minute. The dream. Did Boyle and I share the dream because we were together?'

'The sex.' Connor leaned back, shot his legs out. 'It's a powerful link. Or can be.'

'So if I have sex with Boyle he can get dragged in with me? But it hurt him. His hand. The poison.'

'Which you tended to well. That's good instinct.'

'But the next time it could be worse.'

'You take it as it comes,' Branna reminded her. 'Cabhan hurt him, but Boyle hurt Cabhan as well. Cabhan felt the blow – a human blow and in a dream – and that's interesting to me.'

'It was black, mixed in Boyle's blood. I could see it. If it had spread before–'

'It didn't,' Branna said briskly. 'We deal with what is. You can't cloud what is with what-if, and the emotions.'

'She loves him.' Connor rubbed a hand over Iona's when she jolted. 'Love clouds everything and shines through it as well.'

'I never said I... How do you know what I just figured out?'

'It's coming through you so strong I can't avoid seeing it.' He gave her hand another rub. 'I don't mean to peek through the door, but it's wide open.'

'I haven't said anything to him.' Couldn't and shouldn't, she thought, reminding herself of her vow to be patient. 'I'm just sort of savoring it. I've wanted to feel this way for so long, tried to feel this way. And with Boyle I didn't have to want or try. I just did.'

'That's all well and good, and sure he's one of the best men I know. But you can't let what you have filter through the haze of love,' Branna warned.

'We have different ways of thinking on that,' Connor put in. 'I think love only adds to the power. Where she is, yes,' he said to Branna. 'And being with us. But I'm thinking what she feels is another reason she's gaining so fast. How she knew the poison was in Boyle, and how she drew it out so clean, when she'd never done the like before.'

'I won't argue. It's different for everyone, isn't it? Love, magick, and how we see and deal. And in each, the choices we make. I'll only say you've had but a short time here, and with him, to think of love and the choices that go with it.'

'I knew the minute I saw him. Maybe that was a kind of vision. I don't know. But I felt this flutter.' She pressed a hand to her belly. 'And this rising.' Slid her hand to her heart. 'Attraction, I told myself, because he looked so amazing riding in on Alastar. But it was more. I told myself I couldn't go there because, well, at first I thought he was with Meara.'

She lifted her eyebrows when Connor let out a laughing snort.

'I don't know why that's so funny. They're gorgeous together. Tall and fit and stunning. And they have this connection – it was clear from the start.'

'Sure like Branna and me, for they're as close as brother and sister, and never been otherwise. But you thought they were more, so you pushed aside what you felt or might have felt. That's to your credit. Not all would do the same. I'm wondering if I would myself.'

'Love at first sight's a fairy tale,' Branna said, firmly.

'I love fairy tales.' With a laugh, Iona propped her elbows on the table, her face on her fists. 'I decided it was just attraction, and okay once Meara set me straight. I decided I just wanted to sleep with him, but I've never felt what I feel for him. And I know what it is, and I know it started when I saw him riding up on Alastar, both of them so fierce and furious. I fell for both of them right then and there. I'm trying to be patient, which isn't my nature at all. Alastar figured out he loved me. Now I just have to wait for Boyle to figure it out.'

'You're confident he will?' Branna asked her.

'You can't just hope for happy endings. You have to believe in them. Then do the work, take the risks. Slay the dragon – though I really think dragons get a bad rap – kiss the princess, or the frog, defeat the bad witch.'

'Well defeating the bad witch is happy ending enough for me.'

It shouldn't be, Iona thought, but Connor gave her hand a little squeeze before she said it.

'I've things to see to, but later on, after dinner,' Branna continued, 'we'll practice again. Connor can help you with the visions, the healing. The solstice comes closer every day, and there's still work to be done.'

'You have an idea what to do?'

'You said Boyle hurt him, in a dream, and with only a fist. We can do better than a fist.'

'I've got to go back to the school, check on some hatchlings. But I'll be home within the hour.'

'I'll walk with you,' Iona told Connor. 'I'd like to give Alastar some exercise, even if it's just around the jumps course.'

'Then I'll come back by, walk home with you.'

'I can probably get a ride, but if not, I'll text you.'

'Fine then, go off with both of you, give me some thinking time.' Branna pushed back from the table. 'You said Fin was to do a protection charm for Boyle's bed. Make sure he has before the two of you make use of it again.'

'Okay.'

'The next time you, or any of us, go into a dream, I want it to be a choice, and us doing the pulling in.'

16

Iona changed into riding boots, and took ten seconds to put on some lip gloss in case she ran into Boyle. They both had obligations that evening – his paperwork, her spell casting – but she hoped to talk him into a ride after work the next day, maybe a casual dinner out, then a cozy night in, at his place.

Outside, she hooked her arm through Connor's. The air might have blown cool and damp, but spring rode with it and nudged the blackthorn into bloom.

'Have you ever been in love?' she asked him.

'Sure countless times, and never the way you mean. Though my heart's been bruised and bumped, never has it been broken.'

'I had the bumps, too, and some bruises. When I was in high school, I actively wished for actual heartache, just to know what it felt like. I always wanted those big feelings, you know? The rush and the fall. What I got was mostly even ground. Settling for someone I knew was settling for me. It makes you feel forever mediocre.'

'And now?'

'Now I feel powerful, purposeful.' She circled her fingers, made tiny lights dance. 'Joyful.'

'And all look good on you.'

'Do you want to? Fall in love?'

'Sure one day. She'll walk into the room, beautiful and brilliant, a sexual goddess with the mind of a scholar and an angel's temperament. She'll cook like my aunt Fiona, who can't be equaled in the kitchen, match me pint for pint at the pub, and like little better than to go hawking with me.'

'You don't ask much.'

His eyes, green as the moss, twinkled at her. 'Why not ask for all, as you never know what life's going to hand you?'

'Good point,' she said, and made another dance of lights.

In the stables Boyle brushed Darling as much to soothe himself as to groom her. He'd sent his stable hands home a bit early, as he'd coveted a little time alone. Now, with the sweet mare for company in the quiet stables, he could roll through all the things crowding his mind.

There were bills to pay and orders to make, and he'd get to all that, wouldn't he? He had all evening for that, as he needed.

Wanted, he corrected.

A man needed time and space of his own without a woman expecting his attention.

So he shouldn't be thinking about going by and

scooping her up so she'd be in his time and space.

If anything, once the paperwork was seen to, he should take some of that time to think about all that had happened that day.

He'd have to tell Fin the whole of it, of course, and would whenever Fin got back. They'd talk it out over a pint, so there was no room for Iona, even if he was inclined for her.

Which he was, all the damn time.

What the hell did it mean when a man couldn't keep a woman out of his space, much less his mind?

Bewitched is what he was, by blue eyes and an easy laugh, and a pretty body he couldn't keep his bloody hands off of. And that utter faith in the good and the happy that lived inside her, though he understood, more and more, how little of either she'd had.

Finding himself wanting to give her the good and the happy troubled him more than a little. Hadn't he planned out the entire day with the goal of giving her just that? Not that it had worked out in all cases, considering dark visions and a scare that had near stopped his heart. But he'd planned it all, with her in mind.

Always in his mind, she was.

It was time to remind himself that what a man needed, when it came down to it, was room, work, a good horse, and a pint at the end of a hard day.

'That's it, isn't it, Darling? We've got what counts right here.'

In the next stall Alastar snorted and blew.

'I'm not after talking to you, am I? Bad-tempered beast.'

'And you'd know about that,' Fin said from behind him. 'What are you brooding about, brother?'

The man could sneak up on a body, Boyle thought, like smoke from a flue. 'Who says I'm brooding?'

'I do.' Fin reached out, stroked Darling's neck. 'Sent the men off early, did you?'

'A bit. Everything's done needs doing today.'

'I thought you'd be out rambling still with Iona.'

'We did enough, maybe more than.'

'Trouble then? Of a personal sort or a magickal sort?'

'Both, I'm thinking. It started early this morning, as you know, when I shared a dream with her and came to blows with that cursed bastard.'

'You had more trouble from that?'

When Fin gripped his shoulder, Boyle just kept brushing the horse. 'Nothing serious or lasting. So I'll tell you the rest.'

And he did, from the beginning, right on through to when he carried Iona out of the friary. Only grunted when Fin grabbed his hand.

'I told you she fixed it, and Connor had a look as well.'

'I'll look for myself now.' Once he did, Fin nodded, let Boyle's hand go. 'You said you hurt him. You're sure of it now that some time's passed and you've thought it through?'

Boyle curled his hand into a fist. 'I know when I land a blow, mate.'

'Aye, you would.' Fin paced away and back again. 'I've given it some thought, and we'll use that; I'll think on it more, but use it we will. And I've a protection charm for you before you turn in for the night. Is she coming by?'

'She's not, no. I need a night to myself, don't I? I've work, and I've thinking of my own to do without being crowded.'

Fin lifted an eyebrow at the tone. 'Had a row?'

'We did not. After I carted her out of the cursed friary, she packed away fish and chips like a starving woman. I took her around to Clew Bay, as she wanted to see the water, then she spotted more ruins, another graveyard, so she wandered about, but there was nothing for her there like the other places. And that was a relief.'

'She handles it well, for someone coming into it later than most.'

'I suppose she does, and it's a lot on her plate for all her appetite. And it makes me wonder.'

Fin gestured an opening. 'Wonder away.'

'I want her here, even when I don't. Or I think I don't, then I do.' The words sounded mad to his own ears, but he couldn't stop them now that he'd started. 'And I never have much liked women in my place, as they tend to fuss or leave things behind, or bring little bits over, look to change the order of things.'

'Hmm. And does she?'

'She doesn't, and that's suspect, isn't it?' Boyle jabbed a finger in the air as if his point had been made.

'So if she does those things, she's encroaching. If she doesn't, she's suspect? *Mo dearthair*, you're acting the gom.'

'I'm not.' Insulted, Boyle rounded on Fin. 'It's

not being a fool to wonder if she'd got some plan under there. She talked of weddings, mind you. Of a wedding at Ballintubber Abbey.'

'Which it's famed for. Did she propose to you then, along the Stations? I'm seeing no ring on your finger or through your nose.'

'Smirk if you must, but I'm wondering. I think about her too much. 'Tisn't comfortable. When I have her in bed it's like nothing else ever was. No one else. So I end up staying, or having her stay, and then there's breakfast, and on to work. I have to work, don't I? And she's pushed into my mind even then. It's fucking annoying now that I say it out loud.'

'I can see that. It has to be a trial to you, having a woman as pretty as a spring morning, and as fresh and sweet, taking up your time and attention.'

'I've a life to live, don't I?' Boyle snapped back, as every word Fin spoke made him, well, feel as if he acted the gom. 'And a right to like that life just as it is – was – before.'

'Sure as I'm standing here I'd trade places with you if I could, to have a woman in my mind and heart who was pleased and willing to have me in hers. But you have, of course, every right to live your life without a sweet and fresh and pretty woman in it.'

'She's more than that, as well you know. I've never seen the like of her, and I've seen you, Branna, Connor. But when it's on her, I've never seen the like. It takes my breath. I don't know why that is.'

'I've a speculation on it.'

Boyle mimicked Fin's gesture. 'Speculate away.'

'You sound like a man in love to me.'

'Oh sure and that's helpful.' Boyle resisted throwing the brush only because it would startle Darling. 'I'm telling you, she's pushed herself into my mind, my life, my bed so I've barely a minute to myself. I took a day off work, which I don't do, as you know, to drive her all around Mayo and Galway. I can't get away from her even when I'm sleeping.

'I think she's bewitched me.'

'Oh Christ Jesus, Boyle.'

But Boyle had the bit between his teeth now. 'She's come into it late, as you said, and she's full of the power of it. So she's done a love spell to wrap me up this way.'

'Bollocks. Even if she were inclined, and I don't see it, Branna would never allow it.'

'Branna doesn't know everything,' Boyle muttered, and glanced over darkly as Alastar kicked the wall of the stall. 'She's new to it, Iona is, testing her footing so to speak. She's testing it on me so I'm tangled up taking walks and rides and drives and fixing her breakfast after a night of her sleeping wrapped around me like a vine. So if she's put a love spell on me, you need to break it.'

'Is that what you think?' Very quietly, Iona stepped up to the stall. 'I'm sorry but you were too busy shouting to hear me come in. What a lot you think of yourself, Boyle, and how little you think of me.'

'Iona—'

She stepped back, chin jerking up. 'Do you really think I'm so weak, so sad, so pitiful that I'd

305

want someone who didn't want me of their own free will? That I'd use magick to enchant you into spending time with me, having feelings for me?'

'No. I'm only trying to work it out.'

'Work.' Her eyes filled, killing him, but the tears didn't come. 'Yeah, I know it's so much work to care about me. So I'll make it easy for you. There's no need, and there's no spell. I have too much respect for what I am to use it in such a small, selfish way. And I love you too much to ever use you at all.'

Every word came as a jab to his heart. 'Come upstairs now, we'll talk this through.'

'There's nothing else for me to say, and I really don't want to talk to you now.' Deliberately, she turned away from him. 'Fin, could you give me a ride home?'

'I'll take you myself–' Boyle began.

'You won't. No, you won't. I don't want to be with you. I can call Connor if you can't take me, Fin.'

'Of course I can.'

'You're not just walking away after–'

'Watch me.' She shot him a look so full of both devastation and fury, he said nothing more when she turned and walked away.

'Let it be for now,' Fin said quietly, 'and use some of this famous time and space to learn how to do a proper grovel.'

'Ah, fuck me.'

'And so you have.' He hurried out after Iona, reached down to open the car door for her.

'He's never felt like this for anyone,' he began.

'Don't try to smooth it over, please. If you

could do me one favor, just don't say anything. Anything at all. I just want to go home.'

He did exactly as she asked, kept his silence on the short drive. He could feel her pain. It seemed to pulse from her, sharpen the air in the car so keenly he thought it a wonder it didn't draw blood.

Love, as he knew too well, could slice you to pieces and leave no visible scar.

He pulled up at the cottage, smoke curling from the chimney, an amazing array of colorful flowers twinkling in the evening gloom. And somewhere inside, Branna, as distant as the moon.

'Should I come in with you?'

'No. Thanks for bringing me home.'

When she started to get out, he simply touched her hand. 'You're not hard to love, *deirfiúr bheag*, but for some, loving is strange and boggy ground.'

'He can be careful where he steps.' Though her lips quivered, she managed an even tone. 'But he can't blame someone else for where he ends up.'

'You'd be right. I'm sorry you heard what was—'

'Don't apologize. It's better to see and know you're a fool than to keep your eyes shut and keep acting like one.'

She got out quickly. He waited until she'd gone in the house before driving away. He half wished he was in love with her himself, and could show her what it was to be cherished.

But as that wasn't an option, and it likely wasn't wise to go home and pound on Boyle's rock-hard head with a hammer, he'd go by and fetch Connor. They'd sit down with a bottle of whiskey, the three of them, and as good mates would, get

Boyle drunk instead.

Iona went straight in. She had no intention of crying on Branna's or anyone else's shoulder. She had no intention of crying at all. What she intended to do was hang on to the anger, and that would see her through the worst of it.

So she went straight in, and straight back to the kitchen where Branna sat at the table with her enormous spell book with its carved and well-tended brown leather binding, an iPad, a note-book, and several keenly sharpened pencils.

Branna glanced up, cocked her head in question. 'What, did you just go, turn around and come back?'

'Yep. I'm having a really big glass of wine,' she said as she walked to the cabinet. 'Do you want one?'

Now Branna's eyebrows drew together. 'I wouldn't say no. What happened? Did you have another encounter with Cabhan?'

'Not everything is about Cabhan and ancient fricking evil.' True to her word, she poured an enormous glass of wine, then a more sedate one for her cousin.

'Well now, here's a mood that's come on in under twenty minutes. Wasn't your horse happy to see you then?'

'I never got to Alastar, which is just one more thing I can be pissed about. I never saw my horse, never got my ride.' She handed Branna the glass, tapped her own to it. 'Bloody *sláinte*.'

When Iona flopped down at the table, Branna took a sip of wine, studied her cousin over the rim. Anger, yes, but hurt besides. Deliberately she kept her voice breezy.

'Not Cabhan or the horse, so what does that leave? Let me see, could it be Boyle?'

'Could be and is. I walked into the stables when he was ranting to Fin about how inconvenient it is for him to have me around all the time, in his space. In his way, in his bed. Wrapped around him like a vine in his words.'

'He's an idiot, and I hope you gave him a solid boot for it. Men can be loathsome creatures, especially when they put their heads together.'

'Oh, there's more, as if that wasn't bad enough. He's decided since I've managed to push my way into his life, his head, his bed, I've put a love spell on him.'

'Bollocks to that!' The sympathy Branna tried to keep mild erupted in stunned insult. 'He must've been joking, just having it on with Fin who likely teased him a bit.'

'He wasn't joking, Branna. He was furious, shouting. He didn't even hear me come in. When I did he was saying – loudly – that he barely has any time to himself the way I've pushed myself on him, and I'd put a love spell on him. I'm new at all this, and testing the waters, and decided to test them on him with a love spell. He told Fin to break it.'

'What a pair of right gobdaws.'

'I don't know what that means, but it sounds insulting, so good. Except not Fin. He said bollocks to that, too.'

'I'm pleased to hear that at least. Now we won't be turning him into a slug and drowning him in beer.'

Iona tried to laugh, but it kept catching. 'It's a good word *bollocks*, I'm going to start using it a lot. Bollocks, bollocks, bollocks.'

Her eyes filled, her throat burned. So she shook her head, gulped wine. 'No, no, no. I am *not* going to cry. I have to stay mad so I won't.'

'Did you speak to Boyle, or just turn his penis into a warty little stub?'

'I spoke with him.' Iona swiped at the single tear that got through. 'I let him know I had too much respect for myself to use magick to get someone to want me. To love me. He tried to make excuses, but bollocks to that, right? I asked Fin to bring me back, and he did. He was kind.'

He could be, Branna thought, enormously kind. To some. 'Then I'm glad he was there. I won't make excuses for Boyle. What he said was a harsh and unwarranted insult to those like you and me. And more, it's hurtful because you have such strong feelings for him. I'll only say that while he's got a black temper at times, and is in the way of being, well, gruff's a simple word for it, at other times, I've never known him to hurt anyone like this. It's my thinking he's taken considerably aback by his feelings for you.'

'He doesn't want them. I'm not going to cry over someone who doesn't want feelings for me. I may get a little drunk, but I'm not going to cry about it.'

'A sensible attitude.' Branna's phone jingled. 'It's Connor. Give me a moment. And where are you?' she said into the phone by way of greeting. 'Right here, yes. No, we could do without you, you being a man for all that. That's best, that's

310

fine. And when I want your fine advice, I'll be asking for it. Go on, be jackasses together, and you can tell Boyle he can count his luck I don't make that literal.'

She clicked off. 'Fin went by the school for Connor. I've told him, as you gathered, to go on, as men can just jam things up. I've a mind to ring up Meara, unless you'd rather I didn't. We can sit around, drink more wine, and say all the rude and truthful things about men without any of them around.'

'That'd be great. Really. But you're working.'

'I'll get back to it.'

'You feel sorry for me.'

'A poor sort I'd be if I didn't. But I'm pissed right along with you, for you, myself, and every other self-respecting witch, and every self-respecting woman. Love spell, my arse.'

When Connor and Fin walked into Fin's house, Boyle paced the living room.

'What took you so bloody long,' he began, then spotted Connor. 'Ah, well. Before you jump up my arse I never knew she was there, and was just having a bit of a rant. I'm entitled to have a bit of a rant in my own stables.'

'One question, before we go any further on the matter.' Connor held up a single finger. 'Are you saying Iona used magick to trap you – a love spell?'

'I said it, as you bloody well know, but I'm not saying it. I was blowing off, is all. Or mostly all.'

'Do you think she used magick on you?'

'No, not when I–'

'No's enough for now,' Connor told him. 'No

311

means I'm not obliged to plant my fist in your face, the result of which would be you kicking the living shit out of me, and I'd rather have a beer. Bugger it, Boyle, you know what we're about, and what's over a line for us. You should know the same of Iona.'

'I do. But it's... Well, fuck it, have a swing. I won't hit back as I earned it.'

'There's no satisfaction in punching under those conditions.'

'I'll do it,' Fin volunteered.

'You're not her cousin,' Boyle shot back, then threw up his hands. Jutted out his chin. 'Go on then, have a go.'

Fin only smiled. 'I'll save that offer, and have that go when you least expect it.'

'Why didn't I think of that?' Connor shrugged out of his jacket. 'I want the beer, then you can tell me how you plan to fix this up with Iona.'

'If she'd just be reasonable—'

'That's not the way, mate.' Connor dropped down on the big leather couch. 'Any crisps to go with the beer?'

'I'll take care of it. There's steaks, and Boyle can do the cooking in a bit,' Fin decided. 'To practice being humble and apologetic.'

'Look here.' Boyle sat down, leaned forward. 'You asked if I meant it, right? I said I didn't, and that's that. Reasonable.'

'And you expect her to be the same?'

'I was blowing off,' Boyle insisted. 'When she's calmed herself I'll tell her I was just, what do you call it, venting, and didn't mean anything by it. That's all.'

Connor said nothing for a moment, then glanced over as Fin came back with bottles of Smithwick's and a bag of potato chips.

'I know he's been around and with women before,' Connor said conversationally. 'I've seen that for myself, and met some of them as well. But if I didn't know better I'd swear an oath the man had just crawled out of a cave full grown without having any female contact whatsoever.'

'Ah, feck off.'

'Groveling.' Fin tossed the beers, one to Connor, one to Boyle, dropped down on the sofa, propped his feet on the oversized coffee table he'd found on his travels.

'I'm not doing that.'

'*Mo dearthair*, I wager you will before it's done. I've a hundred I'll put on it. He's mad for her,' he said to Connor.

'Sure that's one more reason he'll make a complete bags of it.'

'I should go talk to her now, get it done and finished.'

'I wouldn't advise it.' Connor grabbed a handful of chips. 'She's with Branna, and my sister isn't too pleased with you at the moment. I reckon she'll pull Meara in, so that'll be all the three of them sending hard thoughts, at the least of it, your way.'

'Well, Jesus, I can't go about fixing anything if she won't talk to me, and she's being guarded by a witch and a woman with a tongue as sharp as a razor.'

'Resign yourself to stewing in it tonight, and maybe a day or two more,' Fin advised. 'After that

'... I'm thinking flowers won't do the trick here.'

Connor washed down the chips with beer. 'She's a romantic soul, our Iona, but flowers are paltry considering the insult.'

'I didn't insult her,' Boyle began, then swore bitterly before gulping down beer. 'All right then, I did. I admit it. Admitting a wrong and apologizing ought to be enough.'

Fin slid down to a slouch. 'I'm forced to agree with you, Connor, though it pains me, about the cave. She's not a man, brother, and you don't handle her as one with a sorry, mate. I'll stand you a round. Flowers, as she's romantic, and something with some shine to it to show you understand the depth of your mistake.'

Astonished, Boyle shot straight up in his chair. 'Now I'm buying her jewelry just for blowing off when she wasn't even meant to be there? I'll not do it.' A man had his pride, and his spine, didn't he? 'It's nothing but a bribe.'

'Think of it more as an investment,' Fin suggested. 'Christ Jesus, man, have you never put your foot in it with a woman and had to find the way to pull it out again?'

Boyle set his jaw. 'If I'm wrong, I say I'm wrong. If that's not enough, well, that's that. I've never gone around with a woman who matters, so...'

'And she does. Matter,' Connor finished.

'It should be apparent enough.' He brooded into his beer. 'I'm not going around buying flowers and baubles to put a patch on it. I'll apologize, for I couldn't be sorrier to have put that look on her face. The mad, that's fine. You shout it out and it's

314

finished. But I hurt her, and I'm sorry for it.'

He pushed up. 'I'll see about the steaks.'

'Mad for her,' Fin said when Boyle left the room.

'And panicked with it, which would be good fun if this hadn't happened. She'll forgive him, for she's tenderhearted and just as mad for him. But she won't shine again until he gives her back what she's so willing to give him.'

'What would that be?'

'Love, given freely and without conditions. The flowers, the bauble will make her smile, when she's ready. But he'll have to give over himself before she shines again.'

'It's what makes us all shine,' Fin observed.

In the living room of the cottage with the fire simmering and candles lit, Iona snuggled into the corner of the couch. Meara had not only come, but with provisions of pizza and ice cream.

'Pizza, cookie dough ice cream, wine, and girls.' Iona lifted her glass in toast. 'The best there is.'

'I keep the pizza and ice cream in the freezer for just such emergencies.'

'It's perfect. We should all be lesbians.'

'You'll have to speak for yourself there.' Amused, Meara took a second slice.

'I think the Amazons were probably lesbians. Or some of them anyway. That's what I thought of you when I first saw you.'

Choking on her bite of pizza, Meara downed some wine. 'You took a look at me and thought: Why, there's a lesbian?'

'Amazon. I hadn't thought about your sexual

orientation, then I saw you and Boyle together and figured you were together, but that was wrong. Amazon,' Iona repeated. 'Tall and gorgeous and built. I'm a little bit drunk.' She smiled at Branna. 'Thanks.'

'Oh, anytime a'tall.'

'We can all be Amazons.'

'You're a bit short for it,' Meara pointed out.

'There had to be some runts in the litter.'

'Word is she's small but mighty,' Branna added.

'Damn right! See what I can do?' She popped a jittery ball of flame into her hand.

'Best not to play with fire, or magick, when you're a little bit drunk,' Branna advised.

'Right.' She winked it out. 'But I can do it, that's the point. I can take care of myself. I'm going to buy a car, then when I want to drive around, I'll drive my own damn self. I've got power and purpose. I don't need a man.'

'If we're to be Amazons, we'll just use them for sex or whatever else comes to mind, then cast them out or kill them.'

Iona nodded at Meara. 'Let's do that. Not the killing, it's a little extreme. But the sex and whatever. I really like sex.'

'Here's to it.' Meara lifted her glass, drank, then glanced at Branna.

'Aren't you drinking to sex?'

'I'll drink to it, as that's the closest I've come to it in some time.'

Iona sighed, a little bit drunkenly. 'You could have sex with anybody. You're so gorgeous.'

'Thanks very much, but anybody doesn't appeal to me at this time.'

'She's particular about the matter,' Meara added.

'Me, too, or I have been. I think I'll stop doing that. Sex with Boyle was spectacular.'

'Do tell,' Meara commented. 'And I mean do. I've all the time in the world.'

With a laugh, Iona sipped more wine. 'Hot and wild and sweaty. Like the world was going to end any minute and you had to have each other first.'

'Ah well, I haven't come close to that particular brand in some time myself.'

'Done now.' Iona swiped a hand through the air. 'It's time for a good dose of cynicism because love sucks. Who needs it when you've got pizza and ice cream and girls, and lots of wine?'

'I've always figured it was the frosting.'

Now Iona stabbed a finger toward Meara. 'Frosting's fattening and gives you cavities.'

'There's the risk of that to be sure, but... Well, you've got to bake the cake, don't you? Bake it well so it satisfies yourself. And maybe you decide to add frosting, maybe you don't.'

'Love as a choice?' No, Iona thought. No. Love just picked you up and tossed you in. 'But how do you choose? You've baked your cake, and there it is, and you're thinking that's a pretty good cake, that's good enough for me. Then you blink and all this wonderful frosting just plops down on it out of nowhere.'

Meara shrugged. 'You could scrape it off.'

'You can,' Branna agreed. 'But it takes some of the cake with it, and you never get all the frosting gone.'

'That's sad. It sounds true,' Iona murmured,

'and sad. We can't be sad. I refuse it. We need music,' she decided. 'Would you play, Branna? I love to hear you play.'

'Why not?' Branna stood. 'I'm in the mood to play. I'll get my fiddle, and Meara, you tune up your pipes.'

Iona got up to stir the fire when Branna went out. 'I know Branna's answer because I've seen her and Fin, and heard the story. But have you ever been in love?'

'Well, sticking with the theme, I've dipped my finger in the bowl of frosting and had a small sample or two, but nothing more.' From her own corner of the couch, Meara shifted. 'I want to say, Boyle can be a idjit.'

'Branna called him a gobdaw.'

'And that as well, as can most men. And I'm sorry to say our side as well has moments of grand stupidity. I want to say as well, I've known him a good long time, and I've never seen him look at another woman the way he looks at you.'

She believed that. She'd felt that. But. 'I wish it could be enough. My problem is I always want more.'

'Why is that a problem?'

'It's a problem when you don't get it.'

She plopped down again as Branna came back with her violin case. 'He's out there,' Branna said.

'Boyle?' And damn it, Iona felt her heart jump. 'No. Cabhan.'

This time her nerves jumped even as she and Meara pushed off the couch.

'There's fog all around the house, pressed right up to the windows like a Peeping Tom.'

'What should we do?' Iona saw it now, the gray curtain of it as she stepped to the glass with her friends. 'We should do something.'

'We will. We'll have music. He can't go past my shield on this place,' Branna said as she calmly took out the fiddle, the bow. 'So we'll have more wine, and we'll have music. And we'll shove the sound of it right up his arse.'

'Something lively then.' Meara shot her middle finger at the window before she turned. 'Something for dancing. I'll see if I can teach Iona a few steps.'

'I'm a fast learner,' she said, as much to what lurked outside as to Meara.

17

The hangover woke her, the steady throb, throb, throb in her temples that picked up the beat from the bang, bang, bang in the center of her skull.

She'd had worse, Iona thought, but not by much.

She considered pulling the covers over her head and trying to sleep it off, but she couldn't – wouldn't – miss work. Cautiously she opened her eyes, then squinted at the living room window.

Not in bed, she realized, but on the couch with a pretty throw in melting shades of purple tucked around her. She remembered now. She'd stretched out on the couch after dancing herself breathless and after joining her friends in a song or two.

She didn't have their quality of voice, but she knew the words thanks to Nan, and could pull off some decent harmony.

Plus it was fun, she thought. And defiant, making song as the fog curled outside.

She'd drunk, eaten, talked, laughed, then sung and danced her way through that first awful punch of pain. And now she had a hangover to distract her, and that was all to the good.

She hadn't cried – or not enough to count – and that was even better.

She'd down a gallon of water, a bottle or two of aspirin, make herself eat something. Then shower for a few days. All better.

And she'd work through the rest.

Sometime between the first glass of wine and the last, she determined she'd go to the stables as usual. She wouldn't crawl off and quit a job she loved because her boss – her lover – had broken her all-too-fragile heart.

If he wanted her gone, he'd have to fire her.

She got up, shuffled her way to the kitchen. She'd gulped down water, some aspirin, and was contemplating trying some dry toast when Meara walked in looking annoyingly bright-eyed and rosy.

'Got a bit of a head this morning, do you?'

Iona gave Meara as close to the stink eye as she could manage. 'Why don't you?'

'Oh, I've a head like a rock and a stomach like iron.' She spoke cheerfully as she put on coffee. 'Can't remember ever being the worse for wear after a drinking night.'

'I hate you.'

'And who's to blame you? We left you where you dropped last night, as it seemed best. Since I'd brought a change with me in case we made a night of it, I slept in your room. You'll want the coffee and some food in your system. Oatmeal, I'm thinking.'

Iona winced. 'Really?'

'Good and healthy. I'll make it up, as Branna won't be stirring as yet.'

'Does she have a head like a rock and a stomach like iron, too?'

'I'd say she does, yes. But then she's careful how much she drinks. She's one to keep her wits about her, always. Here now.' Meara poured the coffee. 'When she's up, ask her to fix you a potion for the head. She has one that's renowned.'

'Good to know. I'd like a clear head when I get to work.'

'So you're sticking with it then?' Meara gave her a light shoulder punch of approval. 'Good for you.'

'I'm not going to deprive myself of work I love, or mope in a corner. I need the job, so we'll figure out how to work together, unless he fires me.'

'He never would. He's not so hard, Iona.'

'No, he's not. Besides, the sun may be out now, but there's always a chance of fog. With that to deal with, we have to put the rest aside. No chinks in the circle, right?'

'You've got spine.' This time Meara gave her a quick rub on the shoulder.

'If you're really making oatmeal, I'll go up, soak some of this hangover away in the shower, and get dressed for work.' She hesitated, then wrapped her arms around Meara in a hug. 'You and Branna got me through a tough night.'

'Ah, well now, what else are friends for if not that?'

By the time she got out of the shower, the throbbing and banging had clicked down a couple levels. But a sober study of her face in the mirror told her more help was needed. Instead of her usual workday slap-and-dash-on makeup, she took some time, some care. She didn't want Boyle to think the pale cheeks and smudged eyes were due to him, though indirectly they were, since she'd overindulged to buffer the hurt.

Satisfied she'd done the best with what she had to work with, she dressed and went back down to face oatmeal.

She found Branna, sleepy-eyed in her pajamas, drinking coffee as Meara hummed a tune while she slapped butter on toasted bread.

'And there's herself now, and looking only half dragged out.'

'That bad?'

'Not bad at all,' Meara said staunchly, and dished out oatmeal.

'Sure we can do better.' Branna crooked a finger. 'Lean down here, since you won't do it for yourself.' She glided her hands gently over Iona's face. 'Just a touch, as we don't want him to think you fussed for him either.'

That brought on a smile. 'You read my mind.'

'It's sensible, so a little glamour adds just the right touch. We women, and witches, stick together. Meara says you've a bit of a head.'

'It's better.'

'Drink that.' She tapped her finger on a glass filled with pale green liquid.

'What is it?'

'Good for what ails you. Herbs and such, and a touch of more. No point going in as you are, feeling less than well, or looking it. You're showing backbone by dealing with what is, so you'll have a reward.'

'And oatmeal.' Meara set three bowls on the table, went back for the toast, then sat.

'Here goes.' Considering it medicine, Iona drank the potion – but found it had a cool, fresh flavor with a faint hint of mint. 'It's nice.'

'Good for what ails you doesn't have to be unpleasant. Eat as well, it adds to it.'

'You're both taking care of me. I want to say if either of you get the crap kicked out of you by love, I'll be there for you.'

'That's reassuring.' Meara dug into the oatmeal.

The hangover slid away, like raindrops sliding down a window pane – a kind of slow, soft, liquid fading that left Iona feeling refreshed and rested.

'You could make a fortune off that single potion,' she told Branna as she pulled on her jacket. 'It's a miracle.'

'Not quite that, and making fortunes isn't all it's thought to be. We work tonight, cousin, and twice as hard for the night off.'

'I'll be ready. I know you're not much for hugs,' she added as she gave Branna a squeeze. 'But I am.' She stepped outside with Meara. 'I don't think Cabhan liked the music.'

'I hope it rings in his ears still. I'll speak with you later,' Meara said to Branna, and strode to her truck. 'I hate I'm saying this,' she continued when Iona sat beside her. 'But don't be too awful hard on him. Oh, he deserves it with no doubt, the donkey's arse, but men can be such fumblers.'

'I don't want to be hard on him. I just want to get through.'

'Then you will.'

He didn't expect her to come to work, and it chafed at him that he couldn't blame her. Before the mucking and feeding, watering and daily morning medications began, he huddled down with the weekly schedule. In a relatively short time, he realized, he'd assigned Iona to so many tasks, students, duties he'd need to do a bit of scrambling to fill in her spots.

Pain in the arse, and really when you thought about it all in a rational way there was no reason she'd get herself in such a state so she'd toss the work in the trash bin along with the rest.

And if he could just have a rational word or two with her, he'd surely climb out of the bin himself.

If women were more like men, life would run along smoother, without a doubt.

He stewed, and finagled the schedule, brooded and shifted hours and students. As he pushed away to pull out his mobile and begin to make the necessary calls, he heard Meara's truck drive up. Hers ran with a cougar's purr rather than Mick's aging lion with bronchitis.

He strolled out, determined to pass the calls to her, and to, very casual-like, pump her for information on Iona, as word was she'd stayed over at Branna's.

So it threw him off stride when Iona hopped out of the passenger's door, dressed for the work-day.

'Morning then,' Meara said with a kind of fierce cheer, and walked right by him into the stables.

He led with: 'Ah...'

'I'm here to work.' In a clipped voice he'd never heard her use, Iona stopped a foot away to speak to him. 'And that's all. I need the work, I like the work, I'm good at the work. If you intend to fire me—'

'Fire you?' Shocked, and once again off stride, he gaped at her. 'Of course I'm not after firing you. Why—'

'Good. Then that's that.'

'Well now, wait a minute there, we need to talk about—'

'We don't.' She cut him off in that same tone, cool and dismissive. 'I know what you feel and think, and on some level I understand it. You're entitled to feel what you feel, and I'm responsible for my own feelings. So it's just work, Boyle, and you have to respect that.'

She turned her back on him, walked to the stables. He could stop her, just pluck her up and haul her off somewhere private where she'd have to talk it out and over. He thought of doing just that for a moment, then let her go.

He stuffed his hands in his pockets, stood in the cool morning air, and wished he'd gotten the damn flowers.

He tried it her way. As he was the one who'd fucked up, he was obliged to give her the room she asked for.

She went about her work, but not all brisk business as he'd expected. Oh no, she had plenty to say to Meara, to Mick and the others, a laugh to share, a question to ask. But not a bloody word did she speak to him unless given no choice.

She managed to be cordial and distant at once.

It pissed him off, then when the mad faded, the guilt piled in.

'You're driving him mad.' Meara watched Iona saddle Spud for a guided ride.

'I'm just doing my job, and leaving the personal out of it.'

'Exactly what's driving him mad. He'd say, being male, and being especially Boyle, the logical thing to do in such situations is separate the business from the personal, but you doing just that's squeezing his balls. He doesn't know whether to yelp or drop.'

'I'm getting through.' After tightening the cinch, Iona put on her riding helmet. 'That's what counts. But I can't say I'm sorry it's giving his balls a good squeeze.'

She led the group out – a couple and two teen-age girls from America taking advantage of spring break – letting them chatter among themselves. But she did glance back, once, and couldn't deny a quick twist of satisfaction at catching Boyle watching her ride away.

As they turned into the woods, she brushed her fingers over the amulet she wore, then tapped them to her pocket where she'd put a protection charm that morning.

She wouldn't fear the woods, she told herself.

She wouldn't fear what came. And she wouldn't fear living her life alone if that's what destiny handed her.

Putting her guide's smile on, she shifted in the saddle, glanced back at the family. 'So, how are you enjoying your visit so far?'

A busy day moved quickly, and for that she was grateful. Knowing she did just exactly what she needed to do didn't make it any easier to do it. She wanted to smile at Boyle, and see him flash her a grin in return. Wanted to feel entitled to touch him, just a hand to his, a hand on his arm, and have him feel entitled to do the same.

She wanted to be easy with him again. Even if they couldn't be lovers, even if she had to find a way to snuff out the light of the love she felt for him, she wanted him in her life.

Needed him, she corrected as she cleaned up at the big stables after her lesson with Sarah. Until Cabhan was defeated, until what Sorcha had begun so long ago was finished, they all needed one another.

What they faced was so much bigger than a bruised heart and some scarred pride.

They'd find a way. If Branna and Fin could work together, she could certainly work with Boyle. It might take some time to find the right way, to smooth out the bumps – and they'd have to talk it out, she admitted.

But not yet. Too tender yet.

She hugged Alastar's neck, pleased when he nuzzled her. 'I've got you, don't I? My guide, my friend, my partner. I've got family who cares about me, and understands me. And I've got a home, a place I belong. It's more than I ever had before.'

She drew back, kissed his nose. 'So no complaints, no pity parties. I'll see you tomorrow.'

She walked out, noted she timed it well when she spotted Connor strolling toward the stables, his whistled tune leading the way.

The perfect Irish picture, she thought, a good-looking man, all lanky limbs and wicked angel face, hands in the pockets of his rough work pants, and the brown path and green, green woods behind him.

'All done for the day then?' he called out.

'Just now. You?'

'Ready to walk my pretty cousin home, and see if our Branna baked any fresh biscuits today. I've a yen for some, and since according to our Branna we're working tonight, I deserve them as well.'

'I'm ready for magick.' She wiggled her fingers. 'And to learn something new.'

'New, is it?'

'Astral projection. I'm doing it in dreams, either on my own or manipulated by Cabhan, I don't know for sure. But I don't control it. I want to.'

'It's a good arrow for your quiver. And so ... how did it all go with Boyle today?'

'Maybe a little awkward and tense here and there, but we got through it. It should be easier going forward.'

'He's feeling a right shit about the whole business.'

She would not feel pleased (maybe just a little). She would not feel sorry, or she'd ignore the sorry.

'He feels what he feels, that's why we're here.

He's your friend.' She gave Connor's arm a quick rub. 'He feels bad he hurt me. You feel bad that he feels bad. We all just have to get past it and not lose sight of what we have to do.'

'And you can do that?'

'I've had a disappointed heart before.' She said it lightly, had to, as it went so deep. 'I think some of us are just destined not to connect that way.'

'But you don't.' He took her hand in his, gave it a bolstering squeeze. 'You don't think that at all.'

'I think,' she said more carefully, 'there's something about me that makes it difficult for others to forge an intimate connection to.'

'Bollocks,' he began, but she shook her head.

'My own parents couldn't. Is that them, or is it me? Who knows, but if they can't, and there's been no one until Boyle I wanted, deep down, to make that connection to, I can't blame him. If it's me, I have to work on me. And I have been. I'm a classic work-in-progress.'

'You're wrong, about the connection, or anything about it being you. You're as easy to love as a summer morning. If we weren't cousins, I'd marry you myself.'

She laughed at that, touched. Then sent him a sultry, sidelong stare. 'We're distant cousins.'

'Cousins all the same.' He slung an arm around her shoulders. 'And it's too odd and tangled for that.'

'Too bad, because you're so pretty.'

'I'll say the same right back to you.'

He opened the door to the workshop, gave his arm an exaggerated sweep to usher her in. Then sniffed the air.

'Ginger biscuits, and what a fine welcome home.'

'Have some and your tea, as we've work to make up.'

At the counter Branna poured white liquid wax into a clear jar, already weighted with a long white wick. Iona wondered how Connor scented the ginger over the summer fragrance of hydrangea.

'How did it all go then?' Branna asked as she tipped up the pan, moved down to the next jar.

'First day down, and not too bad.'

'She thinks she's unlovable.' Connor spoke over a mouthful of cookie.

'Oh bollocks.'

'I didn't say that, don't think that. I meant – never mind.' She grabbed a cookie for herself. 'Do you need help with those?'

'I'm about done, but you can help me with the labels and wick trimming later on. I've made dozens as we were running low, and the tourists come thicker in spring than in winter. Have your tea. We'll work twice as much today for working not at all yesterday.'

'I'm ready.'

'She's after astral projection,' Connor put in.

'Astral projection, is it?' Pursing her lips, Branna studied Iona. 'It wasn't what I had in mind, but well, why not? It's a fine skill to have.'

With the last jar filled, she left them cooling on the rack, pulled off the white bib apron she'd worn to protect her poppy red sweater from drips and spills.

'It's not the same as the active dreaming you've done, but not so very different. Have you been practicing your meditating?'

Iona winced. 'Probably not as much as I should. My mind always wants to go somewhere.'

'Training your mind's part of it. Training it, quieting it, and as I've said, focusing it. Here, bring your tea to the fire. You should be relaxed in body and mind and spirit.'

Iona obeyed, and Kathel stirred from his nap to lay a paw on her foot in hello.

'Just watch the fire, have your tea. You like the taste of it, and the biscuit. Quiet breathing. Inhale, pause, exhale, pause. You can smell the peat fire, and the candles just poured, the herbs hanging to dry.'

'Rosemary especially.'

'Sure it's a favorite. You hear your breath go in and out, and Kathel's tail swishing against the floor, the crackle of the fire, and the sound of my voice. It's soothing, all soothing. The touch of my hand, and Kathel's paw. Soothing all, so you can drift a bit, float a bit. Quiet and peaceful.'

'But I–'

'Trust me. I'll be with you this first time, take you this first time. See where you want most to go, see it in the fire, see it in your mind.'

'Nan's kitchen,' Iona realized all at once. 'I miss her. She's never done anything but love me, believe in me. She's been the only one who has for so long. I'm what I am because of Nan.'

Branna glanced at Connor as he came over to sit on Iona's other side. 'A long trip for a first,' she murmured.

'Her heart takes her there.'

'And so will we. Do you see it, Nan's kitchen,

331

in the fire, in your mind?'

'It's like yours. I mean feels like yours, not looks like. It's smaller, and there's no hearth. I see the walls, they're like a warm peach and the cabinets are dark, dark brown. There's an old butcher block table. When I sat with her there, I could tell her anything. She told me what I am, told me about the first dark witch while we sat at that table having tea and cookies – biscuits. Just like now. She keeps herbs on the windowsill, and the blue and green pottery bowl I gave her for her birthday years ago on the table. There were red apples in it the day she told me everything, not just pieces, but all. Shining red apples in the green and blue bowl. Her eyes are like mine, the same color, the same shape. And when they look at me, I believe.'

'Focus on the bowl, the colors of that, the shape of that. Let yourself lift, let yourself go where you want to go. Quiet breaths, quiet mind, quiet purpose. Lift. Float. Fly.'

She lifted, floated as if weightless. The air, the light all pulsed blue – quiet, soothing. And as she felt the first stirring of its power, of hers, she flew.

Fast, free, soaring over green hills misted by blue, over water – blue under blue.

Branna's voice sounded in her mind. *Breathe. Keep your focus.*

'It's amazing! It's beautiful.' She threw her arms out to the side, laughed with the sheer joy of it.

Hold on now. Nan's kitchen. See it.

She saw it in her mind, and then, she was simply there. Standing by the old butcher block table, with the blue and green bowl. Lemons and limes today, Iona thought, a bit dizzy.

And there was Nan, stepping in the back door, toeing out of her gardening shoes, taking off the wide-brimmed straw hat.

Small statured, small framed, as Iona was. Trim and pretty in her jeans and light jacket. Her hair, maintained a soft golden red, formed a stylish wedge around her face. Light, discreet makeup. Nan wouldn't even garden before taking care of the basics.

She started to walk to the fridge, stopped. Then very slowly turned.

Her hand went to her heart, and eyes wide, she let out one short gasp. 'Iona! You're here. Oh, oh, Branna and Connor as well. Oh, look at you, my baby girl. How much you've learned already.'

'You can see me.'

'Sure I can see you, you're standing right there, aren't you? And so pretty. Sit, sit, all of you, and tell me everything.'

'Can we sit?' Iona wondered.

'There's enough power in this room to light the next fifty kilometers.' Branna pulled out a chair, sat. 'Of course we can sit.'

On a little cry, Iona rushed forward, grabbed Nan in a hug. 'I can touch you. I can feel you. I've missed you.'

'As I've missed you.'

'We can't stay long this time, cousin.' Branna smiled at them. 'It's a long distance for her first time.'

'The first?' With a laugh, a beam of amazement in her eyes, Nan hugged again. 'Oh no, not long then. But long enough to say how proud and happy I am.'

'Will you come? You said you'd come to Ireland.'

'And so I will, when it's time. I'll know. You're happy, but ... there's something unhappy.'

'She's had a ... disagreement,' Connor decided. 'With Boyle.'

'Ah, I see. I'm sorry for it, as I'm well fond of him. If it's right, it'll mend.'

'He doesn't trust me. It's not important.'

'Of course it is.'

'I mean right this minute. I want to know how you are.'

'Fit and fine, as you see. Planting pansies today, as they'll take the cool, and it's been cool this spring. And cabbage, of course, and a bit of this and that. You're teaching her well, Branna, as she tells me. And you, Connor.'

'She learns well. And she's needed.' Branna reached out a hand, took Nan's. 'I want to say to you, you were right to send her, right to give her the amulet. I'm grateful to you.'

'No need for that. It's ours to do. It's our blood.'

'It is, and it will be. He's stronger now that the three are together, but we're stronger yet. I'm sorry we can't have a proper visit.' Branna rose. 'But she's only begun on this skill.'

'Even a moment is a great treat. You take care, my girl. And keep your heart and your mind open, Iona. That's when the best come into them.'

'I remember.' She kissed Nan's cheek, hugged her hard. 'I'll come back if I can.' On impulse, she took a lemon from the bowl. She felt its skin against her palm and, lifting it, caught its scent. 'I know it's silly, but can I take this with me? Is that possible?'

'Let's find out.' Branna took her hand, and when Iona pushed the lemon in her pocket, Connor the other.

'We've missed you back home, Cousin Mary Kate,' Connor told her.

'And I you. You'll take me hawking one day soon, won't you, Connor?'

'It'll be a pleasure to me.'

'Tell your mother, and hers, when you see them, I look forward to a good gossip in person.'

'Come to the Dark Witch,' Branna told Nan. 'There'll be a fire burning for you, and the kettle on the boil.'

'I will, and thanks. My love goes with all of you, and every hope with it.'

'Bye, Nan. I love you.'

And again, she lifted, floated. Flew.

18

She felt amazing, and still Branna pushed a potion on her.

'Your first time. It's best if you level it out a bit now.'

'Can I do it again?'

Branna quirked her eyebrows while Connor grabbed two more cookies. 'Now?'

'No, not this minute. I mean can I do it? Am I capable? On my own?'

'Connor and I were just along for the ride, you could say.' She stepped over to check her candles. 'Helping you prepare, then going along to see you through.'

'Like being on a learner's permit?'

'Sorry?'

'Learning to drive a car – I really have to deal with getting a car. It always gets pushed back, but ... I am a little buzzed,' she admitted, and drank the potion.

'Learning to drive.' Connor considered, nodded. 'Like that in a sense, yes. Where you need supervision until you can handle it on your own.'

'At least one of us should go with you when you try again.'

'You sort of hypnotized me.'

'I helped you find the right meditative state, is all. You've a very active mind, and need practice quieting it.'

'It meant a lot to me to see her. Really see her.' Reaching in her pocket, Iona pulled out the lemon she'd taken from the blue and green bowl, brought it to her face to inhale the scent.

'Family's the root, and the heart. Now, see what you can do with this.' She opened a drawer, took out a printed list.

'A wand tipped with a rose quartz crystal,' Iona read. 'An athame, decorated with a Celtic trinity knot, a silver cup of the Fire Goddess, Belisma, a copper pentagram amulet.'

Frowning, Iona looked up. 'The four elemental tools?'

'Very good, the wand for air, the knife for fire, and so on. Read on.'

'Okay, a sword with a bloodstone in the hilt, and its sheath; a spear with a sharpened tip of hematite; a shield decorated with a pentagram and hematite, amethyst, sunstone, and red jasper; and a cauldron with the symbol of fire. The four corresponding weapons.'

'You've studied. Now you'll do a seeking spell, and find them.'

'Like a scavenger hunt?'

'In a way, yes, like that.'

'Well, I like a good game.'

''Tisn't one,' Connor told her. 'But practice, and important. We'll need to seek him out when we're ready to take him on for once and done.'

'We'll have an advantage if we know when and how he comes,' Branna added.

'Why don't we seek him now? He's got to have a lair of some kind. We could–'

'We're not ready, and if we seek, he may know. He has power, and if we can't block him, he'll see. But when we're ready, we'll want him to see – what we want him to see. When the time comes,' Branna continued, 'the three of us will seek and find, combining our power, as the three.'

'And Fin?'

'I...'

'It's Fin who should seek, and find.' Connor turned to his sister, held her gaze with a quiet look. 'He's of the blood, and that would be for him.'

'You trust so much.'

'And you too little. It's for him, Branna. You know it as I do.'

'All right, we'll come to that when we do. But

now let's deal with this. This is for you to do, Iona. Do the spell, each one in turn, find what you seek, and bring each one in turn, here.'

'Okay.' She glanced at the list again, folded it into her pocket. Then closed her eyes and tried to visualize the wand. 'What I see within my mind, I will seek and I will find. Bring it now before my eyes and I will go to where it lies. Slim and strong it calls to me. As I will, so mote it be.'

She saw it clearly, catching the late light of the sun on the little table by the window in the music room. 'Be right back.'

Connor leaned on the counter where Branna began to meticulously label her cooled candle jars.

'It pains you, I know.' His voice stayed as quiet as his eyes. 'But if you don't accept what Fin is, what he truly is, and believe in him, in his loyalty, it limits us all.'

'I'm trying. I can get past the hurt, or can most days. Trust is a harder thing.'

'He'd die for you.'

'Don't say it,' she snapped. 'Do you think I'd want that? I only want to do what must be done, and I will. I will. You're right that he should be the one to seek, to find. You're right. Leave it at that for now.'

'All right, we'll leave it there.' Then he smiled a little, to soothe her. 'Want to time her?'

'No hurry.' Branna shrugged, relieved he could leave it, that he would, for her sake. 'Some of them are easy to build her confidence. Others will take more.'

'Well then, I'm ready for a pint. Want one?'

'Hmm. A glass of wine might be nice. And don't fool with the pork roast I have in the oven.'

'Pork roast?'

'Leave it be, and what's in with it. I've got a timing spell on the lot as I didn't know how long this would take. Bring the bottle, why don't you, and a glass for Iona. She can have it when she's done.'

Iona rushed in, flushed with victory, brandishing the wand. 'Got it.'

'Nicely done. Set it down there, and find the next.'

'Okay. You're labeling. I was going to help you.'

'There'll be plenty more. The athame.'

'Right.' On a deep breath, Iona began again.

Connor had his pint and played a little tug-the-rope with the dog while Branna finished the first round of candles. Iona traveled back and forth, bringing in the listed items.

'Jesus, this spear.' Iona hefted it, miming a warrior as she strode back in. 'Took me as long to find as everything else so far combined.'

Not quite, Branna thought, but long enough.

'I could *see* it, and the tree you had it leaning against outside, but I couldn't tell which tree. So I did a secondary spell for that after I'd wandered around out there for a while.'

'A good choice. We'll work a bit more so you'll narrow it as we go.'

Iona gave a nod to the items she'd spread on a counter. 'They're all so cool. Anyway, just two more.'

The shield eluded her so long she nearly switched to the cauldron, but Branna had instructed each in turn, so she cleared her mind – a challenge, as it was so damn full – then refreshed the spell.

She found the shield – and oh my God, a work of art it was, hanging in the earthy, herby-smelling greenhouse.

'She's done well,' Connor commented, rubbing the dog with his foot as the game had played out. 'Under difficult circumstances.'

'She has, and they are. She'll be better yet, as the circumstances will worsen.'

'Always a happy note in you, Branna.'

'Always a realistic one.' With the candles she'd finished boxed for transport to her shop, she began to set the ones she'd culled out on shelves.

'Found it.' Iona hauled in the cauldron. 'In the little attic over your room, Branna – that I didn't even know was there.'

'It's not used for much. And so you've found all.'

'Each in its turn.' Iona set the cauldron by the rest. 'Every one of them is beautiful, and unique.'

'So they are. Tools they may be, but I don't see why a tool shouldn't be beautiful as well as practical and useful. So they're yours.'

'Sorry, what?' Because her mind was full again, Iona simply stared at Branna.

'They're yours now.' Branna poured her a glass of wine, passed it to her. 'Connor and I chose them for you, from what has been given to us, or what we collected, or what we found elsewhere since you came to us.'

'But–' Overwhelmed, she couldn't come up with the words that so often rolled out of her mind and straight off her tongue.

'Every witch needs her own tools,' Branna continued. 'And these are the most important of them. You'll find and choose others for yourself along the way.'

'Fire comes easiest to you.' Connor rose to join them. 'So the symbols are yours. And on the athame, the trinity knot for the three in you, and the three of us.'

'The rose quartz on the wand, for it seems your power comes from your instincts – the belly – and then passes through the heart. Bloodstone on the sword for strength.'

'Stones of protection – physical and psychic – for the shield. Hematite for your spear tip, for confidence in your air.' Connor tapped a finger on it. 'And the pentacle of copper, Sorcha's chosen medium.'

'I don't know what to say to you.'

'The sword and shield have been passed down, blood to blood,' Branna told her. 'The cup I found in a shop I favor, as Connor found the pentacle in another. So there's a mix here of old and new.'

Tears she'd denied herself the night before wanted to rush up now, from her heart. In sheer gratitude. 'Thank you, more than I can say. It seems like so much, too much.'

'It's not,' Branna corrected. 'You must be armed for what's coming.'

'I know. A sword.' Carefully, she drew it from its sheath. 'I don't know how to use it.'

'You will. Some will come through it to you.'

'Some,' Connor agreed. 'And Fin can work with you, and Meara as well. She's bloody good with a sword. Either Branna or I can help with the spear, but I think you'll find the tool itself will fit your hand.'

'Once you've cleansed them, and recharged them,' Branna added. 'That's not for us to do. I think we'll have dinner now. We can all use the break and the food. Then you'll tend to them.'

'I'll treasure them. Thank you. Thank you,' she repeated, taking Branna's hand, then Connor's, linking the three. 'You've opened up my life in so many ways.'

'You're part of ours. Come then, we'll eat. I've prepared a special meal anticipating your success here. Bring your wine, as you've yet to drink it.'

'One day I'll pay you back for all you've done.'

'It's not a matter of payment, and can't be.'

'You're right. That was the wrong term. Balance. One day I'll find the balance.'

She started on it by setting the table, and telling Connor he was banned from kitchen cleanup. He didn't argue. Her mood, lifted from seeing Nan, from the gifts, went rising higher when she sampled the little feast Branna had prepared.

'God, this is so good! I know I'm hungry, but this is just amazing. I swear you could open your own restaurant.'

'That's something I won't be doing now, or ever. Cooking, like tools, is necessary. No reason it shouldn't be good.'

'I wish mine was. I really have to learn.'

'Plenty of time for it, and more important things to learn now. Connor, Frannie at the shop tells me Fergus Ryan got drunk as two penny whores on holiday and walked into Sheila Dougherty's house, thinking it was his own, stripped down to the skin and passed out on the living room sofa. Where a none-too-pleased Sheila Dougherty – she who's about seventy-eight and mean as a rattlesnake – found him in the morning. What do you know of that?'

'I know of the black eye Fergus is sporting, and the knot raised on the back of his head from the whack of Mrs. Dougherty's cane. And how he managed to grab only his boots and his aching head while trying to defend himself, and ran straight out with the old woman chasing him and flinging curses and whatever else came to hand.'

'I thought you would.' Branna picked up her wine. 'Tell all.'

So the conversation turned to local gossip, business, stories. The kind of meal, Iona would think as she dealt with dishes and pots, she'd had only rarely growing up, and had craved all the more from the lack.

So, like the gift of her tools, she'd treasure it, and all those that came.

For now, she tried to embrace the quiet, as Branna and Connor were upstairs or about somewhere on their own devices. She had work yet. The cleansing for tonight. And tomorrow she'd imbue and recharge what was now hers.

A good day, she congratulated herself. She'd gone to work, had her first face-to-face with Boyle, and gotten through it without humiliating herself.

Major points.

And she'd flown to Nan's kitchen, a personal high point.

She'd worked seeking spells, and had the priceless reward from it.

To cap it, she'd had a meal with her cousins full of talk and laughter.

And tomorrow, she'd do whatever tomorrow brought her way.

To start on that balance, she cleaned the kitchen to a sparkle. The next time Branna walked in, she thought, giving it all a narrowed eye, it would damn near blind her.

Satisfied, she started to walk through to the workshop to begin her last task of the day, when the knock on the front door stopped her.

Normally, the prospect of company would have pleased her, but she really wanted to get started on her tools. Probably one of Connor's mates or prospective lady friends, she thought. She'd yet to meet anyone who didn't love Connor, or seek him out when they wanted a good time, or needed a shoulder for a bad one.

When she opened the door, her greeting smile faded, as there was Boyle standing there with a big, bright spring bouquet.

She managed an 'Oh.'

He looked so sexy, so appealing, big, scarred hand around stems, his face just a bit flushed, his eyes full of embarrassed determination.

And he shifted his weight and nearly did her in.

'I'm sorry. I need to tell you I'm sorry. These are for you.'

'They're beautiful.' Better, she thought, so much better for herself if she just sent him on his way. But she couldn't do it, not when he'd brought her flowers and a sincere apology. 'Thank you,' she said instead, and took the flowers. 'They're really beautiful.'

'Will they get me in the door, for a minute or two?'

'All right. Sure. I want to go back and put these in water.' She led the way back to the kitchen, using every trick she'd learned to keep her mind, her heart, quiet and steady.

'It shines in here,' he commented.

'I've been balancing some scales.' She found a large, pretty vase of mossy green, Branna's kitchen flower scissors, and the flower food her cousin made herself. And set to work.

'I'm sorry, Iona, for upsetting you, for hurting you. I never would have meant to.'

'I know that.' The flowers, so lovely, the scents, so poignant, helped her with her own balance. 'I'm not angry with you, Boyle. Not anymore.'

'You should be. I earned it.'

'Maybe. But you weren't completely wrong in what you said to Fin. I did push, and I did get in your way.'

'I'm not one to be pushed if I'm not wanting to be. Iona—'

'You were attracted to me. I used that. I never used magick.'

'I know it. I know it.' Trying to find the words, he raked his fingers though his hair. 'I'm not used to all this going on inside me. I lost my seat, and you happened to come in before I'd righted it again. Give me a chance, will you, to make it up?'

'It's not that, or not only that.'

Balance, she thought again. She wouldn't find

it without being honest with herself, and with him.

'Everything about you came on me so fast, and I just went with it. Grabbed for it, and I think, held on too tight. I didn't want it all to slip away. I always wanted to feel all this going on inside me. I've craved it like breath. So I got in your way, I got in your bed, and I didn't let myself think what could go wrong.'

'It doesn't have to be wrong. It's not wrong,' he said, and took her shoulders.

'It's not right either.' Cautious, she stepped to the side so he no longer touched her. 'Do you want a beer? I didn't even ask if you–'

'I don't want a bloody beer. It's you I want.'

Her eyes, blue and beautiful even touched with sadness, lifted to his. 'But you don't want to want me. That's still true. And I can't keep accepting that, keep settling for that just because I always have. It goes all the way back, Boyle. My parents never really noticed when I wasn't there, or cared much when I was or I wasn't. And more awful yet, didn't notice that I knew.'

'I'm sorry to say it, as they're your ma and da, but it strikes me, Iona, your parents are right shits.'

She laughed a little. 'I guess they sort of are. I think they love me, as much as they can, because they're supposed to, but not because they want to. The boys and men I've tried to fall in love with? They'd want me back for a while, but they never wanted me enough, or wanted to want me enough, so it went away. And then I'm left wondering, what's wrong with me? Why can't someone love me without reservations, without all the buffers? Or worse, that I'm a kind of placeholder till someone better comes along.'

Had he done that? he wondered. Had he added to that? 'There's nothing wrong with you, and it's nothing of the kind.'

'I'm working on believing that, and I can't unless I stop accepting less. And that's *my* problem, *my* issue. Maybe I didn't really, all the way, realize that until you punched me in the face with it. Metaphorically,' she added with an easier smile than she'd expected to pull off.

Because he could see her face still, as she'd stood there in the stables, he felt as though he'd struck her. 'Oh Christ, Iona. I'd give anything to take the words back, to stuff them down my own throat and choke on them.'

'No. No.' She took his hands a moment and squeezed. 'Because it knocked me down, I had to get up. And this time deal all the way. Because before that, Boyle, I'd have taken anything you'd given. I'd have wrapped my own gauzy layers around it and convinced myself that it was right. But it would never have been right. I can't be happy, not really down-to-the-bone happy, with less than I need. And if I'm not happy, I can't make someone else happy.'

'Tell me what you need, and I'll give it to you.'

'It doesn't work like that.' And God, she loved him more that he would try, that he'd be willing to try. 'Maybe it is magick after all. What makes us love and need and want one person, over everyone else. Love and need and want them absolutely. I want the magick. I'm not settling for less. You're why. So in a strange way I'm grateful.'

347

'Oh yeah, thank me now and put a fine, foamy head on it.'

'You showed me that I'm worth more than I thought, or let myself think. And that's a lot to be grateful for. I'm the one who rushed in, so I'm the one responsible for the fallout. It was all too fast, too intense. It's no wonder you felt cornered.'

'I never felt... I don't know what I was talking about.'

'You'll figure it out. Meanwhile, the flowers are beautiful, and so was your apology.' She carried them over, put them on the table. 'On second thought, I can tell you some things I need.'

'Anything.'

'I need to go on working for you and Fin, not only because I need to make a living, but because I'm good at it. And because I love it, and I want to do what I love.'

'There's no question about that. I told you.'

'And I need to be friends with you, so we're not awkward or uncomfortable around each other. It's important. I couldn't handle working for you or with you if we held on to resentment or diffi-cult feelings. I'd end up walking away from the job to spare us both, and then I'd just be pissed off and sad.'

'There's no resentment from me. I can't pro-mise no difficult feelings, for that's what they are. They're all tangled for me, and slippery with it. If you'd just–'

'Not this time.' Not with you, she thought, be-cause with him, she'd never get up again whole. 'I don't just. I'm responsible for my feelings, and you for yours. You'll figure it out,' she repeated.

'But we both have good work that matters to us, good friends in common. And more important than anything, right here, right now, we have a common enemy and purpose. We can't do all we have to do if we're not on solid footing.'

'When did you get so bloody logical?' he muttered.

'Maybe I'm borrowing a little from Branna. She's taught me a lot, shown me more than I ever imagined I'd see. I have a legacy, and I'm going to be true to it. I'm going to fight for it. And I'm going to be true to myself.'

'So it's work together, fight together, and be friends? And that's the lot of it?'

She offered another smile. 'That's a lot for most people. And I'm not holding back sex as a punishment.'

'I wasn't meaning... Though now that you say it, it has that effect. It wasn't just sex, Iona. Don't think it.'

'No, it wasn't. But I pushed there, too. Jumping in, as I tend to, well, boots first.'

'I like the way you jump in. But if it's what you need, it's friends.' For now, he thought.

'Good. Want that beer now?'

He nearly said yes, to buy more time, and maybe to soften the line she'd drawn between them. But she'd told him what she needed from him, and he'd give it.

'I'd best be on. I've all that untangling to do, after all.'

'Might as well get started.'

'I'll let myself out, and see you in the morning.' He started to go, turned for a moment just to look at her. So bright, so pretty, with all the flowers beside her. 'You deserve all, Iona, and not a bit less.'

She closed her eyes when she heard the front door close behind him. It was so hard to stand firm, to do and say what she knew was right when her heart ached. When her heart yearned to take less, and make do.

'Not with him,' she murmured. 'Maybe with anyone else, but not with him. Because ... there's only him.'

She'd leave the flowers on the table, for everyone to enjoy. But before she went back to the workshop to cleanse her tools, she found a tall, slim vase, chose three flowers – a magick number – and, sliding them in, took them to her room where she'd see them before sleep. Where she'd see them when she waked in the morning.

19

As spring spread over Mayo, through the green forests, over the lush hills, rains came soft and steady. Wildflowers rose and opened to drink, gardens burst to glorious life. In the fields lambs bleated, ducks plied the lough, while the forest filled with birdsong.

Iona planted flowers and vegetables and herbs with her cousins, scraped mud off her boots, put in long hours at the stables, long hours with the craft.

Bealtaine with its maypoles and songs came and went, and brought the solstice closer.

As the days lengthened, she often rose before dawn and worked well into the night, using the energy that fueled her to push harder.

And in the rain and the mud, she learned how to handle a sword.

Though she couldn't imagine herself in an actual sword fight, she liked the way it felt in her hand. Liked the heft of it, and the fact that – small but mighty – she could strike and block.

She'd never be in Meara's league. Her friend resembled an Amazon warrior even more with her hair braided back and a sword in her hand. But she learned – angles, footwork, maneuvers.

Within the thin veil Branna conjured she sliced and parried while Meara, relentless, drove her back. While the swords sang and Meara shouted insults or instructions, Branna sat on a garden bench like some exotic housewife, calmly peeling potatoes for dinner.

'Put your shoulder into it!'

'I am!' Winded, and seriously starting to ache, Iona shifted her weight, tried to advance.

'Come *at* me, for feck's sake. I could slice off your limbs like you were Monty Python's Black Knight.'

'It's only a flesh wound.' Giggles caught her, distracted her, and Meara moved in like a demon.

'Mind the...' Branna sighed hugely as Iona lost her footing and fell backward into a massive spread of wild blue lobelia.

'Ah well.'

'Ouch. Sorry.'

'You've got the basics well enough.' Sheathing her sword, Meara held a hand down to help pull Iona to her feet. 'And you take your lumps like a woman. You've good speed and agility, and endurance enough. But you've no killer in the blood, and so you'll always be bested.'

Iona rubbed her butt. 'I never planned on killing anyone.'

'Plans change,' Branna pointed out. 'Fix those flowers now, as it's your rump that crushed them.'

'Oh yeah.' Iona turned back to them, considered.

'No.' Branna snapped her fingers. 'Don't stop and think, just do.'

'I'm just catching my breath.'

'You may not have time for that. Sword, magick, a blend of both. And wit to tie them together. Just do.'

So she held out her hands in instinct rather than plan. The crushed blue flowers plumped.

'I gave them a little boost while I was at it.'

'So I see.' With a faint smile, Branna plied her paring knife.

'I could use a shower and a beer. No, beer first.'

'We'll go again, then a beer,' Meara told her. 'Don't hold back this time. Didn't Branna tell you she'd charmed the blades as dull as our first form science teacher? Remember her, Branna?'

'To my sorrow, I do. Miss Kenny, who could out-sister the sisters for the hard eye and bore your brain to liquid between your ears.'

'I heard she moved to Donegal and married a fishmonger.'

'I pity him.' Branna rose with her bowl of

potatoes, her compost bucket of peels. 'I'll put these on and fetch the beer while the two of you hack at each other.'

Stalling, as she really did need to catch her breath, Iona studied her sword. 'You don't really think we'll use these, this way, against Cabhan.'

'There's no telling, is there? And as I don't have what you do, this may be what I'll use and need should the time come.'

'Why don't you sound scared?'

'I've known of the legend all my life, and the hard fact of it since I've known Branna, which seems forever. That's the one part. And on the other...' Meara looked around her, the new plantings, those from past years spreading and spearing, the woods beyond in their rainy evening gloom.

'It doesn't seem real, does it? That come the solstice we'll try to end all this by whatever means we can. Blood and magick, blade and fang. It's not life, but a story. And yet it is. I'm caught up in that, I think. Above that, when it comes, I'll be with people I trust more than any others. So, the fear's not there. Yet.'

'I wish it were now. Some nights I think, let it be tomorrow, so it can be over. Then in the morning, I think, thank God it's not today, so I have another day. Not just to practice, to learn, but–'

'To live.'

'To live, to be here. To be a part of all this. To ride Alastar, to work, to see my cousins, and you and...'

'Boyle.'

Iona shrugged, almost managed casual. 'I like seeing him. I think we've been dealing with everything really well. Being friends was the right answer.'

'Oh bollocks. You're friends right enough, but that'll never be all. The pair of you send out so much haze that's sex and lust and emotion I don't know how any of us see straight.'

'I'm not sending out anything. Am I?'

'Sure you are. I don't suppose a woman in love can help it. But plenty's coming from his direction.' Meara threw up her hands at the thought of so many she cared about refusing to reach for what they wanted most. 'Iona, the man brought you flowers, and I'm thinking the only woman he's carried bouquets to might be his ma or his granny. And aren't the drinks you like stocked in the little fridge?'

'Ah, now that you mention it–'

'Who do you think's seen to that? And who brought you a toasted sandwich when you couldn't stop for lunch just yesterday?'

'He'd do the same for anyone.'

Meara could only roll her eyes skyward. 'He did it for you. And didn't I hear him with my own ears tell you only days ago that the blue sweater you wore to the pub looked fine on you? And who made sure you sat out of the draft of the door while we were there?'

'I ... didn't notice.'

'Because you're trying so hard not to notice. You're putting everything you can into your work, your practice so you don't have much left to think of him, because it's hard for you. At the same time you've blinded yourself to the wondrous fact that the man's besotted. He's wooing you.'

'He is not.' The heart she'd worked so hard to steady stumbled a little. 'He is?'

'Try to notice,' Meara advised. 'Now come at me like you mean it.' She drew her sword. 'And earn that beer.'

She let herself notice, a little, the next day. She knew she had a habit of letting hope overrule everything else. All logic, all sense and self-preservation could, and usually did, fizzle under the bright light of hope.

Not this time, she warned herself. Too much at stake. But she could notice, a little, if there was something to notice.

He brought Alastar to her, and that was hard not to notice. Boyle rode him over rather than drive the horse in the trailer Alastar detested.

'I thought you might want him today, as you've three guideds on your slate.'

'I always want him.' She cupped Alastar's face, rubbed cheeks with him. And sent Boyle a sidelong glance. 'Thanks for thinking of it.'

'Oh well, it's no trouble, and he's needing the exercise. I've a mind to switch out two of the horses for tomorrow, so I'll be riding Caesar over to the stables tonight if you're wanting to ride this one back. I'll drive you home from there if it suits you.'

'Sounds good.'

Nothing in his tone, she thought, but friendship, as agreed. And yet... 'I'll put him in the paddock until I've checked in the first group.'

She took the reins, rolled her aching right shoulder, gave it an absent rub.

'Are you hurt?'

'What? No. Just sore. Sword arm,' she said, a little cocky, brandishing her arm. 'Meara's a brute.'

'She's a fierce one. Why haven't you fixed it? Or had Connor do it?'

'Because it serves to remind me not to drop my guard.'

She led the horse away, determined not to look back. But she *felt* his eyes on her. And wasn't that interesting enough to let just a little hope eke through?

He didn't stint on the work he assigned. As a result, she stayed busy – body and mind – until midafternoon when he shifted her balance again by bringing her a bottle of the Coke she preferred.

'Thanks.'

'It seemed you should wet the throat you must've worked dry calling out corrections to the student you had in the ring.'

'She's really young.' Grateful, Iona took a long sip. 'And she likes the idea of riding. She just doesn't put much into learning how. I think she mostly likes the outfits she gets to wear, and how she looks on a horse.'

'Her parents are divorcing it seems.'

'Oh, that's rough. She's only eight.'

'It's been coming on awhile, from what I hear. And it seems their way of compensating is to indulge her and her brother. Her with the fancy boots and riding pants and such and him with video games and sports jerseys.'

'It won't work.'

'Likely not, no. I wonder if you have a minute to take a look at our Spud. He's been off his feed today. I thought before I call the vet you could take a pass at him.'

'I'll go right now. I haven't worked with him today,' she said as she hurried out of the ring. 'Barely saw him this morning.'

She worked her way down the stalls, Boyle beside her, and stopped at Spud's.

The horse just gave her a sorrowful look as he moved restlessly in the stall.

'Don't feel good today, do you?' She murmured it as she opened the stall door. 'Let's have a look.'

In answer he kicked at his belly.

'That's where it hurts, huh?' Gently, gently, she ran her hands over him, down and around his belly.

And closing her eyes, calming her mind, she let herself see, let herself feel.

'It's not colic, so that's lucky. And not an ulcer. But it's uncomfortable, isn't it, baby? And you can't do what you like best. Eat.'

'I couldn't even tempt him with a potato, his favorite.'

'He's not sweating,' she added. 'Has he been rolling around on the floor?'

'No. Just barely touched his feed.'

'Indigestion.' Which, it occurred to her, Boyle would've thought of himself. But now there they were, the two of them in the stall together, close, arms brushing now and then as they stroked the horse.

'I think I can take care of it, if you trust me to.'

'I would, and more, he would. He's not fond of the vet for all that. And if indigestion it is, we can always dose him. But he's not in favor of that overly either.'

'Let's see if we can avoid it. Would you hold his head?'

As Boyle moved to do so, she crouched down, hands sliding, gliding over Spud's belly. 'It aches,' she said quietly. 'So hard to understand the hurt. You've been eating too fast, that's all. Slow down and enjoy it more. Quiet now, quiet.'

Her stomach burned a moment as she drew the pain away, but she felt Spud's relax under her touch. Heard his snort of relief.

'Better now, that's better. And I bet you're already starting to think about eating again.'

She rose, saw Boyle staring at her.

'You go to gleaming,' he told her. 'It's a dazzle.'

'It's odd because it feels so calm now to do it. And with little hits like that I'm not immediately thinking about food myself. It wouldn't hurt to put some of that homeopathic potion in his feed, just to cover the tracks.'

'Sure I'll do that, and thanks for this. He's a favorite around here as you know.' He continued to stand at Spud's head, blocking the stable door. 'So, are you faring well, Iona?'

'Yeah. Fine. You?'

'Oh, well and fine. Busier as you know with spring.'

'And summer follows.'

'And summer follows. We're to meet again in another two days, to talk of that. I wondered if there was anything I could do for you in the meantime? If you wanted some time off so you could ... do what you do at home, have more time to put into that.'

'Working here keeps me sane, I think. And balanced. The routine of it, and knowing I want that routine when this is over.'

'If ever you did need the time, you've only to tell me.'

'I will.'

'I could buy you a pint for the vet service after work – in a friendly way,' he added. 'After the workday if you've a mind for it.'

He'd do the same for anyone, she reminded herself. But...

'I would, but Branna's expecting me. She's a brute just like Meara. We haven't much time left before the solstice.'

'No, there's not much left. It's weighing on you.'

'Not being sure what I'll need to do, what I'm meant to do weighs. Both Branna and Connor have blocked any thought of me going to the cabin ruins before the solstice. They seem to think I'll pull more from it the very first time, and that may help.'

'You'd tell me if you ... had more dreams or any encounter with him?'

'It's been quiet. That weighs, too. He's watching, you can feel it. But not too close.' She shuddered, rubbed her arms.

'I don't mean to upset you talking of it.'

'It's not the talking. It's the waiting.'

'Waiting,' he said with a slow nod. 'It's never

easy. Iona, I want to–' Mick hailed him, and came down the stalls with quick boot clicks.

'There you are. I wanted to ask if...' With his gaze shifting from Iona to Boyle, Mick flushed. 'Beg pardon. I'm interrupting.'

'No, that's fine.' Boyle shuffled his feet, turned. 'We're just finished with Spud here.'

'I'll dose him, chart it,' Iona offered.

'Thanks for that.'

Alone, Iona leaned against the horse. 'He's been starting conversations,' she realized. 'He never does that, but he has been, ever since... And he bought me Cokes.' She stepped out, picked up the bottle she'd set outside the stable door, took a long pull.

'Hell, Spud, I think maybe I am being wooed. And I have absolutely no idea how to handle it. Nobody ever really tried before.'

With a sigh, she studied the bottle in her hand, wondered what it said about her that her heart was so easy it could be touched by a damn soft drink.

Just ... see what happens, she warned herself, then went to get Spud's medicine.

Nothing happened really – conversations, small attentions, casual offers of help. But he made no move toward more. A good thing, Iona reminded herself as she helped Branna prepare the group dinner. She'd meant everything she'd said to him when he'd brought the flowers to her, the apology to her.

For once in her life she intended to be sensible, to be safe, to look – both ways – before she leaped.

'Your thoughts are so loud they're giving me a headache,' Branna complained.

'Sorry, sorry. I can't seem to stop the loop. Okay, we'll put it on I've never made scalloped potatoes before. Not even out of a box.'

'Don't talk of potatoes in a box in this kitchen.'

'Only as an insult. Am I doing it right?'

'Just keep doing the layers as I showed you.' At the stove, Branna stirred the glaze she intended to use on the ham she had baking.

'Fancy meal for a strategy meeting.'

'I was in the mood. And now we'll have cold ham for days if I'm not in the mood again.'

Conscientiously, Iona sprinkled flour over the next layer of sliced potatoes. 'I was thinking about Boyle.'

'Is that a fact? Never would I have guessed.'

Rolling her eyes at Branna's back, Iona added the salt and pepper, started the butter. 'How do you know? I can't figure out how you know, sensibly, and that's what I'm working on. Is he just missing the sex, maybe even the companionship on some level? Is he feeling guilty because he hurt me, trying to be nice to make up for it, to be friendly because that's what I asked? Or, does he, maybe, care more than he thought?'

'I'm the wrong one to ask about matters of the heart. Some say I barely have one.'

'No one who knows you says that.'

Some did, and there were times she wished they had the right of it.

'I don't know about men, Iona. Whenever I think I do, think I've got it all in a box, just as it is, it all scrambles out when I'm not looking.

361

When I get it all back in, it's something else than it was.

'I know my brother, but a brother's a different thing.'

'Love shouldn't be hard.'

'There I think you're wrong. I think it should be the hardest thing there is, then it's not so easily given away, or taken away, or just lost.'

Stepping away from the stove, she moved over to check Iona's progress. 'Well, it's taking you long enough as you've all but placed each slice of potato like an explosive, so careful and precise. But you've got that done. Take it over and pour that hot milk right over it.'

'Just pour it over it?'

'Yes, and not drop by drop. Dump it on, put on the cover, stick it in the oven. Timed this first part, for thirty minutes.'

'Okay, got it.' And as if it might explode, Iona let out a breath of relief when she had it inside the oven with the ham.

'You know they shouldn't both fit in there.'

'They fit as I want them to. Now I think we'll do a side of the green beans I blanched and froze from the garden last year, then we'll... There's someone coming now,' she said as she heard the sound of cars. 'Let's just see who it is, and how we can put them to use in here.'

'I'm all for it. You know,' Iona continued as they walked to the front of the cottage, 'I think my goal should be to be able to put one really good meal together – figure out what that is, make it my thing. Oh, Iona's making her brisket. I'm not even sure what brisket is, but it could be mine.'

'A fine goal indeed.'

Branna opened the door. Outside Meara stood beside her truck, Fin climbed out of his, and both Connor and Boyle shoehorned their way out of a bright red Mini.

'Isn't that the cutest thing?' With a laugh, Iona stepped closer. 'How did you guys fit in there?'

'It wasn't a simple matter,' Connor told her. 'Nor was driving it, as Boyle's knees sat at his ears the whole way. But she cleaned up well, and runs fine enough. Seems a better fit for you.'

'Get in and see,' Meara suggested.

Obliging, Iona slid in, put her hands on the wheel. 'Much more my size. Is this from the friend you told me about?' she asked Connor. 'It's great. It's really adorable, but I don't think I can afford adorable at this point.'

'But you like it,' he prompted. 'The look of it, the color and feel and so on.'

'What's not to like?' In fact, she could already picture herself driving around like a little red rocket. 'It's just perfect. Do you think he'd consider holding it, letting me pay some now, some later?'

'Well, he might, but it's already sold.' Connor glanced at Branna, got her nod. 'Happy birthday.'

'What?'

'It's Connor and Boyle who found the car, and we all put in a share to buy it. For your birthday,' Branna added. 'Do you think we didn't know it's your birthday?'

'I didn't – I thought with everything that's going on it was better to– But you can't just... A

363

car? You can't.'

'Already have,' Connor pointed out. 'And whatever else there is, a birthday's a thing to remember. We're your circle, Iona. We wouldn't be forgetting yours.'

'But it's a *car*.'

'One that's over ten years old, and truth be told, wheezes like an asthmatic on damp mornings. Which is nearly daily,' Fin commented. 'But she'll do for you.'

She began to laugh, and to weep. On a combination of both, she scooted out to throw her arms around Connor as he stood closest. Then she spun to each one in turn.

When her body pressed to Boyle's, her arms squeezed hard around him, he struggled not to make it more. To just let it be.

'I don't know what to say. Don't know how to say it. It's amazing! Beyond amazing. Thank you so much. All of you.'

'There'll be a bit of paperwork to see to,' Fin put in, 'but you can see to it later. Now you should try it out, shouldn't you?'

'I should drive it. I should drive it.' On another laugh, Iona spun in a circle. 'Someone has to go with me on my first voyage. Who wants to go?'

Every man stepped back as one.

'Cowards,' Meara said in disgust. 'What do you say, Branna? We could squeeze in.'

'I expect we could, but I've dinner on.'

Meara only let out a snort. 'Well, I'm not afraid. I'm with you, Iona.'

She jumped in, waited while Iona slid behind the wheel.

Iona started the car, bounced on the seat, wiggled into it. She lurched forward three times. Fit, start, fit, start, fit, start, then zipped down the road weaving like the cloth loop on a potholder loom.

'Ah God,' was all Boyle managed.

'I told you I put a little charm for safety on it,' Connor reminded him. 'She just needs a bit of practice as she's a Yank after all. So Fin here's contributed bottles of champagne to the birthday feast, and being Fin, it's fancy and French. I say we have the first bottle waiting for her.'

'We've important business to discuss as well,' Branna reminded him. 'And should be doing that with clear heads rather that French bubbles.'

'It's her birthday.'

'Ah well.' On a sigh, Branna relented. 'One bottle among us shouldn't hurt anything.'

'I should've been afraid,' Meara muttered to Connor on the return as Fin popped the first cork. 'She's a right terrible driver.'

'Only needs practice.'

'Please the gods and be right on that as I thought she'd do us both in the first kilometer. Still, it's worth it. She never expected such a thing. Not just the gift, but the whole of it. And I think for all my family is fucked, I've never given a thought but there'd be a bit of a fuss for my birthday.'

'We've cake as well.'

'I never doubted it.' In the mood, Meara gave him a quick and affectionate one-armed hug.

He linked his arm around her before she could

pull away, did a quick step. Laughing, she mimicked the footwork, then reached for the glass Fin held out. 'I'll take that for certain.'

'I'm going to make a toast,' Iona decided. 'Because I've thought of what I want to say. In addition to thank you, which just doesn't cover it. All of you, you're mine, and that's a gift I'll always treasure. Every one of you is a gift to me, a blend of friends and family that's stronger and truer and brighter than anything I ever imagined having. So, to all of us, together.'

She sipped. 'Oh God, that's really good!'

'A fine toast, and fine champagne.' Branna opened a cupboard, took a wrapped gift off a shelf. 'And from your grandmother. I put it aside for her as she asked me.'

'Oh, Nan.' Delighted, Iona set the glass aside to open the gift, took out a sweater in dreamy blues. 'She'd have made it,' Iona murmured, rubbing it to her cheek. 'It's so soft. She'd have made it for me.'

She took out the card, opened that.

For my Iona. There's love and charms and hope in every stitch. Wear it when you want to feel most confident and strong. With wishes for your happiness today, and all days.
Love, Nan

'She never forgets.'

'Put it on,' Meara urged her. 'I've never seen a lovelier jumper.'

'Good idea. I'll be right back.'

'When you're back, we'll begin,' Branna said.

'We've time before the food's done to talk of the solstice, and what we'll do. We do it well and right,' she added, 'and on Iona's next birthday, we'll have nothing but friends and food and wine. And that's a gift for all of us.'

'Well said,' Fin murmured. 'Put on your gift, as it brings your grandmother close. Branna and I will shroud the house. No eye, no ear, no mind but ours will know what we do here, say here, think here tonight.'

20

They used light, not dark, to cloak the cottage and all in it. If Cabhan looked, as shadow, as man, as wolf, he would see only the light, the colors, hear only music, laughter.

It would, Branna explained, bore him, or annoy him. And he would think they simply played while he plotted.

'At moonrise, on the longest day, we form the circle on the ground where Sorcha lived, and where she died.'

Candles flickered throughout the kitchen where Branna spoke. The scents of cooking, the simmering hum of the fire, the steady breaths of the dog who slept under the table all spoke of ordinary things while they talked of the extraordinary.

And that, Iona realized, was the point.

'It's for Fin to seek him, to lure him. Blood to blood.'

'You still doubt me.'

Branna shook her head. 'I don't. Or only a little,' she admitted. 'Not enough to stop doing what has to be done. What I understand is this can't be done without you, and shouldn't be. Isn't that enough?'

'It'll have to be, won't it?'

Their eyes held, a long, long moment. In it Iona felt thousands of words, scores of impossible feelings passed between them. Only them.

'I'll get him there,' Fin said, and broke that moment.

'Meara and Boyle must stay inside the circle – at all costs. Not just to protect yourselves.' Branna turned to them. 'But to hold it strong. And Fin as well must stay within it.'

'Damned to that.'

'Fin, you must,' Branna insisted. 'Within the circle he can't use what runs in you against you, or against us. And what you have will hold it without chink.'

'Four of us outside it, against him, are stronger than three.'

Facing him, Branna lifted her hands, palms up. And the flames of every candle burned brighter. 'We are the three. We are the blood, and we must be the way.'

'Within the circle I'll stay,' Fin told her. 'Until or unless I feel we've more chance ending him with me outside of it. It's the best bargain I can give you.'

'We'll take it.' Connor spoke up, shifted his gaze from Fin to Branna, left it coolly on her. 'And done.'

Branna started to speak, sighed instead. 'And done then.'

'We have to take our guides,' Iona realized.

'We do, yes.' Branna drew her amulet from under her sweater, ran a thumb over the carved head that so resembled Kathel's. 'Horse, hound, hawk. And weapons and tools. I have a spell I've worked on for some time, and I think it's an answer, but only if we draw him to the right place, the right time. And then we'll need his blood to seal it.'

'What spell is this?' Fin demanded.

'One I've worked on,' Branna repeated. 'I've used bits of Sorcha's spells, others that have come down, something of my own.'

'And practiced it?'

Irritation flickered over her face. 'It's too risky. If he learns of it, he can and will block against it. It must be done the first time on Sorcha's ground. You need to trust I know what I'm about.'

'You must be trusted,' Fin repeated.

'Bloody hell.' Branna started to shove back from the table, but Iona raised a hand.

'Just wait. What kind of spell? I mean, a banishing, a drawing, a vanquishing spell? What?'

'A vanquishing, a light spell, a fire spell. All of them in one, sealed with blood magick.'

'Light defeats the dark. Fire purifies. And blood is at the heart of all.'

Branna smiled. 'You learn well. But it may come to nothing if not done at the right time, at the right place. It will come to nothing if we all, each one, don't agree and stand together, in that time and place.'

'Then we will.' Iona lifted her hands as she looked from face to face. 'We all know we will. You'd do anything you could to destroy him,' she said to Fin. 'For Branna, for yourself, for the rest of us. In that order. And Branna would do anything to sever whatever link he might have with you, so you'd be free of it. Connor and Meara would stand for love and friendship, for what's right and good whatever the risk or cost. Boyle would fight because that's how he works. You just have to say when and where, and he'd be with you. And because, whatever's changed between him and me, he'd never want anything to happen to me. And I would never want anything to happen to him.

'For love and friendship, for family and friends, we'll stand together in the right time, in the right place and fight with each other. Fight for each other.'

After a moment's silence, Fin picked up the champagne he'd ignored, lifted the glass toward Iona. 'All right, *deirfiúr bheag*. We'll be your happy few.' He shifted toward Branna. 'Trust,' he said, waited.

'Trust.' She lifted her own glass, touched it to his. In that quiet clink a spark of light flashed, then softened away.

'With that settled, let's get down to the nitty of it then.' Connor leaned forward. 'Step-by-step.'

Boyle said nothing as Branna walked them through her plan, as that plan was revised, questioned, adjusted. He said nothing because looking at Iona as she'd spoken had given him all and every answer.

He'd hold on to them until it was time to give them back to her.

She counted down the days as May drifted into June, and let herself cling to each one for itself. She could prize the blue skies when she had them, welcome the rain when it fell. She came to believe that whatever happened on the longest day, she'd had these weeks, these months, and these people in her life, and so her life, even for that short time, had been richer than ever before.

She'd been given a gift and learned how to use it, how to trust and respect it.

She was, and ever would be, of the three. She was, and ever would be, a dark witch of Mayo, charged with power and with light.

She believed they would triumph, her nature demanded she believe. But that gift she'd been given demanded the respect of caution and care.

As the solstice approached, she wrote a long letter to her grandmother – pen and paper, she thought. Old-school, but it was important, felt important, to take the time, make the effort. In it she spoke of love, for her grandmother, her cousins, her friends. For Boyle, and the mistakes she'd made.

She spoke of finding herself, her place, her time, and what it meant to her to have come to Ireland. And to have become there.

She asked only one thing. If something happened, her grandmother would find the amulet, take it and Alastar, and pass them both to the next.

There would be a next if she failed. That, too,

she believed absolutely.

However long it took, light would beat back the dark.

On the morning before the solstice she went down early, the letter in her back pocket. She tried her hand at cooking a full breakfast fry, and though she thought she'd never be more than a half-decent cook, it didn't mean not making the effort.

Connor walked in, sniffing the air.

'And what's all this then?'

'We'll be busy tomorrow, so I thought I'd take the opportunity to do it up right and spare Branna the time. She was up late again, wasn't she?'

'Barely sleeping the past week or so, and no amount of cajoling or arguing changes it.'

'I hear her music, like last night, and it smooths me right out. She does it on purpose.'

'Claims she thinks clearer when the two of us aren't thinking.' He snagged a sausage from the plate. 'You're worried.'

'I guess I am, now that it's down to hours instead of days. Why aren't you?'

'We're meant to do what we're doing. If something's meant, what's the point in worrying over it?'

For comfort, she leaned against him a moment. 'You smooth me out as much as Branna's music.'

'I have every faith. In you.' He wrapped an arm around her waist for a squeeze. 'In Branna, in myself. And in all the others as well, and as much. We'll do what's meant, and do our best. And that's all anyone can ever do.'

'You're right, on all of it.' She eased away to pile a plate full for him. 'I feel him lurking, don't you? I feel him around the edges of my dreams trying to get in. He nearly does, and part of me realizes I'm allowing it. Then there's Branna's music, and the next I know it's morning.'

Iona got down another plate, arranged about half as much on it as she had for Connor. 'I'm going to leave this warming in the oven for Branna.'

When she turned around, Connor just wrapped his arms around her. He had, Iona thought, the most comforting way.

'There now, stop the fretting. He's never faced the like of us three, or the three with us.'

'You're right again. So let's eat, then I'm going to drive to work, taking the long way for practice.'

'You'd be there in half the time if I walked you.'

'True, but I wouldn't practice.' Or be able to stop off at the hotel, ask if they'd post her letter the next day.

She kept her eyes peeled for any trace of fog, of the black wolf, of anything that alarmed her instincts or senses. She made it to Ashford Castle without incident or accident. Really, she thought she handled the Mini, the roads, the left-hand drive very well, whatever Meara said to the contrary.

Just as she believed she handled the throbbing nerves of the waiting, of the silence, very well.

Maybe her pulse jittered every time she looked out a window of the cottage to scan forest, road, hills. Maybe she recognized the ache of stress in her back and shoulders every time she prepared to lead a group through the green shadows and thick woods.

But she continued to look from the window, continued to guide groups. And that, Iona told herself as she pulled up to the stables, counted most.

As she was the first to arrive, she opened the doors, shifted to flip on the lights.

And there in the center of the ring stood the wolf.

The doors slammed behind her; the lights flashed off. For one shocked moment, all she could see were three red glows. The wolf's eyes, and its power stone.

They blurred when it charged.

She threw up a hand – a block, a shield. The wolf struck it with such force she felt the ground tremble. Just as she felt the cracks zig across her block like shattering glass.

She watched the shadow of its shape bunch to charge again.

She heard the cries of the horses, full of fear. And that decided her course.

As the wolf charged, she vanished the shield, jumped to the left. The momentum carried it through so it struck the doors with the force of a cannonball. When they burst open, it was Iona's turn to charge.

She rushed out, threw the shield behind her this time. It wouldn't get through, wouldn't harm the horses. Bracing her feet, she prepared to protect even as the wolf circled back. Even as it rose up on two legs and became a man.

'You're a quick one, and clever enough.' As in

374

the dreams, his voice was like cold hands gliding over the skin. And still, somehow seductive. 'But young, in years and in power.'

'Old enough in both.'

He smiled at her. Something in her spirit repelled even as something in her body stirred.

'I could kill you with a look.'

'Not so far.'

'Your death isn't my wish, Iona the Bright. Only give me what has come so late to you, what is still so young, so fresh in you.' Dark, dark eyes holding hers, he edged closer as he spoke in that silky voice. 'I want only the power you don't yet understand, and I'll spare you. I'll spare all of you.'

Her heart pounded, too hard, too fast. But her power stirred, in the belly, and would rise. She would make it rise.

'Is that all? Really? Ah ... no.' She heard the cry of the hawk overhead, and now she smiled. 'Company's coming.'

'You'll be the death of them. Their blood will stain your hands. Look. See. Know.'

She glanced down at her hands, at the blood staining them, dripping from them to pool on the ground. The sight of it, the warmth of it, sliced true fear through her belly, through her heart.

When she looked up Cabhan was gone. And Boyle rode like a madman on Alastar up the dirt path.

'I'm fine,' she called out, but her voice sounded tinny, and her knees wanted to buckle. 'Everything's fine.'

The hound streaked to her side as Boyle leapt

from Alastar's back. 'What happened?'

When he started to grab her hands, she instinctively pulled them back. Then saw, both shocked and relieved, they were clean.

'He was here, but he's gone.' She leaned against the horse, as much to soothe him as for his support. The hawk landed as lightly, as neatly on Alastar's saddle as he might on a tree branch. And Kathel sat quiet at her side.

All of them here, she thought. Horse, hawk, hound.

And Boyle.

'How are you here?'

'I'd just saddled Alastar to ride him over when he let out a bloody war cry and bolted for the fence. I barely had time to jump on his back before we went over it. Let me look at you.' He grabbed her, spun her around. 'You're not hurt? You're sure of it?'

'No. I mean yes, I'm sure. Alastar heard me.' She laid a hand on the horse's neck. 'They all heard me,' she murmured as the hawk watched her, as Kathel's tail gave one quick thump. And her cousins pulled up in Connor's truck, spewing dirt and gravel with the slam of brakes.

'They...' She paused as Fin's truck, then Meara's sped into the stable yard. 'They all heard me. He couldn't stop that. It couldn't stop that from getting through.'

'What the bloody, buggering hell happened?' Boyle demanded.

'I'll tell you. All of you,' she said, speaking to the group. 'But we need to check the horses. He didn't hurt them. I'd know if he did. But they're afraid.'

She brought Alastar with her, felt the need to keep him close as she went back inside.

They would purify the ring, she thought. Branna would see to it.

She soothed the horses, one by one, and so doing soothed herself. By the time the stable hands arrived to see to the morning routine, she huddled with the rest, crowded in Boyle's little office, and told the tale.

'There's a sexuality, on the most elemental level,' she added. 'He uses it like a weapon. It's powerful, and it pulls. But more, he was stronger this time. Maybe he's been storing it up somehow. I don't know the answer, but I know when he hit the shield, it cracked. It wouldn't hold him back.'

'So you removed it, took him straight out the doors. Clever,' Fin told her.

'That's what he said. Right before he promised to spare all our lives if I gave him my power.'

'He's a liar,' Branna reminded her.

'I know it. I know. But the blood on my hands.' Fighting a fresh shudder, she pressed her palms together. 'It felt real, and it felt like yours. He knows I'm still the weak spot.'

'He's wrong, and so are you if you believe it.' With the lack of space, Boyle couldn't pace off the anger, so he just balled his fists into his pockets. 'There's nothing weak in you.'

'He wanted to scare me, and tempt me. He managed both.'

'And what did you do about it?'

She nodded. 'I like to think I would have, could have kept doing it if all of you hadn't come

377

so quickly. But the point is I'm still his focus. Take what's mine, and he believes he can take the rest.'

'So we'll use that. We will,' Fin said before Boyle could object. 'The slightest adjustment to the plan, and he'll see her as vulnerable, see it as the time and place to close in, and have it done.'

'It's more complicated,' Branna began.

'And since when have a few complications buggered you up?'

'More dangerous,' Connor added.

'If we're in it, we're in it.' Meara shrugged. 'Today proves Iona can't even come to work in the morning without a risk. Why should she live that way? Or any of us?'

'The next time he might hurt the horses,' Iona added. 'To damage me, to distract me. I won't have that. I couldn't live with that. What adjustments?'

'He thinks you'll go alone tomorrow, to the ruins.'

Iona stared at Boyle, saw the fury behind his eyes. 'I'm bait. But bait with knowledge and power. And a very strong circle.'

Before Boyle could curse, Branna laid a hand on his arm. 'She's never alone, never will be. You've my word, and the word of all of us here.'

She gave his arm a rub, then considered. 'It could be done. I think it could be done well enough.'

'You'll work with me on just that today then?'

Branna looked at Fin, fought her nasty internal war. 'I will, for Iona. For the circle.'

'We'll get started. Keep in the company of

others,' Fin added, tracing a finger over Iona's cheek. 'For the day, keep others close, will you, little sister?'

'No problem.'

It was easy enough, especially since Boyle or Meara hovered.

Boyle took her off guided rides for the day – a frustration to her – and stuck her on stable duties.

She groomed, fed, cleaned stalls, repaired tack, polished boots.

And the day dragged.

She rode Alastar to the big stables – Boyle on Spud beside her – to deal with the lesson she had scheduled for the end of the day.

This time tomorrow, she thought, she'd make the final preparations. And she'd take the next steps toward her destiny.

'We're going to win this,' she said to Boyle.

'Cocksure's a foolish thing.'

'It's not cocksure, or not cocky.' She remembered Connor's words, and her feeling with him, in the morning kitchen. 'It's faith, and faith's a strong, positive thing.'

'I don't care for you being the tip of the spear in this.'

'I sure didn't plan to be, but because I am, he's the one who'll be cocksure and foolish. Think about that.'

'I've been thinking of it, and considerable else.'

At the stables he dismounted, waited for her to do the same. 'I've something to show you.'

He started into the stables. Before one of the hands could speak, Boyle signaled him away, jerked a thumb and sent him out. Then led the way to the tack room with its scent of leather and oil.

'It's that.'

She followed the gesture, hummed in pleasure at the gleam of the saddle sitting on its stand.

'That's new, isn't it?' She stepped to it, ran a hand over the curve, over the smooth black leather. 'Beautifully made, and just look at the stirrups shine! It's hand-tooled, isn't it? It's–'

'It's yours.'

'What? Mine?'

'It's made for you, specifically, and for Alastar. For the pair of you.'

'But–'

'Well, I didn't know, did I, the others would be after buying the car for you, and this was meant for your birthday.'

If he'd offered her a pirate's chest of gold and jewels she'd have been less stunned. 'You... You had this made for me, for my birthday?'

His brows drew together, just short of a glower. 'A horsewoman of your caliber should have her own saddle, and a fine one.'

When she said nothing, he lifted the saddle, turned it over. 'See, it's your name there.'

Gently, she brushed her fingers over her name. Just Iona, she thought. Just her first name, and a symbol of flames beside it – Alastar's name, and a trinity knot, across from it.

'I know a man who does the work,' Boyle continued, flustered when the silence dragged out. 'The leather work, and the ... ah, well, it seemed fitting to me.'

'It's beautiful. It's the most beautiful gift.'

'You'd sold your own.'

'That's right.' She looked at him then, just looked. 'To come here.'

'So ... sure now you have another. And if we're to do this tomorrow, you should have it. You and Alastar should use it.' He started to turn it over again, secure it. Iona put a hand over his.

'It's much more than another saddle. Much more to me.' She rose on her toes, brushed her lips over one of his cheeks, the other, then lightly over his lips. 'Thank you.'

'You're welcome, of course, and happy birthday again. I've things to see to now. Fin'll be keeping an eye out, as he let me know he and Branna are done for today.'

'All right. Thank you, Boyle.'

'As you've said.'

She let him go. She had a lesson to prepare for. And decisions to make.

She walked over to Fin when her student left. Gave a short sigh. 'I didn't give her my best today.'

'I wager she'd disagree. And if you're a bit distracted today, there's cause enough.'

'I guess.' She glanced toward the rooms over the garage. 'And you and Branna?'

'Did what we set out to do, with little drama. That's a blessing in itself. I'll take you back to the stables if you're wanting your car, then follow you home to be safe and sure.'

'Oh, thanks, but ... I want to – I need to ... I have to talk to Boyle. About something. He can take me home, I think.'

'All right then.' With an easy smile rather than

the laugh in his heart, Fin took Alastar's reins. 'I'll just see to our boy here.'

'You don't have to–'

'I'll enjoy it. And I'll say he and I have things to discuss as well.'

'You do talk to him, and the other horses. The way I can.'

'I do, yes.'

'And the hawks – your own, Connor's, the others. Kathel, our hound. Even Bugs. All of them.'

Fin moved his shoulders, a kind of half shrug that managed to be elegant and a little sad. 'They're all mine, and none of them mine. There's no guide for me, as there is for you. No connection that intimate. But, well, we understand each other. Go on now, say what you need to say to Boyle.'

'Tomorrow...'

'You'll shine, brighter than you ever have.' He cupped her chin a moment, tapped a finger on her jaw. 'I believe it. Go see Boyle. I'll be around and about if you need me.'

She took two steps, turned. 'She loves you.'

Fin just stroked a hand over Alastar's neck. 'I know it.'

'It's harder, isn't it, knowing someone loves you and can't let it just be love?'

'It is. Harder than anything else.'

With a nod, she walked over, then climbed the steps to Boyle's room. Straightened her shoulders, knocked.

When he answered the door, she had her smile ready. 'Hi. Can I talk to you a minute?'

'Of course. Is something wrong?'

'No. Maybe. It depends. I need to...' She closed her eyes, held her hands out to the side, palms out.

He saw something shimmer, caught the faintest change of the light, of the air.

'He's focused on me,' Iona said. 'So he might find ways to hear, to listen, to see, even when we're inside. I don't want him to hear what we talk about.'

'All right. Ah, do you want tea. Or a beer?'

'Actually, I wouldn't mind some whiskey.'

'That's easily done.' He crossed over to take a bottle down from a cupboard, then two short glasses. 'This is about tomorrow.'

'In a way. I meant what I said before. I believe we'll win. I believe we have to, that we're meant to. And I know what blood feels like on my hands. I know, or I believe, the good, the light, defeats evil, the dark. But not without cost. Not without price, and sometimes the price is very high.'

'If you weren't afraid, you'd be stupid.'

She took the glass he offered. 'I'm not stupid,' she said, and tossed the whiskey back. 'We can't know what will happen tomorrow, or what the price may be. I think it's important, tonight, to grab what good we have, what light we have, and hold on to it. I want to be with you tonight.'

He took a careful step back. 'Iona.'

'It's a lot to ask, considering I asked you exactly the opposite not so very long ago. You gave your word, and you kept it. Now I'm asking you to give me tonight. I want to be touched, to be held. I want to feel before tomorrow comes. I need you

383

tonight. I hope you need me.'

'I never stopped wanting to touch you.' He set his whiskey aside. 'I never stopped wishing to be with you.'

'We'd both have tonight, whatever comes. I think we'd be stronger for it. It's not breaking a promise if I ask you to throw it away. Will you take me to bed? Will you let me stay till morning?'

There were things he wanted to say, yearned to say. But would she believe them, even with her shining faith, if he said them here and now?

The words would wait, he told himself, until the dawn after the longest day. Then she'd believe what he'd come to know.

Instead of speaking he simply stepped to her. Though they felt big, clumsy, he cupped her face with his hands, then lowered his mouth to hers.

She leaned into him, her arms wrapping, her lips heating.

'Thank God! Thank God you didn't send me away. I've—'

'Quiet,' he murmured, and kissed her – soft, soft, tender as a bud just opened.

They had till morning, he thought. All those long hours, only that finite time. He would do what he'd never thought to do. He would take each minute, make it precious. Show her, somehow, she was precious.

'Come with me now.' Taking her hand, he led her to the bedroom. Then crossed over to pull the blinds down on the windows. The light went dim and dusky.

'I'll be a moment,' he told her, left her there.

He had candles. For emergencies rather than

atmosphere, but a candle was a candle, wasn't it?

He might not be a romantic sort of man, but he knew what romance was.

He unearthed three candles, brought them in, set them around. Then remembered matches. He patted his pockets. 'I'll just find the matches, then...'

She trailed a finger through the air, and the candles flamed.

'Or we could do that.'

'I'm not sure what we're doing, but you're making me nervous.'

'Good.' He went back to her, ran his hands down, shoulder to wrist and back again. 'I wouldn't mind that. I'd like feeling you tremble,' he murmured, opening the buttons of her shirt. 'I'd like looking in your eyes and seeing you can't help yourself. That nervous or not, you want me to go on touching you.'

'I do.' She reached up, managed to open a button on his shirt before he stopped her.

'I want you to take what I give you tonight. Just take, just let me give. I've missed seeing the shape of you,' he continued, and drew her shirt off her shoulders. 'Missed the feel of your skin under my hands.'

He circled her nipples with his thumbs, then gently brushed the pads over them, over them until the tremble came.

He took his hands over her, took her mouth with his – everything slow, everything dreamy, even the thick thud of her heart against him.

'Take what I give.' He backed her to the bed, brushing, stroking, eased her onto it. Watched her in the candlelight as he drew off her boots, set them down.

'Come lie with me.'

'Oh, I will. In time.'

He unbuttoned her jeans, drew the zipper down. Slow. Followed its path with his lips.

What was he doing to her? She found herself clutching at the bed covers one minute, going limp as water the next. He undressed her so slowly, inch-by-inch torture. And yet the pleasure was sumptuous, a banquet of exotic delicacies. The heat of it enervated. The weight of it left her arms too heavy to lift.

She knew nothing but the feel of his hands, his lips, the sound of his voice, his scent. Him. Him. Him.

Once, twice, a third time he guided her to the shuddering edge, held her there, poised, desperate for the leap, only to ease her back again until her breath sobbed with need, with the speechless desire for the next.

Then with lips, tongue, ruthlessly patient hands he slid her over that edge.

Not a leap, but a fall – breathless, endless, a tumble of senses and sensations. And the world revolved.

'Oh God. God. Please.'

'What do you please?'

'Don't stop.'

His mouth, on her breast, her belly, her thigh. Then his tongue, sliding over her, into her until she fell yet again, then mindlessly craved the next climb.

He hadn't known he'd wanted her helpless, or

what it would do to him to know he'd made her so. But to see her alight – she couldn't know she glimmered like one of the candles – to feel her body rise up to take what he offered, to feel it fall again as she grasped that pleasure. It was more than he'd known, more than he'd imagined.

And the wanting of her filled every part of him – mind, body, spirit.

'Look at me now, Iona. Would you look at me now?'

She opened her eyes, saw his in the candle glow. Saw nothing else.

'I'm with you,' he said as he slipped into her. 'I'm with you.'

They climbed again, eyes and bodies locked. Climbed until she swore the air thinned. And when her eyes gleamed with tears, they fell together.

21

Today, Boyle thought as he drank brutally strong coffee at his kitchen window.

He couldn't stop it, or her. And in some part of himself he knew, even accepted that he, that she, that all of them had prepared for this day all of their lives.

Hard enough, it had always been hard enough to understand what his closest friends in the world might face one day – today – but with Iona it was only harder.

Whatever he could do he would to see her safely through it, to help her and the rest end it.

And then?

Once this day was done there would be a great deal more to do, if only he could figure out the hows of it all.

Sure how could he figure out anything when the day was to be filled with magick and violence, struggle and destinies? And very likely life and death.

His life, he thought, would've been easier by far if she'd never come into it.

Then he sensed her, turned, saw her standing outside his bedroom door, that short halo of hair still damp from her shower, her eyes deep and a bit sleepy yet before her coffee.

And he knew without a shadow, easier wasn't what he wanted.

'Should we talk?' she asked him.

'Probably so, but it's a strange day for all that.'

'It is, yeah. Later's better.'

He nodded. 'After, yes. There's a lot to be said after this day.' Get busy, he told himself. Get moving. 'You'll have coffee, won't you?'

'Absolutely.' But she didn't move to pour it for herself as she'd done before.

He'd done that, he knew, made her feel a guest again. Words wanted to be said, but he held them back, and would until this long, strange day was done.

So he got down a mug, poured it for her.

'Thanks. I'm going to go down, spend some time with Alastar. Do you have any problem with me riding him home today, keeping him there until it's time?'

'I don't, no. He's yours after all. I'll ride with you.'

'Actually, I think Fin will. He and Branna need to refine any details of the magicks with Connor and me.'

'All right, but you don't ride alone.' Carefully, he touched a hand to her shoulder. 'Are you afraid?'

'No. Not afraid. I thought I'd be revved, pumped, with some good, healthy fear mixed in. I'm just not, and not sure why. I feel almost unreasonably calm. Today's what I've been working for, training for, learning for. And that was ordained, I guess is the word for it, on the night Sorcha sacrificed herself.

'We finish what she started. And then…'

When he said nothing, she sipped at her coffee. 'And then,' she continued, 'we do good work, we lead good lives. That's enough for anyone.'

'Your work and your life are here.'

'Yes.' On that, at least, she had no doubts. 'My place is here.'

'I'll fix us up some breakfast.'

'Thanks, but I feel like I ought to be a little hungry, and … light for now. I'll be down with Alastar until it's time to go back home.' She set her coffee, barely touched, aside. 'I needed you last night, and you were there. I won't forget it.' She walked quickly to the door. 'I'll see you, an hour before moonrise.'

She slipped out the door and left him wondering over her.

She groomed Alastar carefully, thoroughly so his

389

coat gleamed like pewter. Her calm remained as she brushed even the threat of tangles out of his mane, his tail.

Today he was a warhorse, and she believed that he, too, had prepared for this day all of his life.

'We won't fail.' She circled around to his head, laid her hands on either side of his face and looked into his deep, dark eyes. 'We won't fail,' she repeated. 'And we'll keep each other safe as we do what we're meant to do.'

She chose a saddle blanket – red for battle, for blood, then retrieved the saddle Boyle had given her.

She felt Alastar's pleasure, his pride when she put the saddle on him. And she felt his courage, drew some of it for herself.

'There's magick in a gift, and this was given to both of us. He thought of us when he had it made, so there's more magick there. And last, it bears our names.'

She'd braid charms into his mane, she decided. When they got home she would choose ones for strength, for courage, for protection. And she would carry the same with her, under the sweater her grandmother had made. Another gift.

'Time to go.'

She allowed herself one moment to wonder if she'd ever be back in this stall, then set any doubt aside and led her horse out.

She found Fin waiting outside, and the sleek black he called Baru saddled.

'I've kept you waiting.'

'Not at all. There's time enough. Odds are Branna's just getting her wits about her by now in any case. I see Boyle gave you the saddle.'

'It's wonderful. You knew?'

'When you live and work so close with another, secrets are hard to keep.' Fin linked his hands into a basket to help her mount.

'You look a picture, the pair of you,' he said when she sat the horse.

'We're ready for what's coming.'

'It shows.' He mounted Baru, turned so they could walk down the narrow road together.

In the workshop, closed, locked, shielded for the day, Iona listened to the plan – its step-by-step progression – to the spell she was charged to make, the words to be said, the actions to take.

'You're quiet,' Fin commented. 'Have you no questions?'

'The answers are on Sorcha's ground. I'm ready to go there, and to do what I'm meant to do.'

'It's a complicated spell,' Branna began. 'Each piece has to fit.'

'I can handle it. And as you've said, I won't be alone. You'll be there, and so will Boyle and Meara. If I pull this off, on my own, he won't know that, won't see that. Advantage us. Then you come in from here, here, here,' she said, tapping the map Branna had drawn. 'That distracts him, throws him off balance, and takes the heat off me. All non-witches inside the circle, and Fin, too. They'll need you to keep the protective circle strong,' Iona said as temper flashed into Fin's eyes. 'So will we. We'll need that time when he tries to get to you for the three of us to finish it. Finish him.'

'You're bloody calm about it,' Connor muttered.

'I know. It's odd. Why worry when it's meant, right? And still I should be jumping out of my skin, but I just feel ... right. Maybe I'm saving the jumping for when it's done. Then I'll probably babble like an idiot until you want to knock me unconscious. But right now, I'm ready.'

'If you're so ready, tell me all the steps, from the beginning,' Branna ordered.

'All right. We gather here, an hour before moonrise.'

Iona walked her way through it as she spoke, envisioned it, every step, every motion, every word.

'And when Cabhan is ash,' she concluded, 'we perform the final ritual and consecrate the ground. Then comes the happy dance and drinks on the house.'

Gauging her cousin's expression, Iona reached for Branna's hand. 'I'm taking it very seriously. I know what I have to do. I'm focused. I trust you, all of you. Now you have to trust me.'

'I'd wish for more time, that's all.'

'Time's up.' To demonstrate, Iona rose. 'I want to change, and get everything I need from my room. I'll be ready.'

When she walked away, Connor rose as well. 'I'd take some of her calm just now, but I'll have to make do with too much energy. I'm going to check on the hawks, yours and mine, Fin, and the horses as well.'

As the door closed behind him, Branna got up to put the kettle back on. Though she doubted a vat of tea would drown the anxiety.

'You think we're asking too much of her?' Fin asked.

'I can't know, and that's the worry.' One that ate at her, night and day. 'If I try to see, and he catches even a glimmer, all could be lost. So I don't look. I don't like putting the beginnings of it all in her hands, even knowing it's the right choice.'

'She asked for trust. We'll give her that.'

'You don't think it's too much for her?'

'I can't know,' he said in an echo of her words, 'and that's the worry.'

She busied herself making tea for both of them. 'You care for her a great deal.'

'I do, yes. For herself, as she's charming and full of light, and such ... clarity of heart. And again, as my friend loves her, even if he buggered it up.'

'He did that. And still she went to him last night.'

'She forgives, easier than others.' Fin rose to walk toward her, to stand near her. 'There are things for us, Branna. Words to be said. Will you forgive me, at last, when this is done?'

'I can't think about that now. I'm doing what I have to do. Do you think it's easy for me, being with you, working beside you, seeing you day after day?'

'It could be. All those things used to make you happy.'

'We used to be children.'

'What we had, what we've been to each other wasn't childish.'

'You ask for too much.' Made her remember,

far too clearly, the simple joy of love. 'Ask for more than I can give.'

'I won't ask. I'm done with asking. You don't reach for happiness, or even look for it.'

'Maybe I don't.'

'What then?'

'Fulfillment. I think fulfillment contents me.'

'You wanted more than contentment once. You ran toward happiness.'

She had, she knew. Recklessly. 'And the wanting, the running hurt me more than I can bear, even now. Put it away, Finbar, for it only brings more hurt to both of us. We've important work to do tonight. There's nothing else but that.'

'You'll never be all you are if you believe that. And it's a sorrow to me.'

He walked away, walked out. And that, Branna told herself, was what she needed.

He was wrong, she told herself. She'd never be all she was, never really be free, as long as she loved him.

And that was her sorrow.

At an hour before moonrise they gathered. Branna lit the ritual candles, tossed ground crystals into the fire so its smoke rose pale and pure blue.

She took up a silver cup that had come down to her, stepped into the circle they formed.

'This we drink, one cup for six, from hand to hand and mouth to mouth to fix with wine our unity. Six hearts, six minds as one tonight as we prepare to wage this fight. Sip one, sip all, and show each one here answers the call.'

The cup passed hand to hand three times

before Branna placed it in the center of the circle.

'Power of light, strong and bright, bless us this night, shield us from sight.'

Light erupted in the cup, burned like white flame.

'Now his eyes be blind until this magick I unwind. Not heart nor mind nor form will he see. As we will, so mote it be.'

She lowered the arms she'd lifted. 'While it burns we're the shadows. Only you, Iona, when you break this vial. Wait,' she added as she pressed it into Iona's hand. 'Wait until you're on Sorcha's ground.'

'I will. Don't worry.' She slid the vial into her pocket. 'Find him,' she said to Fin.

'So I will. Find, seek, lure.'

He took a crystal, round as a ball, clear as water, from his own pocket, cupped it in the palm of his hand.

As he spoke in Irish, the ball began to glow, to lift an inch above his hand. And to revolve, slower, then faster, faster until it blurred with speed.

'He seeks, blood to blood, mark to mark,' Branna told Iona quietly. 'He uses what he is, what they share, to see, to stir. He...'

Fin's eyes began to gleam, to glow, as unearthly a light as the crystal.

'Not so deep! He can't–'

Connor caught Branna's arm before she lurched forward. 'He knows what he's about.'

But for a moment, something dark lived behind the light in Fin's eyes. Then it was gone.

'I have him.' His face a mask, Fin closed his fingers over the crystal. 'He'll come.'

'Where is he?' Boyle demanded.

'Not far. I gave him your scent,' he told Iona. 'He'll follow it, and you.'

'Then I'll take him where we want him.'

'We're behind you.' Meara grasped Iona's arms. 'Every one of us.'

'I know.' She breathed slow, kept her calm. 'I believe.'

She touched her fingers to the hilt of the sword at her side, looked from one to the other, and thought what a wonder it was to have them all, to have what was inside her, to have such a purpose.

'I won't let you down,' she said and started for the door.

'Bloody hell.' In two strides Boyle caught her, whirled her around, crushed his mouth to hers with everything that lived inside him.

'Take that with you,' he demanded, and set her aside.

'I will.' And she smiled before she walked out into the soft light of the longest day.

Alastar waited, pawed the ground at her approach.

Yeah, she thought, we're ready, you and I.

She gripped his mane, hurled herself into the saddle. She closed a hand briefly around her amulet, felt heat pulse from it.

Ready, she thought again, and let Alastar have his head.

Faster was better. The others would come as quickly as they could, but the faster she reached her ground, the less time Cabhan could plot, plan, question.

Wind rushed by her ears. The ground thundered. And they flew.

When she reached the downed tree, the wall of vines, she drew her sword.

'I am Iona. I am the Dark Witch. I am the blood. I am one of three, and this is my right.'

She slashed out. The vines fell with a sound like glass shattering, and she rode through.

Like the dream she'd had that night at Ashford, she thought. Riding alone through the deep forest, through air so much stiller than it had a right to be, where the light went dim though the sun showered down.

She saw the ruins ahead, vine- and brush-covered as if it grew out of the trees. She walked the horse toward it, and toward the stone that bore Sorcha's name.

Now her skin vibrated. Not nerves, she realized, but power. Energy. Alastar quivered under her, let out a bugle that sounded of triumph.

'Yes, we've been here before. The place of our blood. The place where our power was born.' She dismounted, looped the reins, knowing Alastar would stay with her, stay close.

She took the vial from her pocket, crushed it under her boot.

So it would begin.

From the bag she'd secured to the saddle, she took the flowers first. Simple wood violets, then a small flask holding bloodred wine.

'For the mother of my mother and hers, and all who lived and died, who bore the gift with its joys and sorrow, back to Teagan who is mine, and the Dark Witch who bore her.'

She laid the flowers by the stone, poured wine

397

over the ground in tribute.

Speaking the words of the spell only in her mind, pulling power up from her belly, she took the four white candles from the bag, set them on the ground at the compass points. Next, the crystals, between each point.

As she laid them, Alastar let out a warning chuff. She saw fingers of fog crawling over the ground.

We're with you. Connor's voice sounded in her ear. *Finish the circle.*

She drew her athame, pointed north. Flame sparked on the first candle.

'You think that can stop me?' Cabhan spoke with amusement. 'You come here, where I rule, and play your pitiful white magick.'

'You don't rule here.'

The second candle flamed.

'See.' He threw his arms high. The stone around his neck flamed with light both dark and blinding. 'Know.'

Something changed. The ground tipped under her feet as she struggled to finish the ritual. The air turned, turned until her head spun with it. The third candle flamed, but she fell to her knees, fighting the terrible sensation of dropping from a cliff.

The vines drew back from the ruin. The walls began to climb, stone by stone.

Night fell like a curtain dropped.

'My world. My time.' The shadows seemed to lift from him. The stone pulsed, a dark heart over his. 'And here, you are mine.'

'I'm not.' She got painfully to her feet, laid a

hand on Alastar's flank as he reared. 'I'm Sorcha's.'

'She sought my end, gained her own. It's she who sleeps in the dark. It's I who live in it. Give me what you have, what weighs on you, what it demands from you, what it takes from you. Give me the power that fits you so ill. Or I take it, and your soul with it.'

She lit the last candle. If they could come, they would come, she thought. But she couldn't hear them through the rush in her ears, or sense them through the stench of the fog.

No retreat, she told herself. And never surrender.

She drew her sword. 'You want it? Come and get it.'

He laughed, and the sheer delight on his face added a terrible beauty.

'A sword won't stop me.'

'You bleed, so let's find out.' She punched power into the sword until it flamed. 'And I bet you'll burn.'

He swept an arm out, and from feet away, threw her back, knocked her to the ground. Winded, she tried to push to her feet. Alastar reared again, screaming in rage as his hooves lashed out.

She saw Cabhan's face register pain, and shock with it. Then he hunched, dropped to all fours, and became the wolf.

It leapt at Alastar, scoring the horse's side.

'No!' Like lightning, Iona surged to her feet, charged.

Her sword whistled through the air, but the wolf streaked to the side, then barreled into her

399

with a force that propelled her, had her skidding on her back, and her sword flying away.

The wolf straddled her, jaws snapping. And became a man again.

'I'll burn him to cinders,' Cabhan warned. 'Hold him back or I set him on fire.'

'Stop! Alastar, stop!'

She felt his rage even as he obeyed. And felt the amulet she wore vibrate between her and Cabhan.

His gaze lowered to it; his lips peeled back in a snarl.

Then he smiled again, terrifyingly, into her eyes.

'Sorcha betrayed me with a kiss. I'll draw what's in you into me the same way.'

'I won't give it to you.'

'But you will.'

Pain exploded, unspeakably. She screamed, unable to stop. Red everywhere, as if the world caught fire. She heard Alastar's screams join hers. Ordered him to *run, run, run*. If she couldn't save herself, she prayed she could save him.

Above all, she would never give up. She would never give her light to the dark.

'A kiss. You've only to give me one kiss, and the pain will vanish, the burden will drop.'

Somewhere in her frantic mind she realized he couldn't take it. He could kill her, but he couldn't take what she was. She had to surrender it.

Instead she groped, found her athame with a shuddering hand.

She wept, couldn't stop that either, but through the screams and sobs she managed one word. 'Bleed.'

And plunged the knife into his side.

He roared, more fury than pain, and, leaping up, dragged her with him, holding her a foot above the ground by a hand clamped around her throat.

'You're nothing! Pale and weak and human. I'll crush the life out of you, and your power with it.'

She kicked, tried to call for fire, wind, a flood, but her vision grayed, her lungs burned.

She heard another roar, and flew, hitting the ground hard enough to shock her bones and clear her vision.

She saw Boyle, his face a mask of vengeance, pummeling his fists into Cabhan's face.

With each hit, flames leapt.

'Stop.' She couldn't get the word out, no more than a croak, even as Boyle's hands burned.

She managed to gain her knees, swayed as she fought to find her center.

The man dropped away. The wolf slipped out of Boyle's hold and bunched for attack.

The hound streaked into the clearing, snarling, snapping. Hawks dove, talons slicing at the wolf's back.

An arm circled her waist, lifted her to her feet. Hands linked with hers.

'Can you do it?' Branna shouted.

'Yes.' Even the single word cut her throat like shards of glass.

The fog thickened, or her vision grayed. But all she could see through it were vague shapes, the flash of fire.

'We are the three, dark witches we, and stand this ground in unity. Before the longest day departs, we forge all light against the dark. On this ground, in this hour, we join our hands, we join our power. Blood to blood, we call on all who came before, flame to flame, their fires restore. Match with us, your forces free. As we will, so mote it be.'

Light, blinding, heat churning, and the wind that whirled it all into a maelstrom.

'Again!' Branna called out.

Three times three. And as she cast the spell, her hands caught tight with her cousins', Iona felt she was the fire. Made of heat and flame, and a cold, cold rage that burned in its core.

Even as she pushed to finish, the fog vanished. She saw blood, smoke, both Fin and Meara at the edge of – not in – the circle, swords in hand. And Boyle, kneeling on the ground, pale as death, his hands raw and blistered.

Alastar, blood seeping from his wounds, nudged his head against Boyle's side, while the hound guarded him. Two hawks perched in branches beside the stone cabin.

'Boyle.' Iona stumbled forward, fell to her knees beside him. 'Your hands. Your hands.'

'They'll be all right. You're bleeding. And your throat.'

'Your hands,' she said again. 'Connor, help me.'

'I'll see to it. Here now, this isn't for you. You're hurt, and I'll do better without you.'

'Here, little sister, let me help you.' Fin crouched down as if to lift Iona into his arms.

'I'll tend her.' Briskly, Branna took Iona's arm. 'Help Connor with Boyle as he's taken the worst of it.'

'His hands were on fire.' When her head spun,

402

Iona simply slid to the ground. 'His hands.'

'Connor and Fin will fix him right up, you'll see. Quiet now, cousin. Meara, I want his blood. Find something to put it in. The blood, the ash. Look at me now, darling. Look at me, Iona. It'll hurt a little.'

'You, too.'

'Just a little.'

It did, a little more than a little, then relief, cool and soothing on her throat. Warm, healing down her sides where the bruising ran deep.

'It's better. It's all right. Boyle.'

'Shh. Hush now. That'll take a bit longer, but he's fine, he's doing fine. Look and see while I finish.'

Through streaming tears, Iona looked over, saw Boyle's hands. Still raw, but no longer blackened and blistered. Still, he'd gone gray with the treatment, and the pain.

'Can't I help?'

'They've got him. I've just your ankle left here. It's not broken, but it's badly wrenched.'

'I wasn't strong enough.'

'Hush.'

'Alastar. He hurt Alastar. He said he'd burn him alive.'

'He's cut a bit, that's all. Why don't you see to that? See to your horse.'

'Yes. Yes. He needs me.'

She gained her feet, walked, a bit drunkenly, to the horse. 'You're so brave. I'm so sorry.'

Swallowing tears, she laid her hands on the first gash, and began to heal it.

'I've used two of the vials from your bag.' Meara

handed them to Branna. 'One for the blood, the other for the ash. I felt a bit like one of those forensic types.' Then she let out a shuddering breath. 'Oh God, Branna.'

'We won't talk of it here. We need to get home.'

'Can we?'

'I got us here. I'll get us back.'

'Where did he go, bloody bastard?'

'I don't know. We hurt him, and he lost blood – plenty of it – but it's not finished. I saw him slide away, using the fog, into the fog. Our fire scorched, and well, but didn't take him. It was not finished tonight, for all we thought it would be. I'm taking us back,' she called out. 'Are you ready?'

'Christ, yes.' Fin put an arm around Boyle, helped him stand.

'I'm fine now, I'm fine. Help her get us home, the both of you.'

Nudging the other men aside, Boyle walked to Iona. 'Let me see you.'

'I'm okay. Branna took care of it. Alastar. I can't heal this scar. He's scarred.'

Boyle studied the slash of white over the gray flank. 'A battle scar, worn with pride. We're going home now, all of us. Up you go. And none of that,' he added as the tears rolled. 'Stop that now.'

'Not yet.' She leaned forward, wrapped her arms around the horse's neck as the ground tilted, as the air turned and turned.

And kept her silence as they left the clearing, and the ruins.

EPILOGUE

Iona accepted the whiskey, with gratitude, and curled into the corner of the living room sofa. The fire snapped, but brought comfort instead of fear and pain.

'I'm sorry. I wasn't strong enough. I wasn't good enough. He rolled right over me.'

'Bollocks to that.' Connor tipped more whiskey in his own glass. 'Bloody, buggering bollocks to that.'

'Well said,' Branna agreed. ''Tis I who's sorry. Every step in place, every detail. But one. I never thought of him slipping through time like that, not on command. I didn't know he could so quickly, and with us so close.'

'No.' Fin shook his head when she glanced at him. 'I never saw it coming. He's too clever by half, changing the ground to one where his power burned stronger than we knew.'

'And where we couldn't get to Iona. Where she was alone, after all.' Boyle reached over, took her hand, held it firmly in his.

'But you came, all of you.'

'Not as fast as I would like. It's not enough to know where, but when. We might not have found you, but you called so strong. You believed, just as you said, and you called. You finished the circle, even with all that, you finished the circle, opened the power, and we could find you. And nearly

405

took him.'

For a moment, Branna closed her eyes. 'Nearly, I swear it was close.'

'It's no fault of yours,' Connor told Iona, 'or anyone's come to that. It's true enough we didn't finish him, but we gave him a hell of a fight, and we hurt him. He won't forget the pain we gave him this night.'

'And he'll be more prepared for next time.' Meara lifted her hands. 'It's true, and needs to be said, so we don't walk into that kind of trap again.'

'That's fine, but ... you're burned.'

Meara glanced at her wrists, the backs of her hands, and the scatter of burns. 'Blowback, mostly. What about you?'

'Fin and I took care of each other. Why didn't you say something? Stubborn arse.' Connor rose, gripped her hands.

'I've worse cooking breakfast.'

'There's no need for pain. Are you burned as well?' he asked his sister.

'Not a fucking mark. We have his blood, and the ash his torn flesh turned to. We'll use it against him. We'll figure out just how, and we'll use it against him when next we come at him. And it won't be his ground the next time. We'll be sure of it.'

Iona didn't ask how. Sitting there, with those she loved, with her hand in Boyle's, she felt her faith come back.

'He couldn't take it,' she said slowly, and touched her free hand to her amulet. 'Even when I was helpless, or as close to helpless as I've ever been, even when he hurt me, he couldn't take it from me. He needed me to give it to him. He could kill me, but he couldn't take what's in me. That pissed him off.'

'Good.'

Iona smiled. 'Damn good. I stabbed him with my athame.'

'Did you now?' Fin rose, walked over, and, bending down, kissed her hard on the lips. 'That's our girl. A weapon of light against the dark. It may be why there was so much blood left for us.'

'We'll use that as well. I'm putting a meal together. I can't promise what it might be, but we'll eat well tonight. And there's a bottle yet of that French champagne. We didn't finish it, but I'd say the first battle is ours, and we'll celebrate that. You lot can give me a hand. Not the two of you,' Branna said to Iona and Boyle. 'You took the worst of it, so you'll sit there and drink your whiskey by the fire a bit.'

'I've not finished with the stubborn arse yet.'

Meara punched Connor's shoulder. 'Mind your own arse.'

'Why when yours is not only stubborn but shapely as well?'

'In the kitchen, I said.' And this time Branna rolled her eyes at Connor to give him a clue.

'Fine, fine, I'm half starved anyway.'

He trooped out, dragging Meara with him.

'I'll take a look at the horses. So you can rest your mind there.'

Iona smiled at Fin. 'Thanks. They're fine, but it never hurts.'

Then she leaned her head back, closed her eyes. 'I was fire,' she said softly. 'Not just making it, being it. It was terrifying and glorious.'

'It was, looking at you with Connor and Branna, burning like a torch, all white and heat. It was terrifying, and glorious.'

'And still, it wasn't enough. I wanted it to be over, now. Tonight.'

'Some things don't happen as fast as you like.' Boyle turned her hand over in his, then gave in and pressed it to his cheek. 'It doesn't mean they won't happen.'

'That's right. And Branna's right. When we weigh it all, we tipped the scales on this one. The way you flew through the fog. You and Alastar, you're my heroes.'

'Since I know what store you put by the horse, I'm in fine company.'

'When I close my eyes and see your hands. See them on fire.'

'Look at them here. See that? Same as ever.'

Big, scarred. Precious.

'I didn't think we'd get to you.' He spoke slowly, and with great care. 'I didn't think we'd get to you in time if at all, and that I might never see you again. I didn't have your faith. I want you to know I have it now. So, you can say you're my hero as well.'

She tipped her head to his shoulder a moment.

'And I think, all things considered...'

She took a sip of whiskey. 'What things?'

'I'm saying, I think considering all of it, and the fact we're done for now, and don't know as yet what might be next. Considering all that, and all the rest, I think it would be best all around if you married me.'

She lowered the glass to stare at him. 'I'm sorry, what?'

'I know all you said after I was, well, just a raving git, and I've done what you wanted, or tried my best to. But I think it's time we were past that now, and considering it all, we'll get married and put all that away.'

'Married.' Had the battle, the bruisings, the flaming addled her brain? 'As in married?'

'It's the sensible thing. We're good for each other, as you've said yourself. And ... we have horses in common.'

'Can't forget the horses.'

'It matters,' he muttered. 'You love me. You said you did, and you're a woman honest about her feelings.'

'That's true.'

'So, we're good for each other, and have the horses. You love me and it's the same for me, so we'll just get married.'

She decided her brain was working just fine, thank you. 'What's the same for you?'

'Jesus.' He had to stand for a moment, circle around the room. Stall by tossing more peat on the fire. 'I never said it to a woman not my mother or related in some fashion. I don't toss such things about as if they're nothing.'

His hair, caught between brown and red, was a tumbled mess. She hadn't noticed before, she realized. Or the blood on his shirt, the way his jaw set, so stubborn.

But she could see, very clearly, the intensity in his eyes.

'I believe you.'

409

'Some words matter more than others, and it's one of those.'

'What's one of those, exactly?'

'Love is. I know what love is, damn it, because you put it in me, and you've given it to me. And I'll never be the same again. I'll never feel it for anyone else.'

'It.'

'I love you, all right then?' He punched the words out like an argument waiting to happen, and she was totally, utterly done for.

'I'm saying it clear enough.' His brows drew together in that half scowl as he threw up his hands. 'I love you. I ... want to as well. I want all that I feel for you, as I'd only be half alive without it. And I want to marry you, and live with you, and have a family with you some time or other. But for now, I want you to stop making me run around it all, and just say it's all right with you.'

She only stared at him a moment, as she wanted it all, every tiny detail of it, etched forever in her memory. 'This is the most romantic thing that's ever happened to me.'

'Oh bugger it. You want fancy words? Maybe I could pull some Yeats out or something.'

'No, no, no.' Laughing, she got to her feet, and felt stronger and surer than she'd ever felt before. 'I meant it. This is romance, for me, from you. If you could say it just one more time. The three words, the word that matters more than others.'

'I love you. Iona Sheehan, I love you. Give me a bloody answer.'

'It was yes as soon as you opened your mouth. I just wanted to hear it all. It was yes the minute you asked.'

He blinked at her slowly, then narrowed his eyes. 'It was yes? It's yes?'

'I love you. There's nothing I want more than to marry you.'

'Yes?'

'Yes.'

'Well good. Grand. God.' He lunged at her, and she met him halfway. 'God, thank God. I don't know how much longer I could've done without you.'

'Now you'll never have to know.' She gave herself over to the kiss, and all the promises in it. 'You'll never have to do without me.' She held on, tight, tight. 'We did win tonight, in so many way. In ways he'll never understand. We have love. He doesn't know what it means. We have love.'

'I'm marrying a witch.' Hauling her off her feet, he circled with her. 'I'm a lucky man.'

'Oh, you really, really are. When?'

'When?'

'When are we getting married?'

'Tomorrow would do me.'

Delighted, she laughed. 'Not that soon. Talk about boots-first. I need a fabulous dress, and I need Nan to be here. And I haven't met your family.'

'A lot of them are right in this house.'

'That's true. We won't wait too long, but long enough to do it right.'

'I have to buy you a ring. The boys were right, after all. I need to get you something shiny.'

'Absolutely.'

'And you're right, too, it has to wait a little bit

of time. At least long enough to get a booking at Ballintubber Abbey.'

'At...' Joy all but drowned her. 'You'd marry me there?'

'It's what you want, isn't it? And by God, it seems it's what I want as well. There, in the ancient and holy place. It's what's meant for us.'

He grabbed her hands, yanked them to his lips, then laughed down at her. 'You'll be mine, and I'll be yours. That's what I want.'

She laid her cheek on his heart. Love, she thought, given freely, taken willingly.

There was no stronger magick.

'It's what I want,' she murmured, then smiled when she heard Alastar bugle. 'He knows I'm happy.' She tipped her head back. 'Let's go tell everybody else, and pop that champagne.'

With wine and music and light, she thought. They'd come through the fire, beaten back the dark for another day.

And now, on the longest day, when the light refused to surrender, she was loved. At last.

Deep in the woods, in another time, the wolf whimpered. The man inside it cursed. And with arts as black as midnight, slowly began to heal.

Carefully, began to plan.

This Large Print Book for the partially sighted, who cannot read normal print, is published under the auspices of

THE ULVERSCROFT FOUNDATION